Tangled Web of Friends: Book IV

THE HOLLOW

By Valerie Lofaso

To Paula,
May your days be
filled with peace, joy,
and love!
Valerie Lofaso

Runestone Publishing
Portsmouth, New Hampshire, USA

Tangled Web of Friends: Book IV – The Hollow

ISBN 978-1-59648-014-8

Cataloging in Publication Data
TBD

Library of Congress Control Number: 2023943205

Editing by Charles Richard, Lin Richard, and Nomar Slevik
Front cover image by Raena Wilson sunrae-artworks.com
Book design by Runestone Publishing

Printed in the United States of America

Runestone Publishing
120 Ledgewood Dr. #10
Portsmouth, NH 03801

First Edition

For Juliana
Always and forever, no matter what!

And in memory of my uncle
Steve Gerstein
The original "The Great Salami"

Prologue

"It's been almost a year since I started to see, to talk to, dead people. But for some reason it didn't really make me think much about death until I saw death. Being there, witnessing someone I love stop living, but at the same time seeing her soul go on… it was awful and strange and amazing all at once. It was weird. A part of me was sad, but another part of me was… happy for her, and no one around me understands," Josie said. It was more than she'd ever said at one time to this woman, and truthfully, she wasn't sure *she* would understand either.

"Do you feel guilty for how you feel?" she asked. Her name was Dr. Gilbert, and she was Josie's therapist.

"No. It's just that no one gets it. Like, really gets it, and that just makes me…."

"Angry?" Dr. Gilbert asked. When Josie continued to stare at her hands, the woman went on. "You've been angry a lot lately."

Josie looked up at her, waiting for more. She wasn't going to respond. It wasn't a question, it was bait, and she wasn't going to bite.

Dr. Gilbert gave in first. "Okay, Josie, why don't we talk about the anger so we can get to the root of it?"

She pursed her lips, trying to hold it all in, but she just couldn't. "But I know what the root of it is. It's the fact that my own father thinks I'm crazy."

"He doesn't think you're crazy, Josie. He just doesn't understand."

"He's not trying to understand!" Josie replied, anger flaring up from deep inside her. She'd taken the bait. "He doesn't want to understand and neither of them get it. They just don't get that it's not just… *that* stuff. It's so much more!"

"Okay, then tell me about the other stuff," said Dr. Gilbert.

Josie saw a look of victory flash across Dr. Gilbert's face. "No. I'm tired of talking about it." She folded her arms across her chest and sank down in the chair.

"But you haven't talked to me about it," said Dr. Gilbert. She leaned forward, resting her elbows on her knees. "And I can't help you if you don't talk to me. Tell me what's going on. Tell me how you feel."

Josie wouldn't meet her eyes. "What's going on is that I feel tired. I feel empty, like everyone that I love and need has been taken from me, ripped from me. I feel like I've given everything inside of me away and gotten nothing in return. I feel… hollow."

PART I

1

Josie stood at the door of the closet in the guest room. It was a deep walk-in closet filled with boxes of holiday decorations, winter sweaters, and other junk. Behind it she could still see the baby-blue paint and border of fire trucks halfway up the wall. How had she never noticed this before? Her heart pounded wildly in her chest.

"Josie, what are you doing in here?" Her mom asked from behind her.

She turned to face Angela. "This was his room, wasn't it?"

Angela flinched. Her eyes gave away her dismay. "Wh-who do you mean?"

"Ethan. This was Ethan's room," Josie told her. "The whole room used to be like this, right? Blue with fire trucks...."

"Josie, go down to the kitchen and we can talk about this," said Angela, her voice suddenly tinged with something hard.

Josie held fast. "I want to talk about this now. Here."

"We will talk. In the kitchen," Angela replied. Her jaw was clenched, and she suddenly looked much older to Josie.

"But—"

"No buts! Downstairs, now!"

Josie, startled by the strangled, anxiety-filled pitch of her mother's voice, gave in, and headed to the kitchen while her mom went back to her bedroom.

Josie topped off her coffee and waited for what felt like an eternity before her parents arrived in the kitchen, her dad's hair disheveled and his eyes barely open. He poured coffee into an oversized mug with a palm tree handle and "Florida" written across it in bubble font, a souvenir Josie brought him from her recent trip.

He looked at his wife. "Now will you tell me why you dragged me out of bed so early on a Sunday?"

Angela looked at Josie. "Why don't you tell him."

Josie took a bracing sip of her own coffee. "Dad, I know about Ethan."

Charles suddenly looked wide awake. "But… but how… what…?" He looked from Josie to Angela and back to Josie, then sighed heavily. "How did you find out?

She took another sip. "He told me."

Charles laughed.

"Josie, be serious with us please," said Angela.

"I am being serious, Mom. I see his ghost and he talks to me."

"Josie, honey, ghosts aren't real," said Charles.

Josie looked at her mug. "I knew you'd say that. I knew you wouldn't believe me. But it's not just Ethan. Uncle Frank, Aunt Pauline's husband, comes to me, too, and he confirmed it all."

Charles let out a strong puff of air and looked at Angela. Josie watched as the two of them had a brief, silent conversation.

Then Angela looked at Josie. "Did Aunt Pauline tell you?"

"No!"

"It's okay, Josie. You don't have to lie for her," said Charles. "She's an old woman. She's getting fragile, forgetful, and a little… weird."

"No, Dad, I'm not lying!" Josie stood in anger, her chair scraping back across the floor. "Aunt Pauline didn't tell me. I can see and talk to ghosts, and I do it all the time. *That* is why Jenna's gotten so into paranormal research!"

"Okay, okay. Let's all calm down and take a breath," said Angela. "How you found out isn't important. What's important is that you know about him, and you must have a lot of questions."

"Not a lot. Just one. I want to know why you hid from me the fact that you had a child." She reluctantly sat down.

Charles sighed again and looked at Angela, again having a wordless conversation. "It had nothing to do with you, Josie," said Charles.

"Losing Ethan was one of the most difficult things we've ever been through," said Angela.

"Ethan told me that you guys almost divorced," said Josie.

Charles frowned. Angela's brows went up in surprise.

Angela shook herself. "We needed to put it behind us in order to move on and heal. We needed to do that so we could be the best parents we could be… for *you*."

"But it's like he never existed!" Josie replied. All she heard from her parents were canned answers she was sure they had rehearsed for when this day inevitably came. She wasn't going to accept that. "There are no mementos, no pictures. Just all of it erased. You wiped Ethan from this home, from your lives. Would you do that to me if something happened to me?"

"Of course not, Josie," said Charles, reaching across the table for her hand, which she ripped away. "And that's not what we did. We didn't erase him."

"How can I believe you? Why didn't you guys just tell me about him?"

"Josie, please just listen to us," replied Angela. "Talking about him was— is hard for us. By the time you were at an age when we thought you'd understand, well… it just became easier not to say anything."

"And you took the easy way out," said Josie angrily.

"You can't judge us," said Angela, her face stern. That strangled tightness returned to her voice. "We made choices that were right for us at the time. Maybe they weren't right for the long term, but we can't go back and change that now."

Josie stood. Her parents looked like strangers to her at that moment. "I don't know if I'll ever be able to trust you guys ever again." She strode from the room.

A flood gate opened in Josie then. She ran a hot shower, sat under the stream of water, and let the tears flow. But she wasn't crying for Ethan, or for Simon, or for Ophelia or Mark or any of the other spirits she'd encountered. She was crying for the life she once had that she knew she would never have again. She cried for the life where Simon was merely a dream at a distance, a life where there were no ghosts, where her parents were exactly who she thought they were. She cried for the life where all her dreams revolved around ballet and theater, and her only nightmares were about not having a date to Prom.

That was all gone now. Dead and reduced to nothing but dust. It was all gone with a bump on the head, washed away in a river that almost took her life with it. But Simon rescued her, and her life changed forever. For almost a year she thought she was grateful to him for saving her life. She was no longer sure of that.

She cried until she had nothing left inside of her but a dull, throbbing ache where her heart once was. Then she dragged herself from the shower and back to her bedroom. Uncle Frank, Ethan, and Hanover were waiting.

None of this is Simon's fault, said Uncle Frank. *You were not meant to die that day.*

"Great. Fine. Whatever. Where were you guys earlier when I was talking to Mom and Dad? I could have used your help, you know," she glowered at them.

Everything happens as it needs to happen, Uncle Frank replied, in his usual vague, cryptic way. *This is your life, Josie, and you cannot depend on us to navigate every turn for you.*

Ethan approached Josie and put a small hand on her arm, causing her skin to tingle with a static-charged warmth. *We know that's not what you want to hear, and I'm sorry.*

Josie shrugged. "Fine. Whatever." It wasn't just the typical teenager response. She didn't care. She no longer had anything left within her to care. She had washed away the ashes of her former life, of her former self, in the shower, and now she was empty.

After her guides faded away to wherever it was that they went – she had asked many times before, but they never answered –

Josie forced herself into normal behavior. Picking out an outfit, blow-drying her hair, putting on makeup… it made her feel like life was almost normal. She didn't allow any of it to creep back into her mind. The only thing she allowed herself to think about was asking to go see Aunt Pauline. It was the only thing she cared about at the moment. Josie had worried about her ever since she saw her appear in her bedroom in Florida.

Josie was contemplating how to ask Aunt Pauline about that when a knock came at her door. "Yeah?"

Her parents walked into her room. "We need to talk to you," said Angela. They sat on the bed while Josie remained seated at her makeup table.

"We're worried about you, honey," said Charles. "All that stuff that happened before spring break, and now you come home and tell us you talk to ghosts…."

"We understand that sixteen is a difficult age and finding out about Ethan has made you lash out at us, and we understand why, honey. We really do," said Angela.

"Wait, you think *I* did those things because I'm mad at you?"

"It's perfectly normal, Josie. And with our circumstances, you're probably feeling even more confusion and anger," said Charles.

"What do you mean by 'our circumstances'?" Josie challenged, with a frown.

Charles and Angela exchanged an uncomfortable look. "We just think that maybe… because you're adopted… this situation is even more complicated," Charles replied.

Anger rose in Josie, but she held it back. "Okay, I can see why you guys might think that. I even thought for a while that I might be the one doing those things, but it wasn't me! It really was a ghost! He was there in Florida too, and there's so much I need to tell you guys about that trip, and Rachel will confirm it all—"

"Josie, stop it!" Charles said, his face red and contorted with anger. "There's no such thing as ghosts. You're under a lot of stress right now, and we're sure Aunt Pauline and Jenna have told you stories that sounded cool or exciting or whatever, but you need to stop this right now."

"Stop what? I'm telling you the truth! I can prove it! Ethan told me about how when you guys were on that cruise last summer, it was his birthday. And at breakfast that day you ordered his favorite meal: chocolate chip pancakes shaped like Mickey Mouse with whipped cream and chocolate milk. How would I know that unless I was telling you the truth? Would Aunt Pauline know that?"

Charles's face went almost purple with rage. "That's enough of that talk!"

"Why can't you believe me?" she asked.

"We want you to go to counseling, Josie," said Angela, her calm, saccharine tone a stark contrast to Charles's anger. Good cop, bad cop.

"Why?"

"To help you sort through all these feelings."

"What feelings? I'm not confused! Please, talk to Jenna and her parents!"

"I'm starting to think Jenna might be a bad influence in all this," said Charles through clenched teeth. "So, if you want to have a friendship with her, you'll go see a therapist."

Josie looked from her mom to her dad. Realization froze her insides in shock. "I don't believe this. You guys think I'm crazy."

2

The day Josie told her parents that she could talk to ghosts turned her life upside-down and turned their home into a war zone.

"She hears voices, Angela. She talks to things that no one else can see! That's a defining characteristic of schizophrenia, which means she needs help! Real, serious, medical help!"

"Josie is not schizophrenic, Charles. She's not hearing voices telling her to kill people or burn the house down. Please, calm down and let's talk about this rationally!" Angela replied.

"I am the only one here who *is* being rational. Maybe the voices aren't telling her to do those things yet, but don't you think maybe they're the ones telling her to break things, hide things, destroy things, and lie to us? It would explain so much."

As Josie watched them fight about her right in front of her, she pleaded silently with her spirit guides to help her. They appeared, Ethan on one side and Uncle Frank on the other, while Hanover manifested in his usual spot around her neck, the warm tingle of him bringing her peace and strength. *Please, will one of you tell me what I can say to stop Dad from saying these things?*

Both Ethan and Uncle Frank placed a hand on her arms and warmth radiated up her limbs and through her body. *Now is not the time for such things,* said Uncle Frank.

Are you kidding? Now is the perfect time! He's threatening to have me put in a straight-jacket and hauled off to the loony bin!

We cannot interfere at this time. But we are here for you, to tell you that it will all work out.

Seriously? That's all you have for me, some new-age mumbo-jumbo crap? 'It will all work out', you say? How does that help me in this moment?

You must be patient. And remember, we are here for you, Josie, said Ethan, and though they faded from view, she continued to feel them. The warm tingle of their presence seemed to behave like a shield against her parents' argument, keeping the pain of their words from completely reaching her.

But over the next few weeks, things only got worse. Angela was in a tug of war between Josie and Charles. She wanted them all to go to counselling to deal with the Ethan situation, but she needed her husband's support. Charles dug his heels in. Angela tried to plead with him, to reason with him, to threaten him, but he wouldn't give in.

The atmosphere in their house was like a boiling pot of water about to spill over – literally and figuratively. The more they all fought, the hotter it became outside. It was not even summer yet and it was 90 degrees with 77 percent humidity. New England was experiencing a heat wave outside while the York family experienced a heat wave inside.

And once again, Josie sat at the kitchen table – the window fans doing nothing to cool the air – and listened to her dad accuse her of being mentally ill. Inside, she could feel her anger rising like the thermometer. She couldn't take it anymore. She was hot, and she was tired, but she wasn't crazy. She wasn't certain of much anymore but *that* was one thing she knew.

In that realization, Josie reached her final breaking point. She had no more tears left to shed, and she didn't have the energy to argue anymore.

She slammed her hand down on the table. "Dad!" she said with force. Angela and Charles stopped mid-fight and looked at her. Josie rose slowly and faced him, her chin lifted, her spine strong as steel, and her eyes blazing. Josie looked into her father's eyes and calmly asked, "What are you so afraid of?"

For a moment Charles's eyes softened, but then the fire matched her own. "Don't you *dare* speak to me like that!"

Josie opened her mouth to rebut, and then the phone rang; the land-line house phone, loud and shrill, cut through the room. For a moment Josie, Charles, and Angela looked at each other as though they didn't know what the sound was, and then Angela lunged for the receiver.

The person on the other end did a lot of talking in only a minute or two, and Angela's face spoke volumes as her forehead wrinkled and her mouth turned down in a frown. She hung up and looked at Charles and Josie.

"It's Aunt Pauline."

3

On the Sunday that Josie got back from her trip to Florida with Jenna's family she went to visit Aunt Pauline with her mom. Josie was anxious to speak with her alone and had to wait for over an hour and a half for her mother to go to the bathroom, finally allowing her to ask Aunt Pauline a very important question.

As soon as the bathroom door shut Josie said, "When I was in Florida, I had a dream, well maybe it wasn't a dream, and—"

"Josie, dear, it wasn't a dream," said Aunt Pauline, a playful smile curling the corners of her mouth. "I came to visit you."

"I don't understand. How?"

"It's called 'astral travel'. I've done it before, but not often. I find that as I get closer to… well, to going to the other side, that it's easier. I didn't mean to wake you. I merely wanted to check in on you, see your face…. I'm sorry if I frightened you."

Josie frowned as so many questions crowded her brain that her face twisted in confusion.

Aunt Pauline chuckled. "Astral travel is when a soul leaves its body temporarily to travel to other parts of the world. It's an out-of-body experience in which the person has some control over where and when they go."

Josie looked at her in surprise. "That's like what Ophelia did!" she said. She wished she could tell Aunt Pauline all about it, but she couldn't with her mom there. "In Florida, this girl I met—"

"What are you girls talking about?" Angela asked as she glided back into the room.

"Josie was about to tell me a little about her vacation," said Aunt Pauline.

Angela sat next to Josie. "Well, I hope you don't mind if that waits. There's something I'd like to talk to you about."

"Does it have to do with why Charles didn't come with you?"

Angela looked momentarily surprised. "Yes. He's rather upset right now. Josie told us that she found out about Ethan."

Aunt Pauline's eyebrows raised as she glanced at Josie. "And did she tell you how she found out?"

"That's the thing, Aunt Pauline. Josie says… well, she says…."

"That she sees his spirit," Aunt Pauline finished for her.

"Yes," she said with surprise. "Charles didn't take it well. There's been a lot going on with Josie lately, and he seems to think that this is just another… I don't know. It's all a mess, Aunt Pauline. He doesn't believe Josie. He thinks you told her about Ethan and influenced her to lie about seeing spirits."

"Charles always was stubborn in his beliefs. Or rather, lack-thereof," said Aunt Pauline lightly, shaking her head with a smile. "But you didn't tell me what you believe."

Angela pursed her lips, looked at Josie with such sadness in her eyes, and then looked back to Aunt Pauline. "Well, first, I don't believe you told Josie about Ethan but I… I guess I never really believed ghosts existed. I have wanted to believe, and thought it a fun idea, but, really, I didn't. Until… well, Josie told us something that she couldn't have known. And I don't know how else she could have known other than…."

"Other than if Ethan told her himself?" Aunt Pauline again finished Angela's words.

Angela nodded. Tears had sprung to her eyes. "I want to believe Josie. I'm her mother. I feel like I have no choice but to believe her, but… if he really is here, with Josie, doesn't that mean…? I've spent all these years, over twenty years now, telling myself that he was somewhere good and pure, and that he was at peace. But now… I don't know what to think."

Josie felt her mother's anguish and wanted to say something comforting, but the words weren't there. *What can I say?* Josie asked in her mind to Ethan, Uncle Frank, and Hanover, though she couldn't sense their presence. *Can I tell her you are somewhere safe? Can I tell her you're at peace? Are you?*

No answer came for Josie's questions. It seemed she had a lot of questions for them that never got answered, but that wasn't going to stop her from asking. There was a phrase her mom often said that was "the squeaky wheel gets the grease", and it had worked before. She had pestered her guides for information about her birth parents, and though she didn't get answers about them, they did tell her about Ethan. Of course, that led to more questions and problems than she had ever anticipated. *That was part of the lesson, wasn't it?* she said to them. She knew the answer without their response, but she didn't regret any of it. Despite the reaction of her parents, she was glad it happened, that she knew about Ethan and that they knew she could talk to ghosts. She had dealt enough with Simon's skepticism that she was hardly surprised by her dad's response. It hurt a little. Okay, a lot. But it could only get better. Eventually he'd come around and everything would go back to normal. At least, that was the hope she clung to.

"Angela, there's no reason to believe he's not at peace," Aunt Pauline said, passing Angela a box of tissues. "Josie told you Frank is with her too, right? His soul, like Ethan's, is with her to help her, to protect her, to *guide* her. They wouldn't be able to do that if they weren't coming from somewhere *good*!"

Angela blew her nose. "How can you be sure of that?"

Aunt Pauline looked at Josie. "Have you told her about all the souls you've helped because of this ability, and with the help of your guides?"

Josie shook her head. "I didn't get the chance."

"Now's as good a time as any, don't you think?"

Josie shrugged and looked to her mom who looked back at her, her hazel eyes filled with eagerness and tears. So, with a deep, bracing breath, Josie told her mom all about it, from how it started in the woods of Maine, to seeing Ethan for the first time in the back seat of their car, to the ghosts that tormented her at Halloween. On and on she went, telling Angela everything. It poured from her like a flood that had been building up behind a dam. She told her mom everything, including everything that happened in Florida. Well, except for seeing Aunt Pauline. That she kept to herself.

By the time Josie stopped talking Angela had stopped crying, and instead was looking at Josie in awe.

"I know it's a lot to take in, Mom, and it all sounds so crazy. Believe me, for a while I thought I might be going crazy, but I'm not. I'm not crazy. And I want you to talk to Rachel and Greg, and even Jenna. Dave and Simon, too, if you want. They can all back me up."

"Rachel knows?" Angela asked. "She knew about all this before me?"

"Only because of what was going on with Lynette's family while we were in Florida, Mom. And she made me promise to tell you when we got home. She didn't like that I asked her not to say anything to you, but it wasn't something any of us wanted to tell you over the phone from 1,500 miles away. So please don't be mad at her. Be mad at me."

"I'm not mad, Josie, not at anyone. This is just a lot to process."

"Of course it is," said Aunt Pauline. "How about I make us some tea?"

"Thank you, but I think we should go. I need to think. And I need to talk to Charles."

Aunt Pauline was visibly disappointed for a moment, and then smiled. "Of course. I understand."

Josie hugged Aunt Pauline's frail body as tight as she dared, filled with so many questions. "Don't be too hard on your parents, Josie," said Aunt Pauline. "They are dealing with things you can never understand until you have children of your own. Okay?"

"Okay," Josie nodded.

"Please come back soon," Aunt Pauline said. Josie could see Uncle Frank behind her as she closed the door.

At home, they found that Charles had shut himself in his office. When Angela went to tell him that a fresh pot of coffee was in the kitchen, he said he was working and didn't want to be disturbed. Angela went to her bedroom and shut her door.

Angela knew her husband and best friend of 27 years was lying. He wasn't working. He was shutting down, shutting her out. Just like he had in the aftermath of Ethan's death. She told herself not to be worried. She told herself that this was what he needed. He needed time on his own to process it all, to sort through everything before making any more moves or saying anything else. It would be okay, she told herself. She and Charles made it through one of the worst things a husband and wife can experience, and they were stronger for it. If they could make it through that, then they could make it through this.

Angela sat on the edge of the bed and braced herself with her hands on her knees. She felt a sob rising within her, but she took a deep breath and pushed it down. When Ethan died, she fell apart. It had been okay to fall apart then because she no longer had anyone to take care of. But that wasn't true now. She was a mother again, and she had to hold it together for her daughter who, whether she was telling the truth or not, clearly needed her.

"Ethan," Angela said to the air and took another deep breath. "I don't know if you can hear me, or if you're with Josie right now… or even if any of this is truly real…. No, I believe it. I do, Ethan. I believe that the sweet little boy who loved to help me and Daddy with cooking and cleaning and fixing things around the house would be here helping our daughter. Your sister. I want to thank you for that. Thank you for helping Josie through something that… that we cannot understand. Thank you for helping her, and please know that I love you. That Daddy and I love you and will always love you. You will always be in our hearts."

Ethan watched as the woman who was his mother in life walked past him without being able to see him and went into the bathroom and shut the door. *But now it's your turn to help Josie, to be there for her through this,* he said before fading away in a shimmer of light.

4

Over the next few weeks Josie tried to go see Aunt Pauline again. Every Friday – no matter if she had been fighting with her parents that day or not – she would ask if they were going to visit Aunt Pauline that weekend. Each time she asked, her mom had an excuse why they weren't going. "Next weekend, I promise," Angela said each time. Josie even tried to get a ride from Jenna and Dave a couple times, but it never worked out. Josie felt a dread in the pit of her stomach that told her time was running out. She hoped that maybe Aunt Pauline would visit her through astral travel like she did in Florida, but if she did, Josie never saw her. Then, when the phone rang that night, interrupting the explosion that was about to come from her father, Josie's worst fears were realized.

"She's gone?" Josie finally broke the silence as Charles drove them to Aunt Pauline's, her voice shaking.

"No, but they don't expect her to last much longer," said Angela. "I just feel terrible. She kept calling, inviting us over, but with everything that's been going on, well… and now…." Angela broke into sobs in the passenger seat. Josie saw her father reach over to comfort her, but Angela pushed his hand away.

When they walked into Aunt Pauline's bedroom, Josie drew in a breath. The room was full of people, but they were people only Josie could see. Uncle Frank was there, as expected, standing right next to Aunt Pauline's bed at her head. She didn't know most of the others but recognized many of them from photo albums or from one of the many photos in frames around the apartment.

Josie rubbed at her arms like there was a chill, but that wasn't it. There was something else going on in the room. There was a feeling in the air, like static electricity in cold fog. A feeling of light-headedness overcame her for a moment, as though her head were a helium balloon trying to lift her entire body off the ground. Josie thought of an elementary school field trip to the science museum and the big plasma ball that you could touch to make your hair stand up on end. If you could walk inside one, she thought, this is what it would feel like.

She shook herself and met Uncle Frank's kind, blue eyes. *Is she...?*

Not yet, but soon. She's waiting for you.

* * * * *

Angela pulled a chair to Aunt Pauline's bedside and took the woman's near-lifeless hand in hers. Aunt Pauline opened her eyes and smiled, then said one barely audible word, "Josie…."

Josie moved through the room, carefully navigating her way through the people her parents couldn't see, to stand next to her mother. Aunt Pauline focused on Josie and smiled wider.

"Aunt Pauline," Angela said, "you know how much we love you, right?"

Still looking at Josie, Aunt Pauline nodded, and then closed her eyes. After more than fifteen minutes passed without Aunt Pauline opening her eyes, Josie said, "Mom, I'm gonna sit over there," pointing to a chair at the back of the room.

Angela nodded and sniffled and then wiped her nose with a wad of crumpled tissues she'd been gripping since the car ride. Josie again navigated her way around all the people to the chair, careful to avoid her father's eyes as she passed him where he stood stiffly in the doorway.

Josie sat back and watched Aunt Pauline's chest rise and fall in slow, shallow movements. She looked around at the others in the room. Some of them turned and acknowledged Josie with a smile or a nod, but mostly they were all focused on Aunt Pauline. She could tell by the soft glow around each of them, each one a different hue, and from the feeling of pure love that filled the room, that they were all crossed – not stuck – spirits. Then came the familiar warm tingle around her neck that signaled the arrival of Hanover, and Ethan shimmered into view standing at Uncle Frank's side.

An hour passed. At some point, another chair was brought in for Charles. The nurse came in and out a couple times to check on Aunt Pauline and then to bring them all cups of coffee.

Another half hour ticked by. Josie was doing her best to remain patient, but Charles frequently stood, sighed, left the room, and then would return a few minutes later and sit again. And then it started. Aunt Pauline's breathing became raspy and sporadic. There were moments when it looked like her chest wasn't going to rise again, and then it moved slowly once more. As this pattern continued, Josie noticed a soft, pale lime-green glow start to radiate around Aunt Pauline, diffusing further out with each laborious breath she took.

Then Aunt Pauline sat up. Only Josie and the other spirits in the room saw this because it wasn't her physical body that moved. It was her soul. To Josie's astonishment, she looked only remotely like the woman she'd known all her life. She looked about forty years younger with smooth skin and long, wavy, chestnut hair. Aunt Pauline looked around the room at each of the spirits standing in waiting. A few moved closer and reached out their ethereal hands to her. The static-electricity feeling in the air jumped and crackled. Josie felt a pulse-like vibration fill the room and move through her whole body. Tears sprang to her eyes.

Aunt Pauline reached her hands out, one to her husband and one to a woman who looked remarkably like her. *Hello, Mom,* Josie heard her say to the woman. As the two of them helped her rise from her body on the bed, Josie noticed Aunt Pauline's body was still struggling to breathe.

How is that possible? Isn't she dead? Josie asked.

The dying process isn't always quite as cut-and-dry as most living people believe, Hanover said in her ear.

But she is dying, isn't she....

Yes, Josie. Watch and learn, said Hanover.

The spirits in the room formed a tight circle around Aunt Pauline's soul. Then Josie heard Uncle Frank say, *Pauline, is there anything you need to do or say before you go?*

Yes. There are a few things I need to say to my family first, she said. Uncle Frank nodded, and the circle parted. She moved forward to where Josie sat.

Tears poured from Josie's eyes as she looked up at Aunt Pauline. *You look beautiful*, Josie said, with her mind.

Thank you, Dear. Will you help me talk to them? She nodded at Charles and Angela.

Josie nodded. "Mom? Dad?"

Angela turned to look at Josie, but Charles didn't move. "What is it, Josie?"

"Aunt Pauline is asking me to tell you both something," Josie said. She saw her father tense.

Angela frowned. "Josie, how is that possible? She's not gone yet."

"I don't really know. I think... well, I guess she's preparing to go. And before she goes, she wants me to tell you something."

"This is ridiculous," Charles growled. "Now is not the time to be pulling this crap. Not while she is lying there dying!" He stood with such force that his chair slammed back against the wall.

"Actually, Dad, this is *exactly* the time for this. I don't care if you don't believe in any of this right now, but I need you to at least listen to what she has to say!" Josie railed back, her voice high-pitched and cracking with the beginnings of grief.

"Okay, Josie," said Angela, shooting a formidable look at Charles. "We're listening."

Josie sniffled back tears and calmed her breathing while Aunt Pauline talked. "She says that you and Dad have been like her children to her, that you treated her better than her own son, and she wants you to know how grateful she is for that."

"Anyone would know that," Charles mumbled.

Josie ignored him, and Angela shushed him.

"She wants you to go into the chest, the one under the window. Inside, under the quilt, there is a box of stuff that's for you both."

Angela rose and went to the wooden chest and lifted the top. She moved a large quilt and found a broad cardboard box underneath. She put the quilt back and closed the lid, placing the box on top. When she lifted the lid off the box, she gasped and started to cry. "Charles, you have to see this," she said through her tears.

He sighed and reluctantly went to his wife's side. He didn't say anything, but he bowed his head and Josie could see his jaw muscles twitching.

Angela turned toward Josie. "Please tell her thank you for us."

"She can hear you, Mom."

"Right… um… Aunt Pauline, I just want to say… oh, I feel rather ridiculous…." Angela said as she gripped the box lid to her chest. She then shook herself and looked at the ceiling. "Aunt Pauline, I'm sorry—" Her voice caught in her throat. She took a breath. "I'm sorry we didn't come sooner."

After a pause, Josie said, "She said that she knows. She's not angry with you. She loves you very much." Josie's cheeks were drenched in tears. Her dad went back to his chair and sat with his head in his hands, elbows propped on his knees, while Angela returned to Aunt Pauline's side, the box in her lap. The nurse slipped quietly into the room.

It's time for me to go now, Josie. Remember that I love you, and I promise I will come see you whenever I can, said Aunt Pauline.

Josie could only nod through her stifled sobs.

Ready? said Aunt Pauline's mother.

I'm ready.

The rest of the spirits who had waited silently and patiently once again moved in close and circled Aunt Pauline. The glowing auras of each spirit began to stretch and fuse together in a tapestry of shimmering colors, and then it began to flow like a gentle wave circling the group. The pulsing vibration quickened as the swirling auras flowed faster and faster, like a high-speed rainbow merry-go-round. Josie could feel the wind it created though it didn't disturb anything in the room, not even a hair on her head.

She watched as the colors brightened, the flowing energy quickened, the vibration thrummed through her whole body, and the images of the spirits blurred together. Josie was filled with an intense feeling of love that made her heart pound hard and fast in her chest. Her breath caught as though it was being sucked out of her. And then in a blink it was over, and they were all gone. The room was empty of all spirits except Hanover.

Josie looked at Aunt Pauline's body and saw that her chest had ceased its struggle to rise.

"She's gone," said Josie. Angela sobbed at Aunt Pauline's side, and Charles went to his wife. He put his hands on her shoulders and this time Angela didn't push him away.

You should leave the room now, said Hanover from his place on Josie's shoulder. Without a word, she stood and quietly slipped from the room.

Uncle Frank and Ethan were standing in the living room, and when she saw them, she frowned.

What are you still doing here? she asked.

Josie, we've come to say goodbye, said Uncle Frank.

Josie's heart dropped to her feet, and she felt sick. She looked from Uncle Frank to Ethan. *You're leaving me?*

We have served our purpose for you. Now, it's time for me to be with Pauline, he said.

How am I supposed to argue that? she scoffed, shaking her head. *I can't very well ask you not to be with your wife who just died. But what about you?* Her eyes looked at Ethan.

I have served my purpose for you as well, Josie. I am now nothing more than a burden, a thorn between you and your parents.

You mean our *parents, don't you?*

Right now, they are your parents, and they need to be focused on that. You need to be focused on that, too.

Josie felt like her insides had turned into cement. *But what if they need to hear a message from you?*

If they do then I will return and pass along my message with or without your help, but you do not need me as your guide anymore. It's time for someone new to take our place.

Someone new? Josie's entire body tensed in fear.

Yes. But Hanover will still be with you, so you are not alone, Josie. Even with us gone, we will still be watching over you, said Uncle Frank.

More tears poured from Josie. Her whole body ached.

You have an amazing life's journey ahead of you, Josie, said Ethan. *Don't lose faith in that or in yourself.*

And with that, they were gone. "No! Don't leave me!" Josie yelled and collapsed on the floor in sobs.

She didn't know what was happening when she suddenly felt hands on her shoulders. Then she heard her mother's voice. "It's okay, Josie. It's okay to be sad about Aunt Pauline," she said in Josie's ear as she was guided to the couch.

"No, no it's not that," Josie sobbed.

"Of course, honey. Just let it out. We're all really sad right now," she said. A box of tissues was placed into Josie's lap.

Josie looked up at her mom, her dad standing at the periphery again, and she shook her head. "You guys wouldn't understand," she said.

"Help us understand, then," said Angela.

Josie shook her head. She had just lost Aunt Pauline, the one living person who understood better than anyone what she was going through, and then in the next breath she lost two of the dead people who understood her. They had helped her so much since they first made their presence known to her and now, they were gone and she was alone.

"Can we just go home now?" Josie wiped at her wet cheeks.

They rode in stony silence, each in their own personal cocoon of mourning and brooding. When Charles spoke to Angela, she snapped at him. When Angela spoke to Josie, Josie snapped at her. Then the sky opened, and rain poured down, drumming loudly on the roof, bringing a bit of relief to the atmosphere outside the car if not inside.

The drive home seemed to take forever, not just because of the tension in the car but because Charles was driving slower than normal because of the torrential downpour. Josie just wanted to be home, to lock herself in her room where she could wallow in her grief. Within it all, she felt a small bit of joy at what she had witnessed as Aunt Pauline passed on, but it was like the sun trying to peek through storm clouds during a hurricane.

But when they got home, Josie realized that it was the last place she wanted to be. "I'm going over to Jenna's."

"No," Angela said, shaking her head. "Not tonight, Josie."

"Mom, please. I really need to be with my friends right now," Josie replied.

"You need to listen to your mother, Josie," Charles growled.

"And I think we should all be together as a family tonight," added Angela.

"As long as Dad thinks I'm a mentally ill freak, we are *not* a family," Josie snapped. She turned and walked out of the house.

5

Once outside, she called Jenna. The rain had stopped, and the temperature had dropped significantly. "Where are you?" she asked when Jenna answered.

"With Dave on our way to my house. Why?"

"Can you come get me?"

"Sure, we'll be right there. Everything okay?"

"No. I'll tell you about it when you get here."

Josie walked to the end of the driveway and kept walking. She was two streets away from home when Jenna and Dave saw her and stopped the car.

"You look awful," Jenna said with shock.

"Yeah, well, I got to witness Aunt Pauline die today and then Uncle Frank and Ethan told me they were leaving me, too. So, yeah, you could say I've had a bad day."

"Oh my god, Josie! I'm so sorry!" said Jenna.

"Geez, that sucks," said Dave.

"You're not kidding. And you should probably know that my parents didn't want me to come over, so just I walked out."

"Wow, I can't believe you did that!" said Jenna.

"I just… my dad, he thinks I'm crazy. Aunt Pauline wanted me to give them a message and he didn't want to listen. It was the weirdest thing. Jenna, her body was still breathing – barely, but it was – and her spirit was standing before me. All these other spirits were there. Uncle Frank, of course, and her mother, and all these other souls. And she looked younger. She was beautiful. And they took her away and her body… stopped."

"Wow," Jenna said again.

"Today hasn't been a good day for families," said Dave.

"What do you mean?" Josie frowned.

"My parents are getting a divorce," he said.

"What? Oh, geez, Dave. I'm so sorry. Why did you guys let me go on and on about my stupid problems?"

"Josie, it's fine. Really," said Dave.

"I feel like an idiot. I had no idea." Josie said.

"Why would you? We didn't know. Came as a total shock to us all."

"That's crazy. I mean, I only met them a couple times, but they seemed happy."

"Yeah, they were good at looking happy, but they weren't good at actually *being* happy. Turns out that my dad's been having an affair with a woman from work and she's pregnant. He's moving out today and going to live with her."

"So, I'm guessing you also feel like you've been hit by a truck?" Josie asked him.

"That about sums it up," he said.

"Jenna, please tell me your parents are still disgustingly wonderful and happily married people," said Josie.

"As far as I know, but after what you two have been through today, I'm kind of afraid to go home and find out."

A minute later they pulled into Jenna's driveway to see Jenna's mom heading to her car.

"Hi guys," Rachel waved at them. "Josie, I'm on my way to your house. Your mom needs a friend right now."

"Okay, good," Josie said with a sigh of relief. For a moment she thought Rachel was going to drag her back home.

"Dad's got dinner cooking. You and Dave are welcome to stay and eat, but Jenna, make sure you all help clean up, okay?"

"Sure thing, Mom," Jenna smiled.

Inside, amazing smells greeted them.

"Chicken Marsala," said Dave. "Jenna, I love your family."

"You love our food," she teased.

"I love *you*, and I appreciate the food," he said, planting a kiss on her cheek.

"Jenna, can you come set the table?" Greg called from the kitchen.

"Sure, Dad," she replied. They all followed her toward the kitchen. "Dave and Josie are staying for dinner. Mom said it's okay."

"Fine with me," said Greg. "Sorry about your parents, Dave."

Dave frowned. "Word travels fast," he grumbled.

"Yeah, well, your dad was trying to enlist Simon and me to help him move some of his stuff."

"Figures. My brother and I refused to help him."

"Yeah, well, so did we," said Greg.

Dave released a breath. "Thanks."

"No thanks needed. Your father dug himself into a big, bad hole and I have no interest in helping him out of it."

"Yeah," Dave nodded, his voice caught in his throat.

Greg stopped what he was doing and put a hand on Dave's shoulder. "You're like another son to us, Dave. If you or your mom or brother need anything, you let us know. Got it?"

Dave nodded again.

"And Josie," said Greg, "my condolences on the passing of your aunt."

"Thanks," she replied.

Jenna handed Josie the plates and headed into the dining room with hands full of flatware. They quickly laid the table while Dave followed with cups and napkins. They brought the food to the table just as Simon appeared from somewhere in the house.

Josie was suddenly very aware of the fact that she couldn't remember the last time she'd looked in a mirror. She'd done a lot of crying since then and knew she must look like a wreck. She stole a glance at Simon, but he wasn't looking at her. She was both relieved and disappointed.

"Where's Mom?" Simon asked.

"She's at Josie's house. Angela's aunt passed away today," said Greg.

“Oh, I’m sorry to hear that, Josie,” he said, but still didn’t look at her.

“Thanks,” she replied half-heartedly and stifled a sigh. She always hoped for more with their interactions, always hoped that he would say more, do more, see more. She was always disappointed. Except for when they were in Florida. They had finally talked and confessed their feelings for each other. Well, she confessed her feelings for him while he confessed confusion. But then they kissed! Finally! And it wasn’t just an ordinary kiss. Something happened in that moment, something strange and wonderful. At the time it felt so real. Time stopped. The ocean and seagulls froze in their rolling and whirling as though captured in a photograph. The only thing moving was a shower of energy forming a dome around them and a cord of sparkling silver and gold energy that that linked her and Simon together. But was it real? Or was it something else, like seeing a ghost, real but only she could see it? Did Simon experience it that way? They never had a chance to talk about it. They kissed a second time but then he broke the connection and ran off. She wanted to talk to him about it, to clear the air and figure out a way to move past it all, but in the weeks since spring break, he had either skillfully avoided her or somehow made sure they were never in the same room alone.

Now, however, Simon was the least of her worries. Her head was spinning with other questions. *What am I going to do without Uncle Frank and Ethan? When will my new guide come to me? How will I know I can trust them? What will they look like? How will I know they’re a guide? How long do guides stay? Why did they have to leave me now?* Her stomach churned with these new anxieties as she tried to force herself to eat a bite of chicken.

It was only when Josie heard a huffy voice say, *Excuse me! What am I? Chopped liver?* that she realized Hanover and his tingling warm presence hadn’t left her shoulders all afternoon.

No, Hanover. Come on, you know what I meant! I just lost three people! Not just Aunt Pauline. And that’s a lot for anyone!

I'm sorry if you don't get that, she said, stopping herself from scowling. *I am very grateful for you and that you're still here. It's just... a big shock. Okay?*

Alright, Josie, I understand. That's why I'm here, to help you through this time. Just try to enjoy your time with your friends. We can talk about it all later, he replied.

"Earth to Josie!" said Jenna.

"What?" Josie asked, her head snapping up.

Jenna raised her eyebrows at her friend. "You okay?"

"Yeah, sorry, I was lost in thought," Josie replied.

"Well, I was just saying that with the guys away for Senior Week next week, you and I will have to plan something fun to celebrate once finals are over," said Jenna.

"Yeah, that sounds great," said Josie, her manner lacking the enthusiasm of the words.

Jenna frowned at her friend, sympathetic but helpless. She looked at Simon and raised her eyebrows at him in a silent plea to help her cheer Josie up, but he ignored her.

Simon didn't have to see the strain on Josie's face or the distracted look in her eyes to know that there was a war going on inside her, an internal conversation filled with emotion. But then he realized that maybe it wasn't as internal as he thought. Josie had demonstrated time and again that she could talk to her spirit guides without speaking aloud. Was that what he felt? He wouldn't look at her. He couldn't allow himself to, because looking at her made it harder to deny everything he felt. But not looking was difficult, too. It was like when your friends would say "whatever you do, don't turn around," and then all you wanted to do was turn around. Or like a door that says, "Keep Out" and you just have to know what's behind that door.

He took a deep breath and looked up from his dinner plate to see Josie doing her best to focus on the food in front of her. But her eyes were red and puffy. She'd been doing a lot of crying. Of course she had, she'd just lost her aunt. He knew they were close.

Simon heard her talk about the woman even if Josie didn't believe he was listening. But there was something else there, too. Something bigger weighing on Josie.

He wanted to do something to help. Whether they were friends or not, he would want to help her, because Josie was a good person who always tried to help others, even if her way of helping was very unconventional in his mind. But he didn't know how to help. He knew science, and he knew medicine. He knew physics and calculus and biology homework. He could tutor her in any subject in school. But he was sure that what she was dealing with went way beyond that. Plus, he needed to sort his own stuff out first. Getting too near her fried him like lightning to a circuit board, and he had a lot to figure out before dealing with that.

Dinner passed with Jenna and Greg driving most of the conversation around a lot of awkward silences. When they finished eating – or pushing food around their plates like Josie – Dave and Simon went to the basement to play video games at Jenna's insistence while Josie and Jenna cleaned up the dinner dishes. Josie didn't mind. She was grateful to have time alone with Jenna.

"I don't know how I'm going to get through finals this week," Josie said as she loaded a plate into the dishwasher.

"What's the deal with your spirit guides? Did they tell you why they were going?"

Josie shrugged one shoulder. "Uncle Frank is going to spend time with Aunt Pauline," she said.

"Oh, well… that's really kinda sweet," Jenna said, rinsing a glass and passing it to Josie.

"I know, right? And Ethan said that he would be more in the way than he would be helpful now, and that my parents need to focus on *me* not him."

"I guess I kinda get that," said Jenna, "but it seems pretty harsh. I mean, couldn't they at least have spaced it out for you? Like, Uncle Frank leaves today, and Ethan leaves in like a week or two. You know, give you time to adjust."

"Ha, yeah, that would have been nice. I don't know why they did it like this. But Hanover's still with me. He's been with me almost all day, which is actually kinda cool because none of them ever hung around for such a long time like this before."

"Well, I guess he knows you need all the support you can get," replied Jenna.

Josie felt the tingle around her neck ripple warmly as if he was confirming this. "Yeah, and I feel bad complaining about all this when Dave is going through something so huge."

"Don't feel bad, Josie. You've both experienced huge losses today. But you can't compare them. They're different. One isn't better or worse than the other."

Josie shook her head at Jenna. "You're far too wise for sixteen."

"Yeah, well, my parents always said I was an old soul. Whatever that means. If only I had a spirit guide that would give me some clue."

"I'm sure you have a spirit guide," said Josie, thinking back to the female spirit in a white robe she saw near Jenna a couple times, pretty sure that she was Jenna's spirit guide. "In fact, I've been thinking about that. There might be a way we can find out who yours is."

"Really?" Jenna said, her face brightening.

"Yeah, but I need to wait until after finals. Okay?"

"Sure! Of course. Wow, Josie, that would be amazing." She loaded the last of the dishes into the dishwasher, closed the door, and started the machine. "So, did your guides tell you anything else?"

Josie shook her head. "Just that a new guide will come to me at some point. But Hanover did say that we could talk about it later. He wants me to just have some down time right now."

"Cool. Maybe we should bake some cookies and watch a movie. And you could take some home. Isn't that what people always do when there's a death in the family? Send food?"

"Yeah, I guess," Josie shrugged. "Do you think Dave is okay? I mean, how is he doing with his stuff?"

"I don't really know," Jenna said, as she started to pull the ingredients for the cookies from the cabinets. "I haven't had a chance to talk to him about it. And I don't want to push it. My guess is that he's angry. At least, that's how I'd feel."

"Sure, but Dave's a pretty sensitive guy. Make sure he knows you're open to talking about it. Don't just wait for him to talk."

Jenna looked at Josie with raised eyebrows. "Where is this coming from?"

"What? I meant that in a good way."

"I know. That's why I'm confused."

"Don't be. I like Dave. When we were in Florida and I was dealing with all that weird stuff with Ophelia, and Simon was being such a jerk, Dave was really cool to me. We had a nice talk at one point."

"Where was I? I don't remember that."

"I think you were in the shower."

"What did he say?" She started measuring flour into a large glass bowl.

Josie's cheeks burned so she turned away, focusing intently on scooping brown sugar into a measuring cup. She couldn't tell Jenna that she and Dave had been talking mostly about her feelings for Simon. "We were talking about relationships – you know, Ben not telling Ophelia how he felt – and he said a lot of nice things about you."

"Of course he did," Jenna beamed. "We are soul mates."

"Do you really believe in that?" Josie asked, genuinely curious. "That you are meant for each other on a soul level?"

"Of course. Why? Don't you believe in soul mates?"

"I did before but now I don't know. I guess it's taken on a whole new meaning now that I can actually see and talk to souls."

"Sounds like Uncle Frank and Aunt Pauline are soul mates," Jenna said, cracking an egg into the bowl. "I mean, he spent fifty years with her in life and wants to spend time with her in death. Sounds like a soul connection to me."

Josie nodded. Tears sprang to her eyes.

Jenna looked at Josie. "Sorry," Jenna said, cracking another egg and tossing the shell in the sink.

Josie shook her head again. "It's fine. It wasn't you. I just started to think about all the questions I had for her. She understood this stuff, you know? She couldn't see spirits, but she could sense them, hear them, and she knew what it was like. I knew I didn't have much longer with her, and I tried to visit her, talk to her, but things kept getting in the way. And now…."

Jenna wiped her hands on a towel and hugged Josie. "And now you can still talk to her, it will just be a little different. Right? I mean, how cool is it that you know she's not truly gone? Some people have faith in it, but not everyone gets to know it and experience it the way you do."

When Jenna released Josie from the hug, she grabbed a paper towel and wiped her cheeks. "You're right. Most of the time it's amazing to have this perspective but… it's just not the same."

"I know it's not the same, but eventually you won't be so sad. Eventually her not being physically here won't hurt so much, and maybe she'll have even more wisdom for you from *there* than she had from *here*," said Jenna.

"I hope you're right," Josie sighed. "Ugh. Seriously, why do we have to have exams this week?"

"I just can't wait for it to be over. Can you believe we're almost Juniors? I am so excited for summer. Did you know our parents are talking about us all going away somewhere together?"

"What? No, I haven't heard a word about it. But my parents don't talk to me about much these days," said Josie. "Do you know where they want to go?"

Jenna shook her head as she mixed the cookie dough. "I think they're still figuring it out. I don't really care where we go. It will just be fun for our families to vacation together."

"Definitely. I don't think I'd survive without your whole family as a buffer between me and my dad," said Josie, pouring chocolate chips slowly into the bowl as Jenna stirred. "That is, if I'm not locked away in a mental hospital first."

"He'll come around eventually," said Jenna.

"I hope you're right and I hope it's sooner rather than later. I can see how hard this is on my mom. She's stuck in the middle of it all. I'm afraid if we keep fighting the way we are, they'll end up divorcing too."

"I don't think that will happen," Jenna shook her head.

"Did you think Dave's parents would end up divorced?"

"Well, no. They seemed happy. They seemed like an awesome family."

"Yeah, so it just goes to show, you never know."

* * * * *

"There's nothing better than fresh-baked cookies," said Dave. He hovered behind Jenna as she pulled the cookie sheet from the oven and placed it on the stovetop.

"They need to cool first," she said, batting him with the oven mitt. "You guys want to watch a movie?"

"Sure, babe," said Dave, taking a swipe of dough from the bowl as Jenna scooped another batch onto a second cookie sheet.

"Okay. Josie, can you start the popcorn? Dave, you and Simon pick a movie, but make sure it's something we *all* will like, okay?"

"You got it," Dave replied.

"I'll get drinks," said Simon. "What do you guys want?"

"Coke for me," replied Dave.

"Me too," said Jenna.

"Water, please," said Josie.

Jenna got another batch of cookies in the oven while Josie popped the popcorn, and then they joined Simon and Dave in the living room. Jenna and Dave snuggled together in the double-sized chair leaving Josie and Simon to occupy opposite ends of the couch, an ocean of awkwardness between them. Memories tickled the edge of her mind of him telling her that when he was near her, he felt things he shouldn't feel. She remembered how time came to a stand-still when they touched, how a shower of energy rained down around them as they kissed, and how they *both* gave into the kiss... deeply. But she wouldn't let her mind give in to those memories, she wouldn't allow herself to wonder what he was thinking, what he was feeling. She wouldn't allow herself to wonder if he regretted the kiss or if he wanted more or if he would even allow himself to feel any of those things now. He and Mary Alice had broken up right after they got back from Florida, but that hadn't motivated Simon to talk to her in the weeks since.

Josie shook her head and put up a wall in her mind against those thoughts. It was the last thing she wanted to think about after the day she had.

* * * * *

They finished the movie, half the cookies, all of the popcorn, and were debating on another movie when they heard Rachel's car in the driveway.

"Ugh, she's probably going to tell me I need to go home," moaned Josie. "I don't want to go home. I want to live here."

"Me, too," said Dave. "But I'm gonna go. I need to be home with my mom tonight." He stood to go.

Simon gave Dave a wave and a "See ya" as he bolted from the room. Jenna walked Dave out to his car and came back in a minute later with her mom.

"Hi Josie," said Rachel.

"Hi. How's my mom? She wants me home, right?"

"She's doing a little better," Rachel replied. "She knows that you understand that this is all taking a toll on her. But she also knows it's hard on you too, and she is willing to give you some space. So, she packed up a bag for you if you'd like to spend the night."

"Really?" Josie looked at Jenna who smiled and nodded.

"Yes, but on the condition that you text her to let her know you're staying, and she'll pick you up around eight thirty tomorrow morning to get you to rehearsal."

"Deal! Thank you!" said Josie, taking the bag of stuff from Rachel and pulling her phone from her pocket to text her mom.

"Speaking of rehearsal, did you get us the tickets for your recital?" Jenna asked as they settled back on the couch to watch another movie.

"No, I'll get them tomorrow at dress rehearsal. Are you sure the guys want to come?" Josie asked.

"Yes, I'm sure. Josie, you come to almost all of our games. We want to support you the way you support us. Dave and Simon both agreed."

"You'll have to sit through a lot of little kids dancing. You guys are gonna hate it."

"It's part of the show, so we'll deal with it."

Josie shrugged. With Jenna there she had no doubt Dave and Simon would behave. "Okay. Well, I'm really excited you'll all be there."

"I'm excited to see you dance. How many different numbers are you in?"

"Four. I'm in group dances for ballet, contemporary, and jazz, and then I have my ballet solo, which I am super nervous about," said Josie.

"Is that the dance you choreographed yourself?"

Josie nodded. "Miss Jillian helped me polish it up a bit. It's pretty amazing. I'm just nervous I'm going to screw up. I've never done a solo in front of so many people. But as soon as I showed her the choreography, she told me I had to do it in the recital."

"That's amazing, Josie."

Josie shrugged again. "I guess. Thanks. I just need to get through finals and.... Oh no!" She sat up, poised on the edge of the couch cushion.

"What?"

"The funeral! There's going to be a funeral for Aunt Pauline. What if it's at the same time as the recital? Or my final exams?"

"Josie, you have enough to worry about without worrying about that. I'm sure your parents will take care of everything."

Josie sunk back onto the couch. "You're right. I know. God, I feel like I'm losing my mind. My brain just won't stop."

"Sounds like you need more cookies," said Jenna.

"Yes, please! Let me drown my worries in chocolate chips."

* * * * *

When Josie got into her mom's car in the morning, she could see the strain on Angela's face immediately.

"Did you have fun?" Angela asked.

"Yeah, I guess," replied Josie. "We made cookies and watched a couple movies and just hung out."

"Just the two of you?" she asked.

Josie sensed her mother was fishing. "No. Dave and Simon watched the first movie with us, but then Dave went home, and Simon disappeared. Did you know Dave's parents are getting a divorce?"

"No. That's too bad."

"Yeah. His dad was cheating on his mom and got his girlfriend pregnant, so he's moving in with her."

"What? Oh, that's awful. That poor family," said Angela.

Unable to control herself, Josie asked, "Are you and Dad going to divorce?"

"No, of course not! Why would you say that?"

"Because you're hardly speaking to each other and when you do, you're fighting."

"We are not fighting, Josie. I'm sure to you it seems that way, but I promise you, your dad and I might be disagreeing about some stuff right now—"

"Me," Josie interjected.

"—but we're in a strong marriage. If he and I could make it through...," she sighed, "if we can make it through losing Ethan, then we can make it through anything. And we will make it through this, Josie. I promise you."

Josie crossed her arms and sunk down in the seat. She wasn't convinced. "Don't make promises you can't keep."

Angela opened her mouth to respond but closed it with another sigh. She wouldn't admit aloud that Josie was right. She couldn't guarantee it, but she was going to do everything in her power to keep her family together.

After a few minutes of silence, Josie asked, "When's Aunt Pauline's funeral?"

"I don't know, honey. Cousin Gary is flying in tomorrow to take care of the arrangements. Why do you ask?"

"Well, it's just with final exams this week and my recital on Saturday, graduation on Sunday...." Josie didn't know how to say what she meant to say without sounding selfish.

"I know. I've thought about that too, but we can't worry about it until Gary makes the arrangements," she replied, pulling to a stop in front of the high school auditorium where rehearsals would take place.

"Ugh. Fine. Bye," Josie said.

She was about to shut the door when Angela said, "Josie?"

"Yeah?"

"I love you."

"I love you, too, Mom," Josie replied, shut the door, and walked away. But she wasn't sure she believed it. She wasn't sure she believed anything her mother just said to her.

6

"I don't know if I can make it through two more days of this," Josie said to Jenna as they climbed in Jenna's car.

"Seriously, final exams are *way* harder this year."

"Where are Simon and Dave today?" Josie asked. Seniors took final exams the week before, and while everyone else took exams this week, the Senior class was having fun. Monday, they had a barbecue and a day full of games like corn hole, volleyball, and a three-legged race that Simon and Dave won, and the day before was spent at Hampton Beach.

"They're at Canobie Lake Park."

"Oh, I love that place! I haven't been there in years."

"I don't picture you as an amusement park kinda person," said Jenna.

"Really? I love roller coasters," said Josie.

"Look at that, I just learned something new about my best friend," Jenna smiled. "We totally need to go there this summer, all four of us. That would be so fun!"

"I'm in. I could use some real fun instead of the roller coaster that is my life right now."

"Once finals are over some of that should go away, right?"

Josie shrugged. Jenna came to a stop in Josie's driveway. Josie looked at her house. "Finals are the least of it right now. School seems ridiculous compared to all this other stuff going on."

Jenna tilted her head at her friend. "It will get better, Josie."

Josie nodded. "I know. I just wonder what else is going to happen between now and then." She shivered, telling herself it was the car's air conditioning that chilled her and not her own words.

Inside, Josie could hear her mom and dad in the kitchen. She tried to slip by unnoticed, but not even halfway up the stairs, Angela called, "Josie, come here, please!"

Josie groaned and rolled her eyes as she turned around and made her way slowly back down the stairs. "Yeah, what's up?" she said with what she hoped sounded like cheer and not dread.

"How did your exams go today?" Angela asked.

Josie shrugged with one shoulder. "I don't know. Good, I think. They were hard."

"School should be hard. It means they're challenging you," said Charles, his back to her as he slowly poured himself a glass of water.

"I'm sure you did just fine," said Angela with a forced smile. "But I have some bad news."

Josie's stomach dropped to her feet. "What is it?"

"I was with Gary today, helping him with everything for Aunt Pauline. The funeral is going to be Saturday at ten, followed by the burial, and then a gathering afterwards with lunch. This is all taking place over in Hudson."

"What? But that's like an hour away! I'll miss my recital! My solo!" Tears stung her eyes and gripped her throat.

"Well, maybe not. I need to be there the whole time, but you don't. Your dad and I talked about it, and since the recital doesn't start until two, if we take two cars, you and he can leave after the burial and go to the recital."

"But you're not going to be there? That means you'll miss my solo!"

Angela sighed. "I'll head there as soon as the gathering is over, but there's no telling how long that will take, so I can't guarantee I'll make it. I'm really sorry, Josie. But Dad will be there, and if I miss it, I'll get to see it on the DVD. I'm not crazy about it, Josie, but unfortunately, it's the best we can do. There's just too much going on and not enough of me to go around."

Josie sighed too. She was hurt and disappointed and frustrated. She wanted her mom there. "Okay, whatever. That's fine. Can I go study now?"

"Sure," said Angela. "Dinner will be ready in an hour."

"Okay."

When Josie reached her bedroom, she shut the door and flopped down onto her bed. "How am I going to be alone in a car with my dad? He thinks I'm crazy!"

She groaned and heaved her backpack onto the bed. Studying for her Geometry and Earth Science finals the next day was a welcome distraction from thoughts she didn't want to give in to. When a warm tingling formed around her neck and shoulders, she smiled.

"Hi Hanover," she said.

We will get you through this, he replied.

"We? Who is we?"

* * * * *

On Friday afternoon Josie and Jenna celebrated the end of final exams with a pizza at Centerwood Village Pizzeria.

"Have you heard from Dave much?" asked Josie.

Jenna shook her head as she swallowed a bite of pizza. "I got one picture of a humpback whale from him and a text telling me how upset he was that no one had gotten seasick yet."

"That's so Dave," said Josie, shaking her head and smiling.

"I know. It's so weird. I haven't seen him since he left my house on Saturday. I think this is the longest I've gone without seeing him since I was, like, six years old."

"Well, I guess it's a taste of what it will be like when he's at UNH next year, right?"

"Good point. I really haven't thought a lot about that."

"You haven't?" Josie was surprised. She thought too much about what it would be like next year with Simon away at school.

"Yeah. I guess it seemed so far away, so unreal. But...." Jenna took a sip of root beer and Josie thought she saw tears glisten in Jenna's eyes. She waited for Jenna to swallow and continue. "He leaves in something like nine weeks. I still can't really believe it."

"How's his mom doing?"

"He says she's okay. More angry than sad. His dad moved out completely, and none of them are talking to him. His mom has one of the top divorce lawyers in the state, and I guess he's not even fighting the charge of infidelity, so she's gonna be well taken care of with alimony."

"Wow, she's not wasting any time."

"I can't blame her. It's not like there's any chance of reconciliation. If it was me, I'd want to get him out of my life as fast as possible."

"I don't know. It's giving him exactly what he wants – to be free of the family he should be responsible for so he can go have fun with his mistress," Josie said, emphasizing the last word with a sour expression. She shuddered. "I would want to make the process slow and painful."

Jenna laughed and shook her head at Josie. "I don't think he'll be having much fun. Most of his money will go to alimony and college tuition for both of his sons, and his girlfriend is going to have a newborn soon, which means living with a screaming baby. If there is any justice in this world, he will soon find himself very miserable. I'm trusting in karma."

"I hope you're right," said Josie, tossing a crust of pizza on her plate. "Alright, I can't eat anymore. Ready to go?"

Jenna nodded as she finished chewing her last bite.

At the nail salon, Josie chose a pale pink that she felt complemented her skin tone and Jenna picked a vibrant blue.

"My dad and I got into another bad blow-out last night," Josie said from the chair next to Jenna, their feet soaking in a warm bubble bath while their fingernails were being filed and polished.

"Again?" Jenna asked.

Josie nodded. "I had some time after my Earth Science exam yesterday, so I started doing some research into Schizophrenia."

"Uh oh. What happened?"

"Well, I'd read through a few websites on the symptoms and stuff, and the only symptom I have is hallucinations."

"What? You don't have hallucinations!"

"Technically, a hallucination is seeing and hearing things that aren't there. So, yeah, I am by that definition."

"But what you hear and see are things that are really there!" said Jenna.

"I know that, but really, how do you know that?"

"Because I trust you. And we've been able to validate a lot of the things you get. Ethan and Uncle Frank are just two examples."

"So why can't my dad trust me?"

"You said it before. Fear. He's afraid of something."

"But what?"

Jenna shrugged. "Only he can answer that."

Josie shook her head.

"What happened last night?" Jenna prompted.

"Well, I confronted him about it, and told him I didn't have any of the symptoms, but he came back at me with a list of symptoms found in teenagers with it."

"Like what?"

"Let's see… withdrawing from friends and family – which he said I had withdrawn from him and Mom. He wouldn't admit that that only happened *after* he accused me of being crazy. Let's see, what else? Oh, a drop off in performance at school, which he conceded I *didn't* have; trouble sleeping – not going there; irritability or depression – again, not going there; and lack of motivation."

"So, normal teenage behavior is also a sign of Schizophrenia?"

"That's exactly what I said! But he had to go through each one and explain what they mean and how it's different."

"Geez, he's serious, isn't he?" said Jenna, her tone grave.

Josie nodded. "I told him that if that was how he really felt, if he really believes I'm mentally ill, then he should take me right then to the hospital while Mom wasn't around to stop him."

"And obviously he didn't because you're sitting here."

"But I think it was only because he's afraid of how Mom would react."

"You don't really believe that, do you?"

"Yeah, kinda. I mean, he was so convincing that I was almost starting to think he was right. And I'm actually surprised Simon never brought it up with all his scientific and medical knowledge."

"He would never," insisted Jenna, "because he knows the truth. He might not like it, and he might have trouble admitting it, but he knows the truth, Josie."

Josie sighed. She knew what it had taken to get Simon to believe her, and she still blushed at the memory of the secret she had whispered in his ear that night back in October. But what would it take for her dad to believe her? He wasn't convinced by what she knew about Ethan and about his marriage. So, what would it take? Would he ever believe her?

When their fingers and toes were dry, Jenna drove them back to Josie's house. Her parents were at Aunt Pauline's wake which Josie was excused from attending because of exams. When she felt some guilt at not going, Hanover appeared and assured her that it was okay. *These are rituals for the living, Josie, not the dead. She takes no offense to your not being there.*

You talked to her? Did she tell you that herself? When can I talk to her? Josie asked eagerly, but the questions went unanswered.

As Josie unlocked the door and let them in, Jenna said, "I don't want to bug you about it, but last weekend you said you had some thoughts on connecting me with my spirit guides. I'm not expecting to do it right now, but can you at least tell me what you're thinking?"

Though Josie was exhausted and not in the mood for ghost talk, she was amazed when she realized that Jenna hadn't said a word about it all week. She decided that the least she could do was indulge her best friend a little. "Okay. Let's go to my room," said Josie.

Jenna sat on Josie's bed while Josie took the chair at her desk. She picked up her spirit guide book. "So, you know how I started meditating during spring break? I still can't believe I am a person who meditates. But anyway, when I was meditating on the beach, I was getting messages from my guides and from Ophelia – I think. They're not always easy to understand. I just figured out most of it recently when I started looking into this stuff for you. But it is a way to connect with them. I'm thinking you and I should try meditating together with the intent that we communicate with a guide and see what happens."

"Okay," said Jenna, nodding eagerly. "Can we try now?"

"Actually, there's more to it. I've been reading through my book, and there's a section on connecting with spirit guides. I'd always skipped that part before because I didn't have a problem talking with mine. But with Uncle Frank and Ethan gone, I thought I should check it out. One of the suggestions they make is to create a ceremony to honor them, to thank them for being with you. It can be as simple as lighting a candle for them each night before you go to bed, but you have to do it every night, and it helps if you try to do it at the same time every night."

"Okay, so you want me to do that?"

Josie nodded. "My hope is that if you do a ritual for them, it will draw them to you more, or stronger, or whatever, so then when we meditate to try to communicate with them, it will be easier."

"How long do you think it will take?"

Josie shrugged. "We could try in a week, if you do your ceremony every night consistently."

"Oh my god, Josie, this is amazing! Thank you so much!"

"I know how important this is to you."

"More than you know," Jenna shook her head.

"I think I have a pretty good idea of your obsession," Josie laughed. "Do you want to try out some ideas for your ceremony?"

"Sure!"

"Okay, I'll run downstairs and get a candle," said Josie. "Be right back."

Josie disappeared from the room. Jenna got up and crossed to the desk to get the book. As she lifted it off the desk, she bumped a notebook with a glossy picture of ballerina's pointe shoes on the cover and it tumbled to the floor. It landed on the carpet open and face up. Jenna bent down to pick it up and gasped. Written across one page in large letters was "Why can't I just stop being in love with Simon?" The date on the page was a week prior.

Jenna sunk down onto the desk chair with the spirit guide book in one hand and Josie's journal in the other, staring at those words written by her best friend.

"I found a brand-new white pillar candle that I think will be—" Josie stopped in her tracks when she saw Jenna holding the journal, the words on the page clearly visible from where she stood frozen in the doorway.

Jenna looked up at Josie. "You're in love with my brother?"

"Why were you going through my journal?" Josie frowned, fear setting her on the defensive instantly.

"I wasn't. It fell open to this page when I picked up the other book, so don't turn this around on me," said Jenna, tossing the spirit guide book aside. "How long have you been in love with Simon?"

"Jenna, is this really—"

"How long, Josie?" Jenna repeated, her jaw clenched and her face red, her blue eyes flashing.

Josie's eyes widened. She'd never seen Jenna so angry. "Since the beginning of Freshman year," Josie replied quietly.

"You've felt this way for almost two years? Longer than we've been friends! Why didn't you tell me?"

"Because I couldn't! Remember last summer on the hiking trip? You told me about Reagan using you to get to Simon and I didn't want you to think that's what I was doing! You hated her so much. I didn't want that to be me!"

"But staying close to him sure is a nice benefit of our friendship, right?"

"No! Jenna, no! Being your friend is the most important thing to me!"

"If it was that important, you would have told me," Jenna said.

"I wanted to, but… it was hard. And nothing is ever going to come of it. I'm trying to get over him because he is never going to return my feelings, and I know that. I've known that since the summer camp. He thinks of me as a sister. He says so all the time!"

Jenna suddenly dropped her chin to her chest and chuckled, shaking her head. She looked up at Josie again smiling but it was not a happy smile. "Now I know the real reason why you never wanted to date, why you never let me fix you up with anyone."

"Simon is only part of it, Jenna. When I told you that I'm too busy, I meant it. When I said that I didn't want to date someone because I would have to lie and cover up all this ghost stuff, I meant it."

"But you also didn't want to date someone while you were still in love with my brother." Again, she shook her head. Josie didn't like the way she was speaking so calmly now. "I can't believe you didn't tell me."

"Jenna, please believe me. I wanted to, I just didn't know how," said Josie. Her eyes filled with tears.

"I have to go. I can't… I just… need some time." Jenna stood, walked to where Josie still stood in the doorway, shoved the journal at her, and slipped away. Josie remained frozen in place. She listened as Jenna's steps retreated down the stairs, heard the front door slam, and then heard Jenna's car door slam and the engine start.

When she could no longer hear the car, Josie finally moved. She put the candle and journal down on her bedside table and sat on the bed. "Wow, the only thing that could make my life worse now is if I failed all my exams," she said, falling back on her bed and letting the tears flow.

* * * * *

All of Josie's calls and texts to Jenna that night went unanswered. At around one in the morning, when she had moved on from distraught to enraged, she considered texting Dave or Simon for help, but fear of incurring even more of Jenna's wrath stopped her.

When morning finally dawned, Josie dressed in a simple black silk dress with one of her black dancer's shrugs, black tights, and black shoes. She then opened her jewelry box and took out the hourglass necklace Aunt Pauline had given her and placed it around her neck, tucking the pendant under the dress where it would lay closer to her heart. Next, she put on the necklace with the chunk of polished amber she had been given by a woman in Salem after Josie passed on a message from her dead daughter. It was only fitting that her jewelry be related to death and dead people.

She looked at her image in the mirror. She looked miserable, and her outfit matched her mood perfectly. Fortunately, no one would know that her red, puffy eyes weren't only for Aunt Pauline. "Hanover, can you hear me?" she asked aloud.

She felt the familiar tingling warmth around her shoulders and neck, and then she saw the form of Hanover the Opossum manifest around her shoulders in the mirror. *Of course, Josie.*

"Will there be a lot of ghosts at this funeral? I don't think I can deal with all that today," she said.

Remember your protection, your bubble, he replied.

"Oh, yeah," she said, shaking her head. "How can I be so stupid? I forgot all about that."

You're not stupid, Josie. You're learning, and you have a lot on your mind. Don't be so hard on yourself.

Josie sighed. "I know. It's just… I've had a rough few weeks, months…."

I know. That's why I'm here, to help guide you through it as much as I can.

"Am I going to get another guide soon?" she asked, then felt bad for asking. "It's not that I don't appreciate you. I just got used to having three voices, opinions… however annoying they could sometimes all be." She smirked just a little.

Hanover smiled at her, his small black eyes twinkling in the reflection. *You cannot worry about that now. Let's get your protection in place so you can get through your day.*

"Okay," she said with another sigh.

It took about ten minutes of back and forth with him for Josie to form her bubble of protection into a fortress of gray stone around her. *Set your intention into the structure, Josie,* Hanover said. *Tell it what you want it to do.*

"I want it to keep all ghosts away from me for the rest of the day," she said.

Good. And if you do encounter a spirit while your protection is in place, what does that mean?

"That my protection sucks?"

No, Josie. Please be serious.

"But I don't know!"

It means that whatever you are encountering is something – or someone – you need to encounter. If it gets through your protection, there's a reason for that.

"Oh," said Josie.

Have faith in your energetic protection.

"I'll try."

Just then, Josie heard her mom yell, "Josie! We need to go!"

She sighed and checked her reflection once more where she saw Hanover wink at her before fading from sight. She then lit her phone screen to see that Jenna still hadn't responded to any of her texts. With another sigh, she made her way downstairs.

* * * * *

The funeral was quiet for Josie. Either her protective bubble worked or there were no ghosts there. She found it a welcome distraction to chat with the many distant relatives she pretended to remember, as well as friends of Aunt Pauline and Uncle Frank, who asked her the same questions over and over about school, theater, and dance. But still her thoughts continually turned to Jenna.

YOU HAVE EVERY RIGHT TO BE MAD AT ME, BUT PLEASE TALK TO ME! Josie texted to Jenna again and again. Her phone and her friend remained in silent vigil.

Later, as she rode from the cemetery with her father, Josie became increasingly anxious. She didn't want to admit to herself that she was disappointed that she didn't at least see Uncle Frank and Aunt Pauline at the funeral. Despite Hanover's assurances that funerals are for the living, not the dead, she thought maybe they would make an appearance and that her protective bubble would let them through. She needed them now more than ever.

Charles drove in stoic silence beside his daughter, and Josie hoped it would stay that way. She couldn't handle fighting with him again on top of everything else. She decided that the only way she would make it through the rest of the day was to push all thoughts of Jenna, of funerals and ghosts, of lies and truths, out of her mind and focus only on the dances she would have to perform in less than two hours. In her mind, she pictured herself on stage, and went through each step of each routine.

When Charles stopped the car in front of the school's theater entrance, Josie spoke for the first time in more than an hour. "You have your ticket?" she asked Charles.

"Yes," he replied, patting the breast pocket of his suit jacket.

"Can you save three seats for Jenna, Dave, and Simon?"

"I already told you I would. Don't worry, Josie. You're going to do great," he said. Josie forced a smile, feeling slightly uncomfortable at the normalness of their exchange.

As Josie busied herself with her costume and makeup in the dressing room below the stage, Dave was across town pounding on Jenna's bedroom door while Simon stood behind him.

"Jenna, if we don't leave now, we're going to be late for Josie's recital!" Dave yelled. He turned to Simon and said, "Dude, are you sure she's in there?"

"Unless she climbed out the window, she's in there," said Simon.

Dave pounded again on the door. "Jenna, what is going on? Jenna!"

Simon joined in, pounding on the door and jiggling the doorknob. "Jenna! Open up!"

Finally, the door swung open. Dave looked at her in her running shorts and sweatshirt and said, "I thought we had to dress up for this thing!" He motioned to himself and Simon, standing there in khakis and button-down shirts.

"We're not going," she said with a scowl.

Simon frowned. "What? Why?"

"What part of 'we're not going' don't you understand?" Jenna barked.

"Hey, go easy on us!" said Dave, his eyebrows raised. "You need to tell us why. You know how important this is to Josie."

Jenna crossed her arms but didn't say anything.

"What happened with you and Josie?" asked Simon. "You were supposed to sleep over her house last night, but you were here when I got home. What happened?"

Jenna looked at Simon and Dave from under her scowl. "It doesn't matter. We're just not going."

"No. Uh-uh. You wouldn't let either of us get away with that, so we're not gonna let you get away with it either," said Simon.

Jenna frowned at him. "Why do you suddenly care so much about this?"

"Excuse me?" replied Simon, matching her frown. "What does that mean? Does this have something to do with me? Did I do something I don't know about?"

Dave's face lit up with realization. "You found out," he said.

"Found out what?" she asked, narrowing her eyes at him.

"Nope. I'm not falling into that trap. You need to tell us what happened," said Dave.

Jenna sighed. "Josie's been keeping from me the fact that…," her eyes flicked to Simon, "…that she's had feelings for Simon for almost two years."

No one moved or spoke. Jenna's eyes widened. "You knew! You *both* knew!" she accused, the fury rising quickly in her. "So, I'm the last to know! I thought she was my best friend! And you! My own boyfriend, keeping this from me! Ugh, you both make me sick." The door slammed shut.

Simon and Dave both sighed and stood there for another minute before realizing it wasn't going to do any good. Dave followed Simon downstairs to the kitchen.

Simon sunk onto a stool at the counter and Dave grabbed two bottles of water from the fridge. He passed one to Simon and opened the other. "How long have you known?" Dave asked Simon and then took a long swig from his water.

Simon shrugged. "Not long, I guess. I mean, she said something about it at the beach the day we left Florida. We had this… this weird thing that happened... I don't know."

"But you weren't surprised, right?"

"No," he admitted, shaking his head. "Looking back, I guess I kinda could tell."

"And?"

"And what?"

"Dude, don't make me ask the question," said Dave.

Simon shook his head. "I don't know what you want from me. This is a really complicated situation, and I just... I don't know what to think."

"You're not supposed to think. You're supposed to feel."

"And now that Jenna knows...," Simon went on, ignoring Dave's comment, "it's even more complicated."

Dave sighed and shook his head. "Josie's going to be destroyed if we're not at her recital."

"What do you suggest we do?" asked Simon. "Go break down Jenna's door and drag her kicking and screaming?"

"And biting. Don't forget, she's a biter."

"Hey, that's my sister you're talking about," said Simon.

"I didn't mean it like that, perv," said Dave. "Come on, we need to go talk to her about this. We can't let this ruin their friendship."

"You're right" Simon stood. "Let's go."

* * * * *

Josie stepped quietly through the dark wings of the stage. On stage was a group of five-year-old ballerinas trying their best to stay in time with each other as they followed the directions of Miss Jillian. Josie peeked through the curtains to see the audience. She easily spotted her dad, seated about seven rows back with three empty seats next to him.

Josie's stomach plummeted into her pointe shoes as her worst fear was realized. She knew Jenna was mad, and she didn't blame her, but she thought she would still be at the recital.

What good is this ability if it ruins every relationship in my life? Josie asked as she headed backstage. *First things with Alex got screwed up, then my dad thinks I'm nuts, Simon barely speaks to me, and now Jenna....* A tear threatened to escape Josie's eye and ruin her makeup. Quickly, she hurried back to the dressing room and grabbed for a tissue, carefully dabbing at the corner of her eye.

"Are you okay, Josie?" asked Bonnie, one of Josie's friends from dance classes and theater.

Josie looked at Bonnie and nodded. "Yeah, I've just had a crazy day. I was at a funeral this morning."

"Aw, I'm sorry. Was it someone you were close to?"

"Actually, yeah. She was my great-aunt, but she was a very cool lady," Josie said.

"That stinks. You going to be okay to dance?" asked Bonnie.

Josie shrugged. "Dancing is pretty much the only good thing in my life right now, so yeah. I can't wait to get out there."

"Good, cuz our Jazz routine wouldn't be the same without you," said Bonnie.

Josie forced a smile. "Thanks."

Why aren't they here, Hanover? Is what I did really that bad? She felt a slight tingle around her neck, but no response came. *Maybe they're just running late. Maybe by the time I get on stage they'll be here.*

* * * * *

After another round of pounding on Jenna's bedroom door, she finally let Simon and Dave in.

"I'm not mad that Josie has feelings for Simon, I'm mad that she never told me!" Jenna yelled at them.

"Did you ask her why she didn't tell you?" Dave asked.

Jenna sunk onto her bed and crossed her arms over her chest. With the same deep scowl as before, she said curtly, "Yes."

Dave tilted his head at her. "And what did she say?"

She looked from Dave to Simon and back to Dave. "She said that she was afraid I'd think she was using me, and that she knew Simon would never return her feelings, that he only thinks of her like another sister, so she didn't want to risk getting me mad."

Dave shot his friend a look. "And here you are, mad anyway," said Dave, shaking his head.

"Yes! She's my best friend! I tell her everything. And she's kept something major from me! So yes, I am mad, and I'm going to stay mad."

"You're being unfair to Josie," Dave said.

"Are you kidding me?"

"No, I'm not, Jenna. When Simon found out I had feelings for you, he didn't flip. Honestly, you can be scary sometimes, and I'm betting that Josie was afraid of telling you for this very reason."

"Yeah, but we told Simon. We didn't hide it from him," she replied.

"Yes, we did," said Dave.

"What? No. We didn't."

"Yes, Jenna, we did. You and I both had feelings for each other long before we said anything to him about it. We didn't go running to him the second we felt something. I know that on my end it was because first, I wasn't sure you felt the same, and second, I didn't want to piss him off. So, I waited until I *knew* you felt the same and that we both wanted something to come of it."

Jenna's jaw muscles twitched as she clenched her teeth and narrowed her eyes at her boyfriend. She then turned her eyes to her brother. "You're being awfully quiet about all this, Simon? What's *your* opinion?" she snarled.

Simon sighed. "I don't think you should be mad at Josie over this."

"That's it?"

"That's all I'm willing to say right now."

Jenna shook her head. "You both need to get out of my room and leave me alone. Now."

* * * * *

After Josie's second performance with her contemporary class, she managed to see past the lights into the audience. The three seats next to her father were no longer empty, but they were filled with people she did not recognize. Guessing that he was unable to continue to hold the seats for her friends when they didn't show up, he gave them up.

I've really screwed up, she thought. *I've screwed everything up. And I have no idea how to fix any of it.*

7

Josie had just finished her final routine of the recital, her solo, and the audience was on their feet with thunderous applause. She curtsied, breathless and exulted, completely unaware that way in the back of the auditorium, Dave and Simon were in the shadows watching.

"Dude, that was…," said Dave.

"Wow…," said Simon. A shiver ran up his spine at all the realizations that came crashing down on him as he watched her dance. He shook himself. "We should go."

"What? Shouldn't we wait and say hi?"

Simon shook his head. "She'll be upset that Jenna's not here, and she'll have a thousand questions we can't answer. We should just go."

Dave shrugged. "Okay."

* * * * *

Josie found her dad waiting for her in the lobby after the recital. As she approached, another parent shook his hand and walked away.

He turned and saw her and threw his arms around her in a hug. An action that was once so natural now felt strange to her. "Josie! Honey, you were terrific! I can't tell you how many parents have come up to me saying how beautiful your solo was. Did you see the standing ovation you got? You were the star of the show!" He beamed at her.

Josie felt herself flushing with embarrassment. “No, I wasn’t. Can we go home, please?” she said, turning and heading for the front doors.

In only a few steps he caught up to her and was by her side. “You’re being modest. There were other standing o’s but when you finished, everyone jumped to their feet!”

“Dad....” Josie tried to protest.

“I’ve never seen anything like it before, Josie. I really haven’t. I’m blown away! I’m so proud of you.”

“Thanks.” She was thankful they had reached the car. She put her costume bag and makeup case in the back seat and climbed in the front, pulling her sweatshirt up around her neck in an attempt to hide.

“Mom is going to be so upset that she missed this,” he continued as he climbed in the driver’s seat and started the car. “You really are so talented, Josie.”

“Thanks,” she repeated softly, flatly. She could sense something in the tone of his voice that told her there was more there.

“You could go really far with this stuff, you know. I don’t understand why you’re jeopardizing it with all this ghost nonsense.”

“And there it is. Can we *not* do this now?” she moaned and sank further down into the seat.

“But doesn’t something like today help you to see how—”

“How what?”

“How different things could be for you?”

She turned to look at her dad. “Do you really think I am doing this on purpose? That I have *chosen* to experience this stuff?”

“I don’t know, Josie. I suppose… yes. I guess I do.”

She shook her head and sunk back down in her seat, crossing her arms over her chest. “I don’t know why you can’t believe me.”

“You’re so young, Josie, and you don’t seem to understand that these things you’re claiming have serious consequences in the real world.”

"The *real* world? You mean the non-crazy world?"

"I mean in the world where I want you to grow up to be happy and successful at whatever you do."

"And you think I can't be in that place if I go around telling people that I talk to ghosts, right?"

"Well, no, of course not. That's not normal. It's not real!"

Josie shook her head. "Tell me something, Dad. Look at that car next to us," she said, pointing to the car in the turn lane at the stop light, "and tell me how many people you see in it."

"Why?"

"Please, just do it."

Charles sighed and looked over quickly. "I see one person. The woman driving the car."

"Right, well, I see two. I see her, and in the passenger seat I see an old man who is so hunched that his chin barely comes up to the bottom of the window, and he's wearing one of those tweed newsboy caps. His nose is big and hooked, and he's looking at me, smiling and winking. He seems really happy to be out for a ride in the car."

"Josie, why—"

"Because I'm trying to get you to understand that I'm not asking to see these things! I'm not making it up, and I'm not crazy! I am not hearing voices telling me to do bad things like break expensive vases and spill wine on antique carpets."

"And you want me to believe ghosts did all that?"

"Not ghosts... *one* ghost. His name was Mark Darcy, and he was a Lieutenant Commander of the Union Navy in the Civil War. His boat sunk off the Gulf Coast of Florida and he was captured by the Confederates at Fort Roday where he was then tortured until he died. Only he didn't know he died. In death, he was confused, and he became mischievous. His spirit suffered for over 150 years. Can you imagine that? He was from Wakefield, Massachusetts, and he had a little sister named Nancy, and he was truly distraught that she didn't know what happened to him. If this isn't real, then how do I know all that? You think I just made it all up?"

"I don't know. But I don't know how to believe that this ghost you say you saw in Florida did all that stuff in our house. It doesn't make sense!"

"And I can't give you an explanation that would satisfy you, so I'm not even going to try."

"You agree that this is unexplainable!" said Charles, sounding triumphant.

"Well, yes and no. It's not unexplainable, just really hard to explain. We don't have the vocabulary for some of this stuff, and we certainly don't have the science for it. Simon can attest to that. But even if it's unexplainable, that doesn't mean it isn't real. There was a time when people thought thunderstorms were the work of angry gods!"

Charles frowned, and this time Josie felt triumphant.

But then Charles said, "I'm sorry. None of it makes sense to me. I've never heard a single intelligent person that I respect talk of ghosts being real. Not a single scientist has evidence. I just can't believe it. Until you can offer me real proof, I'm sorry, that's just how I feel."

As the car pulled to a stop in the driveway, Josie said, "I shouldn't have to convince you. As my father, you should have faith and trust in me that I'm telling you the truth."

Angela had pulled into the driveway only seconds before Josie and Charles arrived. Josie jumped out of the car and grabbed her stuff from the back seat.

Charles jumped from the car after her. "As your father it is my responsibility to provide for you, to guide you, and see that you have the best life possible, but I feel like I'm failing you miserably."

"Well, you know what? Since that's the way you feel, why don't you send me back?"

"What?"

"Send me back. Un-adopt me. Why not? You think I'm crazy and a liar, and the great thing is, I'm not really your kid, so you can send me back."

"Josie, don't say things like that," said Angela.

"Why not, Mom? It's the reality of the situation. I'm not really your kid. I'm not your flesh and blood. I've met your real kid, not that you believe me. So why not just send me back? That way you two can stop fighting over whether or not I'm crazy, and you can live a happy, ghost-free, Josie-free life."

Josie stormed into the house, leaving behind a shocked Angela staring at her husband.

"What was that all about?" Angela asked.

Charles shook his head. "I keep making things worse. Ang, what are we going to do?"

She sighed. "I don't know, but I want my family back."

* * * * *

Josie debated whether or not she should still go to graduation the next day, but she decided she wasn't going to let Jenna's vigil of silence keep her from seeing Simon and Dave graduate.

"Unlike Jenna, I am not going to let this make me miss an important event in my friends' lives," Josie said to herself in her mirror, pleased with her reflection. She wore a baby blue sundress with a light cardigan in amethyst purple and left her hair down and straight. She added the amber amulet and hourglass necklaces as the final touch once again.

At school, Josie made her way to the bleachers at the back of the gymnasium where a section was roped off for students. The rest of the seating was reserved for families and graduates. She sat in an end seat and checked her phone. She didn't expect to see a text from Jenna, but she kept checking anyway. She sighed, thinking about their original arrangements for that night. Jenna would be sitting in the family section with her parents and grandparents, but Josie was going to meet up with them afterwards and join them back at the LaPage's house for a celebratory barbecue. Dave would be there also with his mom and brother. But now, Josie guessed that Jenna didn't want her there.

Her thoughts were interrupted when Bonnie and Caitlyn found her. "Are you saving those seats?" Caitlyn asked, pointing to the empty bleacher space next to her.

"Nope," she forced a smile and slid over so they could sit. She then switched into actress mode. For the next two hours, she played the part of a girl whose whole life was not falling apart. While on the outside Josie was showing everyone a normal, happy person, chatting away about the ceremony, inside she was thinking about what would happen if her parents took her seriously and unadopted her. She didn't know if it really was possible, but if it was, what would it look like? She had less than two years until she was a legal adult, so she would probably be put in a group home or a foster home until then. No one would adopt a sixteen-year-old, and she was fine with that. She didn't want to go through all this again, loving and losing more family. She would be alone, and she would probably be better off that way.

As she watched Simon cross the stage to collect his diploma, she maintained her act as a happy friend. A tiny thread tugged at her heart that she ignored when Jenna's whole family stood and cheered for him, her former-best-friend's signature strawberry curls clearly visible. She told herself that she was not the Josie that was Jenna's friend, that she was now playing the role of a different Josie, one whose life was very normal, with a happy home life and intact friendships. That other Josie clapped and smiled and felt proud of Simon for his success, because the real Josie would have been dying slowly inside and would have felt the distance between her and Jenna as wide and insurmountable as the Grand Canyon. That Josie would have felt ridiculous for making such a clichéd statement. That other Josie would be in tears seeing Simon accept his diploma, seeing that he was moving further and further away from her and taking a large piece of her heart with him.

There was no room for that Josie in this place. The bleachers were full, so this Josie told her to go away. Maybe she would let her come back later, or maybe she would just keep her locked away somewhere deep inside herself, and keep her there until... well, she wasn't sure how long she would need to keep her there, but it would be for as long as was necessary.

It wasn't long until Dave crossed the stage to accept his diploma, and Jenna's family went equally wild for him, their second son. Another lost friend of the other Josie, a friend she had only recently come to appreciate. This Josie clapped and cheered and smiled for him as though none of that existed.

When the ceremony was finally over, Josie, Bonnie, and Caitlyn slowly made their way out into the lobby where students and families were milling about, hugging, smiling, laughing, and taking photos.

"Josie, do you want to go get pizza with us?" Bonnie asked. "Or are you doing something with the LaPage's?"

This Josie, the pretend Josie, smiled and said, "The LaPage's are doing a family thing tonight so yeah, I'd love to get pizza." She followed behind them as they pushed their way through the crowds heading for the exit when Caitlyn stopped to talk to someone Josie didn't know. As she introduced Bonnie and Josie, a break in the crowd revealed Simon across the lobby. He turned and saw her and caught her eyes. He smiled and waved. She was surprised by the friendly gesture, and the other Josie threatened to break from her enclosure, but she managed to suppress her. This Josie forced a smile and a wave back.

Simon frowned as the crowd once again moved in and blocked his view of Josie. What he had seen was not the Josie he knew. It was like seeing a shell of her, with someone else piloting.

Seeing the distress on his face, Rachel asked, "Simon, is everything alright?"

He shook himself. “Yeah, Mom,” he replied, but made a mental note to pull Jenna and Dave aside later to talk to them about what he saw.

8

Josie sat slumped in an uncomfortable chair. If Miss Jillian saw her sitting like that, she would have given her a stern lecture on dancers' posture. But Josie didn't care. Miss Jillian wasn't there, and it wasn't any ordinary therapist's appointment. It was family counselling, which meant that her mom and dad were sitting in their own chairs, their postures stiff and their faces anxious.

They were all there at Angela's insistence. After Josie's declaration that they should un-adopt her, Angela called it the last straw. Josie tried to protest, but Angela's eyes filled with tears, and she declared, "I just lost Aunt Pauline! I am not going to lose the rest of my family, too!" Charles finally caved.

Now, they all sat together, facing Dr. Porter, waiting.

Dr. Porter was recommended to them by Josie's therapist. When Josie asked Dr. Gilbert why she couldn't do it, she said that she couldn't counsel her family and remain Josie's individual counselor. It was an ethical thing for therapists.

Dr. Porter was much older than Dr. Gilbert, very short and plump with a soft voice, rosy cheeks, and sparkly hazel eyes. She smiled at each of them. "I'm glad you're all here, and I can see that you're nervous, but don't be. I understand your situation, and I want you to know, it is hardly unique."

"You're kidding!" Charles scoffed.

"Of course not," said Dr. Porter. "Here you have an adopted teenage girl who feels like her adoptive parents don't understand what she's going through."

"It's a little more complicated than that," said Charles, returning to his pained posture.

"Respectfully, Mr. York, it really isn't. I understand that the threads of the situation are more unique," she said to him, "but when you step back and look from a distance, you have a classic misunderstood teenager. Being adopted adds an extra layer, because children who grow up with their birth parents who experience this have a genetic connection, they have that innate sense somewhere inside that tells them that no matter how bad things get, they still belong. But here you have Josie who has already been abandoned by her birth parents, feeling like her adoptive parents might change their mind about her."

"We would never!" said Angela.

"That's not the point. The possibility is there regardless of how unrealistic it might be. It's there for Josie when it isn't there for other kids. So, what we need to do is find a way to bridge the gap that's been created."

"We didn't mean to create this... this gap," Angela said, looking to Josie with tear-filled eyes, but Josie refused to look at her mother.

"Again, that's not the point. Whether it was intentional or not, the gap is there, and for Josie it is filled with tremendous uncertainty. It is my hope that together we can figure out how we can do away with the uncertainty and bridge the gap."

"But what about all that other... stuff?" Charles asked.

"Actually, because that is something I have no experience with or frame of reference for, I consulted some colleagues – confidentially, mind you – and I was given the name of a psychic medium who works with young people like Josie and their families to help them learn how to deal with their abilities." Dr. Porter held out a piece of paper, holding it loosely in the air between Charles and Angela.

Josie sat up straighter at Dr. Porter's words, but she waited to see how her parents would react to this. She wasn't surprised to see Angela reach out and take the piece of paper while Charles looked at it like it was a snake that might bite him.

"Thank you," said Angela. "But if you can't help us with this stuff, then what *can* you help with? Why are we paying you?"

"As I said before," said Dr. Porter, "that is only part of the problem here. And the premise of the problem is exactly like many other kids her age. A wedge has been driven between you, and we need to work together to remove it. Calling the number on that paper, going to see the psychic, supporting Josie in that way is going to be part of the solution. The other part is finding your way back to trusting each other and giving her back that sense of security that all kids need, giving her the knowing that she has parents who love and support her unconditionally."

Charles cleared his throat. "I understand what you're saying, but how can we find that trust and give Josie that support if we can't sort the truths from the lies?"

Josie slumped again in her chair. *Here we go,* she thought.

"Let me ask you a question," said Dr. Porter. "Before this all started – go back a year or more if you have to – would you have considered Josie a problem child? Was she a child who was prone to telling 'tall tales' and who was caught in lies a lot?"

Charles and Angela glanced at each other. "Well, no," said Charles. "Not at all. Which is why it has been so disturbing that the change happened so quickly."

"And why do you think her personality changed so much?" she asked.

"I don't know. Hormones do crazy things to teenagers," he shrugged.

"Did they do crazy things to you? Did your personality change so drastically when you hit puberty, either of you?" Dr. Porter looked from Charles to Angela.

"Not me," said Angela, shaking her head. "Nothing like this."

"No," said Charles. "I mean, sure I had my moments, but no, nothing drastic."

"So then why should her teenage years be any different from yours?"

"Well, because she's not really—" Charles stopped himself, and his face turned ashen. His jaw hung open.

"For the sake of your family, for the sake of getting trust back, you have to be completely honest and finish your sentence," said Dr. Porter.

Charles looked to Angela, who looked at him like a deer in the headlights. Josie's head hung, her hair falling forward in a veil covering her face.

He swallowed hard. "I- I was going to say… that she's not really… ours."

Josie had heard somewhere, in science class maybe or a movie, that if you were too close to an explosion, it could make you instantly deaf. The silence in the room after Charles's words was like that, as deafening as if a bomb had been dropped between them. Angela squeezed her eyes shut and tears ran down her cheeks.

* * * * *

Two weeks followed with more family counseling sessions as well as sessions on her own. Josie felt little progress had been made and she didn't want to talk about it anymore. There was still no word from Jenna, and when she allowed herself to think about it, she felt as though she were slipping down into a thick mud puddle of hopelessness. Instead, she let the other Josie think about it and wallow in sadness while she moved about as if she were an emotionless robot. The only time she felt almost normal, almost happy, was when she was in dance class. After the recital, Miss Jillian had asked Josie to help her with summer camp, which consisted of three different sessions over the course of summer vacation for kids four to twelve years old. When Josie wasn't helping with the campers or taking her own summer classes, she was vacuuming, cleaning the office and bathroom, organizing paperwork, and doing anything else Miss Jillian needed done. Josie was willing to do anything to keep from having to go home where she would just sit in her room alone, staring at her lifeless phone, willing it to ring.

She also didn't want to think about what was to come on Saturday. Her mom had called the medium that Dr. Porter told them about and made an appointment for the three of them to meet with her. Initially, Josie was excited to meet another medium but now that it was so close, she was becoming apprehensive. What if she told Josie that she was a fraud, and it really was all her imagination? Her father would be happy about that. He would have just cause to lock Josie away and forget about her.

Without Jenna's constant positive outlook on life, Josie had lost the ability to reason with herself, to realize that she had dealt with enough ghosts and received enough confirmation of her abilities to validate the reality of her gifts, so instead her fears took over. In turn, she channeled all that into the dance studio whenever she could. That way she didn't think about how scared she was that she may have lost her family and about how much she missed Jenna and Dave. In her mind, they were pretty much one person at this point, and she had grown used to it. Dave proved over and over again that he was a truly good person. His mellow steadiness was a compliment to Jenna's optimistic enthusiasm, and Josie had come to think of him as one of her closest friends. He knew her biggest secrets and had been there for her through it all. She knew he was only there because of Jenna, but he never protested, never gave her a hard time like Simon did, and he was always willing to help.

Josie didn't want to think about what life with ghosts would be like if it was also a life without Jenna and Dave.

In that moment, though she wouldn't admit to herself that she was thinking about it, Josie realized that Jenna and Dave had become far more important to her than Simon. If forced to choose, she would pick Jenna. Josie didn't realize she already had, time and again, chosen Jenna's friendship over Simon.

When she got home from the studio that night, she sent one more text to Jenna saying, PLEASE FORGIVE ME. YOUR FRIENDSHIP IS MORE IMPORTANT TO ME THAN ANYTHING. PLEASE. I MISS YOU. After sending the message, she put her phone down, not wanting to see that Jenna was not going to respond once again.

At the same moment Jenna's phone received Josie's text, Jenna was at the dinner table with her family where phones were not allowed.

"Simon, pass the potatoes," said Rachel. "Jenna, didn't you invite Josie over?"

Jenna shrugged. "She's busy again."

Simon shook his head at his sister's lie. Rachel met her husband's eyes and raised her eyebrows.

"Oh, well, I owe Angela a call later, so maybe I'll invite them all over on Sunday for a barbecue. How does that sound?"

Jenna shrugged again. "I'm sure they're all too busy, Mom."

Rachel put her fork down with a clatter. "Okay, that's it. Why are you lying to me?"

Jenna's head snapped up and she looked at her mom, her face full of guilt. "But—"

"Come on, Jenna, I talk to Angela all the time and I know something happened. You and Josie haven't seen each other in weeks, and I want to know what's going on."

"Nothing's going on. I just… needed a break from her, and I've been busy helping Dave and his mom …."

"Does this have anything to do with all the ghost stuff?"

"No, of course not!"

"Well, it just all seems weird to me. I know Dave is going through a tough time right now, but from what Angela tells me, Josie's going through a really hard time, too, and could probably use her friend's support."

Jenna's stomach twisted with guilt.

"I can't even imagine what that family is going through. I can't imagine thinking that Josie isn't telling her parents the truth, especially after everything that happened in Florida," said Rachel, speaking quickly, almost as if she was trying to fill the uncomfortable silence that hung in the air. "Did I ever tell you that I thought I saw a ghost once?"

This got Jenna's full attention. "What? No. When? Where?"

Rachel pursed her lips and scrunched her face in thought. "Well, it was about thirteen years ago. We lived for only a few months in a big old house over in North Hampton when Dad's work transferred us out here and we were looking for a house of our own. We celebrated your third birthday there. Grandma and Grandpa McElroy were visiting. It happened right after they left. I'd gone up to the guest room to strip the bed. As I did, I saw a woman walk into the room out of the corner of my eye. I asked Mom if she'd forgotten something and looked up. Standing across the bed from me was this weird, creepy old lady. I screamed and threw the sheets at her in my panic, and she disappeared. Just vanished. I was so confused, and I guess I just wrote it off as my eyes playing tricks on me."

"Wow, Mom! I can't believe you never told me about this!"

Rachel shrugged. "You know, I'd forgotten all about it until just now."

"Hey, was that where we lived when Jenna had her imaginary friend?" asked Simon.

"Wait, I had an imaginary friend? I don't remember that!"

"Well, you were little, honey, and he didn't come with us when we moved to this house," said Rachel.

"What did she call him? Mr. Shuts?" asked Simon.

"Yes! Mr. Shuts!" said Greg laughing. "Because she said he shut things like doors and drawers and windows."

"That imaginary friend is a mother's dream the way Simon leaves the kitchen cabinets open. Too bad he didn't come with us," said Rachel.

"You know, I did have doors close on me a few times while we lived there, and a window once," said Greg. "Nearly caught my fingers."

"I remember asking you if Mr. Shuts was all packed for the move, and you said no, he didn't want to move to our new house, and when I asked why, you said that he wanted to stay in *his* house where he'd always lived. You cried a little when we left him behind. It was really cute."

Rachel, Greg, and Simon laughed over the shared memories while Jenna gaped at them.

"*Are you serious*?" Jenna yelled over their laughter. She was not smiling or laughing. "Are you all messing with me?"

"No, of course not, honey. Why?" asked Rachel with a frown.

Jenna looked at each of them in turn, her mouth hanging open, waiting for one of them to crack and tell her they're pulling her leg and tricking her. When none of them did, she said, "Do you have any idea what you're saying to me? I've read tons of accounts of children whose 'imaginary friend' turned out to be some dead person! And now you're telling me that I had an imaginary friend that would close doors and windows in the same house where you saw an old hag vanish!"

"I'm sorry, Jenna. I was a mom with two little kids moving into a new house in a new neighborhood, and I forgot all about it. I never thought Mr. Shuts was anything other than your imagination," said Rachel, shocked at Jenna's anger.

But Jenna's anger suddenly turned to excitement. "I can't believe this. You saw a ghost, and I *interacted* with a ghost, and I never even knew it. After all this time, and after all the research. I can't believe this!" But her excitement was gone as quickly as it had come when her next thought was, *I can't wait to tell Josie about this,* and she realized she still wasn't speaking to her best friend.

"We don't know for sure that either of them were ghosts," said Greg.

"I wonder if they're still there. Mom, do you remember the address of the house?"

"I'm sure I have it somewhere, but I am not going to give it to you if you're going to go harass the poor family that lives there," said Rachel.

"Mom, no! I just want to do some research. I promise."

She didn't see Simon shaking his head again. He knew his sister well, and he knew what she was thinking.

"So, Mom, let me know when you talk to Angela, if they're all coming over Sunday," Jenna said with an uncomfortable smile. Simon rolled his eyes.

* * * * *

Angela and Charles picked Josie up at the dance studio Saturday afternoon.

"Where did you say we're going?" Josie asked.

"The Four Gables Inn," Angela said lightly. She was determined that this be the turning point for her family, because if something didn't give, she was going to snap. She was so stressed out that she wasn't sleeping, she was gaining weight, and she and Charles had hardly said a civil word to each other in weeks. It wasn't for his lack of trying. He was immediately remorseful after he said those words at their therapy session, that Josie wasn't really theirs, but the damage was done. She didn't understand how he could feel that way. Josie was a baby when she came to them, and since then, they'd been by her through her first words, her first steps, her first dance class, every fever, every joy, and every sorrow. She didn't come from their bodies, but Angela knew that Josie was meant to be their child. How could Charles not feel that, too?

"Isn't that like an hour away?" she asked.

"Forty minutes with no traffic," replied Angela.

"So why are we meeting there?"

"I guess because it's a central location to everyone who'll be there."

"Wait, what? Who else is going to be there?"

"Well, I didn't want to tell you before because I thought you might not want to go, but there are going to be several families there with kids like you," said Angela.

"Oh, great, so I get to make an idiot out of myself in front of a bunch of people? This is fantastic," Josie grumbled, folded her arms across her chest, and sank down into the seat.

"Josie, I think you're overreacting. This is an opportunity for you to meet other kids who can do what you do."

Josie didn't reply. Instead, she put her earbuds in and turned her music up.

Angela glanced at Charles. "I suppose you're unhappy about this too," she said to him.

He sighed. "I'm trying, Angela, I really am. This is not a situation I want to be in, but I *am* trying."

"I know you are," she said, her sigh matching his. He *was* trying, and for that she was grateful, but it would take a lot more than that to repair the canyon between both him and Josie and between him and herself.

They all rode the rest of the car ride in silence, each cocooned in their own anxieties.

When they arrived at the inn, Josie's stomach plummeted to her feet. The place was a large Victorian mansion, and she could already hear the ghosts inside. It was that buzz of voices like when Aunt Pauline had been in the nursing home.

As they walked slowly towards the front door from the parking lot, Angela said, "Oh, Josie, I forgot to tell you. Rachel has invited us all over for a barbecue tomorrow. So that's something to look forward to, right?"

Josie's heart did a flip-flop and she grabbed at her phone to check for a message from Jenna, but all she saw were her last few unanswered texts. "Sure," Josie said. She forced something resembling a smile and wondered how she could get out of going without confessing to the whole mess with Jenna to her parents.

But it didn't really matter at that moment. She had other things to worry about.

Angela led the way up the broad steps to the wrap-around porch, past the rocking chairs, and through the double front doors inlaid with intricate stained-glass designs. A crystal chandelier hung over the entryway, and a thick red rug guided them over a dark, polished wood floor to the front desk.

"How can I help you?" asked the man behind the counter. He was tall and thin with a shiny bald head on top, fuzzy brown hair ringing his head from ear to ear, and impossibly smooth skin on his face. Josie found him oddly pleasing to look at.

"We're meeting someone here. Her name is Zara White."

"Of course. You'll find her in the Lilac Room, down the hall, second door on your right," he said with a broad toothy smile.

Angela headed down the hall with Josie behind her and Charles following last.

A brass plaque on the door told them they had found the Lilac Room. Angela knocked and opened the door. The room was silent as all heads turned to look at them. All Josie could hear was the squeaking of the floor under their feet and her own heart pounding in her chest.

There was a large round table in the center of the room with all but three chairs full. A woman with sleek black hair cut in an angled bob stood and smiled a bright white smile behind bold red lipstick. "Welcome! You must be Josie and family," she said. She was thick-set but shapely in a tight black dress and high-heeled booties with a simple dark blue stone on a thin strand of gold around her neck. Her dark blue eyes sparkled as she smiled. "Please come in and sit down."

Josie and her parents moved into the room and took the three remaining seats at the table, her parents flanking her.

"Alright. Now that everyone's here, let's get started. I want to welcome you all. My name is Zara, and I am a Medium which, as you know, means that I talk to dead people. I've had the ability all my life, however, it became unmanageable around the age of thirteen. It took me many years and a lot of heartache to learn how to manage my abilities, and now I've made it my mission to help young people like you, to give you a resource that I didn't have but desperately needed. This gentleman here to my left," she motioned to the guy sitting next to her with short brown hair, a large bushy beard, arms covered in tattoos, and a warm smile in his big brown eyes that were rimmed with thick-framed glasses, "is my wonderful husband, Gareth, one of the few people in this world who I trust completely with what I experience on a daily basis. Having people that you trust, people who support you, is so important, because we live in a world where being a Psychic or a Medium, saying that you talk to ghosts or do any of the things you all do, is still not 'normal'." She hooked her fingers around the word. "And we need people around us to help us redefine what normal means for us."

Josie thought of Jenna and was overcome with sadness. She had had that. She had those people that were helping her redefine normal. She felt normal when she was with Jenna, Dave, and even Simon, but she didn't know if she would ever get that back or if she would ever have it with her parents.

"So now I'll have Gareth give you his own introduction, and then we'll go around the table and you can each introduce yourselves," she said.

"Hi all," he started with a wave. "As my amazing wife said, I'm Gareth, and I'm here not just to support her but to support all of you. Though I have developed my own intuition over the years, I use my intuition differently. I have a degree in psychology and social work, and I've been in social work for about ten years now, working closely with families who are experiencing all sorts of challenges. In this setting, I will use those skills along with my intuition to help you adults find ways to best support the young intuitives here tonight."

Next to introduce herself was a fifteen-year-old girl named Romy who said she had prophetic dreams of disasters like plane crashes and tsunamis. Romy's mother made a short introduction, and then a boy of twelve introduced himself as Jacob and said he'd been talking to ghosts since he was three and his grandfather died. He had both mother and father there, but his mother Nigella introduced them both. Next was a girl named Miranda who said she was thirteen but said no more. She was there with only her grandmother, a tall woman with thick gray hair cut into a sever bob. She reminded Josie of a mean substitute teacher she once had.

Angela introduced herself next and then it was Josie's turn. "Hi, my name is Josie. I'm sixteen, and I've been able to talk to ghosts for just about a year, ever since I hit my head while on a camping trip and then ended up in a haunted house." Josie didn't know what else to say. It was hard to sum up all she'd been through in an introduction, so she said no more. Charles then quickly introduced himself and shifted uneasily in his chair.

"Okay, now that introductions are out of the way and we're all feeling sufficiently awkward, I'm going to ask the parents to go with Gareth into the room across the hall where there is tea, coffee, and pastries, while the kids stay here with me and chat for a bit," said Zara.

Gareth stood up and Angela followed suit. Slowly, the other parents did the same, and Gareth led the way out of the room.

When the door closed behind them, Zara said, "Okay, let's all move away from the table." She stood and went to the far corner of the room where there was an antique-style couch with an ornately carved dark wood frame and red velvet padding, and two chairs of a similar style. They all quietly followed. Josie and Romy both took seats on the couch while Jacob took one chair and Miranda took the other. Zara pulled a chair from the table and sat in front of them to form a rough circle.

"Alright, now that the parents are gone, let's get to the real talk. I want to know what the hardest part of all this has been for you, and so you are sure it's a safe place, I'll go first," said Zara. "As I said earlier, things became unmanageable for me with spirits when I was thirteen. I grew up in a family where this stuff was common. My mother was a free-spirit hippie-type who did reiki and ate organic before it was ever a thing, and I was always kind of a weird kid who talked to things that other kids couldn't see. Somehow it never mattered much. We had a big family, so I had lots of cousins around all the time who were as weird as me, so I never felt friendless really. But when I turned thirteen, something happened within me. Suddenly I wanted to be normal. I saw the girls around me starting to be interested in boys and makeup and clothes, and I wanted to be part of that. I begged my mom to let me have a big birthday party – a boy-girl birthday party – and I invited everyone in my class. I wasn't shocked when almost everyone came because they were all about parties and really didn't care whose party it was, but I was so excited. I got a special new outfit that was pink and frilly – and I am not a pink-and-frilly girl, if you can believe that." They all chuckled. "Everyone came, the party was going great, kids were dancing, and I was working up the courage to ask a boy I liked to dance when… can you guess what happened?"

She looked around at each of them, but it was Jacob who said, "A ghost messed things up?"

Zara nodded. "Yes! Standing between me and… um, I can't even remember the boy's name… Billy? Danny? Maybe Jimmy? Anyway, suddenly standing between me and the boy I liked was this ghost. It was this craggy old man who started talking fast and kind of slurred, and I couldn't understand what he was saying. He became frustrated that I couldn't understand him and was basically ignoring him, so he got louder and louder, repeating himself over and over again until I finally shoved my fists in my ears," she demonstrated, "and screamed at him to shut up and go away. I was crying at that point, and when I looked around, everyone was staring at me. Within ten minutes they had all fled my house. The ghost was still there, yammering away. And when I went to school on Monday, they were all talking about me, whispering, pointing, laughing. It got so bad – the kids making fun of me and the spirits needing my attention – that I stopped going to school part way through my freshman year of high school. My mother home-schooled me for about a year and a half until I passed all the exams to get my diploma. But in all that time, the spirits didn't leave me alone, so I then decided to find out what they wanted and how I could help them. It was about five years ago, when I finally felt secure in my gifts, that I started to wonder if I could use my own experience struggling with this stuff to help others, especially younger people. With the help of a few friends, I got my name out there and started to work one-on-one and in groups like this with other young psychics. And now here I am with you all. Now, who would like to share next?"

The silence that followed the question was as palpable as the awkwardness. Josie realized that after Zara, she was the oldest one there. She summoned up her courage and once again pretended she was on stage.

"I'll go," Josie said. "Like I said before, I've only been able to do this for about a year, though it feels like it's been a lot longer. And I guess the worst part for me has been the secrecy around it. Right away I felt like it was something I needed to hide, I think because I wasn't quite sure if it was real or if I was crazy. Then the longer I kept it secret, the harder it was to tell. I always assume that if someone hears that I can talk to ghosts they'll think I'm crazy. And that is exactly how my dad reacted when I finally told my parents, and that's why we're here."

"And what about other people in your life? Friends? Do any of them know?" Zara asked.

Josie nodded. "Some of them. The friends that were with me on the camping trip when it all started, yeah, they know, and for the most part they've been a great support system. My friend Jenna is now researching all things paranormal to help me. But…."

"But what?" Zara urged.

Josie sighed. "There are lots of people that don't know, mostly because I don't know how to tell them, and I'm afraid of how they'll react. It's hard to start new relationships because of it, and most of the time I feel like I'm living a double life," she said. She thought of Alex and how messed up that was; she thought of her teachers, like Mr. Wade, who she spent so much time with; Miss Jillian at the dance studio, Bonnie, and Kaitlyn; none of them had a clue she had this other part of her life. Then, Josie realized that she had been speaking more openly than she had in weeks. The other Josie had snuck in and resurfaced, the real Josie.

Zara nodded and smiled sympathetically at Josie. "I can relate because your worst fear is what happened to me. It can be hard to accept this part of ourselves, especially if we don't have much support from those around us. When we do find those people, whether it's friends or parents or grandparents, it's important to foster those relationships. I hope you will all leave here today with several new friends in your support system.

"Okay, thanks, Josie. Who would like to share next?"

"I will," said Romy. "The hardest part for me has been the dreams. I dream of these events, big events, like a tornado ripping through an entire town or a hurricane destroying a whole island. And I can't do anything about it. I don't always know where it's going to happen, and then I'll see it on the news, and I'll see all the devastation and the families crying over their lost family. I knew about these awful things that would happen, and I couldn't do anything to stop it. It… it's awful. I feel so helpless, and I get really depressed. All those people died, and I could have stopped it, but I don't know how."

Romy shifted in her seat and her short, light brown hair fell forward over her face. She brushed it away with a tear.

"Romy, can I ask you a question?" asked Zara.

Romy nodded.

"Aside from seeing the disaster in your dream, whatever it may be, what else happens? Do you see anything besides the cause of the destruction or the destruction itself?"

Romy frowned in thought and then said, "Yeah, I see the souls of the people who die. They come to me for help."

"And what do you do to help them?" asked Zara.

Romy shrugged. "It depends. I talk to them, I hug them, I tell them it will all be okay. But it's not okay because I can't stop these things from happening to them."

"You're right, Romy. You can't stop these things from happening and I don't believe you're *supposed* to stop them. This isn't like in the movies where someone has a prophecy, and then they race around to avert disaster at the last minute. But you are helping. You are a spiritual witness for those people. You are helping them to move on. I can guarantee that every one of those souls that you see in your dreams are real people that cross over to the other side because of you. If you weren't there, they might have no one, and they could become lost and stuck. But they don't because of you."

Romy's eyes lit. "I never thought of it like that before."

"Next time you have one of those dreams, I want you to try to remember this conversation, and try to remember the feelings and sensations that come from that part of your dreams where you're interacting with the spirits. Maybe keep a journal of each incident and the people you encounter, as much as you can remember. Okay?"

"Okay," said Romy with a smile.

"Miranda, will you share next?" asked Zara.

Miranda shook her head, her eyes wide in terror at being spoken to.

"I'll go next," said Jacob. "Nighttime is the hardest for me. The ghosts don't bother me much during the day, but as soon as night comes, they're in my room, in my face bugging me. I was driving my parents nuts because I would be up all night talking to them, and finally my mom suggested I just write down what these people wanted. That seemed to help a little. I write down the things the spirits want, and they go away. But more always come."

"You know, I once met a boy who had a similar problem," said Zara, "and what he did was make a bunch of posters for his walls and his bedroom door that said different things like 'no trespassing' and 'keep out' and he'd draw castle walls. Each night at bedtime he would tell the spirits that they weren't allowed in his room, but if they needed help, they could meet him in the living room in the morning. It worked, he was able to sleep, and it got to the point where he'd wake up every day and go to the living room, turn on cartoons, and cross over a dozen spirits as he ate his Pop Tarts before school."

"Cool," said Jacob.

"Yeah, I know, right?" replied Zara.

"I'll try that too," he said.

"Good, and I want you to let me know how it goes, okay?"

"Okay," he nodded.

Zara then looked again at Miranda. "Are you ready to share with us?"

Miranda shrugged. "I don't know. I'm not sure what the hardest part of it is because it's all awful and scary. But… I guess the hardest part… is the reaction of friends… former friends…and their parents."

"Yeah, it's tough when other people don't understand what we're experiencing, or if they think it's bad," said Zara.

Miranda nodded. "I wasn't like Josie, I didn't realize it was a bad thing to talk about it, and I mentioned it to my friend Sarah when I was at her house watching TV. One of those shows was on. You know, the kind that has a Medium doing readings for people, and she was saying how cool it was, and so I said, 'I can do that, too.' It was neat because I could actually see the spirit that the Medium was talking to on the TV. I was surprised because some of them really are scammers. But my friend flipped out. She called me a liar and got mad, then she told her parents who flipped out, too. She hasn't talked to me since, and she spread it all around school that I'm a freak."

"Let's talk about friendships for a minute," said Zara. "Raise your hand if you've ever lost a friendship somehow because of the ghost stuff."

All four kids raised their hands. Zara did, too.

"It can make you very mad, and sad, and frustrated, right? And it's not just difficult because of people who are afraid, calling you names, and whispering behind your back. You might also encounter people who find out what you can do, and they want you to use your gifts for them because you are friends. They come to you with personal problems and don't want your advice as a friend but want you to talk to the spirits to get them answers. But like with anything, there are spectrums that these people fall on, and it's up to you to decide where that is and what you want to do about it."

Miranda raised her hand. Zara nodded at her to speak. "I don't understand what you mean," said Miranda.

"Well, one way to look at it is like this: Aside from doing these types of gatherings, I also do readings for people. They pay me, and I connect with their deceased loved ones and spirit guides to give them guidance to better their lives. But say you own a house, and there's a storm that causes a tree branch to fall and damage the roof. And you have a friend whose job is a roofer. Wouldn't you call that person and ask them to help? Maybe you would hope they wouldn't charge you anything because you are friends. But is that fair? If they're doing work that requires their time and energy, they should get paid for that. Does that make sense?"

They all nodded, including Josie.

"I think it is the same with anything. Doctors get asked for free medical advice all the time. People ask for favors of each other depending on the unique skills of that other person. Right?"

Again, they all nodded.

"But if you do this stuff professionally, you have every right to tell your friend that you cannot give them a free reading, but maybe you'll give them a discount, or trade them for whatever their unique skill is."

Josie thought of Jenna.

“I’ve gotten frustrated with my best friend a lot,” said Josie. “Jenna is very into the paranormal investigation thing, and sometimes I feel like I’m one of her pieces of equipment for finding ghosts.”

“Have you told her this?” Zara asked.

“Yes, and she always insists that she’s not using me, and she never forces me. But now that you’ve put it the way you just did, I guess we’ve been exchanging skills. She’s a really amazing researcher, and she’s helped me to understand a lot about what’s going on with me. I guess I didn’t really realize until right now that we have a pretty good give-and-take system going on.”

“Good, Josie. That’s really good,” Zara smiled. Josie liked her. “Okay, so what other questions, problems, or whatevers do you guys have for me?”

Sandwiches, chips, and drinks were brought in then. They moved back to the table and as they ate, they talked. Soon they were all relaxed, laughing at each other’s fumbles, and having fun. Miranda even started to open up more. They talked a lot about the different ways they each experienced ghosts and spirits, and Josie was surprised at how varied they were even though they all seemed to have so much in common. They talked more about their individual insecurities and then they shared stories of the good things that came of it all. Zara was impressed by all of Josie’s experiences crossing over spirits, and they were all impressed by Jacob’s stories of seeing people’s auras.

Gareth appeared in the room as Miranda was finishing a story about a child ghost that made her pee her pants a little when it frightened her, and they were all laughing again. “Are we ready for the next phase of things?”

“I think so,” Zara smiled. “Just give me a few minutes to explain to them what’s going to happen.”

“Okay. Be back in five,” he replied and left the room.

“Alright, next I’m going to put you guys on the spot. I know it’s uncomfortable, but you are all talented, and I want you to see the strengths of your abilities. To do this, the staff at the Inn has found four volunteers to receive readings from the four of you. Your parents will be in the room because whether or not they have been supportive through this, seeing you guys in action, doing good for someone else in this kind of setting, is always eye-opening for them.

"We're going to have your parents come in the room first, and then we'll have the four volunteers come in."

"A-are you g-going to tell us who we're supposed to read?" Jacob asked with a stutter.

Zara shook her head. "Nope. I'm trusting that the spirits that come through will pick one of you to communicate with."

"Does that work?" asked Romy.

"I've done this with several other groups, and it always works." She looked at them all. "Any other questions?"

No one spoke up. "Okay, I know this is scary, but I also know you'll all do great. I just want you to remember to relay the messages from the spirits with kindness, compassion, and love, without judgment or your own interpretation. Our own experiences can cloud messages, so just pass on what you get as directly as possible. Okay… ready?"

They all nodded. The door opened, and Gareth came in, followed by the parents.

Josie stood and went to Zara who had approached Gareth. She tapped her on the shoulder. "Zara, can I have a bathroom break?"

"Oh, yeah, me too," said Romy.

"Me three," said Jacob.

"Of course! Down the hall on the left. Miranda, do you need a bathroom break?"

She shook her head, looking frozen with nerves once more.

Josie and Romy headed out of the room and down the hall with Jacob at their heels. He disappeared behind the door labeled "men" as they found the door marked "ladies". Once inside, Romy grabbed Josie's shoulder and said, "Oh my god, I am so terrified to do this!"

"I don't think you need to worry. Zara wouldn't put us in a situation that we can't handle," said Josie. She was nervous too but wasn't about to admit it.

"You think so?"

Josie nodded. "I do."

"Have you ever done anything like this before?"

Josie shrugged. "Kind of, but not on purpose."

"Really? Wow, I've never done anything like this."

"Try not to stress about it. I'm sure Zara will be guiding us through it, and I'll be there to support you," said Josie.

"Oh, thank you!" Romy threw her arms around Josie, which made Josie uncomfortable, though she couldn't help liking the girl. Her perkiness reminded her a little of Jenna.

Josie took her time in the bathroom to allow Romy to leave before her. When Josie was alone, she took several deep breaths and closed her eyes. In her mind, she said, *Hanover, you're with me, right?*

The tingle that was already around her neck grew stronger and morphed into the familiar warmth. *You know I am*, he said with a smile in his tone.

Do you think I can do this?

You can do anything you want to do. And you know you want to do this. You want to prove it to your father. And yourself.

You're right, she sighed, *which is why I'm nervous. I'm afraid that my motivation of wanting to prove something will mean that it won't work, and I'll be humiliated.*

You're correct to think that impure motivation can hamper your ability, but not where the underlying purpose is more important.

The underlying purpose? What do you mean? Josie frowned.

She felt Hanover shift his position around her neck. She moved into view of the mirror over the sinks and saw Hanover smiling at her from his position on her shoulders. *There are real people in that room who have loved ones they want to connect with. Remember the girl in the store in Salem? You passed on messages which helped her mother. You brought her peace and gave her life a new direction that she needed and might not have gotten otherwise.*

So, you're saying that the need to help those people overrules my selfish motivations?

I'm not guaranteeing it, but it's a strong possibility, he said, winked one small black eye, and faded from view.

Josie took another deep, bracing breath, straightened her shoulders, and headed back into the hallway. A beautiful woman was approaching from the direction of the Lilac Room, but something about her was off. Her dark hair was piled high on her head in an intricate array of braids and curls, a bejeweled butterfly clip sparkling in its depths, and she wore a dress of a deep blue velvet trimmed in ivory lace, high collared and tight on top, with a large, full skirt. She glided gracefully past Josie as though she didn't even see her, and as she passed, Josie noticed the tears that rolled down the woman's cheeks.

"Excuse me, are you okay?" Josie called after her.

The woman stopped and turned back to Josie. It was only then that Josie noticed that she was slightly transparent but didn't have any sort of glow, indicating that she was stuck.

Though Josie didn't see the woman's mouth move, in her head, she heard a deafening shout of "Get out!"

9

The woman's telepathic shout sent a stabbing pain through Josie's head, like brain-freeze times a thousand. She clutched at her head and leaned against the wall, squeezing her eyes shut until it passed.

"Josie, there you are!" Zara called from behind her. "Everything okay?"

"What?" Josie jumped and spun around. "Oh, yeah, sorry." She glanced back nervously to make sure the woman was gone as she followed Zara back into the Lilac Room.

The table had been removed and more chairs brought in. Jacob, Romy, and Miranda were already seated along the wall facing what now resembled an audience. In the front row sat four people she'd never seen before and behind them were the kids' family members. Josie saw her mom looking anxious but happier than she was earlier while her dad looked strained and apprehensive.

Josie took the empty seat between Miranda and Romy. She squeezed her eyes shut for a minute to reinforce her bubble of protection, which made it easier for her to not look too closely at the strangers in front of her or the haze of spirits who now gathered in the room. Gareth took a seat next to Jacob while Zara stood in the empty floor space between the kids and the spectators.

"Alright, let's get started," Zara said with a bright smile. "First, I want to thank you all again for coming and being a part of this. What we are doing right now is a demonstration of the abilities of these amazing young people behind me. Over the years I've found that the best way of getting validation as a Psychic or Medium is to connect with a perfect stranger.

"These four people before me have been kind enough to volunteer to be with us tonight. Before tonight I never met any of you. Is that correct?" She looked at the four people in the front row and they each nodded or spoke their concurrence. "Have any of you met any of the people in this room before tonight?" Again, she looked for their answers and they all shook their heads.

"Okay, now I would like to ask that everyone remain quiet unless you are the one being addressed by one of the Readers. I am using that term because their talents range across the spectrum of Psychic or Medium. If you do believe that they are connecting to your energy or a loved one of yours, please speak up, but don't give too much information. Because they are new to this, I will do my best to guide them without interfering.

"Any questions?" Zara paused. When no one spoke, she turned to Josie and the others. "One of you will be approached by a spirit or other energy. When you feel you have some information to pass along, please speak up. Alright. Let's begin!"

Josie felt a ripple run through the room and her stomach clenched with nerves. Her eyes were glued to the floor, examining the wide wooden floorboards where they were visible from beneath the thick red, black and white Oriental rug. *This is just like being on stage,* she told herself. *I'm an actress, acting the part of a Medium. That's all. I'm playing a part.* It was the same thing she'd been doing for weeks, only she didn't feel so confident now. Like Hanover said, the people in this room were real people hoping to connect with someone they lost. When Josie connected Danielle with her mom in Salem, she didn't know that's what she was doing. She didn't go into that store to do that. It just happened. But now she had to perform, really perform, and these people before them had hopes and expectations pinned on the four of them.

Don't panic, Josie, came Hanover's soft, purring voice in her ears. *Take deep breaths, and focus. You've done this before. It's just a different stage, that's all.*

Nice, using my theater terminology on me! She chuckled inwardly.

She was so busy panicking that she hadn't realized that a male spirit had stepped forward and was standing in front of Jacob. She looked at Jacob, his face drawn and tense as he too fixed his gaze on the floor before him. Gareth put a hand on his shoulder in support. Then, in a small voice, Jacob said, "I have a man here with me. He's old like my grandpa, and he's wearing a fishing hat and vest. I can see the little things on it, the hooks and lures on the vest. I think his name is A-Ant-Anthony. No, Arthur. Art, most people called him. And there's something in his hand. He's holding it out toward me. It looks… like a table with four chairs, but it's in the palm of his hand."

A woman with short, graying hair let out a sob. "That's my husband," she said. "He carved doll house furniture for a living."

"Okay, Jacob. Very good," said Zara. "Keep going. Ask him if there's a message that he wants you to pass on."

Jacob sat quiet for a moment, and then said, "He says… he says that she's there with him. I asked who, and now he's taking something from inside his vest. I think it's his wallet, and he's opening it up. He's holding it out for me, and I can see a photo of a girl, a teenager. It looks like a school photo, but not… not like my school photos. Her clothes look old-fashioned, and her hair is in two braids."

The old woman's wet eyes widened. "That's Liza."

"I can see her now. She's standing with Art, holding his hand," said Jacob. He then raised his head and looked at the woman, his brows furrowed. "Did you not know she was dead?"

She shook her head. "We were never certain, but we suspected."

"She disappeared… on a school trip… is that right?" Jacob asked her.

The woman nodded. "It was her Senior class trip to Niagara Falls. They stopped at a diner on the way home. She went to the bathroom and was never seen again."

Josie heard a gasp from one of the parents. Everyone in the room was equally gripped by the story.

"She's showing me a map. I see... Weedsport... it's a small town in New York I think, and she's pointing to a street... Rosewood Circle. I think her body is buried in the basement of an abandoned house on that road. She's saying that she wants to be buried next to her father."

The woman nodded but was crying too hard to speak.

"She's also saying that the man who took her is long since dead, but he received justice for what happened to her and the others before he died."

"The others?" The woman squeaked out between tears.

Jacob nodded. "I think that when they find her, they'll find bodies of about six or seven other girls."

"Thank you," she sobbed again. "You have no idea how much this means to me and my family. This has haunted us for almost forty-five years."

"Is there anything else they want to say, Jacob?" asked Zara.

He shook his head. "No, they're gone now."

"Well, that was a great job, Jacob. And Mrs....," Zara said.

"Richards. Mary Richards," she finished for Zara.

"Mrs. Richards, I have a police officer friend who does a lot of work with Psychic information. I would like to connect the two of you so he can help you validate this information and find your daughter."

The woman nodded as she wiped at her nose with a handkerchief. "Yes, please. That would be very helpful."

"Alright. Let's see who's next," Zara smiled and turned back to Josie and the others.

They all sat in silence. Someone shifted in their seat causing a floorboard to squeak under their chair, and a clock ticked steadily somewhere.

Josie knew there were a lot of spirits in the room and waited for one to approach her, but then Romy, with a slight tremor in her voice said, "I don't have a spirit presenting to me, but I keep seeing a gold chain, a thin link chain, and at the end is a round medallion a little smaller than a quarter, and it has a peace symbol engraved on it."

"Okay, that's good, Romy," said Zara. Turning to the audience, she said, "Does that sound familiar to anyone?"

No one spoke at first, but then the younger of the two men in the audience reached into his jeans pocket and pulled out a chain. He held it up so they could all see the medallion Romy had just described. He was tall and slender with short, spiky, dark hair and a large nose below dark eyes that were set in a skeptical scowl.

"M-may I hold it?" Romy asked.

He nodded. Zara hurried over and took the necklace from the man and handed it to Romy. Romy pooled it in her left palm and covered it with her right while closing her eyes.

"This belonged to your father," she said, her eyes still closed.

"Yes," said the man.

"Michael?" Romy said.

"That was his name and mine. I'm a Junior," he responded.

"I'm not, like, seeing your dad's spirit, but I think I'm feeling stuff from him."

Zara said, "That's good, Romy. Can you tell us what you feel?"

"I think I feel just a lot of his energy in this necklace. Like, he wore it all the time. He grew up in the sixties and was a real hippie but ended up working a suit-and-tie job, so he wore this medallion as a reminder of who he was under that stuff."

"That's right," Michael said, his scowl relaxing just a little.

Romy's eyes remained shut. "I feel that he died when he was… forty-four, yes?"

"Yes."

"And you're approaching your forty-fourth birthday," she said. He nodded, and his scowl almost completely disappeared. Romy continued. "I am sensing a lot of anxiety around that for you because your father and… and his father, too… they both died at age forty-four and you're afraid that it's hereditary and you're going to die also."

"Yes, that's true," he said, his voice catching in his throat.

"I feel like you should go see a doctor, but only to get your anxiety under control and have a physical. You are a very different man from your father and grandfather, despite your similarities. Their story is not your story."

Again, he nodded. He wiped the corner of his eyes.

"You've been living a very daring life these past few years, going sky diving, zip-lining, hiking huge mountains and exploring caves all over the world, and you're always wearing this necklace, aren't you?"

"Yes," he said.

Romy finally opened her eyes. "You have experienced a lot of amazing things in your life so far, and because of your fear of dying at the same age as your dad and granddad, you had the courage to do things that they never did. They were both with you on these adventures. But your story isn't over. I feel that it's time for you to reevaluate your priorities. Figure out what you want the rest of your life to look like and go for it. I think it's going to be just as awesome as the past few years have been, but maybe in a different way."

Romy smiled and stood. She walked across the floor and held out her hand with the necklace to Michael. He took it from her. "Thank you so much," he said quietly to her.

When she returned to her seat, she leaned over to Josie and whispered, "I don't know how I did that, but it was amazing!"

Josie tried to smile at Romy, but a heaviness in her chest told her that it was her turn next.

She didn't hesitate, knowing what would happen if she waited. "I have a female spirit here with me," Josie started. She felt like her voice echoed in the room. "She… well… I… I don't think she's crossed over yet." Josie looked at Zara.

Zara nodded. "That's okay. Keep going but take it slow if you need to."

Josie returned her focus to the girl. "She looks older than me, maybe in her late teens or early twenties. She's...." Josie wrung her hands and looked again at Zara. She was used to talking aloud to Jenna about the spirits she encountered, but not in a roomful of people.

"It's okay, Josie. Say what you're seeing," said Zara.

Josie nodded and rubbed her lips together in nervousness. "I think she was sick," Josie finally continued. "She's wearing a hospital gown and a robe and slippers. But everything looks... dirty and worn. Her hair looks matted and tangled, and she's very thin. I think she's confused because all she's saying is 'Dad, not Dad,' over and over."

Josie paused, unsure of what to do next, but the man sitting almost directly in front of her cleared his throat. "I think that's my daughter—" He cleared his throat again. "Stepdaughter, technically."

"Oh, so you're literally her 'Dad, not Dad,'" said Josie, feeling a little more confident. Suddenly, the other people in the room melted away for her and her only focus was to connect the girl and her father.

The man nodded.

"Did she die in a... hospital?" Josie asked.

He nodded again. "A psychiatric hospital," he said, his face stern and set, but he cleared his throat again.

Can you please give me something more? What's your name? Josie pleaded with the girl standing before her. She was about a foot from Josie, and she held out her arm. Josie saw the white hospital bracelet, not unlike the one Jenna had on her wrist a couple of months ago after she was in a car accident with Dave. Josie peered at the bracelet and saw the name on it.

"Her name is Cynthia," she said aloud.

"Yes," the man confirmed.

You need to talk to me, Cynthia, Josie said. *You're here for a reason. What do you want him to know? What can I tell him?*

Cynthia started to turn around and Josie thought she was going to walk away. But she turned back to Josie with a large brown leather photo album in her hands. She opened it up and started moving through the pages.

"She's showing me pictures. I see her as a young child, she's in a uniform and holding a bat. Softball, I think? And you're in the pictures with her. Each picture she shows me, she looks a little older but in all of them she's playing softball, and you're in all the pictures."

The man was nodding.

Where's your mom? Josie asked.

The next page in the album showed the back of a woman as she walked out the door. The next picture showed only the door.

"Her mother left, and she was afraid that you wouldn't keep her because you weren't her real dad, but you did," said Josie. "You had bonded over your mutual love for softball when she was little."

He nodded again. "She was on track to go to the Olympics, and then to be a professional if she wanted to," he said. "But then…."

"Something went wrong," Josie finished for him. Cynthia was showing her a picture of a bonfire, her as a teenager, friends around, laughter. She moved through the pages of pictures so fast it was almost like a movie. The pictures got weird, and dark, and then bloody.

"I don't know what happened…." Cynthia's dad said.

"She and her friends dabbled in black magic," Josie said, a deep frown furrowing her brow as she put the pieces together from the pictures to form a conclusion. "They didn't think it was real. Cynthia included. But one of them… one of them knew what they were doing, or at least, knew enough to cause serious trouble. Cynthia didn't know that. And then she started hearing voices."

Josie saw more pictures, images of Cynthia with large, dark, shadowed figures clinging to her, their long fingers like claws piercing her.

"I thought she was doing drugs," he said. "I thought the voices were from drugs, drugs that were making her sick in the head. I thought she feared the success she was having, of the changes it meant for her. I thought she was rebelling. And I was trying to deal with it on my own…."

"It was hard. She knows that. She knows you did your best," said Josie.

"She tried to tell me. But I didn't believe her."

"They had a hold on her," Josie said. "Spirits… or ghosts or... I don't know exactly what they were. I hate to say it…." She looked at Zara again.

"Okay, take a breath," said Zara. "Just tell him what Cynthia is trying to say."

Josie sighed and frowned. "Well, it's just that, I don't know for sure, but I guess some people might call these things… demons. You know, evil spirits. I don't know for sure if that's true, but whatever they were, they were there to do really bad things. Their purpose was to mess with the lives of the living people they encountered. They were controlling her, making her say and do things she wouldn't normally do."

"It was my job to protect her," he said, his voice cracking. "And I failed her. I failed her."

"She doesn't want you to feel guilty. She knows you did the best you could."

"How do I know?" he asked, his brows in a scowl again.

"What?" asked Josie.

"How do I know she's really saying that?"

Josie was shaken, but said to Cynthia, *Please, give me some detail of something only you and he would know.*

Cynthia flipped through more pages of the photo album, faster and faster as Josie tried to put the pieces together. "You went to the hospital every Sunday to visit her. You would stay for lunch if she was having a good day. There was one visit about a month before the … accident … she was having a really good day. Things were particularly quiet for her. And you arrived early. You walked the grounds together, you had lunch, you talked about the softball championship the year before and the trips the two of you had taken. You talked about going back to the Polar Caves and driving the Kancamagus Highway when she was feeling better. You spent the afternoon together coloring in coloring books like when she was a little kid. She colored a mountain scene and before you left, she gave it to you. She'd added into the scene a car with a father and daughter and a moose on the side of the road that they were looking at. She told you that it was a picture of the day you'd have together soon, that you'd finally see a moose. You took that picture home, and after the accident, you framed it and put it on your bedside table where it still sits to this day."

He was crying. Tears streamed down his cheeks, but he looked angry. "What did I give her for her thirteenth birthday?"

Josie frowned. Cynthia showed her another picture. "A fishing pole," said Josie.

"Tell me what's in my pocket," he demanded.

Charles stood abruptly, his face full of anger. Gareth stood as well. Zara held her hand up to her husband motioning for him to stay and said, "Sir, that's not appropriate."

But Josie said, "You have thirty-five dollars' cash, some loose change, your driver's license and credit cards, and an emerald ring that was Cynthia's."

"Sir, I'm going to have to ask you to leave," said Zara.

"No, wait," said Josie.

Zara and the man both looked at Josie in surprise. "Cynthia isn't crossed over. I need to cross her over and I don't think I can do that if he leaves."

"Okay, if you're sure, Josie," said Zara.

Josie nodded. She couldn't leave Cynthia like this, still in the form of a sick, confused girl.

"What… what do you mean she isn't 'crossed over'? What does that mean?" asked Cynthia's dad.

"It means that when she died, she didn't completely move on. Part of her is hanging on, keeping her here in a form similar to her living form, as opposed to her soul form," said Josie, remembering how Aunt Pauline became a beautiful young woman when she passed.

What is keeping you here? What do you need your dad to know? Josie asked Cynthia.

"What is keeping her from moving on?" asked her dad.

Josie held up her hand. "I'm asking her that right now." When Cynthia finished moving through more pages of the album, Josie said, "She stayed because she was worried about leaving you all alone. She's telling me that she visits you a lot. You've seen her in dreams, yes?" asked Josie after seeing an image of Cynthia standing next to her dad while he slept.

He nodded.

"She tries to get your attention in the house, too, but… well it's hard for her to make her presence known, especially where you aren't… um, well, very receptive to the idea of ghosts. That makes it even harder for her. But I think maybe she did get the lights to flicker once, and a photo in the living room of the two of you going to the father-daughter dance fell off the table in a way that didn't seem quite possible."

"That was her?" he said, his eyes wet again. Josie felt sorry for him at that moment. He'd been through the gamut of emotions in such a short amount of time.

Josie nodded. "I think she's worked hard to get you here. You're a landscaper? She's showing me an advertisement for your company that ended up on the desk of the manager of the Inn. I think she put it there. They called you in for a meeting about doing landscaping for them, right? The meeting was earlier today. And you were waiting outside the manager's office when his assistant was going around looking for volunteers for tonight. She's showing me you, sitting in the chair, talking to the assistant, and

Cynthia was sitting next to you, yelling as loud as she could in your ear, begging you to agree to come."

"But why? Why did she want me here?" he asked, his tone bordering on pleading.

When Josie saw Cynthia's answer, she squeezed her eyes shut tight. The image of the man before her hanging lifeless from a banister in his house was burned into her mind. *How am I supposed to say that to a stranger?*

Hanover responded, *Say it as gently as possible.*

Josie sighed and opened her eyes. "She wanted you here so she could tell you that she doesn't want you to… to end your own life."

10

His chin fell to his chest and his shoulders shook as sobs wracked his body. Cynthia was now standing at his side, her hand resting on his shoulder. Everyone in the room was silent, feeling like intruders in a very private moment.

When he lifted his head, his face was red and wet. "I don't think I would have actually done it," he said. "But I was thinking about it."

"She saw you looking at things on the computer… things like doses of different medications, if it needed to be combined with alcohol, that kind of thing," said Josie.

"Yes. But I couldn't actually do it. It's just been… so hard since…."

"She wants you to know that your suffering is not going to take back anything that happened. She wants to be able to move on, to be at peace, knowing that you are also moving on from this, and that you will work to find a way to be at peace." Josie paused and frowned, then went on. "She is showing me scales, like the old-fashioned kind. Does that mean anything to you?"

He chuckled through his tears. "Yes. We called it our 'Scales of Justice Bargain'. It's something we used to do when she was younger. I would ask her to do something like clean her room or do the dishes, and she would bargain for extra TV time or an ice cream cone. She would call for the Scales of Justice. I don't even know how she came up with that, if she learned it in school or from a friend."

"She learned it by watching something on the history channel, but she doesn't remember what. She's showing me herself standing with her hands out like this," said Josie, holding her hands out, palms flat and facing the ceiling, her elbows slightly bent. "You would ask her to do something, and she would tip one way depending on the weight of it, and then she would ask for something in return, and tip the other way until you both agreed it was even. Right?"

He nodded and smiled again.

"A friend of yours gave you information about a support group, right?" Josie asked.

Again, he nodded. "I threw it away."

"She's showing me that it is in your bottom right desk drawer. She wants you to go to the meetings. She will only move on if you promise to go to the meetings."

He nodded. "I promise."

Josie looked at Cynthia who smiled and nodded as she faded away into a shower of pale blue glittering light.

Wait! Josie shouted in her mind. She was surprised when Cynthia's form started to come back into view a little. *What happened to those entities or whatever they were that attached to you at the party? Where did they go when you died?*

She replied with a shrug and showed Josie one last photo.

Josie frowned, and Cynthia was gone.

"She's moved on. The last thing she wanted you to know was that you should open the envelope the hospital sent you after she died. I think there's a special letter in there for you from her."

Again, the man nodded.

Josie saw her mom lean forward, handing the man a packet of tissues over his shoulder which he took.

Then Josie felt herself crumble inward. She was suddenly exhausted. She heard murmuring around her but didn't have the energy to hear the words that were being spoken. She wanted to leave, to crawl into the back of the car and lay down and sleep for the whole rest of the night, but she knew she couldn't. So, she stayed where she was, unaware that next to her Miranda was assuring a brand-new mom-to-be that it was safe to tell her family she was pregnant, that after two miscarriages and years of trying, this pregnancy would go full term. Cynthia's dad handed the pregnant woman the packet of tissues to dry her tears of joy.

"That was amazing!" Josie heard Romy whispering at her side. "I can't believe we all just did that. That was amazing!"

Josie pulled herself from the brink of exhaustion and focused on her surroundings. The room had come alive with chatter as everyone stood and started to mill around. Josie thought all the ghosts were gone, but as the living people in the room shifted, she saw a transparent figure standing at the back, a tall woman with long, straight, raven black hair, a heart-shaped face with almond eyes of a golden color, a full mouth, and skin of a reddish-brown tone, so very like Josie's own, dressed in a long dress made of a light-colored tanned animal hide.

Josie stood tall and straight at the realization of who she was seeing. *Hello, Mother Elk Spirit,* said Josie.

She smiled, and Josie heard, *I'll be calling for you soon. I expect you to be ready.* And in a blink, she was gone.

What was that all about? Josie asked, hoping Hanover would answer, but there wasn't time to listen for an answer because Cynthia's dad was approaching her.

"Josie, I want to thank you," he said, reaching out for her hand which she gladly gave. "And I want to apologize if I was… well, not 'if'. I was rude and difficult, and I'm sorry."

"It's really okay," said Josie just as Angela and Charles appeared at her side.

"Hi, I'm Josie's mom, Angela, and this is her dad, Charles," Angela said, smiling but eyeing the man as only a protective mother would.

He shook hers and Charles's hands. "I'm Jerry. Your daughter… she's amazing, you know that, right? I'm just… well, it's amazing what these kids can do. There's no way she could have known any of that. And to see all of you parents here supporting the kids through this…. I wish… well, I know I can't go back. It's just great to see that you aren't making the same mistake I did."

Josie felt her face flush at his words while Charles's face went pale, almost green.

"Thank you, Jerry. It hasn't been easy," Angela replied, glancing at Charles, "but we're trying."

"Well, good luck to you all, and Josie, again, thank you so much," he said.

"You're welcome. I'm honored to have met Cynthia, and I'm glad I was able to help her," Josie replied.

"You folks have a great night," said Jerry.

When the four guests had gone, Zara called their attention. "Alright! So now that that's done, let's gather around and chat for a bit. I want the parents to stick around for this. We have more drinks and goodies coming in a moment."

As she said that, the door opened, and trays were brought in. There was coffee, tea, cocoa, and water as well as platters of chocolate covered strawberries and assorted cheeses and crackers. Josie helped herself to a plateful of strawberries and bit happily through the chocolate that gave way in a satisfying snap.

When everyone was seated, Zara said, "I hope you are all very proud of yourselves for the amazing job you guys did. I am truly blown away with how well you handled yourselves. Now, the reason I wanted you all to do this is because it is a great way to validate what you're experiencing, and it's an opportunity to use these abilities of yours for good. And this was only one way. Or, actually, in Josie's case, two ways since she did a reading *and* crossed a spirit over. But that's another way, helping stuck spirits cross over is a great way to use your abilities. There are endless possibilities, as unique as each of you are. I would like to meet with you all about once a month to go through some techniques and tools to use, and give you guys a safe place to practice as well as a safe place to talk about the challenges you experience. And I promise that all our meetings won't be this intense. I needed to throw you guys in the deep end to prove to both you and your families that this is real and that it has real benefits in the human world."

Zara then went on to talk a little about each of them and the readings they did, offering praise and gentle constructive criticism. When she got to Josie she said, "I've never done this where we've had a stuck spirit come through. That was a new one for me, so I'm guessing that is part of your calling, to help stuck spirits. I was very impressed with how you handled yourself with both the daughter and the father. And what you experienced with him is something all of us can learn from. Even if someone comes to you for a reading, that doesn't mean they are open and receptive to all you may have to say, and they may push back. You need to remember that you have no control over how another person is going to receive the information that comes through, and that's okay. All you can do is pass on the information and let them do with it what they will."

Zara paused for a sip of tea and then went on. "One of the greatest things about doing this work is seeing things like what happened with Miranda's reading. She was able to bring comfort and reassurance to someone in a very delicate state, both physically and emotionally. Because you were able to assure her that her pregnancy would go full term, you gave her a gift of peace of mind, which in turn will make her a healthier person and will also help her baby grow healthy.

"I want you all to remember these moments of success that you had tonight whenever this stuff gets overwhelming, whenever you feel you aren't up for the challenge. You are all talented, intelligent, capable, and kind young people, and I'm really looking forward to seeing how you grow with it all.

"Now, what questions do you all have for me?"

Jacob and Romy overflowed with questions while Josie and Miranda stayed quiet. Josie had a lot to process, most of which stemmed from what Zara had said to her about how helping stuck spirits might be her calling. She wasn't sure how she felt about that. She always thought dancing and theater was her calling, but then that stupid accident happened while whitewater rafting, and everything changed. She didn't want to admit that it made sense. From the start, she's helped stuck spirits cross over: first Philip Stillwater, then the men at Fishkill Pond and the people in Aunt Pauline's nursing home. Even just a few weeks ago she helped Ophelia and Mark. Technically Ophelia was a stuck spirit even though her body wasn't dead and thankfully her life was saved.

Maybe it is my calling, thought Josie. A part of her heart sank. *I might go crazy if I can't still dance and sing, so maybe I can find a way to do both.*

"Alright, well, it's getting late so I guess we should call it a night," said Zara. "I'm sure you guys are exhausted. I want to thank you all for coming and participating, and I want to thank all the family members for coming and supporting the kids. Please make sure you take one of my business cards on the way out so if any of you have any questions or need anything before the next time we get together, you can call, text, or email me. Thanks guys! Enjoy the rest of your weekend!"

Before she left Josie exchanged cell numbers with Romy, Miranda, and Jacob, and got a hug from Romy, Zara, and Gareth. At the car, Josie fell into the back seat, relieved to be done. But as they drove away, Josie turned back to look at the mansion-turned-Inn, wondering about the woman she saw in the hallway and wondering what Jenna would think of it. She had so much to fill her in on but didn't know if she'd ever get the chance.

She was just starting to feel sad again at the loss of her best friend when her phone lit up with a notification of a text. It was from Romy, saying, I'M SO GLAD WE MET! LET'S GET TOGETHER SOON. IT'S SO GOOD TO HAVE FRIENDS WHO REALLY UNDERSTAND THIS STUFF!

Josie responded. I AGREE! LET'S DEFINITELY PLAN SOMETHING SOON. HAVE A GREAT NIGHT!

"So, Josie, what did you think? Are you glad you went?" Angela asked from the front passenger seat.

"Yes, I am," she said honestly. "But I'm wiped out. I feel like I could sleep for three years."

"I can only imagine," said Angela. "I have to tell you, Josie, that I am… just so amazed at what I saw tonight. From all the kids, but especially you… it was… well I just had no idea it was like that. It was all so… emotional, and really just wonderful."

Josie's heart swelled at her mother's words. "Thanks, Mom. What did you guys do with Gareth when he took you to the other room?"

"We did a lot of listening and a little talking. It was interesting listening to him. He offered a great perspective of what it's like to support someone who deals with this stuff. I think it will help things be a bit smoother at home," she said. Josie could hear the cheer and hope in her mother's voice, but the ongoing silence from her dad left her with doubts. He said nothing. No praise for Gareth, Zara, or Josie, no awe for what happened in that room, only enduring brooding.

* * * * *

Josie woke from a deep sleep late the following morning. The smell of freshly brewed coffee enticed her to climb from bed, and she made her way to the kitchen where she found her mom at the stove.

"What'cha makin'?" Josie slurred and yawned. She poured coffee into a large mug and sat at the kitchen table.

"Potato salad. For the barbecue at the LaPage's today. They expect us there by noon," said Angela.

Josie's heart dropped to her feet. "I'm not going," she said.

Angela stopped and turned to her daughter. "Okay, what is going on with you and Jenna?"

Josie swallowed a large mouthful of coffee along with some tears. "She's mad at me," Josie said, too tired to find a lie. "She has every right to be mad at me. I don't know if she'll ever want to be my friend again, so I really can't go over there today. Okay? Please say it's okay."

Angela put down the spoon she was using to stir the potatoes and sat at the table facing Josie. "Fine, but I want to know why."

Josie averted her eyes and continued to sip her coffee.

Angela sighed. "Josie, our family is on shaky ground, and I am working hard to keep us together. I am doing my best to support you in what you're going through, but the only way I can do that is if you talk to me. We need full transparency in this family right now. No more secrets."

Josie matched Angela's sigh with her own. "It's just…."

"Is it something you're worried you might get in trouble for?" Angela asked.

Josie shook her head. "It's nothing like that. It's just… embarrassing."

"You know you don't need to be embarrassed about anything with me," she said.

"I know," Josie replied. She sighed again and said, "Well, I don't know if you remember how on my first day of school freshman year, I had trouble with the lock on my locker?"

"I remember that. You said another student came along and helped you."

"Right. That student was Simon. I'd never met him before, but he came along and helped me out in what could have been a disaster for me. You know, I'd heard horror stories about upper classmen torturing freshmen. But he was really nice, and he didn't laugh at me or anything. He was so helpful. He was…."

"Your knight in shining armor," Angela finished for her.

Josie shrugged. "Yeah. And I kinda had a crush on him after that. But I thought it was just a crush, cuz I only saw him once in a while in the hallways at school. Then last summer when you guys made me go to that camp, there he was. I don't know why I didn't tell Jenna. I think partly because I was just so terrified to be on that trip that was so far out of my comfort zone, and she and I became friends so quickly.

"And then there was Reagan," said Josie.

"That awful girl from your group?" Angela asked.

"Yeah. She flirted with Simon the whole time, and Jenna told me how during the previous summer, Reagan had tried to be friends with her and kept asking her to put in a good word for her with Simon, and Jenna saw she was just using her. I really liked Jenna, and I didn't want her to think I was using her too. And I hoped that as I got to know him, maybe my crush would go away."

"But it didn't," concluded Angela when Josie paused.

"No. We've all... we've been through a lot together, Mom. He saved me from drowning and then a ghost shot him, and it seemed so real. He was bleeding, he passed out, and I thought he was dying. Maybe he would have. I think I might have saved him. Then, in October, I told you how we went to this place, it's called Fishkill Pond, and a small village used to be there, and the ghosts there were... they were mean. One of them kind of possessed Simon. But... it's more than just all that. We've all gotten close and have gone through things – weird things and bad things and good things, too – we've gone through it all together. It made my feelings stronger instead of making them go away. But the longer I went without telling Jenna, the harder it got. Then, on the last day of school, she saw something in my journal that I'd written about him, and she got so mad at me for not telling her, and I don't blame her, really. I knew she'd be mad. I keep hoping she'll text me, but she hasn't. Because of that, I don't want to go to the barbecue. She doesn't want me there and I'd just look pathetic if I showed up."

Angela sighed once again. "I understand, and I guess it's okay, though it hurts me to see you going through this on top of everything else. Honey, I don't know how you do it, but you are obviously an amazingly strong girl."

Josie shrugged and shook her head. "Thanks, I guess."

"Can I ask you one more question?"

"Sure," Josie replied, and took another sip of coffee.

"How does Simon feel about you?"

She shrugged again. "For a while, I thought it was just friendship on his side, or sisterly, you know? But now… I'm not sure. I think he might feel something for me too, but it's all so complicated. He's not the biggest fan of the ghost stuff, and he's leaving for college soon so… yeah, I don't really know. At this point, I don't care. I care more about Jenna's friendship."

Angela got up and went around to Josie and wrapped her arms around her. "Thank you for telling me all this," she said, squeezing Josie tight. "Thank you for being honest."

"How do you know I'm being honest?" Josie asked.

"I can just tell," Angela answered. "Matters of the heart… believe it or not, I remember what it was like to be a teenager. I remember how hard it can be, navigating friendships and… well, stronger feelings. I had my heart broken more than once when I was your age, Josie. So, I will make an excuse for you to the LaPage's, but I really hope you and Jenna can work this out."

"You won't say anything to her, will you?"

"No," she replied, shaking her head. "I would like to, but I know that parental interference won't help."

"Thanks, Mom."

Josie refilled her mug and went back to her room where she stayed until her parents left for the LaPage's house. She then went outside to the back patio and stretched out on a lounge chair in the sun. She put in her earbuds, put on her favorite playlist, and thought about everything that happened the day before. She'd already texted with Romy that morning but still hadn't processed everything she had experienced. She had grown accustomed to having Jenna and Dave there to listen to her stories and postulate theories and ideas about the why's and how's. She missed that, and she missed the banter she had with Uncle Frank, Ethan, *and* Hanover. *No offense, Hanover. I love you and appreciate your presence,* Josie said in her mind, directing her thoughts to her one remaining guide. *But it's just not the same without them.*

I understand, came his distant reply. *Change is difficult, but it is also necessary.*

Change. Yes, a lot was changing for her. Her guides, her friends, her relationship with her parents, even things at the dance studio were changing for her. Not all the changes were difficult or bad, but they were still sometimes stressful. Like the fact that she was going into her final two years at the dance studio. Being an upper-level student meant that the end was near. She'd be graduating soon. And that meant a whole lot of other changes that she couldn't even think about yet.

But you've been through a lot of change in the past year, said Hanover, manifesting at the foot of her lounge chair. *And you made it through that, right? Think about how much has changed in the past year.*

Yes, a lot has changed, and I don't think I would have made it through it all without you guys and Jenna and Dave and Simon. But... I don't think they need me. Actually, I know they don't need me. What do I bring to their lives but misery? No wonder I haven't heard from Jenna. I guess I should cut my losses now. We were only friends for a year. Even though it felt longer, it wasn't. And maybe it wasn't meant to be more than that. Now I have Romy and Zara and the rest of the group. I can probably get through this without Jenna.

Do you want to get through this without her? Hanover asked.

No, I don't. But she has no reason to want to be friends with me after what I've done. I've got to get over it. Get over her, get over Simon, and get on with my life. That's all. Easy as that, she replied. But tears rolled down her cheeks.

* * * * *

Butterflies fluttered in Jenna's stomach when she heard a car in their driveway. She looked around the side of the house to see

Angela and Charles climb from their car, but her heart sank when Josie didn't follow. She knew she shouldn't be surprised. Jenna hadn't responded to any of her texts, so why would she come?

Jenna hurried over to them, taking the large bowl of potato salad from Angela. "Hi, Mrs. York," she said. "Josie didn't want to come?"

They walked into the backyard as Angela said, "She had a rough day yesterday so she's home resting."

Rachel came walking up then and overheard Angela. "Oh, is Josie not feeling good?"

Angela embraced her friend and replied, "She's okay. She's just worn out. She had a rough day yesterday and the past couple weeks have been all over the place too, with finals and the funeral and her recital, then all our family therapy appointments on top of it all. The poor kid just needs some downtime."

"That's too bad. I thought maybe time with her friends today would help with that," said Rachel, who looked at the flush on her daughter's cheeks. "Does this have anything to do with the fight you two had?"

"It wasn't a fight," Jenna protested. "I was just…. And I was hoping she'd come today so we could talk."

"Did she know you wanted her to come?" Rachel asked.

"No." Jenna's flush deepened.

Rachel tilted her head at her daughter. "Then what are you going to do about it?"

Jenna looked at Angela. "Is it okay if I go over there to talk to her?"

Angela shrugged. "It's fine with me. Just please go easy on her."

The two moms watched Jenna get the car keys from Greg and head to the driveway. "I wouldn't want to be a teenager again for all the money in the world," said Angela.

"Do you know what this fight is all about?" asked Rachel.

Angela nodded. "You're going to want some wine for this."

* * * * *

Josie was still in the backyard, lost in her thoughts and unable to hear a car approach over the music in her earbuds when Jenna parked in her driveway. Josie also couldn't hear the car door slam, or the knock on the front door, or the ringing of the doorbell. She had no idea that Jenna, knowing where their spare key was, had unlocked the front door and was walking through her house looking for her, calling her name. She had no idea Jenna finally spotted her sunning herself on the back patio until a shadow crossed in front of her.

"Jenna, what the hell? You scared the crap out of me!" Josie said upon opening her eyes.

"Couldn't you hear me calling your name? Pounding on your front door?" Jenna scowled down at her.

"No, I had my music on. What are you doing here?" Josie asked. She sounded angry, but she was surprised, happy, and scared all at the same time.

"I… well, I was hoping you'd come to the barbecue so we could talk."

"Why would I go? You haven't returned any of my texts or calls in the past two weeks, so I thought it was safe to assume you didn't want me there."

Jenna sat on the empty lounge chair next to Josie's. "I know. I was going to text you and ask you to come but…."

"But you're still mad?"

"No, I don't think I am anymore. I just… Josie, why didn't you just tell me?"

Josie sighed. "I've told you. I didn't want you to think I was using you the way Reagan did. When I got on that bus last summer for the hiking trip, I was terrified. I was completely out of my element. But you just sat down and became my friend, and you made me feel so much better about the trip. Knowing I would have you as my partner, someone who knew what they were doing… I was so relieved. And at first, well, I mean I didn't really know you. All I knew was the story you told me about Reagan, and I decided to keep my mouth shut. But the longer I went without telling you, the harder it got. I decided it wasn't necessary, that I would just find a way to get over him, and then it wouldn't be an issue."

"And have you?"

"What?"

"Gotten over him?"

Fresh tears burst from Josie then. Two weeks' worth of suppressed emotion came pouring from her. She covered her face with her hands as she sobbed and shook her head. "No," she squeaked out. When the sobs slowed, she looked at Jenna and said, "My mom and I have agreed that the only way to repair our family is with total transparency. I think you and I need that, too. So, can I tell you my true, honest feelings?"

Jenna frowned, uncertain, but nodded.

Josie took a deep, bracing breath and said, "I just can't shake the feeling that he and I are linked… like on a soul level, like you and Dave, and Aunt Pauline and Uncle Frank. Ever since he was shot by Philip Stillwater, and I watched the life drain from him… he had saved me from drowning and then I saved him from a crazy ghost. We're linked. Connected. I just know we are. But he… he doesn't see it that way. And I'm just trying to be okay with that. I love being his friend, even when he's being impossible about the ghost stuff. So being around him is a constant source of happiness and pain for me."

Jenna listened to this with a deep frown furrowing her brow while staring at her feet.

Josie took another breath and, before Jenna could say anything, went on. "And there's more. When we were in Florida, on the last day, that morning before we left, I ran into him on the beach. I told him… I told him how I felt, and he said… well, he feels *something* but he's… uncertain what it is, and even though we kissed—"

"You kissed!" Jenna yelled, her head snapped up and birds fluttered from their perch in the trees.

Josie sighed. "Yes."

"Did you kiss him, or did he kiss you?"

"We kissed each other, Jenna. It was mutual, but he was mad. He'd just found out Mary Alice had cheated on him, and he said I took advantage of him. And as you know, I've hardly seen him since.

"But none of it matters. I am just so sorry I didn't tell you. I just… I really did think that I could shake it, get over my feelings for him, and then it wouldn't be an issue. I was wrong. About it all. But I really don't care anymore. I mean, about my feelings for him. I can't spend any more time or energy wondering, worrying, trying to talk myself out of it. I don't know what is going to happen, but right now I just really don't care about that. I only care about being your friend."

They sat in silence for a few minutes. The birds settled back onto their perches and squirrels chirped around them. A bee buzzed languidly somewhere nearby, and Josie waited patiently for Jenna to say something.

Finally, Jenna spoke. "I think I was mad at myself, more than at you, for not seeing it. I look back now, and I can see things, or remember hearing things, and I should have known. But I was too wrapped up in other stuff. It was there, though. Dave saw it. He says he sees it on both sides, but that Simon is too stubborn to admit it," Jenna chuckled and shook her head. She went silent again for a minute then continued. "I still wish you had told me, but I… I understand why you didn't."

Josie looked at Jenna, hopeful. "Really?"

"Yes. I mean, I know I can be kinda harsh when it comes to certain things, and I can see how that stuff with Reagan may have scared you. But…."

"But?"

"We need to promise each other that nothing like this will ever happen again. We're best friends. We need to tell each other everything, okay?"

Josie shook her head. "Does that mean that we're friends again?"

Jenna tilted her head at her. "We never *weren't* friends. It was just a stupid fight, all on me, too. We should've just talked about it right away but… well, it doesn't matter. It's over now."

"You're sure?" Josie asked.

"Of course I'm sure! I've missed you so much! And I've been terrible. I'm so sorry I missed your recital. I'm the worst friend in the world. But Simon and Dave said you were amazing."

"What? They were there?"

"Yeah. They knew I was being an idiot, so they went without me," said Jenna.

Tears once again filled Josie's eyes. "I didn't see them."

Jenna shook her head. "They were late, because of me, so they stood in the back and then left right after. They thought you might be upset if you saw that I wasn't with them."

More tears spilled down Josie's cheeks, but she wiped them away. "This has been such a mess. I've missed you guys so much."

"We've missed you, too. And now… can we go to my house? There's a backyard filled with amazing food there," said Jenna.

Josie nodded. "Just let me change." She ran inside with Jenna following. "I have so much to tell you," Josie said over her shoulder, and went into a recap of all the weird things that had happened to her over the past two weeks as she changed out of her tank top and shorts and into a flowy sundress. She was just finishing telling her about her evening with Zara and the other kids the day before as she brushed her hair into a ponytail.

"I hate to ask you this," said Jenna, "but will you—"

"Write it all down for your journal?" Josie finished for her. She turned around and grabbed a folder from her desk and handed it to Jenna with a smile. "Already done. I haven't had much else to do lately."

"You really are the best," said Jenna.

"No, I'm not. If I was the best, I would have told you about… well, you know. But I'm working on it. I will be better."

"If that's true then there's room for improvement on my side, too," said Jenna. "Are you ready?"

Josie nodded.

At Jenna's, Dave greeted Josie with a bear hug. "I missed you, girl!" he said.

"I missed you, too, Dave. I don't know when it happened, but somewhere along the way you became one of my best friends," she said when he'd released her.

Dave patted his chest. "What can I say? I can't help it if I'm loveable."

Jenna punched his arm affectionately while Simon said, "Welcome back, Josie." He smiled and looked unaffected, but Josie felt the chaos underneath. She could see it in the depths of his eyes.

She murmured an awkward "Thanks," and then turned away, unwilling to get drawn in.

"Let's go get some food!" said Jenna.

"You don't have to tell me twice," Dave replied.

After they took seats at the patio table, their plates heaped high with food, Josie said, "So I already said this to Jenna, but I need you guys to be on board with this, too. Being without you guys for the last two weeks really made me see how important your friendship is to me. You are all my *friends*," she said, putting stress on the last word and looking pointedly at Simon. "I don't think I can go through life without you all as my friends. And yes, I'm going to address the elephant in the room."

"What elephant? Where?" Dave asked, looking around. Jenna smacked him on the arm.

Josie sighed but smiled. "My mom and I have an agreement that the only way to repair broken relationships is to be open with each other. And that's why I need to tell Simon...," she paused, meeting his eyes, feeling her insides quiver, "that the only thing I need from you is your friendship. *That* is the most important thing right now. But I want you to tell me if that's not possible. And know that it's okay if it isn't."

Simon frowned, his sky-blue eyes dimming like a cloud passing over the sun. He looked so much older in that brief moment. But then he smiled. "Josie, I've always been your friend. Maybe not the greatest friend, but I've always been your friend, and I always will be."

Jenna clapped. "Yay! I'm so glad our band is back together! And I just want to say again that I'm so sorry I've been so... difficult these past couple weeks."

"You? Difficult? Never," Dave said, his tone dripped with sarcasm and earned him another smack on the arm from her.

"So, if we're being completely honest, then I have a question for Jenna," said Simon.

"What?" she asked.

"Have you told Josie why you finally decided to give in and speak to her again?"

Jenna's face flushed again. "What do you mean?"

"You know exactly what I mean," he said. "Did you tell her about Mr. Shuts?"

Jenna rolled her eyes. "No. I haven't told her yet."

"Who's Mr. Shuts?" Josie asked.

"Okay, in complete transparency," Jenna said to Josie, "hearing about Mr. Shuts was the *last* piece of incentive I needed to know that this thing with us needed to be resolved, but it isn't the only reason."

"I don't really care at this point," said Josie. "It's all in the past, and I just want to move forward. So, please tell me, who is Mr. Shuts?"

"Apparently, he is an imaginary friend I had when I was three. We lived in a house in North Hampton at the time. It was before we moved here. And my mom said she saw a hag of a ghost there, too. I'm pretty sure Mr. Shuts wasn't just an imaginary friend, because my dad said he'd had things close on him like cabinets, doors, and even a window once. They said that I got upset when we moved because Mr. Shuts said he didn't want to come with us because he wanted to stay in his house."

Josie nodded. "If it was your imagination, you probably would have had him come with you."

"Exactly! I was so excited to know that I probably saw a ghost as a kid, in a house where my mom thought she saw a different ghost, but I couldn't share it with you. I didn't like that."

"Can we check this place out?" Josie asked.

"Wait, did I just hear you ask to go check the place out?" asked Simon. "Did we slip into an alternate universe?"

"Oh, you believe in alternate universes but not ghosts?" Josie shot back with a grin. "Yes, I am asking. First, I know how Jenna's mind works, and second, because, well, believe it or not, I'm curious, too."

"I hate to agree with Simon on this, but this does seem like a little bit of a shift in attitude," said Jenna.

"Yeah, well, when I was at that group – yesterday I went to a group for psychic teens," she said to Dave and Simon, "one thing that Zara said really made me think. She talked about how everyone has certain skills, things they're good at, and people often trade those skills with friends. Like with Simon. His skill is healing, and he's constantly bandaging me up, and in return…."

"You keep me from being killed or possessed by psychotic ghosts and being able to help you when you're hurt has helped my confidence in wanting to be a doctor," said Simon.

Josie felt that too-familiar flush rise to her cheeks, but she moved on with a nod. "Jenna, you're a fantastic researcher, and you've helped me so much with all this stuff. In return, I want to do what I can to help your research by communicating with ghosts."

"What about me?" said Dave.

"Dave, you're just consistently, reliably, solidly a good friend. I'm not sure I've given you anything in return, but I hope to," Josie replied.

"Dude, you're a good friend, and you've also opened my eyes to things I never dreamed were real. That's some pretty cool stuff, in my mind."

"Thanks, Dave. So, you guys get my point. It's put it in a different perspective. You're not just some random person at a party who heard I was a medium and is asking me to talk to their dead grandmother. You're my best friends, and we all share our skills and gifts with each other."

"That's cool. I'm glad you went to that group," said Jenna. "Of course, I have a ton more questions, but to answer yours: yes, sort of. I got the address from my mom, and I definitely want to take a drive by, but I promised my mom that I wouldn't bother the people who live there now."

"Well, maybe we can take a drive out there sometime soon and see what I can pick up on," said Josie.

Jenna clapped again, bouncing in her seat, her curls bouncing with her. "That would be amazing!"

"Alright, I'm going back for seconds," said Dave, swallowing the last bite of a burger and standing.

"Same," said Simon.

"I'm stuffed," Jenna and Josie said in unrehearsed unison.

Later, as the sun sank behind the trees, Greg started a fire in the pit next to the patio. Simon and Dave found bottle rockets and some other small fireworks and put on a little show for them. When they'd used them all up, Rachel called for the attention of all the kids.

"I guess I should have done this before the fireworks," said Rachel, "so we could celebrate, but whatever. We've all been talking and planning for weeks, and now we want to let you kids know that next Saturday, we are all going on vacation for a week!"

"What? Really?" exclaimed Josie.

"Where are we going?" asked Jenna.

Charles stood up. "We're going to a place that our family has been, called Red Drum Lake, in upstate New York."

Josie's heart sank a little. She remembered pictures of Red Drum Lake, a lakeside resort of rickety little cabins that looked full of bugs and squeaky beds. It wouldn't even come close to being as nice as the place they stayed at in Florida.

"Oh, and before Jenna asks," continued Rachel, "Dave is invited along as well. We invited your mother and brother along too, Dave, but your mom said she's going to be away."

"Yeah, she's visiting her sister in Seattle," said Dave.

"And your brother said he has plans with some of his college friends," added Rachel.

Josie started to stand. "Mom, what about—"

"Dance camp? I already talked to Miss Jillian, and she has all your classes covered, so there's nothing for you to worry about," said Angela.

"We've rented two cabins," said Rachel. "They're each two-bedroom so Greg and I will take one with Simon and Dave sharing the other room, and you girls will stay in Angela and Charles's cabin."

"Oh, I can't wait! This is going to be so much fun!" Jenna exclaimed.

Not long after the announcement, their parents went inside, and Dave said he needed to get home. Jenna walked him out to his car leaving Josie and Simon alone together for the first time in a long time.

She waited for him to bolt, to find an excuse to disappear into the house. Instead, he said, "Josie, are you sure you're okay with all this?"

Josie looked at him in surprise. "Yeah," she said, feeling inside that she wasn't quite being truthful. *Transparency*, she told herself. "I mean, I'm relieved Jenna and I are good, and I'm okay with her haunted house thing. I really am okay with you and me just being friends. I am. But...." She shook her head and sighed, gazing into the fire instead of his eyes which became an intense violet color in the firelight. "I'm still overwhelmed. You know, Aunt Pauline just died, and then Uncle Frank and Ethan left. Hanover's been around a lot and that's great but it's just so much at once. And my dad is still being difficult."

"It will get better, Josie. He's your dad, and he cares about you," said Simon.

In her head, Josie heard her dad saying the most hurtful words she'd ever heard, *she's not really ours*. "I appreciate you saying that, but the gap that Jenna and I had was a puddle compared to the ocean between my dad and me, and I don't know what, if anything, can fix it."

They fell into silence, the crackling of the fire and the chirping of night bugs the only sounds. Josie realized that she associated those sounds with him, Jenna, and Dave, thinking back to that disastrous camping trip a year ago. No, not disastrous. Cataclysmic. Altering her life in ways she never dreamed of, filled with both positive and negative. She wasn't sure of the balance of the two and wasn't sure she wanted to think about it.

"Josie," Simon said, breaking the silence. "I just want you to know that I'm glad we're friends, and I'm sorry if I'm not always a good friend to you."

"Thanks, Simon. I appreciate that," she replied.

"Josie!" Angela yelled from the back door. "Time to go!"

Josie stood, and Simon did, too. They locked eyes for a moment, and she had the strong desire to move to him, move into him, to wrap her arms around him and be enveloped by him. Instead, she turned to go.

"Good night, Josie," Simon said behind her.

"Good night," she replied, throwing him a quick smile over her shoulder as she joined her mom.

Simon watched her go until she disappeared into the darkness around the side of the house and then he sat back down to gaze into the fire.

He had almost reached out to her in that moment, almost drew her into him. Yes, he was her friend. He cared about her, and although she said she was okay and that she was overwhelmed by other things, he could still sense something off within her that he couldn't put his finger on. It was that same thing that seemed not right when he saw her at graduation. It was not as big and obvious now, but he could still sense it.

Obviously, I care about her, Simon thought irritably, answering the unspoken, unthought accusation. As he sat there poking at the fire with a stick, he could see her as though she was still sitting by the fire with him, as if she hadn't left. He could see her smile and the way the firelight caused her hair to glitter and turned her golden eyes to liquid amber. He remembered noticing all that a year ago on the camping trip, only he hadn't allowed himself to really *see* her. They had been through so much together since then. There was no doubt that he cared about her. He just didn't expect it to mean that he would sit there, imagining himself pulling her close, wrapping his arms around her, burying his face in the thick fall of her hair, and smelling the heavenly scent of the fire on her skin.

What do I do now? he wondered to himself. *If I let this happen, it could be really complicated. Do friendships ever survive deeper feelings?* He could hear his parents somewhere inside, his mom laughing at something his dad had just said. They always said they were best friends. Jenna and Dave said the same thing. *But what if things don't work out?*

He sighed, tossed the stick onto the fire, and let his head fall into his hands.

Part II

1

Josie pushed her plate away with a groan. “That was the best salad I’ve ever had.” She and Jenna had driven to Portsmouth to have lunch at the Friendly Toast before heading south to North Hampton in search of Jenna’s childhood haunted house.

“These crepes are to die for. I have to bring Dave back here. He’d love this place,” said Jenna.

“Do you have any thoughts on what you want to do when we get there? Or are we just gonna be creepy stalkers?”

Jenna sighed. “I don’t know. I promised my mom I wouldn’t bother them, but… I have so many questions. I don’t know what to do. I guess I’ll figure it out when we get there.”

They made their way back to the parking garage, paid the fee, and waited for the gate arm to lift. Following the GPS, they were guided through the one-way downtown streets and then onto Route 1 South. Josie ooh’d and aah’d as they passed buildings and houses with amazing architecture from the city’s beginning. Some of them were now offices, some were apartments, and some were private homes.

They moved out of the downtown area, passing strip malls and restaurants, neighborhoods, offices, and everything in between. Josie became quiet, taking only mental notes of the places she’d like to come back to explore.

Hanover, are you here? Josie asked silently. She immediately felt the tingle around her neck and shoulders indicating he was in his usual perch. *Is there anything I can do to help Jenna through this?*

Of course, there is, Hanover replied. *That’s why you’re with her. This is going to be a time for you to allow Jenna to explore things for herself.*

Josie frowned. *As usual, I don't know what that means, but okay.*

Just guide her the way we guide you, he offered. Josie felt the weight of that statement and frowned.

Jenna turned off the main road by an enormous, beautiful white farmhouse with an even more enormous barn behind it and then continued past fields, trees, and houses that varied from stunning, newly built mansions to centuries-old houses.

Jenna turned a couple more times and Josie felt they were moving further and further away from civilization. "It's so pretty here," Josie said in an attempt to break the silence.

Jenna nodded but said nothing, so Josie resumed her silence too. Jenna slowed the car. Josie could see on the GPS screen that they were getting close. When they reached the yellow star indicating their destination, Jenna pulled to a stop on the side of the road opposite the house. Josie leaned over and peered through the driver's side window at the dark blue Colonial-style house with dark wood trim and shutters and a bright red door.

"Is that it?" Josie asked.

Again, Jenna nodded. "That's it. I remember that red door. I think I've had dreams about that door. About this house. I had no idea it was a real place."

Josie wanted to ask again what Jenna wanted to do, but felt it was better to stay silent and wait for Jenna to figure it out. Josie watched the minutes tick by on the dashboard clock while Jenna stared at the house. Five. Ten. Twelve. Thirteen. Fourteen minutes passed. Then Jenna finally said, "Do you sense anything?" She looked at Josie with wide, hopeful eyes.

Josie shook her head. "I don't think I'm supposed to sense anything. I think this is your house to sense things."

Jenna sighed. "That's what I was hoping but… I don't know. I want to see a ghost so badly, but I don't know if it's wishful thinking making me *think* I feel something…."

Jenna relapsed into silence and continued to stare at the house. Clouds rolled in and dimmed the daylight as though a thick gray curtain had been pulled across the sun. Josie let out a small sigh, hoping it would urge Jenna to make a move. But she didn't do or say anything, and Josie became more irritable.

Then Jenna slammed her fist into the steering wheel. "Ugh! I just don't know what to do!" At that moment, a U-Haul truck drove by, slowed, and pulled into the driveway of the house they'd been watching. A man got out from the driver's side and went to the back of the truck and opened it to reveal the empty cavernous space while a woman got out of the passenger side and disappeared into the house through a side door. The man then disappeared into the house too, and a few minutes later they both reappeared, each carrying a cardboard box.

"They're moving," Jenna said in a half whisper that created a circle of fog on the window. They watched them go in and out and bring out several more boxes.

Josie was getting antsy, and she needed to pee. Then there was a tingle near her ear. *You need to be patient with her*, said Hanover.

Josie frowned and fidgeted with her fingernails, pushing at the cuticles. *I get it, but... can't she just figure it out already?*

Josie... have patience, he repeated, slightly scolding. She sighed and scowled. Then she opened her phone and used the camera to reapply lip-gloss and check her hair. She brushed her hair even though it didn't need it and examined her face with a scowl. She couldn't shake it. She was annoyed and frustrated with Jenna and getting more so by the second. She knew she had no right or reason to be, but she couldn't shake it.

"They see us," Jenna said, snapping Josie from her brooding.

"What?"

"I'm going to talk to them. I don't care what I promised my mom. I need to do this."

Jenna opened her door and Josie saw that the couple were standing at the back of the moving truck looking in their direction.

Josie quickly jumped from the car and followed Jenna across the street.

"Hi there," Jenna called as she strode across the pavement. "I'm sorry to bother you. I can see you're busy, but…," her voice softening as she reached the edge of the driveway, "I used to live here with my family when I was a little girl."

"You couldn't have possibly heard that it's for sale," grumbled the man, rubbing at his neatly cropped beard of dark hair. "The realtor hasn't officially listed it yet."

"If your family wants the house back, they can have it," said the woman, turning to put the box she held in the truck, her pin-straight silver-blond hair swinging like a skirt of fringe. Josie wondered scathingly how much she paid for it to be that color.

"No, sorry," Jenna said. "It's just a coincidence that I'm here."

There are no coincidences, said Hanover softly.

"My family and I were talking the other night about my childhood," Jenna went on. "I had my third birthday party here. And, well, I understand if it's too much of a bother, but I was wondering if my friend and I could maybe take a quick look around?"

The couple looked at one another and the man said, "I don't really care. The place is a mess with boxes, so go ahead but don't sue us if you trip over anything."

The woman shook her head and crossed her too-slender, too-tanned arms across her chest. "You're taking a chance going into that house. I hope you don't mind a little bad luck."

Jenna tilted her head at the woman and frowned. "What do you mean by that?"

"Oh, nothing. I'm sorry. Don't listen to me. Moving is stressful," she waved a hand in the air at the house. "Go ahead and look around quickly, but please be careful."

"Thanks!" Jenna said and headed for the side door.

Josie could hear the couple talking in lowered voices behind them as they went inside. They entered the side door that led into a kitchen that was filled with old dark wood cabinets, wide-board wood floors, and brand-new stainless-steel appliances. It was an expertly orchestrated blend of old and new.

"Jenna, it's weird being in a complete stranger's house," said Josie quietly.

"It isn't a stranger's house. It was once my house," Jenna replied. "I think I remember it. I remember the kitchen. It didn't look exactly like this back then, of course. Not these modern things, but the way everything is laid out… I remember that."

She walked through the kitchen and passed through a low doorway. "Yes!" Jenna exclaimed, pointing to a large fireplace in the inner wall of the next room. "I remember this fireplace! I was shorter then and we – me and Simon – were amazed that we could stand inside it and our heads didn't even come near the top. And we'd hide things in here, in this little hole in the side." She stuck her hand inside as if expecting to find the treasures of a three-year-old, but it came out empty.

"I think that's an oven or a warmer," Josie said, remembering numerous trips through old homes like this with her parents.

Josie followed when Jenna continued through another doorway into the living room that was crowded with boxes. Jenna turned and went down another hall that had the stairs to the second floor. Jenna ascended slowly, the treads creaking under her feet. Josie's stomach dropped, remembering those sounds as though it happened yesterday… just like in that house in the woods in Maine. Everything creaked in that house. She shivered and gave thanks that her parents bought a more modern home for their family.

"This was the guest room where my mom saw the old lady ghost," Jenna said when they reached the top of the stairs, pointing in through a doorway. The hallway stretched the length of the house in either direction. Josie looked around, expecting to see a gnarled old woman ghost lurking in a corner, but there were only cobwebs catching some of the dim daylight coming in through a window. Josie heard a rumble in the distance and knew it would start pouring any second.

"Jenna, I really don't feel comfortable doing this," Josie said, her voice in a whisper. Below them she could hear footsteps and murmurs and assumed the couple had come inside for more boxes.

"Will you relax? They said we could look around." Jenna had left the spare room and headed down the hall, passing a bathroom Josie pondered using but decided against it.

"Didn't you think their reaction was…I don't know, a little odd?" Josie asked.

"No, I didn't," Jenna responded sharply.

Josie sighed quietly. *Okay, Hanover, you told me I need to be here for Jenna, but like this?*

She heard a distant chuckle from Hanover who replied, *Yes, just keep doing what you're doing, Josie.*

"This was my room," Jenna said as she entered a small bedroom at the far end. The walls were covered in pink floral wallpaper. A twin bed and matching nightstand stood on one wall and a dresser and bookcase were on the other. Boxes were strewn about the room, and it looked like things were carelessly thrown into them in haste. Josie shivered again.

I don't like this place, Josie thought.

Then Jenna pulled her digital camera from her pocket and started taking pictures. Josie shouldn't have been surprised, but she was. She didn't think Jenna had brought any equipment with her. "It's all coming back to me. This is where I would talk to Mr. Shuts. I think he would tell me stories and jokes. Mom said she would hear me giggling when I was by myself in my room. She thought it was just my imagination. You don't see him? Or anything? I want to know if he's still here."

Josie shook her head. "I don't *see* anything, but this place gives me the creeps. Like that dang Stillwater house, I feel like there are eyes on me."

Jenna sighed and turned in a circle, her camera set to video now. "I don't get it. I'm here, and I want to see, or help, or just talk to him again. You should be able to help me with that!"

"Don't be mad at me, Jenna. You know I can't control it. And like I said before, I think this is more something for you than me."

Just then Josie heard a hiss behind her. She spun to face the doorway, but nothing was there. "Did you hear that? Was that you?" Josie asked, turning back to Jenna.

"Hear what?"

"A hiss."

"Damn, why do I miss everything?"

"I don't know that it was anything paranormal so don't be mad at me!" Josie repeated.

Jenna was glaring at Josie when a voice cut through the air. "Girls, are you upstairs?" They both visibly jumped.

Jenna went to the doorway. "Yes, we're here," she called back to the woman.

"Would you like some iced tea?"

Jenna looked at Josie and shrugged. "Sure. We'll be right down." She put her camera back in her pocket, though Josie was pretty sure she didn't turn it off, and they hurried downstairs.

In the kitchen, the blond woman was pouring three glasses of iced tea on the center island. "I'm sorry if I was rude earlier. I didn't catch your names."

"I'm Jenna LaPage, and this is my friend Josie."

The woman extended her slender hand and shook both Jenna's and Josie's hands. "I'm Barbara Shultz. My husband – well, soon-to-be ex-husband – Caleb just went to get more moving boxes."

"I'm so sorry…," Jenna said. "And I'm sorry if we're barging in on you here."

"You're not, honestly. I can imagine how fun it is to visit a home you spent time in as a child. But you are young, still. When did you live here?"

"We moved out soon after I turned three, but I remember a lot, now that I'm here. The kitchen, and that fireplace in the next room. When did you move in?"

"Only about two years ago, but this house has been in Caleb's family forever. When you lived here, his family was renting it out to cover the cost of Caleb's father's nursing home. Poor man had dementia and suffered for fifteen years before he finally passed. That's when we inherited the house and moved in."

Josie sipped her iced tea feeling monumentally uncomfortable. It felt almost as if the air was replaced by a thorn bush. She wanted to get away from it all.

"Do you mind if I ask why you're selling if it's been in the family for so long?" Jenna asked.

Barbara shrugged her bony shoulders, too prominent under her emerald-green t-shirt. "As I said, my husband and I are divorcing, and the cost of this place… it's just not possible for either of us to stay here, and no one else in the family wants it. I don't blame them. We've had nothing but misery since we moved in."

"Again, I'm really sorry," Jenna said. "My mom is going to be mad at me for bothering you, but we were reminiscing the other day and I just really wanted to see this place again. But we'll let you get back to packing."

Jenna rose and Josie jumped to her feet. "Thanks for the iced tea," said Josie.

They were at the door when Barbara said, "Can I ask you something before you go?"

Jenna turned back, and Josie froze, disappointed that they hadn't made their escape. "Sure."

"Did you… I mean, do you remember… or maybe your family…," Barbara rolled her iced tea glass between her hands nervously. "Did anything weird ever happen when your family lived here?"

Jenna straightened, and her blue eyes widened just a little. Josie heard thick raindrops start to fall with dull thwaps on the sides of the house. "What do you mean by 'weird'?" Jenna asked.

"Never mind. I'm sorry, I didn't mean to keep you," Barbara said.

"No, don't be sorry," protested Jenna. "Do you mean, like, doors and cabinets closing, or seeing an old lady or an old man that aren't there?"

Barbara looked at Jenna with eyes as wide around as dinner plates.

"That's the real reason why I'm here," said Jenna. "My parents said that when we lived here that I had an imaginary friend. I called him Mr. Shuts because he would shut things. And my mom saw an old woman in the bedroom at the top of the stairs. That's why I wanted to come back, to see if those things were… real."

Barbara's head fell into her hands, her elbows propped on the counter. "I thought I was going crazy. Caleb thinks I'm nuts. But our daughter Abigail – she's seven now – she would talk of 'Pop-Pop' sometimes, and repeat jokes he told her, but we wrote it off as childish imagination and jokes she probably heard at school. Then she started having nightmares. She'd wake up in the middle of the night screaming and crying, saying that a scary old woman was in her room. Caleb and I started fighting all the time, and I was so stressed out that I lost a ton of weight. I mean, look at me, I look like a walking, talking skeleton."

"Did you ever ask Abigail why she called him 'Pop-Pop'?" Jenna asked.

Barbara nodded. "She said that's what he told her to call him. Then we were going through some old photo albums one day and she pointed to a picture of Caleb's grandfather who owned this house before his son, Caleb's father, inherited it, and she said 'Mom, look! There's Pop-Pop!'"

"So, he is her great-grandfather," Jenna said. "And you said your last name is Shultz? I'm assuming that's your husband's family name, right?"

Barbara nodded, and Jenna looked at Josie. "Are you thinking what I'm thinking?" Jenna asked Josie.

"That 'Shultz' might sound a lot like 'Shuts' to a three-year-old?" Josie asked.

Jenna nodded, and as she did, Josie saw a familiar, tall figure in a long white robe appear behind Jenna. She saw Jenna visibly straighten and grow slightly taller as her Spirit Guide put her hands on Jenna's shoulders. Josie also saw a man step into view in the doorway at the other side of the kitchen.

Thunder rumbled overhead, and the rain came down harder. It pattered on the roof one story above their heads and tapped on the walls and windows. Again, Josie had horrible flashbacks to the night they were trapped in that house in Maine with a storm raging outside and a mad ghost terrorizing them inside.

Take a breath, Josie, said Hanover, *and ask yourself if this situation has any other similarities to that one. Ask yourself if it warrants your fear.*

Josie did so, taking one of her slow dancer's breaths in, filling her lungs, and releasing it slowly, letting herself get a feel for the situation. She saw Jenna's guide smile, and Josie said to Hanover, *Similar but not the same. Not enough similarities to be afraid. I have to be here for Jenna.*

Yes, Josie. Fear is a human failing. Don't let it get in your way, said Hanover.

Jenna then looked at Josie. "He's here, isn't he?" she smiled. "I can't see him, but I feel something… something familiar."

Josie nodded. "Yes, he's here."

Barbara looked from Josie to Jenna and back with a brow furrowed in confusion.

"I'm… I'm a medium," Josie said.

"Are you really?" Her face softened and her voice was intoned with gentle curiosity. "And you see this man?"

Josie was surprised at her tone, one of wonder instead of disbelief. "Yes."

"Is he in the doorway over there?" Jenna asked Josie.

"Yes," Josie said, surprised. "Can you see him?"

"No, not really. In my mind I see him, looking just like he did when I was a kid."

"What does he look like to you, Jenna?" Josie asked.

"He's kind of short, like, just a little taller than me. He's wearing a gray suit that looks really nice, like, really good quality, with a waist coat and one of those things… what do they call it? A pocket square, I think, and a striped tie. He has thick, white hair, and a big nose and big lips."

Barbara rose and went into the other room. The spirit of Mr. Shuts stepped aside as she passed through the doorway and then quickly returned with a framed photo. She held it out for Josie and Jenna to see.

Though Josie wasn't surprised that the man in the photo was the same as the transparent man standing before her, she was still amazed to see proof that he had once been a living person.

Jenna nodded furiously. "Yes! That's him!" She took the photo and looked at it longingly. "He was my friend, probably my only friend at the time. So, Josie, what do we do?"

Josie shrugged. "I think he wants you to talk to him, Jenna."

"Me? But I can't. I'm not like you."

Josie had never seen Jenna look or sound so intimidated. "It's okay. I'll help."

"Maybe it will help if we all go sit down in the living room?" Barbara asked.

Josie looked at Mr. Shuts who nodded. "Okay."

Barbara led the way and quickly shuffled boxes to clear space on the u-shaped sectional sofa. Jenna sat in the center while Josie and Barbara each took an end piece. Mr. Shuts was already in the room, standing near another fireplace that was large but not nearly as big as the other one. Jenna's spirit guide remained at her shoulders. Josie tried to meet her eyes, but the spirit's gaze remained fixed on Jenna. *If you need me to do anything, just let me know,* Josie said in her mind, directing the message to the guide. But if she heard Josie, she made no indication.

Hanover?

I'm here, Josie. Just relax. A flash of lightning illuminated the room, and a moment later, thunder rumbled.

"What do we do now?" Barbara asked.

"Jenna, what questions do you have for him?"

"Wait. Can I use my pendulum to do this?" Jenna asked Josie. Josie silently asked the question of the spirits in the room and got a "yes" from Hanover and a nod from Mr. Shuts. Josie then watched as Jenna's guide held two hands over Jenna's head and a dome of white energy descended over Jenna.

"Yes," Josie replied. Jenna pulled from a pocket her pale purple, cone-shaped crystal that hung at the end of a short chain. She apparently had come prepared with more equipment than Josie realized, and she wondered what else Jenna had hidden in the pockets of her shorts.

Josie waited as Jenna situated herself on the edge of the sofa with her right arm bent, elbow pressed to her side, and the chain of the pendulum between her first two fingers with the crystal hanging below. Her left hand was palm up about a half-inch below the crystal's point.

After a moment, Mr. Shuts sat next to Jenna. Josie had expected that she would see him moving the pendulum, so she was surprised when he placed one hand on her shoulder.

"Mr. Shuts, please communicate with us through this pendulum and swing it in the direction that will be a 'yes' answer," said Jenna.

Josie watched as the green-yellow light that he effused moved from his hand to Jenna's shoulder, down her arm, and into her hand. Slowly, the pendulum started to swing up and down along Jenna's left hand, wrist to finger-tip.

Jenna's eyes widened, and she smiled. "It's working!" she said, then recomposed herself. "Please move it in the direction you want to use for a 'no' answer," Jenna said when the pendulum had slowed. It began swinging in the opposite direction from thumb to pinky finger.

"Thank you, Mr. Shuts," she said. "I'm going to start asking you questions now. The first question is, do you remember me?"

Quickly the pendulum swung for "yes".

She was my little ladybug, said a soft, gravelly voice. It was the first time Josie had heard him speak.

Jenna smiled at the pendulum but stayed calm and waited for the swing to slow. "Are you a 'stuck' spirit?"

The pendulum answered "no" by swinging back and forth, pinky to thumb.

"Is your last name 'Shultz'?"

The pendulum swung for "yes" again.

"Are you Caleb Shultz's grandfather?"

Again, she received a yes.

"Were you with me to protect me from the female ghost that frightened my mom?"

This time the pendulum swung for "no." Jenna frowned. That was not the answer she expected.

"Is she a relative of yours?"

Again, he answered no.

"Is she here with us now?"

Another no.

Jenna looked at Josie who shrugged.

"May I ask some questions?" asked Barbara. Josie had almost forgotten she was there.

"Sure," said Jenna.

"How do I do it? I just talk aloud?"

Josie nodded. "He can hear you."

Barbara cleared her throat. "Hello, Mr. Shultz. I'm Barbara, your grandson's wife. We didn't get to meet while you were alive.... Um, are you who my daughter Abigail calls 'Pop-Pop'?"

The pendulum swung for yes.

"Is the scary woman she has nightmares about the same one this girl's mother saw here?"

The answer was yes.

"Is she trying to hurt Abigail?"

It swung for no.

"Why is she frightening her?"

The pendulum stilled and Mr. Shuts – or Shultz – looked at Josie.

"The pendulum can only answer yes or no questions," said Jenna.

"Does this woman have something to do with what's happening to Abigail?"

The pendulum answered "yes."

"Why is she doing this to my baby girl?" Barbara asked.

Jenna rolled her eyes and looked imploringly at Josie. "Maybe I should help," Josie said.

"But the pendulum finally worked for me! I've tried a hundred times before and it never moved, and here it was finally moving," Jenna protested, but she saw the despair on Barbara's face. "Oh, okay. You're right," she reluctantly conceded.

Mr. Shultz took his hand from Jenna's shoulder and turned to Josie. "Can you tell me who the old lady ghost is?" Josie asked him aloud.

Josie listened, and then her brows furrowed.

"What is he saying?" Barbara asked, concerned at the silence and the look on Josie's face.

Josie held up a hand in a motion asking for silence. Barbara shifted impatiently in her seat.

Finally, Josie spoke. "I'm sorry, I'm just trying to sort this out."

"What do you mean? Can't you just tell us what he said?" asked Barbara.

"It's not that easy," she shook her head. "He's telling me things that I've never experienced before, so I'm just trying to make sense of it."

Hanover started to speak to Josie, so she held up her hand again before either Barbara or Jenna spoke again. She listened, and then said, "Okay, so again, this is new for me, so bear with me. Apparently, there are spirits that… that never lived a human life, unlike Mr. Shultz. And these spirits come here with specific tasks. Apparently, this woman appears when there's some sort of illness, although she is not the cause of the illness."

Josie let that bomb drop, and in perfect synchronicity, thunder rumbled overhead again. She didn't know how to say it any gentler.

"But my mom saw her!" Jenna said. "She wasn't sick!"

"Are you sure?" Josie asked.

"Well, no. I was three. But she didn't say anything about being sick."

Josie looked at Barbara whose tanned face had gone pale, and her hand covered her mouth. "Is Abigail sick?" Josie asked her.

Barbara nodded. "They can't figure out what it is," she said, tears falling rapidly from her eyes. "It's one of the things Caleb and I fight about. Is she… does this mean she's going to…?"

She couldn't finish the sentence. Josie looked at Mr. Shultz and listened. "No," Josie said. "She isn't going to die. She doesn't have cancer."

Barbara released a sob and covered her face with her hands. "That was my biggest fear," she said, lifting her face, smiling.

"I know," said Josie. "Or rather, *he* knows."

"Does he know what is making her sick?" Barbara asked. "We've had all kinds of tests run on her and we had this place tested for mold and lead, we had the water tested, we've done everything we could."

"If he knows, he isn't – or maybe can't – say, but… hold on," Josie said, holding up her hand again as she listened. "Okay, he says that there is one simple test that's been missed. A blood test. He says to take her back to the pediatrician—"

"But the specialists are the ones—"

"Barbara, you can take her to whoever you want, I'm just telling you what he is saying, and he is saying that her pediatrician will be the one likely to see which test was missed in order to figure it all out. And he is also saying that she will get better very quickly once they get the test results."

Barbara smiled again and breathed a huge sigh of relief though tears were still running down her cheeks. "And what about my marriage? My divorce?"

Josie waited for the answer, frowning again at the new, confusing information. "This sounds kind of hard to understand, hard to believe maybe, but he's saying that there are places that are… energetically programmed to do certain things for the living people who spend time in those places. Sometimes these seem like bad things when you are experiencing them, but he says that they always lead to better things."

Barbara frowned. "What does that mean?"

Josie shrugged. "He just said that you need to trust your gut that you're doing the right thing."

Barbara nodded but continued to frown. Then she sighed and looked at Josie. "This is all rather overwhelming. I appreciate what you've both done, but think I'd like you to leave now."

Josie looked at Jenna, and Jenna stood, putting her pendulum that had been balled in her fist back into her pocket. "Yes, of course. Thanks again for letting us come into your home. Good luck with everything," Jenna said, and they hurried from the house.

Outside, the rain poured down. They ran across the street to the car. Inside, Jenna put the keys in the ignition but didn't start the engine.

"Are you okay?" Josie asked.

Jenna shook her head, then leaned her forehead against the steering wheel. "Like she said, overwhelmed."

"Yeah, that was… a lot."

Jenna turned towards Josie, still leaning on the steering wheel. "Did he say anything else… for me?"

Josie smiled and nodded. "He called you his little ladybug and said that you were a bright light in a house that had known too much darkness. He said he was glad you didn't live there very long."

"Ladybug? Yeah, I kinda remember that." Jenna smiled, then let out a big, long sigh. "Okay, let's go home. Believe it or not, I think I've had enough of this for today."

Josie chuckled. "I never thought I'd hear you say that."

They rode home in complete silence, each lost in their own thoughts as they each processed what had just happened.

After dropping Josie off, Jenna went home and went through her equipment. When she reviewed her camera, she smiled as she zoomed in on one of the shots of the dresser in what had been her room. In the reflection of the mirror, she could clearly see Mr. Shuts' ghostly face smiling at her.

She rose from her desk and went downstairs to the kitchen where she found her mother unloading the clean dishes from the dishwasher.

"Let me help you," Jenna said, reaching in to grab a glass in each hand.

"Thanks, honey," said Rachel, stacking the clean plates in the cupboard.

A minute or two went by with just the clatter of dishes between them, and then Jenna said, "Mom, can I ask you a question?"

"Of course," replied Rachel, leaning one hip against the counter. "Shoot."

"I need you to promise me you'll be totally honest with me."

Rachel's face became serious. "Okay."

"When we lived in that house in North Hampton, were you sick?"

Rachel sighed and closed her eyes for a moment. Then she looked at Jenna. "This isn't going to be easy to hear," Rachel said.

2

Jenna's heart skipped a beat. "I can handle it, Mom. I want the truth."

"Okay. Well, when we lived there, I was… pregnant. We found out just before your third birthday. But pretty soon I started to feel sick, different from when I was pregnant with you and your brother. I'm… I'm not going to go into detail, but I ended up having a miscarriage and I had to have surgery on my fallopian tube. It had been an ectopic pregnancy which means—"

"I know what that means, Mom," Jenna said.

"Well, okay then. So, yes, I guess you could say I was sick. During the surgery, they found a blood clot in my uterus which they were able to remove. It left me unable to have any more children, but it most likely saved my life."

Jenna put down the cereal bowls she had pulled from the dishwasher and put her arms around her mother. "But we have a really good family just as we are, right?"

"Yes, we do, Jenna. I love our family. And I believe everything happens for a reason. That soul was only meant to be with us for a short time for whatever reason, and that's okay."

"Maybe it was only meant to come save your life. Its job was done," said Jenna.

"Yes," said Rachel, kissing Jenna on the cheek. "I think you're right, my wise daughter."

Later, when Jenna was back in her room, she pulled out her pendulum and did everything she did earlier, but this time – like all the other times before – it remained motionless.

* * * * *

Josie could hear her phone buzzing under the sound of the dryer as she dried her hair. She had been going back and forth in text messages with Jenna all morning about the pendulum. When Josie told her how Mr. Shuts had made the pendulum move the day before, that seemed to ease Jenna's mind.

SO BASICALLY, IT ISN'T WORKING IN MY HOUSE BECAUSE THERE'S NO GHOST THERE TO MOVE IT? Jenna asked.

I GUESS. HARD TO SAY SINCE I WASN'T AT YOUR HOUSE WHEN YOU TRIED AGAIN, BUT IT MAKES SENSE TO ME, Josie replied.

WANT TO COME OVER TONIGHT?

CAN'T. MOM AND I ARE MEETING UP WITH ROMY AND HER MOM FOR DINNER.

OK. IF YOU DON'T GET HOME TOO LATE, LET ME KNOW. WE CAN GO GET ICE CREAM. SIMON AND DAVE ARE BOTH WORKING TILL CLOSE.

OK, I'LL LET YOU KNOW, Josie said.

Josie finished her hair and then checked the newest message from Jenna. REMEMBER YOU PROMISED TO HELP ME CONNECT WITH MY SPIRIT GUIDES? ARE YOU STILL WILLING TO DO THAT?

HAVE YOU BEEN DOING A CEREMONY EACH NIGHT FOR THEM? Josie asked.

YES. EVERY NIGHT!

OKAY. TOMORROW NIGHT.

YAY!

Josie put the finishing touches on her makeup just in time to hear her mother calling to her that it was time to go. Josie grabbed a light sweater and her phone and went downstairs.

"Ready?" asked Angela.

"Yup."

In the car as they pulled out of the driveway, Angela said, "I'm really glad we're doing this. It's been so helpful for me to have another parent who's going through this."

"I'm glad, Mom," said Josie. Angela had seemed a lot happier, and her parents were fighting less – as far as she knew – since they went to Zara's group.

"And you like Romy, right? She seems like a nice girl."

"Yeah, Romy's cool. It's cool to have someone to talk to about this stuff who gets it," said Josie. "Jenna's an amazing friend and everything, but she doesn't always get it."

"Is it… is it scary sometimes?"

Josie nodded. "It's scary a lot of the times, but I think I'm getting used to that part of it. It's all just so… weird."

"And things are going better with Jenna? Friendship is healed?"

Josie nodded again. "Yeah, it's all good."

"Good. I was glad to see you show up at the barbecue with her," said Angela. "And what about Simon? What's going on with that?"

Josie took a breath in and held it, hesitating.

"Transparency, Josie," said Angela in a softly warning voice.

"I know, Mom. I'm not trying to keep anything from you. I'm just not sure how to answer. I mean, I told him on Sunday that we need to be friends, because the friendship I have with all three of them, Dave included, is more important to me at this point. All that other stuff, it's still there, but it needs to take a back seat. For now, anyway."

"And you're sure about that?"

"Yes, I'm sure. I mean… my feelings for him… yes, they seem like they're more than friendship, but if trying to be more than friends is going to take him and possibly Jenna out of my life, then it's not worth it."

"And what if he were to want to be more than friends?" Angela asked.

Josie pulled her lip gloss from her purse and reapplied it in the visor mirror, a nervous habit. "I… I can't know until… unless it actually came to that. But I don't think it ever will. He's leaving for college in August. His life is changing in a major way. I don't think I'd fit into that very well."

"You know, you have a lot more maturity with this kind of thing than I did at your age. You're an amazing young woman, you know that?"

"Thanks, Mom. I probably owe a lot of it to Jenna. She's got life figured out. I've learned a lot from her."

"Well, I'm glad you have such a good friend in your life. It's comforting for me to know that when you aren't getting what you need from your dad and me that you have her, and Dave and Simon, to turn to. That's something that I worry about. Especially now with your dad being… well, anyway. I feel like with Zara's group and everything else, things are going to get better for us."

"I feel it, too," said Josie, hoping her voice didn't betray her uncertainty.

When Josie and Angela arrived, Romy and her mom, Patricia, were waiting outside the restaurant, sitting in the evening sun on a bench. The moms embraced each other as did Romy and Josie before going inside. They were seated quickly by a good-looking young man who couldn't hide his smile when he looked at Josie and Romy, as though they were the first pretty girls to come into the restaurant in a long time.

"My name is Michael, and I'll be your server tonight," he said, handing them each a menu. "Can I get you lovely ladies drinks to start?"

The moms each ordered a glass of wine and Romy and Josie each ordered iced tea, trying their best to suppress their giggles.

Michael smiled at Josie and Romy. "I'll be right back with those and to take your order."

"At least we know we'll get attentive service," Angela joked to Patricia who laughed and nodded.

"He's kinda cute," Romy said as Michael walked away.

Josie evaluated Michael from a distance. "Not my type," Josie shrugged.

"Who is your type?" Romy asked. "Do you have a boyfriend?"

"No, not right now. It's all too… it's just too complicated."

"How do you mean?"

"You know, this stuff is still pretty new for me, and it's hard to talk about. How do you just tell someone who you just met that you talk to ghosts?" Josie said.

Romy nodded. "I get that. It's different for me with my prophetic dreams. I tell my friends about it, and they think it's cool, not weird, but I think it's because they don't think it's anything other than a dream, which is fine, I guess. I probably wouldn't believe it either if it wasn't happening to me."

"It's not just the dreams for you though," said Josie.

Michael returned then with their drinks. "Okay, what can I get you beautiful ladies to eat?" he said to Angela and Patricia.

When everyone had ordered Romy said, "What do you mean that it's not just dreams for me?"

"Well, what you did at Zara's group, you weren't dreaming. When I told my friend Jenna all about the group, she said that what you did is called 'psychometry', which basically means that you can hold an object and get a reading off it, like you're reading the energy of the object, or the energy a person has left behind on it."

"Oh, yeah. Zara mentioned something about that, but I think I was just so excited about the whole evening that I didn't really hear her. Oh, that's so cool! It's called 'psychometry'? Hmm, I'll have to ask Zara more about that."

"If you want….," Josie said hesitantly, feeling slightly like she was in Jenna's shoes for the moment. "We can try an experiment. I have something you can hold and see if you get anything from it. If you want?"

Romy nodded excitedly, the bangs of her short pixie-cut hair falling into her eyes. Josie glanced at their moms who were deep in conversation, then pulled out from under the neckline of her tunic-dress Aunt Pauline's hourglass pendant that she had worn every day since the funeral. She took it off and gently laid it in Romy's outstretched hand, her heart pounding nervously.

Romy covered her palm with her other hand, closed her eyes, and bowed her head. Josie felt her insides quiver in anticipation. She'd never been on the other side of it like this before.

"Wow," Romy said, breathless. "There is so much love coming from this necklace. I feel like it was given to someone with tremendous love, and it was very beloved by that person. That person… she passed it on to you. Is that correct?"

Josie nodded, swallowing back tears. She hadn't seen Aunt Pauline since the day she died, and she was missing her terribly.

"It was given to her in a black, velvet-lined box, and when she received it, she felt… well, it was the equivalent – or maybe better – than winning an Olympic gold medal. It was a special occasion, too. Her… tenth birthday, I think. A big deal because it's the start of double-digits, I remember. And she cherished it right up until…."

Romy opened her eyes and looked at Josie. "She died just recently, yes? And gave this to you in the velvet box not long before?"

Josie nodded.

"You wear it hoping she'll come to you?"

"Yes," Josie said, her throat thick with suppressed tears.

"I think she will. You just need to give her and yourself a little more time," Romy said, handing Josie back the necklace. Josie put it back on, allowing it to rest on the outside of her dress now.

"Thanks for that," Josie said solemnly.

"That was really cool! I had no idea I could do stuff like that!"

"You're really good at it," said Josie. "Everything you said was spot-on."

"Wow," Romy said, smiling proudly. Michael placed their salads in front of them then. "Thanks, Michael," Romy said, giving him a sly look.

When he was out of earshot, Josie said, "So you never told me if you have a boyfriend, or if you're just planning on taking Michael home with you?"

Romy laughed. "Actually," she said, lowering her voice and leaning in, "I kinda do have a boyfriend, but it, like, *just* happened two days ago."

"Okay, so, who is he?" Josie asked, matching her volume to Romy's.

"His name is Landon, and we've been friends for, like, two years. But we both liked each other the whole time. Finally, he said something and asked me out. We're going out with a bunch of our friends tomorrow, but that will be the first time going out as a couple." Romy's grin was ear to ear.

"I'm happy for you," Josie said. "But don't you worry about ruining your friendship? With him or with the other people in your group?"

"No," was her light response.

"Really? Why?"

Romy shrugged. "How else are you going to meet someone and know that you like them if you're not friends? Plus, it just seems silly to worry over something that hasn't happened yet."

"Can't argue with that," Josie smiled. "Keep me posted with how things go with him, okay?"

"Sure! Maybe you and I can go shopping next week or something?"

"Actually, I'll be away. My family and my friend Jenna's family are going on vacation to a lake in upstate New York for the week."

"Oh, that will be fun!"

"Yeah," Josie agreed, though inside she was still unsure. "But let's plan a shopping trip for when I get home."

"Okay," said Romy.

Michael delivered their meals with special attention to Romy who smiled and giggled at him. As they ate, Romy talked about art club, yearbook club, and her mini-Dachshund named Pete.

Josie told Romy about theater and her dance classes, and then it was time to go.

They all hugged again as they parted, and as Angela drove them home, she chatted but Josie wasn't really listening. She thought about what Romy said, about not worrying about something that hasn't happened yet. She wished she could be so… relaxed and optimistic and confident about such things. Josie just didn't have it in her.

As Josie looked back on the prior few days, she realized she should feel happier than she did. Things were good again with Jenna, Dave, and Simon, she had interesting new friends in Romy, Zara, Miranda, and Jacob, and her mom seemed happier. It was summer, and she would be going on vacation with her best friends. *So why is there still this emptiness inside me?*

* * * * *

The following day, Josie assisted in two ballet camp classes, one for five-year-old's and one for three-year-old's, and then had two classes of her own. Afterwards she vacuumed the waiting area, cleaned the bathroom, wiped down the mirrors in the small studio, and took out the trash from the office.

"This place is going to be a mess by the time you get back from vacation," Miss Jillian said as Josie dusted the team trophy shelf.

"Are you sure it's okay if I go?"

"Of course! You've been working so hard. You deserve a vacation."

"Thanks," Josie said.

"No. Thank *you*. Josie, you're such a big help around here."

Josie smiled. "Well, it's my home away from home," she said. Her phone buzzed in her pocket, and she looked at it to see a text from Jenna indicating that she was waiting outside for her. "Do you need me to do anything else before I go?"

"No, really, Josie. You're good. Thanks again and I'll see you when you're back from vacation."

"Bye, Miss Jillian," Josie said as she threw her dance bag over her shoulder and headed out the door.

Jenna was all smiles when Josie got in the car. "Thank you so much for doing this. You don't know how excited I am," said Jenna.

Josie laughed. "Actually, I think I have a pretty good idea."

"So, what's the plan?" Jenna asked.

Her eagerness irked Josie, but she took a breath in an attempt to push it aside. "I don't want to say too much now. I want to go into it with you having no preconceived ideas about what's going to happen. But I have done some research and even texted with Zara to get some help from her."

Jenna squealed as she drove. "This is going to be so amazing!"

"Jenna, please, calm down. There's no guarantee that this is going to work."

"I know, but I have a good feeling about it."

Josie sighed. "I just don't want you to be disappointed if it doesn't work."

"I won't be. Oh, I need to warn you," Jenna said, her face becoming serious.

"About what?" Josie's heart had jumped into double-time.

"Your parents were at my house when I left, and I think they're staying for dinner."

Josie relaxed. "Oh. Well, I guess that's okay. I mean, we'll all be together for the next week, right? Why not start a day early."

Jenna nodded. "Our moms were comparing packing lists and making new lists. They went to the grocery store and came back with a ton of stuff."

"Of course they did," Josie scoffed.

"How are things with your dad?"

Josie shrugged and tugged at her tank top. "Same. We've hardly spoken two words to each other since the thing with Zara."

"I would *love* to meet her sometime," said Jenna.

"I know you would," Josie said, chuckling and shaking her head. "I'm just afraid of what you would say to her."

"What? Me?" Jenna feigned shock.

"I don't want you turning her into a research project."

"What if she was willing?"

"That would be fine, but can you let me spend some time with her before you ask?"

"Yeah, I guess I can do that," Jenna laughed, pulling to a stop in the driveway.

"What are Simon and Dave up to tonight?" Josie asked.

"Simon's working, and Dave's dropping his mom off at the airport."

"Boston or Manchester?"

"Boston," sighed Jenna.

"Is he coming here after?"

Jenna nodded. "She'll be away for three weeks and though his mom said he'd be okay on his own, my mom refused to let him stay home by himself even for one night."

"I'm sure he doesn't mind this arrangement," Josie teased.

Jenna grinned slyly in response.

Inside, Greg was bringing a platter of burgers into the dining room. "Hi, girls! Just in time," he said.

Jenna looked at Josie with pleading eyes, but Josie said, "Can we eat, please? I've only eaten a protein bar since breakfast."

"Oh, okay," Jenna conceded with a roll of her eyes.

Josie turned and went into the kitchen where her mom was putting the finishing touches on a salad. "Hi, Josie! How was dance camp?"

"Good," said Josie, allowing her mother a quick hug. "The kids are so cute. There's this one little girl in my five-year-old group who is actually really good. She's very serious about it all and she asks a lot of questions about technique. It will be interesting to see if she sticks with it and continues to be as good as she is."

"You're all packed up at home, right?" Angela asked her.

Josie nodded. "I have some things in my bag for tonight but that's all coming with me anyway."

"Good," smiled Angela, handing Josie the salad bowl to bring to the dining room.

"We're all heading out around ten tomorrow morning, right?" Greg asked as they all sat at the table.

"Ten sharp," replied Charles. "It's about a four-hour drive, and factoring in pit stops and a lunch break, we should be there just in time for the 3 PM check-in."

Josie piled her plate with a cheeseburger and salad and ate slowly, purposefully trying to delay the inevitable. She had made the promise to Jenna but now she was afraid she would only let her friend down.

"You okay, Josie?" Charles asked.

Josie visibly jumped, not expecting the question from her father. She looked at him. "Huh?"

He gestured to her plate. "You're just picking at your food. Are you feeling okay?"

Like you actually care? she thought. *Probably just trying to look like a concerned father in front of his friends.*

"I'm fine. Just tired from the day, I guess," she said, taking a big bite of her burger.

Her dad just smiled at her, his eyes crinkling at the corners. *When did that start?* She wondered, taking a closer look at him as he turned back to his conversation with Greg. He looked older, more worn than he had before. *Because of me.*

* * * * *

"Okay, what do we do first?" Jenna asked as soon as she closed her bedroom door.

"Jenna, *please* relax. You're making me nervous," said Josie irritably.

"You don't have to be nervous," she replied.

"But I am. Whatever you say, I know you have high expectations. I just need you to take your excitement down a few notches."

Jenna sighed. "Okay. I'm sorry. If nothing happens, I will be disappointed, but I won't blame you. And I'll keep on trying. I'm nothing if I'm not determined."

Josie wasn't quite convinced, but she put her bag down and got out a notebook and her spirit guide book. "Alright, let's get started," said Josie. *I just want to get this over with.* "First, I want you to show me your ceremony."

"Like, actually do it or just show you what I do for it?" Jenna asked.

"I want you to do your ceremony."

"I've been doing it every night at ten o'clock. Is it okay that it's earlier?"

Josie nodded. *Hanover, I think I'm gonna need your help with this,* Josie pleaded.

He tingled into position on her shoulders draped around her neck. *You're doing just fine, Josie. You really don't need me for this,* he replied.

Please stay?

He sighed. She felt a slight breeze under her left ear. *Okay.*

"Do you mind if I record everything?" Jenna asked.

Josie suppressed an eyeroll. "No, I don't mind," she replied.

Jenna turned on her digital recorder, dimmed the lights, then went to her dresser and stood before it, the top of it coming to just above her waist. She opened one of the small top drawers and pulled out a baggie and poured something into her hand that Josie couldn't see. Josie stood and moved closer. On top of the dresser Jenna had laid a scarf that looked like silk in a deep shade of purple with a wispy pattern of lilac and white. On top of that were two tall pillar candles, one on each end, one white and one purple. In between the candles was a small vase of wildflowers. In front of the wildflowers was a small plate with an incense cone in the center, and in front of that was a bowl about the same size as the plate. Jenna took a torch lighter from the side of the dresser and clicked the button to ignite a flame. She lit the incense first and the scent of sandalwood filled the air around them as a swirl of smoke twisted and twirled toward the ceiling. She then moved the lighter flame to the white candle.

"I light these candles in honor of the Lady of the moon, of the restless sea, and fertile earth, for the Lord of the sun and of all the wild creatures, for my spirit guides, and all those who have my best interests at heart." She lit the purple candle and put the lighter down. "I ask you to accept this offering of seeds as an expression of my gratitude for all you do for me, for watching over me and guiding me on my path." Jenna poured the seeds from her hand into the bowl. "Please continue to watch over me and grant me the wisdom and ability to see your presence in all nature around me."

Jenna stood for another minute with her hands on the dresser, her head slightly bowed. Her hair gleamed orange in the candlelight. Josie suppressed a gasp when the woman in white appeared behind Jenna. She was so different from Josie's own guides, impossibly tall and slender with long auburn hair. She wore a robe of an iridescent white that reminded Josie of a pearl. Her whole being emitted a soft, purplish glow.

Should I tell Jenna what I see? Josie asked.

She directed her thoughts at Hanover, but the response came from a distant female voice. *If you tell what you see, she will not learn to rely on herself.*

Fair enough, Josie replied, surprised.

Finally, Jenna turned to Josie. "That's it. What do you think?"

"That was really good," said Josie, genuinely impressed. "How'd you come up with that?"

"Mostly from a book on Paganism, with my own twists, of course," she smiled.

"How'd you pick the scarf and the candles? Why those colors?"

Jenna shrugged. "I was just drawn to the combination."

"Cool," Josie nodded. "Okay, now, let's leave the candles burning if you don't mind. I want you to sit or lie down so you're comfortable but not so comfortable that you'll fall asleep."

Jenna sat on her bed with pillows propped behind her back, her legs crossed in front of her. Josie sat in the desk chair next to the bed.

"Okay, you're comfortable?" Josie asked.

"Yeah." Jenna nodded.

Josie opened her notebook and laid it on her knees. She started an app on her phone that emitted soft music with the sounds of a bubbling brook and birds chirping in the background. "Alright, the music is to help you relax and block out any other sounds from the house. I want you to close your eyes, take a couple deep breaths, long and slow." She waited as Jenna did what she said. "Okay, now I want you to imagine yourself floating in a wide river. The water is flowing gently, warm and soothing, and you're effortlessly floating. There are soft, green roots growing up from the riverbed that attach to you, holding you in place. The water of the river runs over you to cleanse from you any frustration, any anger, anything negative that you might be holding onto. Let it all be washed from you by the river or sucked from you by the roots. You are in a relaxed state, and you are in a safe place. Your breathing is slow and steady. Are you able to see and feel this, Jenna?"

"Yeah, I… I do. I'm there," Jenna replied, her tone drowsy and relaxed.

"Good. I want you to hang onto the imagery. Ask for your spirit guides to come to you, and just wait and see what happens."

Several minutes passed in silence. Josie felt anxiousness start to rise in her.

Be patient, Josie, she heard Hanover say softly.

Josie stifled a sigh. Somewhere below her she could hear the distant sounds of their parents talking. It sounded like her mom and dad were leaving. Josie heard a car door shut, then another, and the sounds of a car engine starting up. Josie looked to the female spirit who was standing at Jenna's shoulder on the opposite side of the bed from Josie. She met Josie's eyes and heard her say, *We are doing all we can. Be patient.*

Josie felt instantly guilty for being annoyed and anxious. She didn't know what was wrong with her. Jenna was always so tolerant and helpful with her. Now the tables were turned, and she was not doing the same for her friend.

Please give her something good, Josie pleaded to her. *She wants this so badly.*

Jenna's guide did not reply.

A few more minutes of silence passed, and then Jenna spoke softly. "Not much is happening, except the sky changed. I couldn't see the sun, but the sky darkened, and it now looks like nighttime. There are thousands and thousands of stars overhead. It's beautiful. And oddly, it's not really dark. Like, not scary dark. It's just… comforting dark."

"Did you ask for the sky to change?"

"No, not at all," said Jenna.

"That's good. Just keep focusing on your breathing."

"Okay," said Jenna languidly.

Josie settled into the silence again and decided to close her eyes also. Simon's face popped into her mind's vision, startling her, and causing her to jump slightly and open her eyes. She looked to Jenna who was motionless as was the female spirit at her side.

Josie was about to tell Jenna to stop when Jenna said, "I see something I think."

"What do you see?"

"A light, I think. Like a column of light, glowing white and purple. There's an amazing… amazing feeling of harmony and hopefulness radiating from it."

Josie looked to the female spirit in the room, and Josie would have sworn she shimmered like a wave.

"It just feels so good, this light and… well, I don't know…."

"Just say whatever it is you feel, Jenna. You can analyze it later," Josie told her.

After a pause, Jenna said, "I don't know why, but I get the feeling that this light is a being. Like it has a consciousness. That seems so weird, but it kind of feels female, too."

Josie waited and anticipated the woman in white to show herself more to Jenna, but Jenna remained silent. Then, "I see something else. Something in the sky, flying. I see large wings, a long body and tail…."

Jenna was frowning. "I think… I think it's… a dragon!" And a second later, Jenna was jumping up from the bed, a grin from ear to ear. The woman in white was gone. "It flew right at me! It had silvery skin and red eyes! Plucked me right from the water with one hand! Scared the crap out of me, it felt so real!" Jenna breathed like she had just run a race. She went to Josie and threw her arms around her.

"That was amazing! That was *so* amazing! Do you think that light was a guide?" Jenna turned in circles, twirling like a little girl in a new party dress.

"Do *you* think the light was a guide?" Josie asked, turning the question around on Jenna. In that moment, she realized the cryptic nature of guides. Josie knew the answer, but she needed Jenna to know the answer.

"You know, I do. It felt… familiar. Is that weird?" Jenna asked.

"Jenna, all of this is weird. But if you mean, do I think it possible? Yes. And you know, I think the dragon might be a guide, too," said Josie, turning the pages in her spirit guide book.

"Really? A dragon?"

"Yeah. I think that might be your animal guide, like Hanover is for me."

"But dragons aren't real."

"Look at this," said Josie. She quickly flipped through the pages of her book and handed it to Jenna on the page for dragon.

Jenna read through the page before her, her eyes widening as she read. She looked at Josie. "This is weird. But like, crazy awesome weird. It sounds just like me!"

"And the thing about practicing Wicca or Pagan magic? You just said you got your ceremony from a book on Paganism, right? I think there might be something more to that. And how it says that people with dragon as their power animal tend to have an endless contagious enthusiasm for life? I mean, that's you in a nutshell."

"Okay… I need to show you something." Jenna turned the lights on bright and went to the shelf that housed her many soccer and track trophies and medals. From between two of the trophies she picked up something small and carried it to Josie and held it out. In her palm was a pewter dragon with its large wings lifted and folded behind its back. It was perched on top of a prismed sphere that was white in the center and purple on the outside. The head was turned and looked at her from red crystal eyes. "This was a gift. I got it at one of those Yankee swap parties for someone in my dad's office when I was… I don't know, maybe eight or nine. I wasn't, like, into dragons, but for whatever reason I *loved* this figurine. I was obsessed with it for the longest time."

"I think you now know why," Josie smiled. She heaved a sigh, relieved at what happened. No, she was amazed at what happened. *I didn't think anything like this would ever happen for Jenna,* she said in her mind.

You need to have more faith in your friend, said Hanover with a ripple of energy tingling around her neck. Jenna's woman in white was no longer in the room – or at least, not visible to Josie.

I know, and I'm sorry.

It isn't me you should apologize to.

Again, Josie sighed. "I feel bad, Jenna, because I didn't think that would work."

"Why do you feel bad? It did work!"

"I know, but I didn't think it would happen."

"That's okay. It turned out amazing, didn't it?"

"Yeah. It did." Josie nodded, realizing she was living up to the dragon description of endless, contagious enthusiasm.

A door thudded in the house below them. "Oh, I bet that was Dave. I have to go tell him what just happened!"

She ran from the room, Josie following behind slowly. Jenna accosted Dave in the living room and spilled it all to him at a thousand miles an hour while Josie turned into the kitchen and poured herself a glass of water. She was happy for Jenna, really happy that she'd been able to help her have an amazing experience, and she was starting to feel excited for their vacation, if for no other reason than to get away and lie on a beach in the sun. But something was still bothering her that she couldn't identify, something that was keeping her from fully enjoying all that was going on around her.

She drained her water glass, hoping that was enough to fill the emptiness inside her.

3

Jenna spent some time with Dave while Josie thumbed through her book and then through the latest issue of Glamour magazine. After saying good night to Dave, Jenna dragged Josie back to her room where she and Josie rehashed her experience, listened to the audio recording, and took notes until they were both exhausted. Jenna then fell quickly into sleep while Josie tossed and turned. It was well past midnight when Josie gave up on sleep. She went to the bathroom where she brushed her hair and washed her face and then went to the kitchen. The LaPage house was quiet. By the front door Josie could see a pile of bags and suitcases ready and waiting for the morning departure. In the kitchen was an empty cooler ready to be filled with the items on the list on the counter.

Josie poured herself a glass of milk and headed back to Jenna's room but stopped short when she found her way blocked by Mother Elk Spirit, a soft peach glow illuminating her. *I'll be calling for you soon. I expect you to be ready.*

"Josie?" The voice that came from behind her startled her. She jumped and spun around to see Simon.

"Simon, you scared me!" Josie said. She glanced behind her, but Mother Elk Spirit was gone.

"Sorry. Are you okay? You look…."

"Yeah, I'm fine," she said, frowning. "You're home late."

"I had to close, and then I hung around for a bit talking to my boss. But I should get to bed," he said with a forced yawn.

"Yeah, me too," she replied.

Simon gestured that she should go first, and she reluctantly headed back into the hallway. The air felt suddenly electrically charged but whether it was from her acute awareness of Simon behind her or a lingering energy from Mother Elk Spirit, Josie didn't know.

"Good night, Simon," Josie said quietly when she reached Jenna's bedroom.

"Good night, Josie," he replied.

Back in Jenna's room she drank the milk and laid down. She thought about Mother Elk Spirit. Every slight sound of movement caused her eyes to pop open, hoping to see Mother Elk Spirit in the room, but she never was. Nearby, Jenna slept soundly. Josie didn't know when she finally slipped into sleep, but she would never admit to herself that it happened while a familiar fantasy involving Simon and a campfire filled her mind.

* * * * *

Down the hall, Simon lay in bed while Dave snored softly nearby. He felt a slight remorse at being so abrupt with Josie, but he hadn't expected to run into her like that, wearing just a small tank top and shorts, her hair free, her face fresh, smelling of lavender and toothpaste.

He shoved his pillow over his face to stifle a groan and rolled over, resigning himself to a restless night.

* * * * *

"It was just so unexpected. I turned to come back here and there she was," Josie told Jenna as she stuffed her books and pajamas in her bag. "Then she was gone."

"And she said the same thing as last time?" Jenna asked as she packed her own bag.

"Exactly the same as when I saw her at the Four Gables Inn."

"I looked up the history of the inn. It was built in 1870 by a man named Arthur McAllister. He had a wife named Sarina who, according to gossip of the time, may have dabbled in things like

Tarot cards and table tipping. They had only one child who died before it was two. Maybe Sarina is who you saw in the hallway."

"Maybe," Josie said.

"I'd love to do an investigation there. I'll have to call them when we get home. I hope this place we're going to will have Wi-Fi so I can do some online research."

Josie smiled at her friend. "Jenna, I want you to enjoy vacation, not do research the whole time."

"You know very well that I enjoy researching this stuff, and I won't do it the *whole* time," Jenna replied with a smile. "I do have a boyfriend who needs some attention."

Josie rolled her eyes at Jenna and then looked out the window to see a large van pull into the driveway. "My parents are here," she said. "I guess we should get downstairs."

Josie's dad had borrowed a twelve-person passenger van from a friend at work, so they didn't have to take two cars. Jenna and Josie carried their bags outside and added them to the pile already waiting.

"Okay, one more bathroom stop before we get in the car," said Josie, hurrying back into the house.

* * * * *

Dave walked up behind Simon. "Dude, are you okay?"

"Fine," Simon replied, staring out the window. Josie had gone back outside and was helping her dad load bags in the back of the van. He couldn't tear his eyes away from her.

"You're lying," said Dave, his eyes following Simon's. "I've known you most of my life, and I know something's up with you."

Simon shook his head and turned away from the window. "I don't know what's wrong with me. I don't know why I'm… I'm seeing her differently. It's like I put glasses on and am seeing…."

"Clearly?" Dave finished for him.

Simon shook his head again and turned back to look out the window. "I don't think I can call this 'seeing clearly.' Things are more muddied than ever."

Dave chuckled.

"What are you laughing at?"

He shrugged. "I just think it's funny that for such a smart guy, you are too stupid to figure out what everybody else knows."

Simon scowled at him. "If you're so smart, why don't you enlighten me?"

"And rob you of the opportunity to figure it out on your own? I'd never do that," Dave grinned at him.

"Simon and Dave!" Rachel yelled from the front door. "We're ready to go. Lock up on your way out, please!"

"You know you can be a real ass sometimes," Simon said.

"Yeah, I know," Dave said, still smiling as he followed Simon out of the house.

* * * * *

They stopped somewhere in Vermont for lunch before piling back into the van for the rest of the drive. Josie had finally managed to get some sleep after the restless night she'd had, but after eating and stretching her legs she felt revived. As Charles drove along hilly roads lined with farmland, Jenna and Dave played a card game. Josie risked a glance back at Simon to find him with headphones on, his head leaned back, and eyes closed. He wasn't asleep, though she didn't know why or how she knew that. She looked at the apps on her phone and decided against playing a game, and instead just looked out the window. Eventually, Vermont turned into New York, though little changed in the landscape. Mountains in the distance were as green in one state as they had been in the other. Only the license plates were different in the driveways they passed.

Josie played two rounds of Uno with Jenna and Dave, then turned back to the landscape. She was starting to get drowsy again. In the distance she heard her dad say something about the Catskill Mountains. Jenna announced that she needed a pit-stop, but Greg stated that they were almost there, so she'd have to wait.

The car slowed as they passed through a busy downtown area lined on both sides with restaurants and shops. Smack dab in the center of it all Josie saw a sign for "Count Dracula's Wax Museum" and distant memories surfaced. A lake sparkled in the sun beyond the buildings, but they passed through town without stopping, following the curve of the lake. Eventually they turned off the main road, continuing around the lake. Jenna was starting to plead again for a stop when they came to the sign for Red Drum Lake Resort. On one side of the road was the office building, the "no vacancy" sign lit in red neon. Charles pulled the van to a stop in the small parking lot near the building. They all tumbled out of the van, stiff and lethargic. Josie looked across the street to where the hill rose. In the center directly across from them was a line of rooms like a motel, and then behind that, rising along the hill in a semi-circle, were individual cabins.

"Come find the bathroom with me," Jenna demanded, grabbing Josie by the arm, and dragging her into the office behind Charles and Greg.

The man behind the counter looked up as they all entered. "Bathroom?" Jenna said, bouncing. He responded by pointing towards the back of the room where a wide doorway showed multiple video game machines, a pool table, and a ping-pong table. Jenna scurried out of sight.

"Hello, Mr. York! Good to see you again," said the man behind the counter. He stretched out his hand and shook Charles's hand and smiled. Josie liked the way the man's eyes crinkled as he smiled, and she looked at the man in wonder. He had long dark hair streaked with only a little gray at the temples, pulled back in a braid. He had a pleasant, round face and almond eyes of a chocolate brown. His skin was tanned a warm brown with a reddish undertone. Like hers. He was like her.

"It's good to be back, William," said Charles.

"So glad you could come visit us again. And brought friends with you!" He reached out his hand to Greg and introduced himself. "I'm William Lightfeather. Anything you need during your stay, you ask me or my son Daniel, who is around here somewhere." He then went through the check-in procedure with them both before he spotted Josie waiting patiently for Jenna to return from the bathroom.

"Mr. York, that cannot be your daughter, all grown up?" asked William, his eyes twinkling.

"You are right, William. That's Josie," Charles smiled at her in a way she hadn't seen in weeks.

"Well, time certainly does fly, doesn't it?" He smiled again. He handed Greg and Charles each a set of keys and ushered them all to the door as Jenna finally rejoined them. "Alright, you all are in cabins four and five, right up there at the top of the hill. Best views in the place!"

"Thanks, William," said Charles.

"I'll send Daniel up to help you folks unload in a few minutes," William added, shaking hands with Charles and Greg again.

They all piled back into the van and rode the short distance across the street and up the hill to the two uppermost cabins. Charles parked in the gravel driveway between the two small wood-shingled structures and they again all climbed out. Rachel and Angela quickly sorted out which cabins they each wanted while Charles and Greg unloaded the bags and coolers. Feeling useless, Josie went to help her dad.

"Mr. York, how can I help?" came a voice. Josie turned around to see a tall young man with broad shoulders and beautiful almond-shaped eyes, the same shape and color as William's, the same shape as her own eyes, and the same long dark hair that went past his shoulders. His skin was like Williams's and like hers, so warmly tanned with a reddish undertone.

Jenna leaned over to Josie and said, "You'll let flies in." Josie looked away from Daniel, blinked at Jenna, then closed her mouth that had been gaping at him as her face flushed with heat.

"You must be William's son, Daniel," said Charles. "These things are going in this cabin, those in the other. Feel free to grab stuff and bring it inside."

Daniel turned and caught Josie's eyes. "Hi," he said with a casual, easy smile.

"Hi," she managed to say back. He turned away, grabbed a bag in each hand and walked into the York's cabin.

"Wow, he's…." Jenna said.

"Yeah," Josie breathed, her eyes on the door he had just disappeared through.

"And he looks just like…."

"Yeah," Josie repeated. She shook herself and turned to Jenna. "I've never… this is so weird, Jenna. I've never seen people who look like me, who are… Native American… in real life before."

"Never?"

Josie shook her head. "Not that I know of. Not like this."

"You've been here before, right?"

"Yeah, but I was a lot younger, and I didn't really… I wasn't…."

"Aware?"

Josie nodded, thankful that Jenna understood.

"Josie, he's hot," Jenna said very matter-of-factly after Daniel had returned to grab a large cooler and carried it into the cabin.

"Yeah, he is," Josie agreed eagerly.

"Well, this vacation just took an interesting turn!" Jenna gave Josie a mischievous smile, grabbed her own bags from the pile, and went into the cabin.

A few minutes later, back outside, Charles and Greg each handed Daniel a bill of cash in tip for his help. Charles closed the back of the van as Daniel said, “Thanks. Oh, and my dad said he forgot to mention that there’s a big barbecue on the beach Monday night and then the fireworks are set off from the lake. It’s a pretty big deal around here. See you around.” He smiled again, looked directly at Josie, gave her a wink, and walked down the hill towards the office.

Simon and Dave stood on the porch of the LaPage’s cabin, watching Daniel walk away.

“Dude, I think you might have competition,” Dave said to Simon with a chuckle. Simon punched Dave in the arm as he turned and walked into the cabin.

* * * * *

Each cabin consisted of two bedrooms, a common bathroom and a small kitchenette and living room. Jenna and Josie took the bedroom with two twin beds and were unpacking when Angela appeared in the doorway.

“Everyone has decided that we’re all too tired from the drive to cook, so we’re going into the village for dinner. The van leaves in ten minutes,” said Angela.

Josie grabbed her makeup bag and hair brush. She’d released her hair from the braid and brushed it out. She was trying to decide on a ponytail or leaving it down, then decided to pull just the top back and leave the rest down.

“A good compromise,” said Jenna teasingly, having watched Josie deliberating before the only mirror in the room.

Josie shot Jenna a look and stepped aside so Jenna could contain her curls with a ponytail. Josie then checked her makeup in her travel mirror and decided she didn’t have enough time to change clothes.

It was still early so they didn’t have trouble getting a table for eight at Village Pizza. After eating they walked around town, checking out the shops selling souvenirs and t-shirts. Dave and

Simon disappeared into the arcade on the corner, and a candy shop and ice cream parlor next door lured the rest of the group inside with heavenly aromas wafting onto the sidewalks from their open doors. When they all regrouped later, they headed back to the car, passing the Count Dracula Wax Museum. Dave and Jenna asked if they could go in, but Charles and Greg moaned protests and Josie flat out refused.

"Let's just go back to the cabins and hang out for tonight, and we'll come back to go through the wax museum another day," said Rachel, putting her arm around her disappointed daughter. "We'll do mini-golf and the arcade and maybe even the paddle boats or something."

Jenna reluctantly conceded and dragged Dave with her back to the van.

Back at the cabins, the parents gathered on the LaPage's front porch while the kids gathered in front of the York's cabin.

"I want to explore," said Jenna.

"Sounds good to me," said Dave.

"Okay," Josie agreed. They all looked at Simon.

"Sure, I guess."

They followed Jenna towards the other cabin. "We're gonna take a walk around and check this place out," she said to their parents.

"Don't be long, it's getting dark," said Angela.

"We'll be fine, Mom. We won't go far," Josie replied.

They walked the semi-circle driveway down the hill, past other cabins, voices floating from the open windows, and headed towards the lake. In the distance on the other side of the lake, mountains caught the last of the day's sunlight. The air was still warm and thick with the day's humidity.

They crossed the street and walked to the small, sandy beach. It was there, behind the office near the edge of the lake, that Jenna found what she was hoping to find.

Josie's heart quickened as Jenna strode quickly ahead of them.

"Hi. Daniel, right?" Jenna said.

Daniel was pulling a canoe up the beach to a rack at the back of the building. He lifted it effortlessly onto the only empty spot and turned to face Jenna and her friends.

"Yeah," he replied, wiping sweat from his brow.

"I'm Jenna. This is Josie. That's my brother Simon, and my boyfriend Dave."

"Nice to meet you all."

"Are you done working? Can you hang out for a few minutes?" Jenna asked. Simon took an unconscious step closer to Josie.

"Yeah, that was the last of it," Daniel replied.

"Cool," she said and headed for a picnic table nearby. "So, Daniel, how old are you?"

"I'm sixteen," he said, taking a seat with them.

"Josie and I are sixteen, too. Simon and Dave are eighteen."

"I know. At least about Josie," Daniel replied, looking at her. "You and I played together and swam in the lake when you were here as a kid."

"We did?" Josie replied. "I… I don't remember."

Daniel smiled again easily. "Honestly, I don't remember, either. My father likes to remember these things and then remind me when guests return. He told me. But now that I see you all grown up, I'm sorry I don't remember you."

Josie flushed and smiled at him.

"So, what's it like growing up here?" Dave asked.

Daniel shrugged. "It's pretty cool, actually. Busiest from May through October. I get to meet a lot of people from all over the place. Most of them are cool."

"What kind of things are there to do around here?" Jenna asked.

"Is there good fishing?" asked Dave.

Daniel nodded. "The lake is filled with trout, bass, perch. We have fishing poles and tackle you can borrow, but I recommend taking out a canoe or rowboat. You won't catch much from the shore. But there's lots to do around here. There are hiking trails, one here that goes all the way around the lake, and others nearby."

Josie groaned and Jenna said, "Josie has a kind of aversion to nature. What else?"

"There's horseback riding. And you have mini golf in the village and the arcade. Canoeing and swimming."

"She has an aversion to water, too," said Jenna, teasing Josie.

Daniel looked at her in surprise. "How can you have an aversion to nature and water?"

"It's a long story, and I don't have an aversion, I just… tend to have accidents everywhere I go," Josie said.

"She got stung by a jellyfish in Florida," Dave said.

"And almost drowned in a river in Maine," added Jenna.

"Not helpful, guys," Josie said, throwing looks of irritation at her friends.

"Well, you have nothing to be afraid of around here. There are no jellyfish in the lake, and the fish are more afraid of you than you are of them. And look," he pointed out at the water. "See the platform out there and the line of buoys that runs from shore to the platform? That's the safe zone, and no fish are allowed to swim within that zone."

Josie frowned. "You're teasing me."

He smiled again. "Maybe a little. It's only because pretty girls make me nervous." He winked at Josie, and she was glad she was sitting down because her legs turned to jelly. She smiled at him. "But I like long stories, so why not tell me yours?"

Josie shook her head. "Really, it's nothing. I don't mind nature or water. I'm here on vacation, aren't I?" She looked at him, wondering if he had bought it. She knew her friends didn't.

"That's good because there's a lot of both around here. If you guys need a tour guide, just let me know," he said, and flashed Josie a bright smile.

"We'll probably take you up on that," Jenna said.

"Cool. Well, I should get going. My dad's probably looking for me. But I'll see you guys around."

"Bye," Josie and Jenna said.

Dave said, "See you."

Simon was silent.

"He seems nice," Jenna said. They all stood and started walking back. Another family with five young children had just arrived at the beach and were gathered around the patio area where there was a fire pit.

"Oh, they have S'mores," said Dave as they walked by. "Hey, Jenna, why don't you make friends with them and see if they want to invite us to join them?"

Jenna rolled her eyes but grabbed his hand, their fingers intertwining, and they walked back up the hill hand-in-hand, leaving Josie and Simon behind in awkward silence.

The sun had set. The air was filled with the sounds of night bugs and distant voices chattering. Rachel's laugh cut through the night and then a dog barked somewhere in the distance. Josie stopped and looked up to see countless stars twinkling into view overhead.

"Wow!" she said. "I've never seen so many stars!"

Simon stopped next to her and gazed at the sky. "Yeah, there's a lot less ambient light here. Perfect for stargazing." He looked at Josie as she looked in wonder at the sky and decided to take the opportunity presented to him. "Do you see the four stars up there, almost straight ahead, that look like an upside-down kite?"

Josie looked but shook her head. "No."

He moved to stand behind her. He put his left hand on her shoulder and leaned in so that his face was almost touching hers, and he pointed into the sky. "Okay, see that bright star right there?"

Josie, startled by his sudden closeness, took a deep breath in, and urged herself not to tremble. When her eyes focused again, she said, "Yes, I think so."

"That's Vega, and it's part of the constellation of Lyra. If you look just to the right of Vega, you'll see the kite," he told her, doing his best to not be overwhelmed by the warm tingle he felt with his hand on her bare shoulder.

"Oh, yeah! I see that now!" Josie breathed.

"That's Hercules, or rather, his torso. And if you follow the stars from that bottom left corner of his kite, those two stars lead to his head. Then, just to the left there, see that star?"

"Yes," she replied, following the long, muscled line of his arm to where he pointed in the sky. On his wrist was the healer's cuff she had given him as a present when he announced which college he was going to. Seeing him wearing it always gave her a little inner leap of joy.

"That's part of another constellation, one of the biggest in the sky. That's Ophiuchus. Legend says that Hercules was positioned in the sky head-to-head with Ophiuchus. Ophiuchus was also known as 'The Doctor'. And the story is that Ophiuchus found the magic formula for immortality, but that made Pluto, the god of the Underworld, angry, because immortality meant he wouldn't have any new souls in the underworld. So, Pluto sent a great serpent after Ophiuchus, and we can see them still battling in the sky to this day. Because there, just below and to the left of Hercules, you can see what almost looks like the Little Dipper only the handle is bent the wrong way...."

"I see that," Josie said.

"That's the head of the serpent, and the handle is the body which if you follow those stars," he moved his hand along the sky, "goes from one side of Ophiuchus to the other."

"Wow, that's amazing," she said, still looking up.

He allowed his other hand to fall and rest on her shoulder, but the electricity from touching her with both hands was too much, so he let go and stepped back.

She turned to face him. "How do you know all that?"

"I wanted to be an astronaut when I was little," he replied, shuffling from foot to foot, and stuffing his hands in his pockets, trying to wipe away the heat from her. "I was obsessed with learning it all, and even applied to Space Camp in fifth grade, but I didn't get in. I was pretty devastated, and that's when I decided I wanted to be a doctor instead."

"You know, you could probably be a doctor for NASA," Josie said.

Simon shrugged. "Yeah, I've actually thought about that, like if I could combine both, but I think my passion now really is in emergency medicine."

Josie started to walk slowly back toward the cabins. "That does seem to be your calling. I should know, seeing as how you've come to my rescue and patched me up more than once," she said. She thought she saw his head nod in the darkness, but they had lapsed into silence.

When they got to the top of the hill, Dave and Jenna were snuggled together in one of the chairs on the porch of the York's cabin. She was about to ask Simon if he wanted to hang out when he said, "Good night, Josie."

"Good night, Simon," she replied. "Oh, and Simon?"

He turned back to her. "Yeah?"

"I'm really glad we're friends," she said.

Simon hesitated, then said, "Yeah, me too."

Not wanting to be a third wheel, Josie went into the cabin and collapsed on her bed. *Why did I say that to him?*

4

Simon grabbed a bottle of water from the refrigerator and threw himself down on the couch wishing he had a TV and video games so he could blow things up. He didn't like feeling like this. In the past, he'd always known what he wanted, and he always knew how to go after it. But then there was Josie, who just scrambled him.

He cared about her. He knew he did, and he was okay with that. And he thought he was okay with just being friends with her. It was what he *thought* he wanted from the start. But seeing Daniel flirt with her, looking at her like she was the diamond in the sand he'd been searching for, and then when she said those words just now, "I'm really glad we're friends," … it cut right through him.

The answer danced at the periphery of his mind, but he refused to let it get closer. He wouldn't allow it. Not yet. He knew, though, that he might be forced to face it sooner rather than later.

He chugged down the water, stood, and went to bed.

In the next cabin, Josie was finishing a similar conversation with herself by putting the pillow over her head in hopes of silencing her thoughts.

* * * * *

Josie was still awake and staring at the ceiling when Jenna came in.

"What took you and Simon so long to get back to the cabin?" Jenna asked, her tone a bad attempt at being casual.

"I'd just noticed all the stars and so he showed me some constellations," Josie said flatly.

"Oh?" Jenna's response was tinged with a combination of genuine surprise and suspicion.

"Jenna, I don't know what to do. Just when I think things are working perfectly, in goes the monkey wrench, screwing everything up."

"Are you talking about Daniel?"

"No."

"He was flirting with you."

"I know," Josie said, sitting up.

Jenna released her hair from its ponytail and sat on her bed facing Josie. "Do you like Daniel?"

"I barely know him, Jenna," Josie replied.

"But…."

"But, yeah, I mean, of course. I've never met any other Indians. I feel weird even saying that. I don't really, well, I'm not really…."

"What are you saying? That you're not really Indian? Josie, that's ridiculous."

"No, it's not, Jenna. I know I look like them and that my DNA says that I am, but I'm not part of that culture. Not like Daniel and his dad. And that, well, makes him appealing."

"And he seems to like you."

"Maybe. He probably flirts with every girl that stays here."

"You don't know that."

"It doesn't matter. We're only here for a week and we live four hours away."

"So what? Whether you feel it or not, you and Daniel share a culture and a history that ties you together in a way that no other girl staying here on vacation can compete with."

"But…."

"But what?"

"Simon…."

"Look, Josie. I get it. Or at least I *think* I do at this point. And let me just say this. I love my brother, but he's an idiot. He knows the deal. He knows how you feel about him, so if he is willing to reciprocate, he needs to tell you. Otherwise, you have no reason not to get to know Daniel better."

She sighed. "You're right," she reluctantly admitted, and Jenna smiled triumphantly.

* * * * *

"You were showing Josie the stars?" Dave said to Simon. "Sounds romantic."

Simon rolled over in his bed, facing away from Dave.

"If you don't want to talk about it, that's fine, but let me say one thing. If you're only thinking of starting something with Josie because of this Daniel guy, and you end up chickening out when it all gets too real for you, it will destroy Josie. And if you do that to Josie, I will punch you in the head. Hard."

Simon sighed and turned again to lay on his back. Staring at the ceiling he said, "Can you just do it now and get it over with?"

Dave shook his head at Simon.

* * * * *

Josie woke early as Jenna moved about the room.

"Simon and Dave were up before the sun and went fishing," Jenna said. "I'm going for a run."

"Okay, I'll be here," Josie said with a yawn.

Jenna jogged from the room as Josie rose from bed. She did a few of her stretches from dance class in the narrow space between the two beds. She'd slept well. It had been warm, but a breeze steadily blew in through the open windows of the cabin to make for a pleasant night. She showered and dressed and then made her way into the kitchen where her mom was putting out a box of cereal, bowls, milk, and a carton of orange juice. She wondered if in the next cabin Greg was making pancakes.

"Good morning, sweetie," Angela said.

"Morning," Josie replied, filling a coffee mug.

"Hungry?"

Josie shrugged and sat at the small kitchen table. "Just coffee for now. What are we doing today?"

"I think the plan is to hang around here for the day, take advantage of the lake. I've prepared sandwiches and potato salad for lunch and Rachel and Greg are going to cook burgers and dogs on the grill for dinner. Sound okay?"

She shrugged again. "Sure."

"Is everything okay, Josie?"

Josie looked at her mom over the rim of her mug as she sipped her coffee. "I'm fine. Why?"

Angela sat next to Josie. "I… I guess I don't know how to ask these questions, but I didn't know if there were any, you know, ghosts hanging around bothering you? You did say you see them everywhere you go."

Josie put her cup down. "Mom, all you have to do is ask. But no, there are no spirits bothering me here. Actually… this place is quiet, paranormally speaking. It has a really great feel to it."

"It does, doesn't it? Your dad and I have always loved coming here. We stayed here when we… when we picked you up for the very first time."

"You did?" Josie said.

Angela nodded. "The home you were in was about ninety miles north, but your dad and I wanted to stay some place… neutral, you know? He picked this place out on a lark, just thought it looked pretty with the lake and the little cabins and all. We have pictures of you in a little pink bathing suit, your diaper sticking out from the bottom, sitting down on the beach."

"I think I remember that photo. I didn't realize it was here."

Angela nodded again, smiling at the distant memory. "You were so adorable, and so happy. It was very scary taking a baby into our home that wasn't born from us. We had prepared ourselves for you to be screaming and crying the whole time, but you didn't. You were calm. You just constantly looked around and took everything in. Then your dad started blowing raspberries on your tummy, and that was it, you were both smitten."

Josie's smile faded. Angela saw but went on. "We came back for vacation when you were five, about to start kindergarten. You played with William's son Daniel on the beach."

"Yeah, he mentioned that to me," said Josie.

"Oh, does he remember?"

"No. He said his dad told him."

"Yes, his father is very attentive, very kind."

"Mom, can I ask you a question?"

"Of course, sweetie. What is it?"

"Did we come here because William's Indian like me?"

Angela sighed. "Not at first. Like I said, your dad just randomly picked this place. And William Lightfeather didn't own it then, but he did work here. When we heard he'd purchased the place from the old owners, we decided to come back. That was when you were five. We did think it was a good idea for you to be exposed to people from the same culture, and we hoped to come back more often. There are a few pow-wows and festivals in the area, and we really wanted you to be exposed to it all, but… things got busy and, well…."

"Life got in the way," Josie finished for her.

Angela nodded. "You got into dance and theater, and you were – are – so good at it and you really loved it, so we focused on that, our jobs, all that other stuff. We came back once a few years ago just for a long weekend, you probably remember, but it rained a lot, and you were at an age where being on vacation with just your mom and dad was pretty boring. This place was all booked up, so we stayed at a little hotel in the village, but it just wasn't what we'd hoped for. So, we let it go until…."

"Until all this ghost stuff came up?" Josie asked.

"That's a big part of it because, well, your dad doesn't agree with me, but I think maybe your heritage has something to do with it. Native Americans are very spiritual people in ways the rest of us aren't and don't really understand. Are you mad?"

Josie frowned. "Why would I be mad?"

Angela shrugged. "I don't know. I don't want you to think we were trying to trick you or anything."

"What, trick me into learning about my roots? A lot of adoptive parents might not be very encouraging of that. No, I'm not mad. I'm surprised, but not mad."

Angela let out a breath of relief. She stood and went to the counter and poured herself a bowl of cereal. "Alright. Well, on that note, I do know that William and Daniel will both be more than happy to answer any questions you might have."

Josie's heart suddenly jumped into double-time. "Okay."

"Want anything to eat yet?" Angela asked.

Josie shook her head just as the door to the cabin opened and Jenna jogged in, shiny with sweat and panting. "I'm so hungry," she said, grabbing a bowl and pouring cereal.

"How was your run?" Angela asked Jenna as she took the seat Angela had recently left.

"Awesome. Went by the lake. It's beautiful here!"

"It is, isn't it," Angela smiled. Josie was happy that her mother was happy.

* * * * *

"Which bikini do you think I should wear?" Josie asked Jenna. She had just told Jenna about her conversation with her mother and was now avoiding Jenna's questions.

"I think you should wear the blue one. You look killer in it, and you can torture both Simon and Daniel."

"You want me to torture your brother?"

"He may be my brother, but you're my best friend, and when my best friend has two guys both drooling over her, then yes, I'm going to encourage a little female manipulation," Jenna smiled.

"This is a side of you I don't see very often," Josie laughed. "I like it!"

When they reached the small stretch of sand by the lake, Jenna spread a blanket and they sat. It was still early, but the sun was bright and warm. Josie scanned the area but didn't see Daniel anywhere.

"Are Simon and Dave still fishing?" Josie asked.

"No, they got back just before we came down here. They should be here in a few minutes."

Josie found her heart pounding fast in anticipation. She was curious to see how Simon would behave around her, anxious to see if he would be like he was the night before. But she was also anxious to see Daniel, to have him flirt and smile at her again.

During a restless night's sleep and a long morning of uneventful fishing, Simon had resolved that nothing would happen again like the night before. He would be leaving for college in a few weeks, and it wasn't a good idea to get involved with anyone, especially Josie. They were friends, and that would have to be enough for both of them.

Then, as he and Dave crossed the narrow street to the other side of the resort, he spotted her. She was standing at the edge of the sand, her toes barely in the water. She was talking animatedly to Jenna who was already in up to her neck. As he walked, he watched her remove her white mesh beach cover-up to reveal a tiny, sky-blue bikini, and he felt himself waver at the sight.

Jenna must have seen them approaching and said something to Josie, because she turned around and waved at them. He and Dave both waved. Dave gave his friend a side-long glance that went unnoticed, knowing what Simon was thinking at that moment and wishing he would do something about it.

"Hey, Josie, how's the water," Dave said when they reached the lake's edge.

"Cold," she said.

"It's not cold once you're in it!" Jenna yelled from a short distance away, floating on her back and paddling her arms along in a circle.

"She wants to swim out to the platform," Josie told them.

"Let's do it!" said Dave, throwing his t-shirt and flip-flops onto their blanket and running into the water. He dove at Jenna and reached her in seconds.

Simon took his t-shirt off and then turned to Josie. "There's nothing to be afraid of, you know," he said.

"As long as you're here to rescue me...," she said with a grin. She turned and ran into the water and dove when she reached knee depth. The water was a cold shock to her bare skin at first, but she quickly grew accustomed to it, and swam slowly to where Jenna and Dave were.

Simon shook himself. Her words had cut through him in a way he hadn't expected. Not in a bad way, but like a swallow of hot coffee on a cold day, her words filled him with warmth. "I don't know how much more of this I can take," Simon mumbled to no one, and ran into the water after his friends.

They swam out to the platform, Jenna with Dave ahead and Simon keeping pace with Josie. When they reached the square of wood floating in the lake, Jenna climbed up first, then Dave. Simon held the ladder and let Josie climb up, but she said, "You go first," so he did. He stood at the top waiting for her, and she reached out a hand for him. Without thinking, he grabbed her hand and pulled her up the rest of the way.

"Thanks," she smiled again, her eyes glowing gold beneath her thick, dark lashes.

"Sure," he replied, letting go of her hand, wanting to shake the electricity from it but not wanting her to see.

All around them at the lake's edge they could see docks with small boats and lake houses just beyond. Further beyond that, there was a bend in the shore that went towards the village which they couldn't see from there. All around were mountains, thick with dark green evergreens.

"This place really is beautiful," Jenna said.

"It really is," said Dave, making like he wanted to put his arms around his girlfriend but instead, he grabbed her and threw her into the water. She screeched with glee as she flew through the air, twisting around at the last minute to dive gracefully into the water.

When she surfaced, she was laughing. "You jerk!" she yelled.

"Who, me?" Dave asked, diving off the platform, over her head, and into the water.

Simon shook his head at them while Josie laughed. She sat and stretched herself in the sun while Jenna and Dave swam back to the ladder and climbed up again.

"Hey, let's see who can dive the best," said Dave to Jenna. "Josie, you be the judge."

Josie rolled her eyes. "Fine. Go ahead."

"Jenna, you go first."

Jenna stepped to the edge of the platform and gave her best dive, hands together and pointed above her head.

Then Dave, stepping to the back edge of the platform, ran and jumped, bringing his knees to his chest and hitting the water like a cannon ball.

"Oh, come on! That wasn't a dive!" Jenna yelled and laughed while splashing water at him.

"At least give me something worth judging!" Josie yelled at him. Dave just laughed and splashed Jenna back.

For the next few minutes, Simon, Dave, and Jenna all took turns diving and jumping off the platform while Josie sat at the edge, her feet dangling in the cool water and the sun warming the rest of her.

Then her eye caught movement on the beach, behind the office where the canoes were kept. It was Daniel. He came out of the office and walked along the deck carrying several bright yellow life vests. He brought them to the boat shed near the water, grabbed a tackle box, two fishing rods, and two other life jackets, and went back inside the office.

Then her attention was caught by a woman standing just below the deck. She was examining the flowerbeds that were a full riot of color. She bent to sniff a flower, then moved on and bent again to touch the petals of another flower. Josie squinted her eyes to see the woman more clearly, but she was hazy. She could only make out that she wore a long white skirt that dusted the ground and a brown patterned shirt. Her hair was long, dark, and straight. Then Josie realized why she was hazy. There was a pale pink glow radiating from her, similar to the ones she saw around all the other dead people she had encountered.

Inwardly she groaned. Josie hadn't seen a single ghost since she and Jenna did the spirit guide meditation two nights before, and she thought maybe she would actually get a vacation. But she should have known better.

Daniel came out of the office again and went to the back of the building. This time he came back around dragging a hose. He moved along, watering the flowerbeds. Josie watched as he neared the ghostly woman and then her jaw dropped. Even from a distance she could see his mouth moving, she saw his head turn in the direction of the spirit, and then she saw him pointing at one of the flowers. The ghost woman did the same. She was pointing at a bush lush with fuchsia colored flowers and saying something. Her aura shimmered as she spoke. Daniel pointed the hose at the roots of the bush, said something, paused, and then laughed.

"Earth to Josie!" she heard from behind her. She turned to see Jenna swimming towards her. "You okay?"

Josie shook her head but said, "Yeah, I'm fine, I was just… thinking about something. But I think I'm going to swim back to shore and sit on the beach for a bit."

"You want me to come with you?"

"No, that's fine. I'll be fine," she smiled.

Josie pushed herself off the edge of the platform, into the water that felt cold again to her sun-warmed skin, and she swam back to the shore. She dared a glance in Daniel's direction, but the ghost woman was gone, and his back was still to Josie as he continued to water the flowers.

She reached the shore and dried herself with a towel before sitting on the blanket. *Hanover? What did I just see?*

She felt a distant tingle and heard him reply, *That is not for me to say.*

Josie frowned. *Well, who* can *say?*

There was only silence. A light breeze blew off the lake, hitting her damp skin and raising goose bumps on her arms. She sighed.

Simon looked to shore, keeping one eye on Josie and one eye on Daniel. Simon knew Daniel had seen Josie on the beach and wondered if he was going to take advantage of her being there alone. Part of him wanted to go back to the beach but he didn't want to be obvious, and besides… did it really matter if this Daniel guy talked to Josie? Flirted with her?

Before he could answer, a hand was on the top of his head, pushing him under the water. Simon reached above his head and grabbed Dave's wrist, yanking and pulling Dave from his perch on the platform back into the water.

When they surfaced, both sputtering water, Dave said, "If you don't make a move, you're going to get run-over."

5

"Can I tell you guys about something weird I saw today?" Josie asked. She was sitting at the picnic table outside their cabin with Jenna, Dave, and Simon, with a feast spread out before them. She had hoped to talk to Daniel before her friends came back to the beach, but when he was done watering the flowers, he disappeared inside and didn't come back out, and Josie didn't have the guts to approach him.

Jenna replied, "Of course," while Dave nodded, his mouth full of potato salad. Simon didn't say anything.

After swallowing a bite of her sandwich, she explained what she saw while sitting on the platform in the lake.

"Wait, he was *talking* to the ghost?" Jenna asked.

"It looked like it from where I was."

"And you're sure she was a ghost," Dave added.

"Yes. Not a stuck ghost, but one that's crossed."

"How can you tell?" Simon asked, surprising Josie with his interest. She had expected him to find an excuse to leave as soon as the word "ghost" left her mouth.

"Crossed spirits have a brighter aura. Stuck spirits don't always even have a glow. Plus, I could see the flowers *through* her," she told him.

"But if she isn't a stuck spirit, then that's a good thing, right? I mean, we don't – or you don't – need to help her. Right?" Simon asked.

"Right, but—"

"But what?"

"But Daniel was talking to her," said Jenna for Josie. "A ghost. Daniel was talking to a ghost. That's a big deal!"

Simon's stomach clenched. "You're sure he was talking to her? There wasn't anyone else nearby that he could have been talking to?"

Josie shook her head. "I didn't see anyone else, living or otherwise."

"Well, that is weird," said Dave, shoving the rest of his sandwich in his mouth.

"What are you going to do?" Jenna asked Josie.

"I want to ask him about it."

"I think you should," Jenna agreed.

"Yeah. Ugh, okay, next time we see him, I'll just ask him," said Josie.

When Jenna and Josie had gone inside to put the leftover food away, Dave turned to Simon. "Your competition just got stiffer."

"What?"

"The guy shares a heritage with her and now shares the whole ghost thing. I'm getting tired of saying it, so this is the last time. If you want her, you need to tell her now. Before it's too late."

* * * * *

Josie and Jenna followed Angela and Charles outside to find Greg and Rachel talking to Simon and Dave.

"Charles and I are going to grab a canoe and go for a paddle on the lake. Anyone care to join us?" asked Angela.

"That sounds like fun," said Rachel who looked at her husband. "What do you say?"

Greg shrugged and smiled. "Sure, I'm in."

"Oh, me too! I want to go, too," said Jenna, hopping up and down. "Josie?"

Josie shook her head. "I'd rather keep my feet on solid ground."

"I'll take you out in a canoe," Dave said to Jenna.

"Okay. Yay!"

They all headed back down to the beach. Simon fell into step beside Josie. "Are you sure you don't want to go out in a canoe? I'll take you, and I promise I won't flip the boat like Dave would."

"Thanks," she replied with a smile, "but I'd rather hang out on the beach."

Simon shrugged. "Okay, sounds good to me."

"You can go if you want. I don't mind hanging out by myself," she said.

"I really don't want to be the third wheel with my parents *or* my sister and Dave."

"Okay, just as long as you don't think I need a babysitter." She hurried her steps to catch up with Jenna. Was she trying to get rid of him? he wondered. Well, if she was, he wasn't going to make it easy on her.

Josie caught up to Jenna as they crossed the street to the beach side. "I want to be the one to ask Daniel about what I saw, okay? So, if you see him, please don't say anything."

Jenna smiled at her friend. "Yeah, sure. He's all yours."

While Rachel, Greg, Angela, Charles, Dave, and Jenna all headed to the boat shed, Josie and Simon went to the beach. Josie spread the blanket, sat, and watched as Daniel lifted canoes down from their racks one by one. She saw him talking to Jenna who pointed behind her then turned to look in Josie's direction.

Josie pretended not to notice.

"Your shoulders are getting red, you know. You should put sunscreen on," Josie said to Simon when he sat next to her.

He reached into the beach bag and grabbed a bottle, then leaned towards her, his bare shoulder touching her bare shoulder. She felt the sparks. "Will you help?" When she looked at him with a furrow on her brow, he said, "Please? It's hard to reach back there, plus I can't see if I'm getting it everywhere it needs to go."

Josie hesitated. Part of her thought she must be dreaming and at any second, she'd wake up in the little twin bed in the cabin or maybe even back home. When that didn't happen, she shrugged and squirted the sunscreen into her palms. Cautiously at first, she spread it over his shoulders, then his back and his upper arms. His biceps. It couldn't be real. There was no way Simon would ask her to do this. Touching him in this way was both bliss and torture. Why had he asked her to do this? Was his reason genuine? Did he not care about her touch the way she cared about his? No, her gut wouldn't accept that. Not after last night. Something had changed. He was acting differently. He showed it at lunch, too, when she talked about the ghost. In the past – the recent past – he would have rolled his eyes and walked away before he could hear anything. But today he listened and even asked questions, almost like he actually wanted to know.

Josie glanced over her shoulder. All the canoers were out of sight, and Daniel had disappeared. She finished with the lotion, and laid down, her sunglasses shielding her closed eyes.

"Thanks," Simon said, turning back to face the lake. He glanced at Josie but couldn't see how shaken she was by what she just did. It took every bit of energy she had to lay there calmly, without trembling, next to him.

Josie thought about asking him straight out what he was doing. She ran it through in her mind, but in every scenario, he denied everything, and so her courage wavered.

After a little while, she got hot laying on her back, so she rolled over. Simon was sitting up, reading a book.

"What are you reading?" she asked.

He put his finger in the book to mark the page. "It's a biography on Frank Sinatra."

"Sinatra?"

"Yeah. It's my dad's book but I picked it up one day when I was bored and found it really interesting. Did you know that he was arrested – twice – when his girlfriend attacked his wife-to-be, Nancy?"

"Why twice?"

"Once for seduction and once for adultery," Simon replied. "And he tried to commit suicide more than once."

"Really?"

Simon nodded. "He came across as cool and confident, but he was a pretty messed-up, insecure guy. He even wore something called 'elevator shoes' because he was only five-foot-seven."

Josie chuckled. She propped herself up on her elbows and looked at Simon. Once more she tried to get the words out, to be bold and just ask him what was going on, why he was being so different towards her. But she couldn't. The words wouldn't travel from her mind to her mouth.

After a few minutes of trying not to jump out of her skin, she got up. "I need to go find the bathroom," she said.

Simon put his book down. "I'll go with you."

She smiled and frowned at him. "I think I can use the bathroom without getting into any trouble."

He sighed and watched her walk away, right towards the office, right towards Daniel.

* * * * *

Josie went into the office. It took her eyes a minute to adjust, going from sunlight to indoors. She looked around. William was behind the desk and smiled at her. She smiled, gave a wave, and then made her way towards the game room where the sign for the bathrooms were. She didn't really have to use the bathroom. She was looking for Daniel, but he didn't seem to be in there. But she went into the ladies' room anyway, washed her hands, splashed a little water on her face, and then brushed through her hair with her fingers.

She went back out into the game room and looked around. There were two pin-ball machines, a Pac-Man game, and a race-car game at the edges of the room. The center space was shared by a pool table and a ping-pong table. No one was at any of the machines or tables. It was too nice outside. And again, Daniel wasn't there.

"Enjoying your stay so far?" William asked.

"Yeah. Having a great time," Josie nodded.

"Well, you and your family just let me know if you need anything," he said.

"Will do," she said over her shoulder, and pushed through the door. On the other side, she crashed right into Daniel's torso.

"Sorry!" she mumbled, bounced backwards, and hit the doorjamb.

Daniel reached out and grabbed her by the shoulders to steady her on her feet. "Are you okay?"

"Yeah, I'm fine," she said. "Just a little embarrassed."

"Why are you embarrassed?"

"Because of my extreme clumsiness. You'd never know I've taken ballet since I was four," she said, her cheeks burning red.

"You're a ballerina? That's very cool," he said.

She looked down at his hands still gripping her arms and looked up at him. "You can let go now," she smiled.

"Are you sure? Don't ballerina's usually have a guy there to hold her up?" He winked and let her go.

"So, got a lot of work to do today?" Josie asked.

"It never ends," he replied. "We don't have any more canoes but if you and your friend want to take a boat out, we have one rowboat left."

Josie looked to where Daniel pointed, seeing Simon still sitting on the blanket on the beach. When Simon saw Josie looking, he turned his head away.

"Thanks, but no. I'm happy to just sit on the beach."

"Okay, well, let me know if anything changes."

"I will." She hesitated, took a deep breath, and said, "Can I ask you a question?"

"Sure. But will you walk with me? I have to get back to work."

"Yeah, okay." She followed him as he went around to the back side of the office where the boat shed was. Her heart pounded in anticipation. "Earlier today I was out there, on the platform, and

I saw you watering the flowers here. And I saw you… talking to a woman."

"So, what's your question?" he asked, sorting through a tackle box on the workbench in front of him.

She hesitated again. "Well, I don't know. I mean, I could see her, but I'm pretty sure she isn't someone that most people can see."

Daniel smiled. "That still wasn't a question."

Josie sighed and closed her eyes, bracing herself. "Can you see ghosts? Because I can, and it's turned my life upside down. I saw you talking to her, this woman, and I know she's a ghost." She let the words fall, then opened her eyes to see his reaction.

"Yeah, that was my mom. And no, I can't see ghosts – usually – but I can hear them and sense them, you know, feel them nearby sometimes. I hear her a lot. She especially likes to help me with the flowers. They were kind of her thing when she was alive."

"You don't seem surprised by this."

"Should I be?"

"I… I don't know. Most people I know… well, talking to ghosts isn't a normal thing."

He nodded. "You were raised in a Honio'on family, right?"

"What does that mean?" she frowned.

"Non-native," he replied, looking over from his work with a grin.

"Oh, well, yes. I was adopted."

He nodded. She wanted him to say more. She wanted to know more. Then she heard familiar voices behind her.

"Hey, Josie," said Rachel. "We're done with the canoe," she said to Daniel.

"Just leave it there. I'll take care of it," he told Rachel.

"Okay. Josie, your parents are still out on the water somewhere. Greg and I are taking the van to the store to get a few things for dinner tonight."

"Okay," she smiled at them. Rachel gave Josie a curious smile as she turned and walked away.

"Well, I'll let you get back to work. Maybe I'll see you around later?"

"Sure thing, Kachina Kai," he said with a grin.

* * * * *

Josie stood in the shower, lost in thought. The water streaming down on her smelled like the lake. The lake reminded her of Simon, of swimming to the platform with him, of lying on the sand next to him, and putting lotion on his shoulders. It reminded her of how he watched her talking to Daniel and how when she went back to the blanket after talking with him, Simon was unusually chatty.

"Did you know Mark Langford started that giant beach ball going at graduation?" Simon had said.

"No, that was him?" Josie replied.

"Yeah. He had the thing hidden under his gown, deflated, and then blew it up during Hailey's valedictorian speech."

"She must have been mad," Josie said.

"He said that he'd heard her speech fifty times already, and he could prove it by reciting the whole thing himself," Simon said with a shrug.

"They're a cute couple."

"They're both going to Penn State."

"That's nice," Josie said. "I guess they didn't want to try the long-distance thing?"

Simon shook his head. "There's a lot of that happening, though. Misty and Evan, Dennis and Amy, Chris and Kirsten. All going to different schools, hours away from each other."

"It's going to be hard on them," said Josie.

"What makes you say that?" asked Simon.

"I don't know. I mean, I have zero relationship experience, but from what I've seen, being in a relationship while living in the same town, going to the same school, is way different from living hours apart. Especially in a college situation where you're going to be in all kinds of new situations, meeting new people, having new experiences. It will be challenging for them to fit a long-distance relationship into all that."

"Maybe, but only if they let it," said Simon.

"I guess, but do you really think it's worth it to try?"

"I... I really don't know. How can anyone our age know if it's worth it or not?"

"Jenna and Dave do."

"You think?" Simon asked.

"Absolutely. I think that even though UNH isn't that far, it's still going to be an adjustment for them both not to see each other every day. But they both know who they are and what they want in life, and a part of that is each other. I think they'll work hard to keep things good between them. Most kids our age have no clue who they are and that's what college is for. How can you find yourself if you have this person holding you back? I don't believe that most high school relationships can survive the transition to college."

"Hmm," Simon said and looked back out at the lake. "Do you know what you want in life?"

"I used to think I did. My ultimate dream was to go to the Boston Conservatory at Berklee, and to be on Broadway. That's all I really knew. But now... this ghost stuff... I just don't know. It throws a wrench into everything. Especially relationships. Things are already complicated and add in this other thing. I mean, my own father thinks I'm nuts, and you're still on the fence with it all. My whole life is just a mess."

"I'm not on the fence, Josie."

"Oh, so you're convinced I'm nuts, too?" she said it teasingly, but when she looked at him, she saw a flash of hurt in his eyes.

"I don't think you're nuts," he sighed.

"I know," she replied.

"Do you?"

Josie was ripped from her memory by Jenna pounding on the bathroom door. "Josie! Are you gonna finish sometime today?"

"Yeah, I'll be right out!" she yelled back. "Sorry," she said as she passed Jenna in the bathroom doorway a minute later.

Josie dressed in a white, off-the-shoulder peasant dress and applied barely-there make-up – just a bit of mascara and lip gloss. She decided to let her hair air-dry and went outside. Dave and Simon had moved a second picnic table over and arranged it next to the other one, and now a feast was spread across the tabletops. There were burgers and hot dogs, corn on the cob, garden salad and potato salad, large slices of watermelon, potato chips and dip, bottles of soda and bottles of wine.

Josie pointed to the latter and said to Jenna, "I think our parents have more fun together than we do."

Jenna laughed. "No way, it's just a different kind of fun."

The sun was setting behind thick clouds creating a glowing sunset across the lake. Lanterns were brought out and placed on the table. As they ate, she told her friends about her conversation with Daniel. Simon was sitting close, so close that every now and then their arms brushed each other.

"That's all he said? Didn't you ask him any other questions?" Jenna said when Josie finished.

Josie shrugged. "I didn't really have time. I guess I'm not as good at interrogating people as you are," Josie replied, feeling inadequate and suddenly grumpy.

"Well, can I talk to him, then?"

"No," she said with a shake of her head. "Let me talk to him some more. Or try, anyway. Please?"

"Okay. Looks like your next chance is heading our way now." Jenna pointed behind Josie. She and Simon both turned to see William and Daniel walking up the hill, Daniel carrying a cardboard box. They stopped at the cabin next to the LaPage's, spoke to the people inside, and then headed for them.

"Good evening, folks!" said William with a wave. "How's everyone doing?"

"Great, William. What brings you and Daniel by? Would you like to join us? There's plenty of food."

"That's very kind but no thank you. We're just letting folks know that there might be a storm tonight, so we brought by some extra flashlights and candles in case we lose power." William reached into the box Daniel held and gave a handful of candles and four flashlights to Charles and Greg.

"Thanks," said Angela. "Is the storm supposed to be bad?"

"Hard to say," William said. "With the mountains all around us it will either be blocked or contained."

"They expect it to pass by sunrise, though," added Daniel, looking at Josie. "I have tomorrow off and was wondering if you guys wanted to come hike the trails around here with me?"

"That sounds fun," said Jenna.

"I'm in," Dave said.

"Sure," Josie replied, and then looked at Simon.

"Yeah, sure," he said with a forced smile.

"Cool. We can meet here around eight, okay?" Daniel then turned to William. "Oh, Dad, I forgot to tell you. Josie saw Mom when she was helping me with the flowers today."

William looked at Josie with a smile. "You saw her? How did she look?"

Josie was startled, but said, "Beautiful."

William nodded. "Yes, Anna was beautiful."

"William, I didn't know your wife was here. I'd like to meet her," said Charles.

"That's very kind of you," William said to Charles, then looked at Josie. "I don't see her. I just feel her presence sometimes, like Daniel. Is she here now?"

Josie shook her head. "No."

William looked back at Charles. "I guess meeting her will have to wait for another time."

"Wait," said Charles, looking from William to Josie. "Is your wife...."

"She is with the Great Spirit," William said to Charles, sweeping his arm over his head in an arched gesture at the sky.

Charles's jaw hung open for a moment and then snapped shut, swallowing hard.

"Alright, well you folks have a good night," said William, his eyes twinkling as he smiled.

"See you tomorrow," Daniel said, his eyes still on Josie.

When they were gone back down the hill after stopping at the other cabins, Angela said, "Josie, what was all that about?"

Josie looked at her dad who continued to look confused, then to her mom who looked curious. "I saw Daniel talking to a woman earlier today. She was a spirit, a crossed spirit. Turns out it's his mom. William's wife."

Charles got up from the table and walked into their cabin, the screen door slamming behind him. Josie rolled her eyes and turned away from the table.

They cleaned up the leftover food and then Greg grilled pineapple for dessert, a treat Josie had never tried before but instantly loved. Then, just as Rachel was pulling the cork on the next bottle of wine, dark clouds rolled in, and the sky opened up. They all ran for cover into the LaPage's cabin, taking with them whatever they could grab from the table.

They were all soaking wet and laughing. Rachel filled the wine glasses and said, "Who's up for a game of 'Cards against Humanity'?"

"I'll go get Charles," said Angela, her voice falsely light.

"Oh, heck no, I am not playing that game with my parents," said Jenna, backing out of the kitchen into the hallway. Dave, Josie and Simon followed. But when Josie got to the hallway, she saw Jenna pulling Dave into the bedroom he and Simon shared. Josie rolled her eyes again with a groan and decided the only safe place to go was the porch.

Simon followed her out. The rain poured down hard. She stepped to the edge of the porch just out of reach of the rain and then retreated and sat in a red Adirondack chair.

"Here," he said, handing her a sweatshirt he'd grabbed for himself before Jenna and Dave took over his room. He sat in the chair next to her.

"Thanks," she said. She wrapped herself in the sweatshirt, the soft fleecy inside instantly warming her chilled, wet skin.

Silence hung between them. Angela and Charles came running through the rain back to the LaPage's cabin. Her dad still looked grim; her mom looked at her with eyebrows raised, then they disappeared inside.

Josie sighed. In the distance, beyond the lake and the village, the mountains were being lit up by lightning. Thunder rumbled. She thought back to another time like this. Just a little over a year ago on the camping trip that started it all. A storm broke out as they paddled down a river in Maine. The river got rough, their raft flipped, and they were all tossed from the boat. With little gear left, they managed to find an old house in the woods and took shelter inside. While rain and wind pummeled the house, Josie warmed herself in one of Simon's sweatshirts. She had been frightened then.

She wasn't frightened now.

A streak of red lightning shot from the clouds to the mountains, and then a streak of yellow. A streak of green followed.

"It's beautiful, isn't it?" said Josie.

"The lightning? Yeah."

"Do you remember last summer on that camping trip, we were stopped, having lunch or something, and Adam was telling us about Baxter State Park, and about Mount Katahdin?"

"Yeah, I remember," said Simon.

"Adam was telling us about the Abenaki who lived there, who believed that Pamola, a storm god that took the form of a bird, lived on the mountain, and protected it with harsh weather. Do you remember that?"

"Yeah."

"I wonder if Pamola is hanging out over there for a change of scenery," she said.

"Maybe."

Silence hung between them again for a few minutes. Several more streaks of lightning lit the sky in a rainbow of colors and thunder chased after it.

"I can't believe it's been just over a year since we took that trip. It feels like a few lifetimes ago," said Josie.

Simon said nothing. The rain pattered on the porch roof and poured off the overhang, splattering into puddles in various musical notes. Josie sighed happily. She didn't mind that her parents were inside playing a game with Jenna's parents, and she didn't mind that Jenna and Dave had disappeared into the bedroom to do God-knew-what. She was content to sit there in mutual silence, watching the lightning, snuggled into his sweatshirt.

"Josie?"

"Yeah?"

"I'm sorry."

She shifted in the chair to look at him. Even in the dim light she could see his bright blue eyes. "About what?"

"I'm sorry I've been so difficult about the whole ghost thing."

She furrowed her brow at him. "It's okay, Simon."

He shook his head. "It's not. It's not okay. My life changed during that stupid summer camp, but I didn't know how to handle it. I still don't have it all down, but I'm trying."

"I know you are. It really is okay. I can't imagine being in your shoes, having someone say the things I've said. I don't always believe it. And I definitely don't understand it all yet."

"That's the hard part for me. Up until that point, everything around me was explainable. It was rooted in science. But then… well, it's just so hard for me to not be able to have solid evidence of what's happening. I want to see it, touch it."

"But you did see it. Don't you remember? When we were trapped in that room. You could see Philip and Harold, and Lily, too. You couldn't hear them, but you could see them. And you *felt* the bullet, right? You felt a bullet and you felt pain that shouldn't exist in scientific terms."

He nodded, looking at her. "You're right. I forget about that part sometimes – seeing them, I mean. I guess because I don't see them all the time like you do. But science can't prove any of it happened."

"Does it need to? Does science need to explain everything?" she asked.

"I would like it to," he said.

Josie shook her head. "It just seems like an impossible task. Science is a man-made concept and you're trying to explain non-man-made things, things made by no-one-know-who-or-what!"

He didn't respond. Then he said, "I still dream about it. The gunshot wound. I wake up at the point when I feel like the last of my life has drained from my body. Sometimes I wake up expecting you to be there with me, like you were in that room."

Silence fell between them again. Josie went back to watching the lightning show. As though the electricity filling the air charged her with courage, she said, "Do you realize that this is the most you've talked about this stuff in the past year? Why is that? Why are you finally talking to me about this?"

He took a deep breath and let it out in a sigh. "You dropped a bomb on me back in the fall, telling me that I'm an Empath. Well, you're right. And tonight, when your dad got up and left the table when you were talking about William's wife, I felt what you felt. I could feel the hurt he is causing you. I don't want to do that to you, too."

The rain softened to just a patter and the thunder rolled away in the distance. Josie stood, and Simon did the same.

"Thank you," she said. She moved to him and wrapped her arms around him. He pulled her close, but only for a second before she pulled away. "Good night," she said, looking up into his eyes and giving him a smile that made his knees buckle. He fell back into the chair and watched her run through the rain until she disappeared into the dark cabin.

Simon leaned back in the chair and put his feet up on the porch railing. The rain became heavier again and thunder rumbled close overhead. Lightning tore through the sky just over the lake now. Behind him, he heard an expression of distress when the lights went out on the card game but moments later, he heard laughter again and saw the flicker of candlelight through the windows. Whatever Jenna and Dave were doing, they didn't notice the power outage.

He watched the storm, watched the lightning streak across the sky and touch down with loud cracks as it hit the ground. He listened to the thunder rumble and crash, rolling through the clouds overhead. He breathed in the air that was washed clean by the rain and felt peace wash through him and relax his body.

He felt something on his left shoulder, a soft depression as though someone put a tender hand of encouragement on him. *Who are you? Are you my spirit guide?* He asked silently.

He didn't hear an answer, but he felt a comforting warmth mingling with the peacefulness in him.

Simon didn't know how long he'd sat there, watching the storm like it was the latest blockbuster movie, when Dave and Jenna emerged from the cabin.

"Good night!" she said and dashed across the grass through the rain to the other cabin.

Dave took the chair Josie had been sitting in. "You okay, man?"

"Yeah," Simon nodded. "It's a good feeling to know exactly what you want, isn't it?"

* * * * *

Josie felt herself rise out of a deep sleep. She rolled onto her back and blinked the sleep from her eyes. The room was dark, but she could see enough to know that Jenna's bed was still empty. She got up and groped for the wall switch, but nothing happened when she pushed it up.

Power must have gone out like William said it might, Josie thought. She didn't know where the extra candles or flashlights were, so she made her way carefully back to the bed, feeling her way to the bedside table and felt for her cellphone. But when she pushed the buttons, nothing happened. "What? The battery wasn't that low when I went to bed. How can it be dead?" she asked. Then she noticed that she could no longer hear the storm.

Josie carefully groped her way into the hallway and across to the kitchen area hoping to find a flashlight. She saw that the master bedroom door was open, meaning her parents hadn't come back to the cabin yet either. Instead of searching the kitchen, she decided it was probably best to go back to the other cabin.

When she stepped outside, she found that the storm had passed. The night was cool, clear, and eerily quiet. There were no sounds of the usual night bugs, birds, or tree frogs. She looked up to see a star-filled sky. She could pick out Hercules and Ophiuchus and the Serpent. She shivered a little and pulled Simon's sweatshirt closer around her body.

Then she noticed that the ground beneath her feet was dry, almost dusty. She looked around. There were no traces of the recent storm. She frowned, and nerves twisted her stomach. She hurried over to the LaPage's cabin. Simon was no longer on the porch. She opened the screen door. The inside door was shut. She reached for the handle and was grateful to feel it turn and to have the door swing open. But the cabin was also dark and quiet.

"Jenna? Mom? Is anyone here?" The bedrooms were empty, as was the kitchen area. There were no signs that anyone had ever been there.

"Where is everyone?" Josie asked aloud, a deep frown furrowing her brow. She went into a panic, thinking maybe she had accidentally gone into the wrong cabin, so she hurried back outside.

Her own cabin was no longer there. There was only the hillside, grass, and rocks protruding from the ground. The other cabins down the hill were gone. She started to spin. The motel rooms at the foot of the hill were not there, and if the office building was still there in the dark distance, she couldn't see it. When she turned back full circle, the other cabins – including the LaPage's cabin – were all gone. She was standing on a bare hillside under the stars.

"Josie."

She heard her name behind her and turned to see a familiar figure, tall and slender with long dark hair like her own, wearing a long dress of soft-looking honey-colored animal hide.

"Mother Elk Spirit! What is going on?"

"It's almost time. I will be calling on you soon," she said.

"When? For what?"

"Josie."

"What?"

"Josie," Mother Elk Spirit repeated.

"What? I can hear you; can't you hear me?"

"Josie!" This time the voice was Jenna's.

Josie blinked. She blinked again. She frowned, confused. The cabins had returned. She was standing before her own cabin, her feet in a muddy puddle. "Jenna?"

6

"Jenna, what's going on?"

"You tell me. I said your name about a dozen times. You looked like a zombie. You were speaking, your mouth was moving, but I couldn't understand what you were saying. Are you okay?"

Josie shook her head, a deep frown furrowing her brow. "I think I was dreaming. Where is everyone?"

"Asleep, hopefully. I was too, but I woke up and the light was on, and you weren't in bed. I went looking for you and found you out here. Did you just sleep-walk?"

"I don't know. I hope not."

"If you weren't sleep-walking, then how did you get out here?"

"I wish I knew."

* * * * *

Josie woke again a few hours later to bright sunlight streaming in the window.

"So, what happened last night?" Jenna asked as Josie sat up.

"No idea. I guess I was sleepwalking, though I've never done that before."

"That you know of," Jenna added.

"True. My new spirit guide – at least I think she's my new guide – was there, in my dream, telling me that she'll be calling for me soon."

"She's very dramatic with her messages!"

"You're not kidding."

"What do you think it means?"

Josie shook her head. "I can't even begin to guess." She groaned and stretched, and finally slid out of bed.

"Daniel will be here in forty-five minutes," Jenna said as they walked into the kitchen.

Josie groaned again. "I hate that you're always perky in the morning." She poured herself a mug of coffee.

"Love you, too," Jenna smiled.

Josie drank half the coffee before her shower and the rest after. Jenna smiled as she watched Josie contemplate her outfit, changing her shorts several times before settling on her black dance shorts and a fuchsia pink athletic tank top, her hair in a high ponytail.

"You are the master of the barely-there make-up," said Jenna as she watched Josie dab on lip gloss.

"I know," Josie smiled proudly.

"I envy it, you know."

Josie looked at her friend. "You have amazing peaches-and-cream skin that needs no make-up. *I* envy *that*."

As they headed outside to get Dave and Simon and meet Daniel, Angela stopped them. "I know you'll be with Daniel, but you all be careful out there."

"We will, Mom," Josie said with a reassuring hug.

Daniel was walking up the hill towards them as they stepped off the porch.

"I'll go get Simon and Dave," Jenna said and hurried away.

"Good morning," Daniel said to Josie with a wave.

"Good morning," she replied.

"How'd you all do with the storm last night?" he asked.

"Fine. I think the power went out for a bit, but I was asleep by then," Josie said.

"Yeah, it happens a lot up here in the mountains, but it doesn't usually last long," replied Daniel. Jenna came bounding back with Dave and Simon behind her. "You guys all ready?"

"Yup! I have a backpack full of water, trail mix, and jerky," said Jenna, twisting to show the bag strapped to her back.

"Me too," said Daniel, showing her his own backpack. "I like the way you think, Jenna."

"Always prepared," she said with a salute. Josie wondered what else she had in that backpack, guessing there was a camera, an audio recorder, an EMF detector, and all the other paranormal equipment she usually had with her "just in case".

"Okay, between the two of us, we should be good for about two weeks if we get lost," said Daniel. "But we won't get lost. I know these woods better than I know my house, and we'll be on trails the whole time."

He led them down the hill and towards the lake. At the far side of the beach there was an opening in a thick clump of small trees and shrubs that was like an archway. Daniel had to duck his head as he went through. Josie followed behind him with Simon close at her heels and Dave and Jenna behind. Once through the initial ten feet of woods, it opened up to a spacious path, and Josie fell into step beside Daniel.

"It isn't weird for you that you can sense spirits?" Josie blurted it out.

Daniel smiled. "No. Should it be?"

Josie shrugged. "I don't know."

"It's just something I grew up with. A soul is an endless thing in a temporary place when it's in the body. So, when the body dies, it doesn't seem so weird to think that it would continue to exist with us, with people they love, to help us, does it?"

"No, I suppose not. Not when you put it that way."

"Our culture has always communicated with spirits. It isn't weird. It's part of our everyday life."

"Yeah, that's not the culture I grew up with."

"You didn't grow up seeing spirits?"

She shook her head. "Only for about a year. I was at summer camp with Jenna, Simon, and Dave. We hiked and whitewater rafted in Maine. During a storm I got thrown from our raft and hit my head on a rock. Ever since then, I've been seeing them."

"Sounds like you're being forced into what was probably already there naturally," Daniel said.

"Maybe. Jenna said something like that. She said that having a head injury, being a Native American, and being a teenage girl was the perfect recipe to enable me to see spirits."

"Sometimes we need something big to wake us up to important things we've been ignoring," he added.

The trail they were on was smooth and flat, something Josie was grateful for, but then at a fork in the path, Daniel turned and went up hill. The trail then narrowed as they climbed, forcing her to walk behind him again, making it harder to talk.

Simon was okay with that. He knew what he wanted finally. He could no longer ignore the fact that he wanted to be with Josie, but he wasn't going to charge into it like a mad bull. Daniel added an extra complication, but he wasn't sure Josie was really into Daniel. Despite the flirting he'd witnessed between them, he couldn't believe it was serious. Not after everything they had been through, after everything she'd said.

The path ascended the hill gently, following the bank of a stream that flowed strongly downhill with rain from the previous night.

"You really don't know anything about our culture?" Daniel said to Josie over his shoulder.

"I know, it's sad, but… I don't know. I just never thought much about it until recently," she replied, her cheeks burning.

"I'm not criticizing," Daniel said. "I'm just curious. Didn't you ever feel a pull to be out in nature, exploring the trees and plants and animals?"

Josie shrugged. "I don't think so. Bugs and dirt? Not really my thing. I've spent more time in nature this past year than ever in my life, and so far, nature does not seem to be my friend."

"Why do you think that?" Daniel asked.

"Remember how I told you this all started for me? That long story I didn't want to tell before? On that camping trip, the river almost got the better of me. I almost drowned. The storm forced us to take shelter in a very haunted house. Then there was Fishkill Pond where, a couple hundred years ago, an angry mob of men ambushed and killed a bunch of women because they thought they were witches. The ghosts of those men tormented me and my friends. Oh, and there was also the jellyfish in the ocean, the sand creatures that attacked us, and the quicksand that almost swallowed Brad."

They came to a part of the trail where it leveled out and then opened into a circular clearing. The stream also leveled out, creating a small pool before moving on down the hill.

Daniel stopped and took off his backpack, searching it for a bottle of water. He handed one to Josie first, then offered water to Simon, Dave, and Jenna, too.

"You're up against a tough case here," Jenna told Daniel, taking a drink of water.

"It can't be that bad," said Daniel. "It sounds like a lot of good came out of all those things: deep friendships and self-discovery. Right?"

Josie looked at Jenna, Dave, and Simon. They might not be such a big part of her life if all those things hadn't happened. "Sure," Josie reluctantly agreed.

"Do you know your animal totem?" Daniel asked, drinking down almost half a water bottle.

"You mean like a spirit guide?" Josie asked.

He nodded. "Yes, an animal that shows itself to you to bring you messages."

"Yes, he's an opossum," she told him.

"That's an interesting totem," he smiled.

"Do you have one?" Jenna asked.

"Of course. Everyone has an animal totem," Daniel replied.

"What is yours?"

Daniel looked at each of them, looked to the sky, and then said, "Do you want to meet him?"

"Um, yeah," said Josie, a furrow of confusion on her brow. She looked at Jenna. "How do we do that?" She was thinking of her friends who didn't see spirits the way she did.

Daniel answered with a wink and a grin. He smiled a lot and she liked that.

He then cupped his hands around his mouth, looking up at the sky above them through the break in the trees, and gave three great, throaty screeches followed by clicking sounds. Then he reached into his back pocket and pulled out a leather glove and pulled it on.

Then there was a screech in reply to Daniel's that echoed in the air above them. They all looked up to see a bird with a thick body and an enormous wingspan silhouetted against the blue sky. It circled in the clearing, spiraling down towards them, closer and closer, until, with a great swoosh of wind, it perched on Daniel's gloved wrist. It fluttered its wings several times before settling.

Josie's jaw dropped at the sight before her.

"This is Achachak. It means 'spirit'. Achachak, these are my new friends: Josie, Jenna, Dave, and Simon."

The bird looked at each of them with large, dark round eyes in his flat white face that was rimmed in a heart shape with caramel-colored feathers. Feathers of the same color and speckled with gray covered his head and his enormous wings. The feathers on his broad chest were pure white all the way down, covering his legs which ended in grayish brown feet with three toes in front and one in back.

"That's an owl," Josie said in awe. She had expected a hawk, not an owl.

"He's a barn owl," Daniel said.

"Can I touch him?" Jenna asked.

Daniel looked into Achachak's eyes and said, "Yes."

Jenna stepped closer and slowly reached a hand up. She stroked the owl's head and back gently, a smile growing and her eyes lighting up. "He's amazing!"

Josie reached her hand toward Achachak, hoping to stroke his feathers, too. But he turned his face to her and nipped at her finger, almost getting her. Josie gasped and jumped back.

"Achachak, be nice to Josie," said Daniel. "I like this girl." He added a wink at Josie.

The owl stretched his head around to the back of his wing and nibbled at himself. He turned his head back with a feather in his white, sharply hooked beak. He leaned towards Josie.

"He's apologizing," said Daniel. "Offering you a gift."

"Really?" Cautiously she reached and took the feather from his beak. She stuck it in her hair just above her ear, and then stroked Achachak's head. "Thank you," she said to the owl.

"I thought animal totems were spirits, not physical animals," said Jenna to Daniel.

"Well, yes and no," he said. He looked at Josie. "Do you only see your opossum in spirit form?"

Josie nodded.

Daniel continued. "Animal totems can come to you in both forms. Because I don't often see spirits, I asked for a physical manifestation."

"Is it always this same owl?" Dave asked.

"It is now. But it wasn't always like that. Achachak's been with me for just about three years now, since just after my mother died. I was upset, so I came out here. I was right in this spot, sitting on that rock over there by the pool, thinking about her. I then asked for Achachak to bring me comfort and come through in a physical representation. A few minutes later I heard a soft thud nearby. I looked and just over there in the leaves was a baby owl. He'd fallen from his nest in the tree up above. I picked him up and held him for a little bit. When I was sure he wasn't hurt, I climbed the tree and put him back in his nest. I came back every day to check to make sure he hadn't fallen again, and as soon as he could fly, he would come down to me and hang out with me. He's been with me ever since."

"That's really cool," said Dave.

"You know, now that I think about it, on the morning we started that summer camp last year, on the way to the YMCA parking lot, my mom and I almost hit an opossum walking across the road. I wonder if that was Hanover," said Josie. She felt a familiar tingle around her neck.

"That was before your accident?" Daniel asked.

"Yes," she replied.

"He was probably trying to let you know that your life was about to change."

The tingle around her neck surged and then eased. She knew what Daniel said was right. "That wasn't a very clear message," Josie scoffed.

"I'm sure you know by now that the spirit world isn't meant to hand us the answers, just to give signposts to help us along the way," said Daniel.

Josie wanted to roll her eyes but refrained. "Boy, do I know that!" she said. Then silently she said, *Hanover, can you manifest for me as a physical creature?*

"I have a question," said Dave, "you said before that everyone has an animal totem, so could I do this? Ask for my animal totem to show up like this?"

"Sure," he said with a shrug. "There's no reason why anyone can't ask for that to happen, but if you're going to do it, I ask that you use caution," said Daniel.

"Why?" Dave asked.

"Well, depending on what your animal totem is, you might not want it to come in physical form."

"How do I find out what my animal totem is?" Dave asked.

"Sometimes you can figure it out on your own. Is there a particular animal that seems to show up in a lot of strange, noticeable ways in your life? Or one that you're just really drawn to? If not, often a talented intuitive – a Medium, a Medicine Man or Woman – can tell you."

Dave frowned in thought. "Hmm. I'm not sure. Do you guys know what mine is?" He looked from Daniel to Josie.

Daniel looked at Josie. "Do you know what his animal is?"

Josie looked at Dave, shrugging, but the knowledge came. "A moose?"

Daniel nodded. "Yes, I agree."

"A moose? Why did you say I should use caution?"

Daniel sighed. He pulled something out of a pouch at his waist that looked like a piece of meat and held it out in the palm of his hand. Achachak leaned down and nipped it with his beak, taking it into his mouth in one swift movement. Daniel leaned in close to Achachak and they locked eyes.

"Meegwech. Manajiwin. Biwabamishinam menawah," said Daniel. Achachak nipped at him, gave a small screech, and rose into the air with several flaps of his enormous wings. He put his glove back in his pocket and turned to Dave. "Despite what you just saw, that was a wild animal. When you call in these creatures in physical form, you are often calling on wild animals. You need to be careful. It's taken me three years to form a bond with Achachak in physical form, and I always treat him with as much respect as I do my own father. What I said to him just now was 'Thank you. Respect. Please come see us again.' It's what I say every time. There's never a guarantee he'll come back, but I do my best to respect and honor him, as I do all the life in this forest.

"Now, Achachak is an owl. He's smaller than me. He can do damage with his claws and beak, but still, he's smaller than me. As is an opossum. They can be nasty when threatened, but humans are bigger. Imagine calling in a moose and having it show up. Even a juvenile moose is two or three times our size. You need to call them in with tremendous caution and always with great respect."

"I don't suppose I could call in my spirit animal," said Jenna with a frown.

Daniel looked at her for a moment. "Dragon?"

Jenna nodded, her smile returning. "How did you know?"

"I'm very connected to the animal world," he replied. Josie was really enjoying the casual, confident way Daniel talked of it all. "And yes, calling in a physical form of a dragon is a little more challenging—"

"A *little* more?" Simon scoffed, slipping back into skeptic mode.

Daniel ignored him. "Your totem is something that lives in alternate realms that our world doesn't quite understand, but that doesn't mean it can't happen. It just might happen in other ways."

"Like how?" asked Jenna.

"You might find a book in your room one day that you've never seen before and it has a dragon on the cover, or you're driving down the road, and a big box truck will drive by with a dragon painted on the side. A dragon figurine could be gifted to you suddenly. There's a number of ways it could show up," said Daniel. He turned and started walking up the trail again. Everyone followed.

"Simon, what's your animal?" Jenna asked as they walked. "Do you know?"

"No," Simon replied, shaking his head. He was trying not to feel dejected. He wanted to give Josie space to discover that Daniel wasn't right for her, but having witnessed him call in an owl, he realized he might be too late, the mountain of a challenge might be too big. He sighed.

"Do you want to know?" Daniel asked.

He didn't want to know. He wanted to surrender, wave the white flag, and go home. And then Josie turned to look back at him, her eyes shining expectantly. "Sure," he said.

"It's a tiger," said Daniel.

"Seriously?" said Dave.

"I will *not* be asking for a real tiger to show up," Simon said.

"Thank you!" said Jenna with a laugh.

"What does it all mean? All these different animals. What's the point?" asked Dave.

"Josie, do you know the answer to that?" Daniel asked.

She was startled to be put on the spot. "Um, well… yeah, I mean, as far as I can tell, from what I've learned so far, each animal represents different characteristics, different personality traits, or brings certain messages. Right?"

"You got it," said Daniel.

"What does a tiger represent?" Simon asked, trying not to sound as doubtful as he was.

"People who have tiger for their totem are usually athletes and healers, they are adventurous, and they are passionate," Daniel replied.

"Simon's going to be pre-med in the fall," said Josie.

"And he was co-captain of the football team and ran track," added Jenna.

"What does a moose represent?" asked Dave.

"Moose would be with someone who's careful with their words and relationships, preferring a few very close people in their life to having a ton of acquaintances. They tend to be teachers, very patient, and have really good intuition."

"That sounds like Dave," said Josie, nodding.

"You're good, Daniel," said Jenna.

"It's not me, really. I didn't assign the characteristics. I'm just passing along the information," he said casually, shooting a smile over his shoulder.

They reached another clearing on the hill, this one giving them a view overlooking the part of the lake that stretched to the village, and they stopped. Snacks were passed around. Boats could be seen moving slowly over the glassy surface of the lake. A few puffy white clouds hung around at the peak of the tallest mountain in the distance where lightning had been dancing the night before.

"The trail curves around here," Daniel said, pointing to his right, "and heads back down the hill."

"Do you know how lucky you are?" Josie said to Daniel.

"What do you mean? I'm very grateful for my life," he said.

"I just mean... talking about the spirit animals and things, it's so easy and natural for you."

"It's how I was raised. It's not better than how you were raised, it's just different," he replied.

"I think it's better. You aren't surprised by these things. I've spent a lot of time thinking I was crazy and with people around me thinking I'm crazy because we don't fully understand this stuff. I don't live in a world where it's normal and accepted. Plus, you still get to talk to your mom. Ever since this happened, I've wondered if I'd be able to see and talk to my birth parents, but...."

Josie didn't notice, but Jenna took Dave by the arm and tugged on Simon. "Let's give them some time to talk," she whispered.

"But—" Simon didn't want to leave Josie alone with him. Her words had cut through him once again. He knew he was one of the people in her life who'd made things difficult, and he was trying to change that, but the more she and Daniel talked, the more he felt her slipping away from him.

But Jenna was strong and stubborn. "No. No buts. Leave them be," she insisted quietly but sternly, dragging him along the path.

Daniel looked at Josie. "I can't imagine how hard it must be. You have a lot of unanswered questions."

She nodded, tears catching and forming a sudden lump in her throat preventing her from speaking.

"I think you need to trust – as hard as it might be – that this is your path. This is how your life is supposed to go. You might not be able to see it, but that's what the spirit world is for. Imagine it like this: We are walking along this trail, and we can see a little way behind us, and we can see a little way in front of us, and we can see where we are right now. But Achachak can go up into the trees, into the sky, and he can see the whole path, from start to finish. And as I walk, if I'm about to step somewhere I shouldn't step, it's his job to come to me and help me find the right way. Does that make sense?" he asked.

Josie swallowed her tears away. "Actually, that makes a *lot* of sense." A comfortable silence fell between them as Daniel bit into a granola bar. Josie watched the boats making small waves as they moved along the lake. Somewhere, Josie heard a screech that she thought might be Achachak.

"Can I ask you something?" Josie said, quietly disturbing the peaceful silence.

"Anything," he said, turning to face her.

"Yesterday you called me something. Kachina… something?"

He smiled. "Kachina Kai."

"What does that mean?"

"It means 'dancing willow tree'." When she frowned, he said, "I thought it fit you because you said you're a dancer, and you're tall like a tree, but there's a… there's a sadness in your eyes, like a weeping willow." He brushed a finger gently down her cheek as spoke.

A happy shiver ran through Josie, and she immediately became self-conscious. She turned to see if her friends were watching and was surprised to find them gone.

"We should probably catch up with everyone else," Josie said, suddenly feeling uncomfortable.

"Okay," he said.

She walked ahead of Daniel, looking for any sign of Jenna, Dave, and Simon down the slope, very aware of Daniel's eyes on her.

"Do you know anything about your birth parents? Their tribe or anything?"

"No," Josie said. "They were killed in a car accident when my mom was almost nine-months pregnant with me. It happened here in New York State, up near the Canadian border, so they think they might have been Cree or Algonquin, but no one came forward to identify them, so I was put up for adoption."

"My mom was Abenaki, which is a tribe of Algonquin," Daniel said. "Dad is from a Mohawk tribe. They're kind of adversaries, or they were at one time I guess, but a lot of that stuff doesn't matter anymore."

"I encountered the spirit of an Abenaki woman in Maine when this stuff started with me," Josie said, surprised at the connection. "She fell in love with a local man – a Honio'on – who ran a logging business with his brother who also fell in in love with her. The brother she didn't love killed her out of jealousy and kind of lost his mind. He killed a lot of other people, too, in his unhappiness. It was a mess."

"That was your first encounter with spirits?"

"That I know of."

"Right. Well, it's no wonder you've had difficulties if that's how it all started."

Josie nodded. "I was completely out of my element. I'd never camped or hiked before that trip. But Jenna and I paired up and became friends quickly. She and Simon and Dave were really helpful to me. They had a lot more experience with that stuff. Simon was the one who pulled me from the river when I hit my head and did CPR. He saved my life."

"And your awakening started," said Daniel. "I've heard of that, where a traumatic experience opens a person to supernatural experiences. But I believe it was something already in you. You just needed something to help you pay attention to it."

"You think so?"

"I believe we are all born with an openness to it all. The difference between you and me is that I was raised in a home where it was natural to talk of it all, to talk to our ancestors and the gods and goddesses. My awareness of it was nurtured throughout my entire life. Yours wasn't. But it was still there."

"Is it something natural just in native people, do you think?"

"No. I think everyone born into this world has the opportunity to be open to it. Your friends and family included."

Josie thought of Simon being an Empath, of his seeing the same ghosts she saw in that house in Maine. She thought of how other people in that house heard and saw things. Christine did, and even Reagan. And she thought of Zara and Gareth, and Romy and the others.

Daniel went on. "Many Honio'on sense the spirits, they just don't know it. Your friend Dave, for example, hears his spirits in his own way, and he trusts them. I can see it in him. It runs deep within him. He might call it instinct; others call it intuition. I call it spirits."

Josie fell into silence as they continued down the hill. She watched and listened for signs of her friends but didn't see them. She walked faster.

"Did I say something wrong?" Daniel asked as he hurried to keep up.

"No. No, you didn't. It's just... a lot to take in." She slowed her steps.

"Sure. Yeah, of course."

Silence fell again. Josie felt something in the pit of her stomach, something in that emptiness, like a ladybug that kept flying into the glass of a window. She didn't like it.

"Can I ask about your mom? What was she like?" Josie said, ignoring the niggling feeling inside her.

"Yeah, she was the best," Daniel said. Josie could hear the smile in his voice. "All she ever wanted in life was to be a mom. Her name, Anna, means 'mother' in the Algonquin language, and that was her. Unfortunately, she was sick when she was a little girl, had some virus and the infection spread to her heart. She recovered but her heart was always weak after that. Doctors didn't think she'd be able to survive having children, but she and my dad had me. It weakened her, but she fought it, she recovered, and for the first thirteen years of my life she was the best mom. They wanted more kids, though, and talked about adopting, actually, but I don't know, I guess it never worked out for them. She was always a mom, though, to everyone she met. Everyone who came here, she treated like family."

"That must have been really nice," said Josie.

"It was. She helped make this place a success. I mean, it was already doing well when my dad took over, but she added a little something extra that our guests loved. And it brings them back year after year. Now my dad and I try to maintain that as best we can."

"You said she had heart problems," Josie said. "Is that why she died? Was it sudden?"

"Yeah, her heart got the best of her. She got the flu which became pneumonia, and it was just too much for her heart. She was sick only a couple weeks and then she was gone."

"I'm really sorry," Josie said, not sure what else to say.

"Thank you. It's hard not having her here with me, to hug her and see her the way I did, but I still talk to her, and I know someday we'll be together again."

"I think that's been one of the best things to come out of all this for me. Knowing that there is an existence of some sort after this life," Josie said.

"Yeah. It gives life a different perspective, doesn't it?" Daniel asked. "Makes some of the ridiculous drama of this world seem like just that… ridiculous."

Josie nodded. "Your dad seems like a really good guy," she said.

"He is. He will never admit how much my mom's death affected him. He just continues to look for the good in everything and everyone around him. He's the strongest person I know."

Josie heard voices up ahead, and coming around a bend in the path, saw Jenna, Simon, and Dave taking a water break.

"Hey, guys!" Jenna said, capping her water bottle and putting it inside her backpack. Josie looked at Jenna with suspicion, but her friend wouldn't meet her eyes. "Do you need a water break? I'm anxious to get back. I'm ready for a swim in the lake!"

* * * * *

They made their way back to the wide lake-side path and back to the resort. When they reached the beach, Daniel said, "I have to go help my dad get ready for the barbecue tonight. See you guys later?"

Josie nodded and Jenna said, "We'll be there."

Daniel ran off with a wave and another smile and wink at Josie. They watched him go and then headed up the hill to their cabins to change into their swimsuits.

When they were alone in their room, Jenna asked, "So, how was it?"

"How was what?" Josie asked, suddenly tired.

"Your time alone with Daniel!"

"You did that on purpose, didn't you? Jenna, you didn't need to do that."

"Maybe not, but I thought it might be easier for you two to talk and… I don't know, get to know each other better if we weren't there, listening and watching."

Josie rolled her eyes.

"So… how was it?" Jenna asked again.

Josie sat on her bed, her bathing suit in her hand. "It was fine."

"Fine? Just fine?"

Shaking her head, Josie said, "It's just that… he's living a life I should have lived. I keep thinking that he has what I would have had if my parents had lived. But they didn't."

Josie shook her head again. The smile fell from Jenna's face.

"Josie…."

"Look, I know I promised complete honesty and transparency and all that, but can I just have some time to think about it all? I need to process everything."

Jenna nodded. "Yeah, sure." She understood, but she was disappointed.

Ten minutes later, Jenna was changed and ready to go but Josie was still sitting on the bed. "Are you coming to the beach?"

"Yeah, go ahead. I'll be down in a few minutes."

"You sure?" Jenna asked cautiously. Josie nodded. "Okay." Jenna frowned as she left. Dave and Simon were walking just ahead of her, so she jogged to catch up.

"Where's Josie?" Dave asked.

Jenna shrugged. "She'll be down soon."

"Is she okay?" asked Simon.

"I guess," said Jenna. Simon stopped and turned to look back at the cabin. "Simon, come on. She's fine."

The annoyance in his sister's voice was the sole reason he turned and continued on, but he wasn't convinced Josie was okay. He couldn't help wondering if something had happened with Daniel earlier. Simon hadn't wanted to leave them alone, and now he wondered if he'd made a big mistake by listening to Jenna.

At the beach, Dave and Jenna ran right into the water. Simon spread the blanket out on an open spot in the sand, then turned to look up the hill at the York's cabin. *What is going on with her?* he wondered to himself.

* * * * *

Josie had finally changed into her swimsuit but was sitting on her bed again, enjoying the peace and solitude, when the cabin door opened with a squeak of protest. She assumed it was Jenna, come to drag her to the beach, but the bedroom door didn't open.

Josie's heart pounded, but she called out, "Hello?" as she moved towards the door.

"Hello? Josie?"

She sighed and relaxed, opening the door. "Hi, Dad," she said.

"What are you doing here? Where's Jenna?"

"She's at the beach. I'm heading down there now," she said.

"Okay." He started to turn away but stopped. "Josie, are you okay?"

"Why does everyone keep asking me that?" Josie snapped. "I'm fine!" She stormed out of the cabin and started down the hill, but tears stung her eyes because all she could think was *What would life have been like with my real parents?*

* * * * *

Simon was relieved when he finally saw Josie. He had waited on the sand for her while Dave and Jenna swam.

"Hey," said Simon.

"Hey," Josie replied. She put her bag down, sat on the blanket, and pulled off her beach cover-up, revealing a bikini with a sunflower pattern on a white background. Simon felt his heart skip and his stomach did a small flip, like he was on a rollercoaster.

"You want to go in the water?" he asked

Josie shook her head, her high ponytail swishing back and forth. "No. You can go in if you want."

He remained sitting next to her. He took a deep breath and closed his eyes and asked himself silently, *What do I feel? What is going on with Josie?*

He breathed slowly and steadily. All he felt was jumpy energy, anxious and agitated. "Josie, are you okay?"

She turned on him, her golden eyes flaring. "Oh… my… god. If one more person asks me that question….!" She grabbed her stuff and stormed off.

7

Jenna and Dave were just coming in from the water as Josie stormed away. "What was that all about?"

"Apparently, she doesn't want anyone to ask her if she's okay," Simon replied, falling back on the blanket and covering his face with his hands.

* * * * *

Jenna followed Josie while Dave sat with Simon.

"What did you do?" Dave asked accusingly.

"I didn't do anything!" Simon replied.

Dave looked at Simon. "Dude, come on."

Simon sat up, his arms resting on his bent knees. "Something's off with her. It's been off for a while. I first noticed it when I saw her at graduation. It was right after she and Jenna got in the fight. I don't know if that's when it started but… I'm worried about her. I didn't like leaving her alone with Daniel, and when she caught up to us… I don't know… I could tell something was wrong. All I did was ask…."

"If she's okay? Yeah, dude, come on. You know how annoying it can be when you're in a bad mood and people keep asking you what's wrong and if you're okay."

Simon groaned. "Ugh, I know. You're right, but I thought…."

"Thought what?"

He grabbed his hair and squeezed his eyes shut before looking at Dave. "I thought maybe I'd show her that I care… like, *really* care, that it might help whatever she's going through."

"You went about *that* the wrong way, eh?" Dave laughed.

"Thanks, Captain Obvious," he growled.

* * * * *

Jenna headed in the same direction as Josie, but she didn't see her. She walked around, checking in the office, the game room, and went all the way back to the cabin but couldn't find her.

Josie had walked in a blind rage and ended up back on the lakeside path in the woods. She walked for a while, fast and angry, until she felt her frustration ease a little. Then she turned around and went back towards the beach but instead of going back to her friends, she took a left turn and went up to the cabin. She was glad to find it empty and the van gone. She looked at her phone and saw that her mom had sent a text message to say that she had gone out with Rachel and the dads were fishing. She sighed with relief. She went into the kitchen and found a kettle and tea bags. She made a cup and went out to the porch and sat. She could just barely see Jenna, Dave, and Simon on the beach, huddled together. *They're probably talking about me,* she thought bitterly.

And what if they are? asked Hanover. He appeared suddenly in front of her, perched on the porch railing.

Josie sighed.

* * * * *

"You couldn't find her?" Simon said, anxiety squeezing his heart.

"No. I looked everywhere, but… she couldn't have gone far, right?" asked Jenna.

"Maybe we should all go look for her," said Simon.

"Do you think she would have gone back into the woods?" asked Jenna.

"Guys," said Dave.

"What?" said brother and sister at the same time.

"She's at the cabin." Dave pointed past them up the hill. They both squinted, just barely able to see Josie's silhouette against the cabin wall.

"But I checked there!"

"Should one of us go talk to her?" Simon asked.

Jenna opened her mouth to speak but Dave jumped in. "No! No. Leave her alone. She obviously wants some space."

* * * * *

Josie felt bad for ignoring her friends, but the time in solitude was worth it. It was all too much. Her brain spun with thoughts she couldn't face, that only screamed louder at her when she was with other people. She needed time to quiet it all, to stuff it down, and close it behind lock and key deep within.

The warm tea helped to settle her mind as she sat there listening to the sounds around her. Birds and bugs chirped and buzzed and danced in the air. She took several deep breaths and felt herself calming.

She didn't know how long she'd been sitting there but her tea was gone, and the sun had swung lower in the sky when saw Jenna, Dave, and Simon heading her way. Apparently, her time was up. She thought back to the day Simon and Dave graduated, and like she did then, she put on her best act. That's all any of this was, anyway. An act. She would act okay. She would act like she wasn't thinking the things she was thinking. Maybe if she acted it well enough, it would become true.

* * * * *

When they went back to the beach later in the evening, it was completely transformed. A fire roared in the fire pit, and all around it tables had been placed, decorated with red, white, and blue tablecloths and centerpieces of glittering patriotic star bouquets. On one end of the beach near the office was a big barbecue grill loaded with burgers, hotdogs, and chicken, and on the other end was a long table set with buckets of ice and filled with drinks, platters of salads and fruit, baskets of fresh baked rolls and chilled dishes of butter, and small bags of potato chips. Strands of white lights were strung between posts and wrapped around the trees.

"Wow, this is... magical," said Angela, her arm linked through Charles's.

"They really know how to throw a party here," said Dave, dragging Jenna towards the food.

Josie had been quiet since they joined her at the cabin, and they were all treading carefully. No one asked her where she was or why she snapped at Simon. No one asked her what was going on or prodded her for any information, which she was very grateful for. She didn't know that they felt like they were walking on eggshells, just waiting for one of them to say the wrong thing that might set her off. She talked a little and laughed with them, but only because she was checking her imaginary script.

The only time Josie's act was almost shaken was when her mom came by their table – the adults were sitting with William and some other guests – and saw a half-eaten burger and untouched piles of potato salad and fruit salad on Josie's plate.

"Josie, you're not eating," Angela said, looking around at the empty plates in front of Simon, Dave, and Jenna. "Are you feeling alright?"

Jenna and Simon braced themselves for an explosion as Josie rolled her eyes and clenched her jaw. "I'm fine, Mom. I'm just not very hungry," she said flatly.

"You sure?" Angela pressed, placing her hand to Josie's forehead.

"I'm fine," she said, pushing Angela's hand away.

Angela forced a smile and said, "Okay, well, you kids have fun," before walking away.

"Are you gonna finish your food?" Dave asked, eyeing Josie's plate. She pushed it towards him, and he grabbed it. He pulled the bun off the top of the half-burger and added more ketchup and relish, then ate it in two bites.

"Sometimes your appetite really grosses me out," Jenna said.

"Come on, Babe. You know it's one of the things you love best about me," he said in between chews, then gave her a crooked smile with a blob of ketchup in the corner of his mouth. Jenna scowled but kissed him, licking the ketchup from his face.

"Eww!" Josie turned away.

Simon shook his head but laughed. "You two are insane."

The daylight faded as the sun dropped closer to the mountain tops. Dinner was cleared away and dessert arrived in the form of an old-fashioned ice cream truck.

William stood near the truck with a megaphone and said, "Ice cream for everyone!"

Dave, Jenna, and Simon stood, while Josie remained sitting. Simon looked at her. "Want anything?"

"No thanks," she replied, avoiding his eyes.

She glanced around, looking for Daniel, and found him clearing used plates and cups from a table on the other side of the beach. Jenna, Dave, and Simon were standing at the end of a long line of people waiting to get ice cream, so she got up and walked to the water, stepping in up to her ankles, then walked along the water's edge towards the boat house. The sun was sinking fast, casting shadows on the lake and lighting the clouds above with a deep shade of orange. The sky above the clouds was purple fading to a pale blue above her head.

When she came to the small dock used for the boats, she walked to the end and sat, her feet dangling in the water. She leaned her head against the post and sighed.

As the first stars twinkled into view, the first fireworks burst in the sky. Josie heard someone walking up the dock behind her but didn't move. She was comfortable and content.

"Is this seat taken?"

Josie looked up at Daniel just as another firework popped and sizzled. "No. Please sit," she replied with another sigh.

He sat next to her on the end of the dock, his legs over the edge and his feet in the water like hers. The water was getting cold, but she didn't care.

"Can I tell you a story?" Daniel asked her as they watched red, gold, and green firework flowers pop.

"Sure," she said. A blue firework popped.

"It's called 'Kanien'kehaka'. It's the creation story of the Mohawks that my dad used to tell me. It goes like this: In the beginning, our world was different from what it is today. It had no land and no people, but there was water as far as the eye could see. High above this was the Sky-World and the people who lived there. They were known as Onkweshona and were similar to humans. In this Sky-World there was a man named Tharonhiawakon and his wife Aientsik who was pregnant.

"In the middle of the Sky-World grew the great Tree of Standing Light. Tharonhiawakon's job was to stop anyone from harming or taking anything from the tree, but Aientsik had a craving for the bark. She begged and begged, and though he knew it was wrong, eventually Tharonhiawakon thought of an idea to give in to her while not harming the tree himself. He dug a hole near the roots of the sacred tree for her. When she came close to the hole in the ground of the Sky-World she saw water below. As Aientsik bent over to get the bark of the roots, she fell through, taking with her some of the roots of the tree. Aientsik fell towards the water below. The water birds saw her falling and caught her on their backs. Then a great turtle came up out of the water, and the birds gently placed her on his back. The woman asked the water animals to bring soil from the bottom so she could plant the roots she had brought from the Sky-World. Many animals died trying but finally the muskrat succeeded, returning from his dive with a crumb of earth in each paw. Aientsik placed the dirt on the middle of the turtle's back and then began to walk in a circle in the direction of the sun. As she walked the earth began to grow.

"She continued to walk and walk and walk. She gave birth to a daughter. Aientsik and her daughter continued to walk and to form Turtle Island. One day the daughter fainted and when she awoke, she found two arrows placed on her chest. She and her mother continued to walk. They knew that she would bear twins. When the twins were born, the right-handed twin was born naturally, the way babies should be born, but the left-handed twin came out of his mother's armpit which killed her. They buried their mother and from her grave they grew corn, beans, and squash. From her heart they made tobacco.

"The grandmother, Aientsik, watched the twins grow into men with powers to create things. The right-handed twin created the plants and medicines that were beautiful and helpful and animals that were harmless. The left-handed twin made thorns and poisons and predatory animals. Soon, the twins were waged in battle against each other and the left-handed twin was killed, his spirit moving to linger within the earth. Aientsik was angry with the right-handed twin. Eventually, he tired of her and cut her head off and threw it towards the Sky-World. The right-handed twin then went to live in the Sky-World where, to this day, he watches humanity fighting amongst each other, under the left-handed twin's influence."

As his story ended, the finale of the fireworks lit the sky in a rainbow of colors and dozens of deafening explosions. When it was over, everyone on the beach clapped.

Josie looked at Daniel and said, "That was a really weird story."

He laughed.

* * * * *

Simon stood near the boathouse watching Josie and Daniel. She laughed at something, looking happy. Maybe he had it wrong, maybe Daniel hadn't upset her. Maybe it was him she had a problem with.

He turned and walked away.

* * * * *

Josie climbed into bed and lay back with a sigh. Her performance was over for the day and now she could rest.

When Jenna came into the room she said, "Hey, Josie?"

"Yeah?"

"No sleepwalking tonight, okay?"

"I'll do my best."

* * * * *

Fireworks burst overhead in the inky black sky, blotting out the stars. They showered down in sparks of red, green, blue, gold, silver, purple; they spiraled and whirred and sizzled; they popped and banged.

Josie sat on the end of the dock, watching the show, the fireworks so close and bright that she could feel the heat from them on her upturned face.

"Josie," she heard, and turned to see Daniel at her side.

"Hi," she replied.

"Can I tell you a story?"

"Sure," she replied.

"There once was this girl who was an orphan. She got adopted by a family that was nice, but never really loved her like their own child who had died. So, she left home and went in search of her birth parents. She walked and walked and walked until she gave birth to twins. The twins fought all the time, and they cut a hole in the sky and pushed her through. She fell up into the sky and burst into thousands of sparks and died, and everyone clapped for joy."

Josie frowned at Daniel. "I don't think I like that story."

"Why not? It's about you!" He replied, laughing.

Tears sprang to her eyes. "Why are you laughing at me?" She stood and tried to move, but realized her feet were still in the lake, and when she looked down, she saw that the lake was completely frozen over, and her feet were encased in ice past her ankles.

"Josie, what are you doing?"

Daniel was no longer on the dock. Now, Jenna was there.

"Josie, what are you doing?"

"What do you mean? Help me!"

"Josie, you need to run!" said Jenna.

"Why?"

"Josie, run! Run! Run!" Jenna pointed behind Josie and then fled up the dock and out of sight. Josie turned to see a giant muskrat charging towards her. Josie tried to move but, struggled, the skin of her ankles being sliced up by the ice, the cold stinging in the heat of the wounds. The animal barreled towards her across the ice, its claws ripping at the ice, nearly at her. She crouched down, covering her head with her arms in an attempt to protect herself. Then she heard a crack like a gunshot, and the ice beneath her gave way.

She slipped under the water and was enveloped in cold blackness. Josie flailed and kicked, hoping to touch something – the dock, the lake bottom – but she was surrounded by nothingness. Icey water filled her mouth and nose and lungs, her heart pounded loud and slow in her ears. The cold started to overcome her, immobilizing her entire body. It was almost over, she knew, and so she started to give up.

Then she felt a hand on her arm, felt herself being pulled upward. She broke the surface and kept rising, but only for a second. Then, she was looking down at herself lying lifeless on the beach. Fireworks were still lighting the sky, illuminating Jenna, Simon, Angela, and Charles standing over her body.

"I'm sorry," Simon said, his voice far away, echoing. "I didn't get to her in time. I couldn't save her."

"That's okay," said Charles. "It's not like she was really our daughter. We'll just get another one."

Josie gasped, pulling a great gulp of air into her lungs, and found herself sitting up in bed. She panted, grasped at her chest, and looked around her. She could see the lump of Jenna in her bed, breathing deeply and sleeping soundly. Pale light of dawn was just starting to show through the open window. A soft breeze caused the pine trees outside to sway gently.

Josie laid back down, pulled the sheet and thin cotton blanket up to her neck, pulled her knees to her chest, and cried silently.

8

"York, party of eight!"

"Thank god, I'm starving!" said Dave.

"You're always starving," said Rachel.

They followed the hostess to a set of square tables pushed into one big rectangle at the back of the restaurant. The aromas of coffee and bacon surrounded them. The hostess handed them each a menu as they sat.

"Dave, look! It's your animal totem," Josie teased, looking at the menu cover image of a cartoon moose sitting at a table full of food, the words "The Hungry Moose" in bubble letters.

"That's a pretty funny coincidence," Dave said.

"I don't believe in coincidences," said Jenna.

A waitress appeared with a pot of coffee in each hand, filling cups around the table. "My name is Mallory and I'll be taking care of you all this morning," she said with a bright smile, a stray clump of mousy brown hair falling from her messy bun across her striking hazel eyes. "And I'll be back in a few to take your orders."

"You know," Dave started, "I just remembered that my grandpa had a moose head hanging in the garage when I was a kid, and I was obsessed with it. I would go out to the garage no matter how cold it was and talk to it. You think it's cuz I knew it was my animal totem?"

"Probably," said Josie.

"Can we keep the ghost talk out of the restaurant, please?" Charles growled.

"We aren't talking ghosts, we're talking—"

"I'm not stupid, Josie. I know what animal totems are. And I'm asking you all to leave it alone. At least for this one meal." His tone was mostly calm and level but somehow it dripped with the threat of anger.

"Sorry, Dad," said Josie, heat flushing her cheeks.

"Yeah. Sorry, Mr. York," said Dave.

"Sorry," said Jenna.

Mallory returned and moved around the table to take their orders. Josie ordered herself a tomato and spinach egg white omelet and an English muffin, then added cream and sugar to her coffee, and took a sip, sighing with pleasure, the warmth thawing her stomach from the chill of her father's words. Plus, she was exhausted. After waking from the nightmare, she tossed and turned without sleeping until Jenna got up and went for her run. She was so tired that she didn't notice Hanover tingling into position around her neck until he said in her ear, *There is something you need to do here.*

You've got to be kidding me, Josie replied.

And then she saw her. She was sitting alone at a vacant two-person table against the wall within Josie's view. Her hair was silver and done in a short, curled style. She smiled at Josie from a plump face, her thin lips painted a shade of raspberry, her eyes crinkling behind large, octagonal-shaped plastic-framed glasses.

Didn't you hear my dad just now? I can't do this! And how did she know I'd be here? Josie asked.

She assumed Hanover would respond, but instead she heard a crackly, feminine voice. *You, my dear, are a shining beacon of light in a very drab existence.*

Not likely, Josie scoffed.

She's not trying to flatter you, said Hanover. *That is how you seem to her.*

Seriously?

Hanover huffed and a wave of tingles went from her shoulders right up her neck to her scalp as though he'd ruffled his fur. *Fine. You don't have to help her. It's a choice. But just know that if you choose not to help her, it may be years before someone else comes in here who can help her.*

Josie sighed. She could feel the woman's eyes on her, but was unaware Simon was also watching her. He could feel a war going on inside Josie, but he didn't dare speak up and say anything.

Then, Josie leaned in, catching the eyes of her friends. "Guys, I don't know what to do," she whispered. Jenna, Simon, and Dave leaned in closer. "There's someone here that needs my help."

"Wait… really? Here?" Jenna said, an excited smile on her face as she looked around, hoping to see signs of the spirit.

"Yes, and I don't know what to do. It's really crowded here. Plus… my dad…."

"Why here of all places?" Dave asked.

Josie shrugged and looked at the woman. *Why are you here in this restaurant?* The hostess of the restaurant blocked Josie's view as she escorted a young couple to the table the ghost-woman sat at. When she moved, the old woman was gone. *Where did you go?*

Their waitress appeared with a tray of glasses filled with orange juice that she placed in front of each of them. "Your food should be ready shortly," she said with a smile. The ghost-woman reappeared behind Mallory just as she walked away, and Josie knew the answer instantly.

"Her granddaughter is our waitress," Josie moaned.

"Ah," said Jenna. "Where is she?"

"Almost directly behind Simon now."

Simon glanced over his shoulder, half-expecting to see her standing there.

He's cute, the ghost-woman said, smiling at Josie. *Is he your boyfriend?*

No.

He should be, she smiled and patted Simon's cheek with a chubby hand decorated with glittering rings on each finger.

Simon reached up and scratched his cheek. Josie chuckled. "What?" he asked her.

"She thinks you're cute," Josie told him with a more genuine smile than he'd seen from her in days.

Simon smiled back, meeting Josie's eyes. "Tell her thanks, but my heart is taken."

His words shook Josie, but she held his gaze. His eyes, always a bright blue, had a different intensity to them, almost like an internal glow. She wondered if it was just the lighting in the restaurant or if it was something else.

Aw, honey, if you don't snatch him up, I think I'll find a way to reincarnate as a gorgeous girl and steal him away! The ghost-woman threw her head back and let out a cackling laugh. Josie relaxed and smiled.

"What did she say?" Jenna asked.

Josie shook her head. "Nothing important," she replied, meeting Simon's eyes again and looking quickly away. "What am I going to do? How can I do this here, now, in the middle of a crowded restaurant? My dad is going to flip!"

"What are you kids whispering about over there?" Greg asked teasingly, leaning towards Jenna. "You've got some secrets going on over there."

Josie's face flushed.

"Josie," said Angela. "What's going on?"

Josie shook her head.

Angela raised her eyebrows at her daughter. Charles kept his eyes on his coffee cup.

Suddenly, Josie was angry. She was angry and she was tired of it all. She looked from her mom to her dad, raised her chin defiantly, and said, "There's someone here who needs my help."

Angela's eyes widened. "By 'someone', do you mean…?"

"Yes, Mom. I mean, a ghost."

"Oh, okay, well… um…." Angela hesitated.

Charles's hand slammed down on the table. Coffee cups clanged in their saucers, spoons rattled, and orange juice splashed out of their glasses. "For Christ's sake, Josie, what did I just say? Do you hate me so much now?"

Oh, he's a feisty one, isn't he? said the ghost-woman, suddenly standing behind Josie. *What's his problem?*

"She wants to know what your problem is, Dad," Josie said, standing firm.

Charles's fists clenched, and his face flushed. "My problem is that we're on vacation, and I thought we could have one meal in relative normalcy."

Josie frowned. "What does that even mean? What is normal? Do you think I'm doing this on purpose? Do you think I *asked* for this to happen here? Now? Oh, wait. No, you think I'm making this all up, don't you?"

The diners around them hushed and glanced in their direction. Josie didn't notice or care.

"You're making a scene," Charles growled through clenched teeth.

"Oh, I'm sorry. Are you afraid that people are going to overhear the fact that your insane daughter thinks she can talk to dead people?"

"That's enough!" Charles shouted, standing so quickly that his chair slid backwards and knocked into a busboy who went crashing forward on top of his bin of dirty dishes. Charles turned and stormed out of the restaurant.

Josie rushed over to help the busboy up. "I'm sorry," she said to him, tears stinging her eyes. Then she turned and walked quickly towards the back of the restaurant. She went to the hallway that had a sign overhead labeled "Restrooms", but when she found the door to the ladies' room locked, she went out the door with an emergency exit sticker on it, thankful when an alarm didn't sound.

Outside it was warm and sunny. She hurried past the dumpsters, her nose stinging from the stench, and sat on a low cement wall. At her feet was a litter of crushed cigarette butts.

Back inside, as the voices around them started to ripple in distracted conversations, Simon and Angela both stood and looked at each other. Simon said, “Let me go to Josie. Please.”

“Okay,” replied Angela with a sigh. “I’ll go after Charles.”

He strode quickly through the back hall, past the bathrooms and storage closet, and out the back door. He saw her sitting on the wall, her head hanging, her straight dark hair covering her face.

She only looked up when his shadow fell across her. He was surprised that she wasn’t crying, and he was even more surprised when she threw herself at him, wrapping her arms around him and burying her face in his neck.

He held her close and tight, feeling her body release the tears she’d been holding on to. He felt them, warm and wet, falling on his neck. He stroked her hair, trying to think of something to say, but words failed him. Instead, he remained silent and waited, taking in the feeling of her pressed up against him, of her hands on his back, her fingers curling and clawing at his shirt as she gripped him tighter. He held on. He wouldn’t let go, afraid she might crumble if he did.

“I’m sorry, Simon,” Josie sniffled into his chest.

“What are you sorry for? You didn’t do anything wrong,” he said, pressing his cheek to the top of her head.

“I yelled at you yesterday. You were just being nice. I’m really sorry,” she said with more sniffles.

He chuckled, pulling her closer. “I’d forgotten all about that.”

“I’m just so tired… all the time… I’m so tired of being scared and confused and angry…. It never seems to end.”

“It will get better, Josie. It will. I promise. You have Jenna and Dave and me to help you when you’re tired. You can yell at me all you want, if it helps. I can take it.” He kissed the top of her head.

Angela tried to make her footsteps obvious as she walked around the back of the restaurant to where her daughter was being held by a – in her opinion – too-attractive young man. His constant presence in Josie's life made her anxious. Her daughter was going through enough without having her heart torn to shreds by his blue eyes.

As the gravel crunched under her feet, Simon finally looked up. When he saw Angela, he released Josie and stepped back. "Simon, can I please talk to Josie?"

"Of course," he replied. He whispered something to Josie who nodded, unable to look at him, wiping the tears from her cheeks that hadn't soaked into his t-shirt, and he headed back inside.

"Let's sit," Angela said. They both sat on the low stone wall. "We can't go on like this, Josie."

"What was I supposed to do? You wanted honesty."

"You baited your father."

"I didn't—"

"Yes, you did, and you know it." Angela sighed. "I get it, Josie. I really do. You're angry and confused and scared."

Josie looked at her mom with a scowl. "So?"

"Well, so is your dad."

Josie rolled her eyes.

"I know you think right now that he doesn't love you, that he isn't… maybe the father he should be, but Josie, let me tell you something. If any of that were true, he wouldn't get so upset. He is so affected by all this, so afraid for you, because he loves you so much. Not because he doesn't love you. He is afraid of losing you to something he doesn't understand, something he can't even begin to know how to protect you from. That's really scary for a parent."

"Mom," Josie started, shaking her head.

"Josie, I'm telling you the truth," Angela said, her voice cracking, tears releasing. "He's not trying to hurt you. He wants so badly to keep you from being hurt. He's not doing it the right way, but he's trying. Someday, when you're a parent, you'll understand… how hard it is to love someone like this, to do everything in your power to protect them, and to then see them in situations that are out of your control. Josie, there's no fear like it in the world. There are no words to describe it."

Angela let her words sink in.

"I didn't realize," said Josie.

"That's why I'm telling you," Angela replied. "Come on. Our food is probably getting cold." She put an arm around Josie.

"Is dad inside?"

"No. He was too embarrassed. He's taking a taxi back to the resort to cool off."

"I'm sorry, Mom," Josie said, hugging her.

"It will get better, Josie," she replied, echoing Simon's earlier words.

Josie ignored the heads turning to stare at her as she went back to her seat. Her omelet was cold, but she picked at it. At least the coffee was constantly refreshed and hot.

Mallory's grandmother was again sitting at an empty table, her hands folded in her plump lap, patiently watching Josie.

What do you want? Josie asked her. She was hoping she could help her without anyone knowing, without having to talk to anyone.

I need to talk to my granddaughter, she replied.

Josie sighed. *Of course you do.*

Mallory approached the table then. "How's everyone doing? Can I get anyone anything else this morning?" She topped off coffee cups as everyone shook their head or said 'no'.

"Just the check," Greg said.

"Alright," she smiled. As she refilled Josie's coffee cup she said in a low voice, "I heard what you said before. Can you really talk to dead people?"

Josie could tell from her tone that she was intrigued and curious, not judgmental. "Um, yeah," Josie replied.

"That's so cool," she replied. "I've always wanted to get a reading done. There's a woman in the village that does palm readings and Tarot cards, but I've never had the guts to actually go see her."

Mallory refilled Jenna's coffee cup slowly. Josie braced herself and asked, "Do you have a minute to talk about that? Maybe a break coming up or something?"

"To talk about the palm reader in the village?" Mallory asked.

"No," said Josie. "To talk about your grandmother, Maxine."

Mallory's eyes widened, and her face went pale.

It's okay, sweetie, Maxine said to Josie. *I knew this would shock her a little.*

Mallory grabbed at another waitress as she passed by, handing her the coffee pot. "Tell Phil I'm taking my fifteen, please?" She reached to steady herself on a chair.

Simon hopped up and said, "Here, sit," gently guiding her into the seat. He then took Charles's abandoned seat.

"Is she really here?" Mallory asked.

"You're named after her, right? Your middle name is Maxine, right?"

Mallory nodded.

"You have her eyes," Josie said, looking from the spirit to the young woman. "And she raised you. She was more like a mom to you than a grandmother, and you called her 'Mama Maxi'."

"How do you know that?" Mallory said, her voice a hoarse whisper, thick with tears.

"Because she's telling me this. She's standing right behind you," Josie replied, keeping her voice low, although she could tell that people around them were watching and listening. She couldn't worry about that though.

"Is she… is she okay?"

Josie nodded. "She wants you to know that she's sorry for what she put you through at the end. Do you know what she means by that?"

Mallory nodded. "She had Alzheimer's. Towards the end, she got really nasty. She didn't know me most of the time, and she'd yell at me and push me and throw things at me. But I knew it wasn't really her, that she couldn't control it." She grabbed a napkin from the dispenser in the middle of the table and pressed it to her face, dabbing at her tears.

"She's also saying that you sacrificed everything to stay with her and take care of her. But now that she's gone, she wants you to take care of yourself. Follow your dreams," Josie said.

She's wasting away in this job, Maxine said.

"She is saying that you wanted to be a chef and own your own restaurant. Is that right?"

Mallory nodded again. "I was accepted to a culinary school in New York City, but then she got sick."

"She wants you to apply again. She's saying that because of your circumstances, you'll be accepted, and you will be able to find financial assistance through the school."

"Why is she saying this?" Mallory asked.

Josie listened as Maxine answered her granddaughter's question, then Josie said, "She wants you to have the opportunities that she never had. Fear held her back, and she doesn't want you to be afraid of what might happen. She wants you to chase your dreams, focus on the good things that could happen for you, of all the wonderful things that could happen in your life. And she wants you to take that first step and go to school."

"Really?"

"Yes, but she says that you need to apply right away. If you apply right away, you'll be able to start in the fall. It's not normal, but she says that it will work that way if you do as she says."

"Okay," Mallory said, nodding again. "I'll do it."

Is there anything else you need to tell her? Josie asked Maxine.

"She's almost ready to go, but she wants you to know that she is so proud of you. She wants you to know that you are stronger than you think, and she said that you need to let go of any guilt associated with your mother, because you were put on this planet for her, Maxine, not for your mom. Does that make sense?"

Mallory nodded, burying her face in more napkins.

Josie watched then as Maxine faded away in a swirl of silvery-blue sparkles.

"She's gone," Josie said softly.

Mallory nodded again, then crumpled the napkins up. She was still crying but she was also smiling. "Thank you so much. You have no idea how much that means to me. What she just said… I always blamed myself for my mother's situation, like it was my fault she couldn't cope with being a parent. Mama Maxi was the best mom, though. Hearing her say that… well, it's really freeing, and, well, there just aren't words enough to express my gratitude." She stood, wiping her face once more with the crumpled napkins. "Thank you so much."

"Wow, Josie," said Rachel. "That's the first time I've seen you do that. That was remarkable." Rachel exchanged a smile with Angela, who turned proud eyes on her daughter.

"Good job," Angela said.

Mallory came back then and said, "Your breakfast is on the house."

"What? No, you don't have to do that," said Angela.

"Really, it's my pleasure. I'm so grateful to you," she said.

"We wish you very good luck with your future," said Greg, handing her a generous tip.

"Thank you. Thank you all," she said.

"This stuff never ceases to amaze me," Jenna said to Josie as they all crossed the parking lot. "Do you realize you may have just changed that girl's life?"

Josie shook her head. "I didn't do anything. It was her grandmother."

"But her grandmother couldn't have helped her without you. That's huge!" Jenna insisted.

"Really, it's not a big deal. I'm just the messenger."

Greg opened the side van door and said, "Your humbleness will take you far in life, Josie."

Josie smiled at him, then looked at Jenna. "I see you get the wise-sage quality from your dad."

She climbed in the van, sliding across the middle bench seat to the window. Simon sat next to her while Jenna and Dave took the row behind them.

Josie leaned her head on the glass of the window, cool despite the morning's heat. It felt good. She was exhausted. It felt like it had been days since she woke from that nightmare. So much had happened since.

Her skin tingled with the awareness of Simon sitting so close by, of his hand resting on the seat so close to her bare leg. Her mind jumped back to the parking lot of the restaurant. She hadn't expected him to be the one to follow her out. She thought it would be her mom or Jenna, but it had been Simon to come to her first and her heart had soared.

She closed her eyes and went back to the moment when she went to him and he held her and comforted her, her face buried in his neck. She could remember the smell of his skin, a mix of soap and something she couldn't place but that was distinctly him. She could hear his heart beating in his chest, feel the heat of his entire torso pressed against her, and the strength of the muscles of his back as she clung to him, doing her best to hang on. She remembered feeling his arms tighten around her in that moment, and she had known that if she had let go, if she had given up and just fallen apart, that he would have held her together.

And then she remembered something he said at breakfast, before that moment, before the thing with her dad, when she told him that Maxine thought he was cute, he had said, "Tell her thanks, but my heart is taken." Had he said that just to put off a flirting old-lady spirit? Or had he meant it? And if he meant it, who was he talking about? Who had taken his heart? The idea that it might be her niggled at the edges of her mind, reminding her of all the little things he'd done over the past few days, the extra attention he'd been paying her. Was he just being nice, or was it a sign that he was feeling something more?

Then Daniel jumped into her mind. Was he the reason Simon was acting differently? Was Simon only expressing interest in her because Daniel was also? She also wanted to know if Daniel was interested in her only as a fling, a temporary bit of entertainment in an ever-changing landscape for him, or if it was something more. They would be leaving on Saturday, giving her only four more days to find out, but did it really matter since they lived so far away?

Josie hadn't realized she'd started to doze off until the buzzing of her phone in the back pocket of her shorts woke her. She shifted in her seat and reached for her phone, her arm brushing against Simon's.

The buzzing was a notification of a stream of text messages from Romy. She was checking in, asking how Josie's vacation was, and sharing a dream she had the night before about a house-fire that killed four people that she helped cross over. She also sent a link to the news article about a house that had burnt down that night and killed four people just outside of Boston.

Josie was texting a response when she heard Rachel say, "This doesn't look like the right street, Angela."

"I don't know!" Angela responded tensely. "You're right, I think. I guess I wasn't paying attention."

"Mom, how did you get us lost? Weren't you using the GPS?" Josie asked.

"You know I don't like those things. I thought I knew where I was going, but I guess not," Angela replied, laughing at herself. "Hold on, I see a place up here where I can turn around."

She pulled over into an overgrown dirt lot, and then Jenna yelled, "Stop!" from the back of the van.

Angela slammed on the brakes and said, "What's the matter?"

"Where… in the world… are we?" Jenna gaped and stared out the window.

9

"What is this place?" Josie asked, her voice barely a whisper.

They all gawked out the van windows at the sight before them.

Angela turned the engine off and got out, followed by Greg and Rachel. When Jenna and Dave climbed out, Simon looked at Josie and said, "You want to go have a closer look?"

"Sure," she said, unable to tear her eyes from the sight outside. She stuffed her phone back in her pocket, the unfinished text to Romy forgotten, and followed Simon out into the heat.

Angela had pulled the van over into what looked at first like just a pull-off on the side of the road, but it opened into a wide expanse of dirt. A once-white picket fence, peeling and splintered and missing boards in many places, separated the parking area from an overgrown grassy field at the base of a tall hill. The only way in was under a wide arch formed by two telephone poles with a faded sign on top that read "Mystery Mountain" in bubble block lettering outlined with long dead and broken neon tubes.

"Oh, look at the house over there!" said Rachel.

On the opposite side of the road was a small white farmhouse. A "For Sale" sign stood by the front walk, looking almost as old and ignored as the rest of the place.

Rachel, Greg, and Angela walked across the street to the house while Jenna, Dave, Simon, and Josie stared at the bizarre scene before them. Beyond the archway, scattered through the field, were the remains of a forgotten tourist trap. A huge geodesic dome, its yellow paint peeling away in large chunks, gleamed strangely in the sun and dominated the landscape. It looked odd, futuristic yet dated at the same time, a man-made pimple on the natural terrain. Further beyond was something that looked like a caricature of a house, eerily similar to the one they encountered in the woods of Maine but with crooked angles and odd-sized features; a Halloween-style ghost looked out from one warped window and a faded sign over the door read "Enter at Your Own Risk". The decrepit, broken siding was a dull, moldy brown, probably weathered on purpose at one time and now was even worse for its neglected state. Just beyond that, what looked like the skeletal remains of a ski lift scarred the face of the hill and not far from there, in the shadow of the hill, was a small Ferris wheel, missing half of its seats and completely entwined by a tree and creeping, choking vines, looking as though they had all grown from the ground together. Near the front of the field, a ghastly sight stood: a merry-go-round that had no horses, but instead carried creatures of all kinds now frozen in their journey; a unicorn, a sea serpent, a phoenix, a werewolf, and others, silent and motionless.

Jenna took out her phone and said, "There's no signal here! How is that possible?"

"It's to keep it a mystery, probably," said Dave.

Jenna rolled her eyes at him, turned to Simon and Josie, and went to them. "What do you think of this place?"

"Looks like a closed-down amusement park of some sort," said Simon.

"Josie?" said Jenna.

"I…." Her stomach had what felt like a flock of geese trying to get out. Her cheeks filled with saliva, and she pursed her lips together and swallowed hard. She took slow, deep breaths, but a cold sweat broke out on her forehead and the hairs on the back of her neck stood up as though a crisp winter breeze had blown by, impossible in the 85-degree weather.

Simon frowned at her. "Josie?"

"I think I'm going to be sick," she said, bending down, her hands pressed to her knees. She braced herself and continued to breathe, slowly and deeply. She squeezed her eyes shut and focused on feeling the rough dirt and gravel beneath the thin rubber soles of her flip flops, hearing the buzz of bugs and the chirp of the crickets in the overgrown grass, smelling the heat and the earth and exhaust from the van. Finally, her stomach calmed, and she straightened, thankful that the moment passed.

Dave, Jenna, and Simon were looking at her expectantly. "I think I'm okay," she told them.

"You sure? You wanna sit in the van for a minute?" Simon asked.

"No," she replied, keeping her breaths slow. She looked at the scene before her. "Guys, something's here. Watching us."

"What do you mean 'something'?" asked Jenna. "Ghosts?"

Josie shook her head. "Maybe. I don't know. I can't see anything," she said, searching for faces, figures, eyes, or anything else anomalous among the already-strange scene but she saw nothing. "I just feel it. But it feels… different. I don't know how to explain it."

Josie took a few slow, careful steps forward, towards the fence, towards the arched entrance with its gaudy sign. She could see evidence of pathways, some disappearing into the overgrown shrubs and grass. Maybe there had been other buildings there at one time.

"Josie, I don't like this place," Simon said from close behind her, quietly, as though he didn't want *it* to hear him.

"This place is amazing," Jenna said, coming up next to them and standing at the entrance. She started taking pictures with her phone. "As soon as we find cell service, I'm looking this place up.

"Come on, guys," shouted Angela from behind them. "Let's get going."

They all hesitated for a moment before finally retreating to the van. Josie couldn't tear her eyes away from the place as her mom drove away, back the way they came.

* * * * *

Angela pulled to a stop in the driveway between the cabins. Josie could see her dad sitting on the front porch, his face gloomy.

Angela was at the side door of the van when Josie stepped out. She knew what was coming. "You, your father, and I need to talk," she said, then looked at the rest of them. "Will you guys give us a few minutes?"

"Sure," said Rachel, and they all moved off towards the other cabin.

Josie walked behind her mom to the porch.

"Charles… inside. Now."

Josie threw herself onto the couch, an old, orange thing with worn-soft fabric and springs that made popping noises when she sat. Charles took a chair from the small dining table and Angela remained standing.

"You two have got me at the end of my rope," said Angela. "I can't do this anymore. We are on vacation. A *family* vacation with our very good friends, who, right now, are more of a joy to be around than the two of you. And I've been killing myself trying to figure out how to fix this. But I'm done. I can't do it. This isn't mine to fix. This is between the two of you, so now it's time for you both to figure out how to fix it.

"To start, you both need to apologize to each other for your behavior this morning."

Angela shot a look at both of them that sent fear into Josie's heart. It wasn't a side of Angela that often showed, so when it came out, they knew to take her seriously.

"I'll apologize for egging him on, but I won't apologize for what I had to do. I can't control it. I didn't want my vacation interrupted by this woman, but it was. And I couldn't *not* help her."

"And you did help her. You helped her granddaughter, and it was truly amazing to watch," conceded Angela. "Charles, I really wish you had been there to see it."

"Was that an apology? Because I didn't really hear one in there," he said, glowering.

"Charles, you'd think *you* were the teenager," Angela admonished.

"Dad, I'm sorry for what I said, for being rude and impertinent," Josie said, mustering as much sincerity as she could in her state of complete exhaustion.

Angela gave Josie a smile and then looked at Charles expectantly.

"Josie, I'm sorry for… how I reacted."

"Good. Now the two of you can figure out the rest on your own. Rachel and I are going shopping, and I don't want to hear one word about how much money I spend," said Angela. She spun on her heel and walked out of the room, the screen door banging behind her.

Josie looked at her toes, waiting for her dad to speak. Somewhere she heard something ticking, like a clock, though she couldn't see one anywhere. Outside she could hear the muffled voices of Angela, Rachel, Jenna, and Dave. Then she heard the van's engine rumble to life again and the crunch of the gravel under the tires as it drove away.

Finally, she stood up. "You know what, Dad, it's okay. We can tell Mom we've fixed it and just pretend it's true until I can get myself out of your hair for good. Okay?"

She didn't give him a chance to respond, but he didn't try to stop her when she walked out.

* * * * *

"Dave and I are going to take a canoe out," said Jenna. "You don't mind, do you?"

"Of course not. As long as you don't mind if I nap on the beach," Josie replied.

They caught up to Dave and Simon. Dave and Jenna veered left to the boathouse while Josie and Simon went straight to the beach. She scouted a clear spot on the sand, not too close to the family with several small, noisy children.

As she spread the blanket out, Simon said, "You know, I wouldn't mind taking a canoe out too, if you want."

She shook her head. "I'm kinda worn out from earlier. I think I'd rather just lay here. You can go if you want."

"No, that's okay. I'll stay here," he said, and sat next to her.

She lay down and put her earbuds in, setting a playlist that was not too happy but not depressing either and she closed her eyes. She focused only on the heat of the sun on her skin and the melodies of the music in her ears. She didn't want to think about anything else at that moment. Not Simon, not her mom or dad, not Mallory, and not Mystery Mountain.

It seemed to be working. She wasn't sure if she dozed or not, but she didn't know how much time might have passed when a shadow darkened her closed eyelids. She blinked her eyes open, expecting to see Jenna or Dave. Instead, Daniel loomed over her.

She pulled her earbuds out and sat up. "Hi," she said, her heart giving a small leap of excitement at seeing him.

"Hey, sorry to bother you," he said.

"You're not bothering me," she replied.

"Good. So, I have a couple hours off, and was wondering if you and I could hang out for a bit?"

"Sure, yeah," she said, then looked at Simon. "You don't mind, do you?"

Yes! Don't go! he wanted to say. "No," he said. "Why would I mind?"

He watched her pull on her beach coverup and walk away, side by side with Daniel, suddenly looking revived and happy. *That's okay,* he told himself. *I was the one holding her this morning. I was the one who comforted her and was there for her when she needed someone. Not him.*

He tried to tell himself that it didn't bother him, her going off with Daniel. He knew Josie was going through something, and she needed to figure it out. He was okay with that. He had felt the turmoil in her that morning at the diner as he held her. He could still feel her skin, exposed by her small tank top, so soft and warm under his hands. He remembered the smell of her hair, a light coconut scent with a trace of vanilla. Physically she was intoxicating. Emotionally, he had felt how fragile and drained she was. When her dad got mad, he felt the energy leave her, he felt the cracks in her shell. He wanted to help her, but he knew enough to know that he had to be careful. He didn't want to push her because that might only push her away.

So, he tried not to mind her spending time with Daniel for now.

When he looked up, he saw Josie sitting in a canoe with Daniel paddling and realized it would be harder than he thought to manage his jealousy.

* * * * *

"Can I take you out on the lake?" Daniel asked Josie as they walked towards the boat house.

"I don't know," Josie replied, shaking her head with reluctance.

"I promise it's very safe. I know this lake like I know the woods and everywhere around here. I'll take very good care of you," he said.

"You won't tip us over?" she asked.

"Josie, I'm not ten," he said with a mocking laugh.

"Sorry, I just… water makes me nervous."

"That's okay. I get it. But you can trust me."

She looked at him, her eyes searching him.

"Okay?" he asked.

"Okay," she nodded.

He effortlessly put a rowboat in the water at the edge of the dock. He stepped in and held out a hand to help her into the boat.

When she sat, he handed her a padded life jacket which she put around her neck with a sheepish smile.

The afternoon was warm, the air was quiet except for the usual birds and bugs and the lap of the oars as Daniel rowed them away from the dock. "I'm sorry if I upset you yesterday," Daniel said, breaking the silence.

"You didn't upset me, you've just given me a lot to think about," she replied.

"Like what?"

"Like, what my life could have been like if my birth parents hadn't died."

Daniel frowned. "I'm sorry for that. But I don't believe anyone lives a life they weren't meant to live."

Josie nodded. "I know, and I try to tell myself that. But I feel so out of place sometimes. I didn't feel that way for the longest time. I didn't think of myself as different. Then my life took this left turn. Everything changed with that one camping trip. Suddenly I'm aware that I'm not like my family, and I'm not like my friends. I don't mean Jenna, Dave, and Simon. Being with them is the only time everything feels almost normal. But like, when I'm at school, it's weird to walk around knowing that there's all this other stuff going on that they don't know about."

"Are you sure about that?"

"What do you mean?"

"Just that it's easy to assume no one else in school thinks about ghosts the way you do, but you don't really know that until you start talking to people."

"And risk being called a freak? Or a witch? Or who-knows-what?"

"Are you a freak or a witch?"

"No."

"Then why do you care if anyone calls you that? Your friends know you're not a freak or a witch. Your family, too."

"Ha, see, that's where you're wrong."

He tilted his head at her.

"My dad thinks I'm nuts. He thinks I'm schizophrenic. I'm in therapy because of it. And…." She shook her head, remembering the horrible things that had been said. "It's been awful."

Daniel nodded. "It's hard to believe that it's all meant to be this way when you're in something so deep and dark."

"Exactly."

"I'm curious about something. You said you aren't, well, friends with nature, right? So how did you end up on that camping trip? Was it just because your friends were going?"

"No," she shook her head. "Actually, I didn't know Jenna before that trip, and I'd only met Simon once. My parents set it all up for me because they were going on a cruise and needed somewhere for me to go. That was the only camp in the time frame they'd be gone."

He chuckled. "In my world, that sounds like fate."

"What do you mean?"

"Just that I have a hard time believing there were no other camps. In my world, it looks to me as though that camp was made to seem like the only option, because it was where you were supposed to be. You were meant to experience the accident to enable you to see the ghosts, to enable you to help them."

"Thinking like that doesn't make me feel better. It makes me angry," she said.

"It really should be comforting. To know that what is happening is just another step in the path should be comforting. Sometimes we need a shove to take the right step."

"Hm," she furrowed her brows. "Someone else said something to me like that one time."

"Who was that?"

"It was in a dream. I think she's one of my spirit guides. I'm pretty sure she's an Indian. She's beautiful. But I've only seen her a few times."

"That's pretty cool."

"Yeah. In the dream she showed me stones going across a river and used it as an analogy for my path in life."

"It's pretty amazing, you know, what you can do."

"Maybe to you. But I think having a relationship with an owl is pretty amazing."

"Yeah, having Achachak in my life has been… well, I hate to use the word 'amazing' again. But it is. He's my best friend."

"And what about other friends? Girlfriends?"

Daniel smiled. "I have friends. Two of them were helping out at the barbecue yesterday," he said. "No girlfriend at the moment."

"Are your friends… do they belong to… are they like…."

"Like us? Some of them. Most of them aren't. They're cool, though."

"Do you date? I mean, have you dated much?"

He smiled again. "Well, I don't know exactly what 'much' means, but I've had a couple girlfriends. Nothing that lasted. But, you know, we're young. What about you?"

"What about me?" Josie replied evasively.

"Well, I've met three of your friends. What about boyfriends?"

Josie shook her head. "Dating has been hard for me. Not just because of the stuff with spirits. I have a lot going on with dance lessons and I do theater. Musical theater mostly. I guess I've really only dated one person." She felt embarrassment filling her cheeks.

"Nothing wrong with that. Like I said, we're young. We should be living life and having experiences. If that includes a relationship, that's good too. You never know what might come along, right?"

"Yeah, you're right about that," she smiled. Then she said, "Hey, how do you say 'thank you' in your language?"

"The Mohawk word is 'Niá-wen'."

"Okay. Niá-wen."

"Io. Means 'you're welcome'," he smiled. "But why are you thanking me?"

She shrugged with one shoulder. "Just for talking and listening. You're really easy to talk to."

Daniel slowed his rowing, gliding the boat in among a mass of lily pads in a cove where there were no houses. He pulled in the oars. Josie looked around and realized she had no idea where they were. She couldn't see the beach or the resort. She saw a couple other boats in the distance.

"I like talking to you, too, Josie. I don't want to offend you by saying this, but… I really like you. I feel like we have a connection. You know? Like, I feel like I've known you longer than just a couple days."

Josie smiled. "Why would that offend me? I like you, too. I've never met anyone like you. And I agree. I feel like we've known each other longer."

He reached forward and took her hand. She was surprised at how large and warm his hands were, how long his fingers were. "So, if you like me and I like you… where do we go from here?" Daniel asked.

* * * * *

Josie and Daniel returned to the dock. He pulled the rowboat in and put it away. They saw Jenna and Dave sitting on the beach with Simon. Jenna waved to them.

"Did you have a good nap?" Jenna asked Josie with a teasing smile when they joined them.

Josie rolled her eyes. "Yeah, it was exactly what I needed," she answered, both sarcastically and honestly. Maybe she hadn't napped, but her time with Daniel was exactly what she needed.

"What are you up to, Daniel?" Jenna asked.

He shrugged. Josie sat on the edge of the blanket and Daniel sat next to her in the sand. "Just hanging out. I have the afternoon off."

"Cool. So, you're going to hang out with us?"

"If that's okay with you guys," Daniel said.

"Sure," Jenna answered, looking at Dave who nodded. Simon remained silent but didn't object. "Oh, hey! I can't believe I didn't think of this sooner. Can you tell me anything about 'Mystery Mountain'? There is almost no information online about it."

Daniel's face fell into a frown. "You don't want to go there. It's closed down. It closed sometime in the 80s, I think. Long before the internet, so that's probably why you can't find anything."

"We know it's closed. That was obvious just by looking at it. What I want to know is, what was it? Why did it close? Who owns it? Why hasn't anything been done with it?"

"Did you go there?" Daniel asked, looking from Jenna to Josie, his frown deepening, darkening his eyes.

"Yeah, kinda," Josie replied. "My mom got lost driving us back from breakfast and she turned around in the parking lot."

"Did you go inside? Inside the fence?"

"No. Why do you seem freaked out by this?" Josie asked.

Daniel shook his head, his frown dissolving. "I'm not. It's just… there's something really off about that place."

"No kidding," grumbled Josie, remembering all too well how she felt just standing in the parking lot. Her stomach gave a small lurch.

"What do you mean?" Jenna asked hungrily.

"I don't know. Like, people go walking through there and they disappear, mutilated animals are found on the property, neighbors report weird sounds and lights coming from there at night. But I doubt you'll find the reports online."

Jenna turned excited eyes, wide and round like dinner plates, on her friends. "Guys, we *have* to investigate there."

"I don't know about that, Jenna," said Josie. She didn't want to admit – to herself or her friends – that she was curious about that place. She wanted to know why it made her feel sick. And she wanted to know who – or what – she had felt watching them.

"What else do you know about the place?" Jenna asked Daniel.

"I don't know," he shrugged. "It's been for sale for as long as I can remember. I have no idea who's trying to sell it. I think it was just a roadside attraction, you know, like a ton of other places. The road it's on was once a main road until they built the new Route 9."

"Maybe someone older would know more. Someone who's lived here for a long time. Like your dad?" asked Jenna.

"Maybe. I don't know," said Daniel, shrugging again. "Right now, I'm hot and I'd like to go for a swim. Anyone else?"

"Sure," said Josie.

"Yeah, me too," said Dave.

"Who wants to race to the platform?" asked Jenna, jumping up and running into the water. Dave ran after her while Josie and Daniel both strolled to the water. Simon remained on the beach alone.

* * * * *

As they were getting ready to leave the beach and go back to the cabins, William approached. "Are you all having a good afternoon?" he asked.

"Great!" said Jenna. "Hey, Mr. Lightfeather, you and Daniel should join us for dinner tonight."

"Oh, that's very kind, but I don't know," William replied.

"Why not?" Jenna said.

"Dad, we don't have anything else going on tonight," said Daniel.

"And you guys worked so hard at the barbecue last night that you deserve to have someone else do the cooking," Jenna argued.

"Well… okay, that would be nice, if you're sure your parents won't mind," William replied.

"Of course not!" Jenna said.

"It really is okay for us to come?" Daniel said quietly to Josie.

"Absolutely, and if it wasn't, Jenna would make it okay," Josie replied, matching his tone so the others couldn't hear. "When Jenna gets an idea in her head, she's a force. It's best for everyone to just go with it."

"Good to know," he said.

That evening they once again all crowded onto the two picnic tables pushed together to form one long feast table. Charles and Angela did the cooking, offering up chicken wings and drumsticks and pork ribs along with the usual abundance of side dishes of salad and fruit.

Daniel stuck close to Josie and got a seat next to her. Simon's first instinct was to elbow his way in to sit on the other side of her, then thought better of it and sat across from her where he could be face to face, but it backfired. Josie spent most of dinner turned towards Daniel, so instead Simon got to see how well they were getting along.

"They make a good couple, don't they?" Jenna said quietly in Simon's ear.

He frowned at her. "Jenna, what are you doing?"

His sister looked at him with suspicious eyes. "You don't care if she hooks up with him, do you?"

"What if I do care?" he replied flatly.

Jenna's shock was obvious.

"Babe, pick your jaw up off the floor," Dave said from her other side. "You're gonna let flies in."

Jenna closed her mouth with a snap and turned to her boyfriend. "Did you hear what Simon just said?"

"Yeah. So? Don't tell me you haven't noticed."

"I've noticed. I'm just shocked he's admitting to it," Jenna replied.

Simon rolled his eyes and shook his head at his sister.

Jenna might have pushed further but she had other things on her mind, more important things than whether her brother liked

Josie or not. So, when she saw an opening, she took it. "Hey, Mr. Lightfeather, do you know anything about 'Mystery Mountain'?"

William turned to look at Jenna. "Oh, that old place?"

"What an unusual place that was!" said Angela. "We just stumbled on it this morning. It was the strangest thing. I took a wrong turn, and when I pulled over to turn around, there it was!"

"It was very bizarre," Rachel agreed. "Just out there in the middle of nowhere. But the farmhouse across the street is exquisite. Do you know how long it's been empty?"

"Oh, must be over thirty years now," said William.

"Thirty years? Geez, that's going to be a tough sell. It must be a nightmare inside," said Rachel. "They'll be lucky to sell it at this point."

William nodded. "The house is part of the property for Mystery Mountain. There've been various developers interested in it over the years, mostly wanting to build condos or retail space on the land, tear down the house and get rid of it all, but none of it ever went through."

"Do you know why?" asked Jenna.

"Something always seems to go wrong at the last minute. One buyer had a lawsuit come up which forced him to withdraw his offer, something with the tenants of another property… endangerment, or something. I became friendly with another buyer. His name was Henry. Very nice fellow. He stayed here whenever he came up for meetings with the realtor. We would talk and he would ask my advice. It was his dream to own a B and B, and he thought the house was perfect and wanted to turn the rest of the property into stables and a spa. Everything seemed to be going well. We were excited, thinking it was finally going to be sold and made into something instead of wasting away. Then the day before he was supposed to come up for the closing of the sale, he was found dead in his bed. Massive heart attack, they said." William shook his head again. Sadness was in his eyes.

Josie met Jenna's eyes. They both knew what the other was thinking.

"I'm so sorry about your friend," said Rachel. "It's all so strange. Everything about that place is strange, isn't it?"

"Yes, it is," said William, his voice tinged with sadness.

"So, what about whoever built Mystery Mountain? How did they get the property? Did something strange happen to them?" asked Jenna.

Josie looked at Daniel, but he was staring at his plate where he was pushing around pasta salad with a plastic fork, but she could sense his discomfort. She then looked at her dad whose face was pinched in anticipation of where the conversation was going. Then she met Simon's eyes, expecting to see reluctance or displeasure at the conversation, but instead, his gaze offered comfort.

"I really can't speak much to it. I came to this area towards the end of the height of its success, which is being kind."

"It wasn't successful?" asked Jenna.

"It brought in curious people, but not enough. It takes a lot to keep a place like that going. Like many places like that, they hit a rough patch and couldn't recover."

"And what about the owner? Did he die in some tragic way?"

"Last I heard, the guy was living in a nursing home down in Glens Falls," said William.

"Still alive?" Jenna's eyes lit up.

"As far as I know," said William.

"Did you go to Mystery Mountain when it was open?"

William sighed, wiped his mouth with his napkin, and looked at Jenna. "I can see that you are very curious about that place. You all seem curious." He looked around the table. "I understand, but I want to caution you not to go back there."

Josie had to suppress a chuckle. If there was any way to get Jenna more interested in Mystery Mountain, it would be to warn her to stay away. Charles let out a huff of air and continued to glower.

"Can you tell us why?" Angela asked with a frown.

William looked at Angela. "Your daughter sees into the spirit world. Many people believe – in one way or another – that there is our human world and the spirit world. But there are more than just those two planes of existence. And there are things in those… other places that none of us understand. They can be dangerous, and they can affect those other planes of existence. It is my belief that the Mystery Mountain land is a gathering place for those things. I believe the people that built it experienced it and built the place to expose people to it. But I don't think it worked the way they wanted it to. It isn't a good place. I encourage you all to forget about it."

"We need to go there," Jenna whispered.

"I agree," said Josie, her voice low.

10

"Dinner was delicious," William said. "Would you folks like to move this party down to the fire pit? I thought I'd break out my old guitar and sing a few songs. I'm not very good, but I'm not terrible."

"Sure, sounds fun," said Rachel. "We'll just clean up here and then we'll be down."

"I should go help my dad. See you guys in a few," Daniel said to Josie.

When Daniel and William had gone, Simon turned to Josie. "Don't tell me you agree with her after what happened to you there."

Softly, she replied, "I felt it when we were there. What William was talking about, whatever that was. I need to know what it is."

Jenna leaned forward. "So how do we do this? We have no way to get there on our own."

"I know what you guys are whispering about," said Charles from the other end of the table. "And I want you all to stop."

Angela put her hand to her forehead. "Charles, don't…."

"I'm sorry Angela," he said. "But you can't tell me you support this. You told me about that place, and it sounds like a death trap."

"I'm not supporting anything," she replied. "I just think that now is not the time for this."

"When is the time? When they've run off to Monster Mountain?" he replied.

"It's Mystery Mountain," Jenna mumbled.

If Charles heard, he didn't show it. Instead, he looked at Greg and Rachel. "And what about you two? It's not like you don't know what's been going on."

Greg stood. "I get it, Charles. Really, I do. I understand how hard this all is to process and understand. Regardless of all that, I think that if Mr. Lightfeather says it's not a good idea to go there, then the kids should respect that. Okay?" Greg looked at Charles and then at the kids.

"Of course, Mr. LaPage," Josie responded quickly but she felt a ball of frustration in her stomach. It was one thing for her dad to be against it all, but if all their parents ganged up on them, they were in trouble.

There were several long beats of silence as Charles seemed to be weighing Josie and Jenna's assurances before he walked away in a huff.

"He does that a lot, doesn't he," said Dave.

* * * * *

When they arrived at the fire pit by the beach, Daniel was just lighting the kindling. He arranged larger pieces of wood over the smaller ones that held a flame, and soon a fire was roaring.

"You guys aren't going to drop the Mystery Mountain thing, are you?" Daniel asked.

"No," said Jenna and Josie in unison.

Daniel sighed.

"I'm sorry," said Josie.

"Why can't you let it go?"

"Because… we just… I felt something out there. We've been to places like that, and I helped. I want to help here."

Daniel busied himself, stacking extra wood by the fire pit.

"Are you mad?" Josie asked.

"Would it make a difference?" Daniel replied, a deep furrow darkening his brow. He tossed another partial log on the fire and then turned to them. "Is there anything anyone could say to keep you from wanting to go there again?"

"I doubt it," said Josie.

"No," said Jenna.

"Dude, you're dealing with two stubborn girls," said Simon, shaking his head.

"We're not stubborn. We're tenacious," smiled Jenna.

"Well, if you go, will you at least let me go with you?" asked Daniel.

"Yeah, sure," said Josie. "Right? It's okay," she added, looking to Jenna and Simon.

"I don't have a problem with it," said Jenna.

"Me either," said Dave.

"Simon?" Jenna looked at her brother.

Simon looked at Daniel. "If you're against us going, why would you want to go?"

"That place is weird. Like I said, bad things tend to happen to people who go there. I'd feel better about you all going if I was with you. I know the area better than you do, and I can probably be of some help."

"Why can't I find anything online about all these bad things?" asked Jenna. "There's nothing in the online archives of the local papers."

"It's not something people around here want advertised. If you put things like that in the paper, it might attract people. Not the right kind of people."

"Are we not the right kind of people?" Josie asked.

Simon perked up and looked from Daniel to Josie and back to Daniel. He was enjoying watching Daniel dig himself into a hole, getting flustered as he went.

"No," said Daniel. "That's not what I mean."

"What do you mean?"

"I don't live under a rock. I see all the TV shows about ghost hunting, UFO hunting, Bigfoot hunting. I hear stories about people destroying places because they think it's haunted. People do rituals, dark rituals. They do drugs and get drunk in those places. They go where they shouldn't go, and mess with things they don't really believe are real until it's too late. We don't want people like that around here."

Josie thought of Cynthia and her friends. "We aren't like that."

"We're investigators," said Jenna. "I don't want to mess with things, I want to do it the right way and find out what's going on."

"And I want to help whoever or whatever is there," Josie added.

"How do you know there's anything there that you can help?" Daniel asked.

"I don't," Josie replied. "But if I go there, I can find out and try. I have to try."

"So, Daniel... are you with us or against us?" Jenna asked.

Daniel sighed. "Look, Josie and I were talking earlier, and I told her that I believe everything happens for a reason. If someone is meant to be somewhere – like on a camping trip when that's the last place on Earth they would want to be – then they will find themselves there. And I can't help thinking that maybe, since you ended up at Mystery Mountain because of a wrong turn, that maybe you guys are meant to go to this place, to help or investigate or whatever."

"Okay," Jenna nodded approvingly.

"But you need to know that I am not happy with it. I've been out there, and the place gives me the creeps. And the fact that my dad doesn't like it... well, I trust what he says. But I don't want you guys going out there on your own."

"Fair enough," said Dave, nodding.

"What's that saying: 'If you can't beat them, join them'?" Simon said with a mocking smile.

"So, what song would you like to hear?" William asked, calling attention to everyone. "Like I said, I'm not very good but I'll give it a try."

"Josie's pretty good with a guitar," said Angela. "I'm sure she'd be happy to play if you want her to."

"You play guitar?" Jenna asked. "How did I not know this?"

Josie shrugged. "It's kind of just something I do just for me."

"She's taken years of lessons," Charles added, a hint of pride in his tone.

"I'd be happy to let someone with more experience play," said William with a smile. He held out his acoustic guitar.

Josie felt her face flush with embarrassment as everyone looked at her expectantly. "I... I've never played for anyone... but.... Okay, I guess."

She took the guitar and adjusted the way she sat by scooting to the edge of the chair, then she plucked at the strings to get the feel for them. It wasn't quite like her guitar, but it wasn't too different.

"Alright, what do you want to hear?" she asked.

The first request was "Leaving on a Jet Plane" by Frank Sinatra. Josie, William, Angela, Charles, Jenna, and Rachel all joined in. Then she played "Hotel California", "Blowin' in the Wind", and "Fire and Rain".

When they finished, Jenna said, "Hey, do you know Cindi Lauper's song 'True Colors'? It's one of my favorites."

Josie swallowed hard. "Yeah, I know that one," she said. She looked at the fire, blazing high in the stone pit. The sun had almost completely set so everything outside of the fire was in shadows. She was grateful for that, as she started the song. Her dad was the only one who joined in singing, and it made a lump of tears threaten her voice. She swallowed again. Did he remember? Josie wondered. *Does he know this is killing me? Does he care?* Josie asked silently. She looked at Charles and then quickly looked away when she met his eyes. *This was our song,* Josie thought. *He taught it to me. We sang it together, and he said that I inherited my singing voice from him. He had said that.*

Nearby, Simon saw the shift in Josie when she started the song and wondered what happened. There was a slight catch in her voice which she moved through as she sang. He realized it had been a while since he heard her sing, and he suddenly realized he'd missed it.

When the song was over, Josie looked visibly relieved. She drank down almost a whole bottle of water that Angela passed to her and accepted a roasted marshmallow from Jenna.

"Any more requests?" Josie asked with forced lightness.

Then Angela said, "What about that song you wrote for class?"

"Um…."

"It's a great song, Josie. Your teacher gave you an 'A' right? I heard you play it a thousand times. It's really great. So, that's my request."

"I don't know, Mom. No one wants to hear something like that," Josie said.

"I'd like to hear it," said Simon. He caught a flashing look from Daniel that disappeared quickly.

"Me too," said Daniel.

"Me three!" said Jenna.

"Come on, Josie. Play it for us," said Dave.

"Really?" She looked around the circle of fire-lit faces, waiting for an objection, but none came. "Okay. Well, I should preface it by telling you that when I wrote the song, I'd been looking for inspiration. At the time I was reading a book about King Arthur, so I wrote this song about that scenario. I call it 'Lancelot's song for Guinevere'.

She started the ballad with a slow, gentle intro. Then she sang:

> I'm walking on eggshells
> navigating through this maze
> dodging peril that I'm begging for
> What will happen if the sword runs through
> me?
> Will she save me or will she flee?

Does she remember where the landmines
we planted will be?
I didn't want to cause trouble
but with one look, wrong became right
and with a kiss I was thrown into the mist

I just couldn't resist the pull of her gravity
She is the moon, and I am her world
I can keep time by her orbit
But she wants to stand in Venus's shell

Oh, patience is a virtue
She's growing it like weeds!
I want to feed it poison
and mow it with my sharpest blade
'cause she's keeping me in suspense
wondering if she's around the next turn
I would give anything to have her there
arms open, smile bright
But she has me on the run
and slips through my fingers like water
Oh, let me drown in her deep end

I just couldn't resist the pull of her gravity
She is the moon, and I am her world
I can keep time by her orbit
But she wants to stand in Venus's shell

I catch a glimpse of her milky flesh
beneath the chain and armor
She says she hates expectation
and holds no empty promise
She has seen strong men fade away
but not this time

'cause she remade my wings of wax
into wings of sterling
and she has set me free

But I just couldn't resist the pull of her
gravity
She is the moon, and I am her world
I can keep time by her orbit
But she wants to stand in Venus's shell
So don't hold her back from giving her all
'cause you shouldn't catch a tiger by the toe
Oh, she brings out the animal in me

She's danced with the Devil
Been to Hell and back
so many times she'll show you the way
'cause like a Phoenix with his sweetest song
she'll rise from the ashes once more
His tears have healed her wounds
Take a look, she'll proudly show her scars
Like chapters in a storybook
They are the guideposts to her soul
A map to where most dare not go
(but I'll go…)

Because I just can't resist the pull of her
gravity
She is the sun, and I am her world
She keeps me warm in my orbit
As she stands in Venus's shell

The last notes of the song faded until only the crackling of the fire and chirping crickets could be heard. Then they all broke out in applause with whoops and cheers. Josie smiled and flushed with embarrassment. Angela beamed with pride.

Charles sat back with a sigh, feeling awed and humbled by his daughter. He resolved in that moment to find a way to fix things with her the way he should have from the start.

* * * * *

Simon took a slow, deep breath. He had never experienced anything like that – something that happened more and more frequently around Josie. He couldn't explain it if he had to, but it was something that left him shaken. His heart pounded hard within his chest.

Josie put the guitar down, smiling but looking exhausted.

"You're very talented!" Rachel said. "That was wonderful!"

"Thank you," Josie replied, avoiding all the eyes that were on her. "I'm pretty tired now. Is it okay if I head back and go to bed?"

"Of course, honey," said Angela.

"I think I'll go, too," said Jenna, shooting a look at Dave.

"Yeah, I'm tired, too," said Dave, standing. Simon stood, too, and so did Daniel.

"I'll walk with you guys," said Daniel.

"We won't be too long," said Rachel.

"Thank you for the music, Josie," said William.

"You're welcome. Thank you for the use of your guitar. Good night," she replied.

When they were out of earshot of their parents, Jenna said, "Okay, so when should we go to Mystery Mountain?"

"I'm working in the morning, so maybe tomorrow afternoon," said Daniel.

"Okay, that will give me time to do a little more research," said Jenna. "Now that I have a few more details."

"I'm surprised you didn't want to go tonight," said Daniel.

"I do, of course," said Jenna. "But I know better. There's no way we'd be able to get past our parents tonight."

"Speaking of which," said Josie. "We'll need to find a way get there as well as what to tell our parents."

"I have a car," said Daniel. "It's a beat-up junker, but it'll get us there."

"We can say we're all going to play mini golf," suggested Dave.

"I don't think so," said Simon. "They could drive by and see we're not there."

"Do you have any ideas?" Dave asked Simon.

"I don't know. It would have to be something that would take time – enough to give us time to wander around Mystery Mountain and check things out," Simon said.

"I can say I'm taking you guys hiking up Black Mountain over by Lake George. I've hiked it a few times with my friends. I think it would allow us enough time."

"Seems legit. I like it." Jenna nodded. "Okay, we have a plan."

"You don't have to do this, you know," Josie said to Daniel. "I don't want you to do something that makes you uncomfortable."

Daniel shrugged. "Sometimes we have to do things that make us uncomfortable. That can be when the best things happen to us."

They reached the cabins.

"I hope you're right about that," said Josie. She turned and looked up at him.

"I should get back to my dad," said Daniel. "See you tomorrow." He leaned down and embraced Josie in a movement that both looked and felt completely natural. Simon had to tell himself to relax, to allow it all to unfold, that his jealousy was natural but unfounded. But still, a part of him wasn't so sure of that. He'd spent the day on the outside looking in, watching Josie spend time with Daniel, talking and laughing and doing who-knows-what when they were out of sight. She wouldn't go out in a boat with him, but she went with Daniel. What did that mean?

"Goodnight, guys," said Daniel, walking away.

When he was gone, Simon said, "Are you really going to bed? Or do you want to hang out for a bit?"

"I'm tired. I didn't sleep good last night," said Josie, "and it's been a really long day."

"I'm tired, too," said Jenna. "Goodnight, Babe." She kissed Dave.

But Jenna didn't sleep. Josie didn't either. She was exhausted and wanted to sleep, but it wouldn't come. Jenna was in bed but on her computer, taking notes and searching for something on Mystery Mountain.

Josie tossed and turned.

"Am I keeping you awake?" Jenna asked.

"No," Josie replied. "My stupid brain is keeping me awake."

"Everything okay? Or am I not allowed to ask that?"

Josie frowned at the annoyance in Jenna's tone. "It's fine. I'm fine. Just a lot on my mind. Trying to sort through it all and make sense of it all. I can't verbalize it aloud until I get it straight in my head."

"Okay. Let me know if there's anything I can do to help," said Jenna.

Again, Josie sensed annoyance in her friend's words. "Is everything okay with you?" Josie asked casually.

"What? Yeah, fine. I'm just frustrated at how difficult it is to find information on this place."

"Okay," said Josie. She rolled over, feeling a disturbance in that pit in her stomach. Something was off with Jenna, she could tell, but she wouldn't push it. Not yet anyway.

* * * * *

"We have a full day of fun stuff planned today, girls," Angela said cheerfully. "I hope you're ready!"

"What do you mean?" Josie asked as she poured coffee.

"Well, we're going first to Fort William Henry Museum, and then over to the Stone Bridge and Caves Park. There's a winery we want to stop at, though that won't be much fun for you kids. Then we have dinner reservations at a steakhouse, and if there's time, we'll go down to the village and do a round of mini golf and maybe the wax museum or whatever."

Josie looked at Jenna, whose face was an impassive mask.

"Wow, Mom, that really is a full day," said Josie.

"They know," whispered Jenna as they left the kitchen. She and Josie brought their coffee to the porch and were joined by Simon and Dave.

"You think?" said Josie, her stomach doing a nervous flip.

"They know we're curious about Mystery Mountain and that we want to go there, so they're going to keep us busy to keep us from sneaking off," said Jenna.

"I have to agree," said Simon.

"What are we going to do about it?" asked Dave.

"We need to tell Daniel," Josie said. "I'll text him and let him know what's going on."

"They can't keep us busy forever, can they?" asked Jenna.

"I hope not," said Josie.

"Ready to go?" Greg called to them as he came out from his cabin and headed toward the van.

"Oh, I have to grab my bag," Jenna said. "Be right back!"

Jenna was the last one to climb in the van.

"What's with all the stuff, Babe?" Dave asked.

"I want to be prepared," she said.

"For what?" asked Josie.

"We're going to a fort! I mean, I'd much rather be going, you know, hiking with Daniel, but if we have to do this, I'm going to be prepared just in case," she smiled.

Josie laughed. "I should have known. I didn't even think of that." Then she sighed.

"Will you be alright?" Simon asked. Once again, he had taken the seat next to her.

"I'll be fine. It's probably safe to assume I'll run into something there, but I doubt this fort will be like Fort Roday."

"Maybe we should say something to your parents," said Dave. "I mean, your dad flips at this ghost stuff, so maybe they will change their mind."

"No, it's fine," said Josie.

"Maybe you should at least warn everyone," said Simon, "so they're not surprised if – or when – something happens."

Josie shrugged. "You can tell them if you want, but I'm in no mood to deal with the wrath of my dad again."

* * * * *

Everywhere they went that day included at least an hour's car ride to get there. First, they went to the fort where Josie was followed around by a man who, in life, had been a tour guide and now, in death, continued to try in vain to educate various guests. When she told Jenna, she tried to take pictures of him but was unable to capture an image of anything but Josie and the fort. Josie also encountered a female ghost that was dressed in a way that suggested she was from colonial times. The woman became irritated when she knew Josie could see her and kicked at the dirt with her worn leather boot, sending a good-sized rock scuttling across the ground that hit Charles in the ankle. Josie said nothing as he hopped in pain while Jenna lamented that she just missed it with her camera. Before they left, while everyone else wandered around the gift shop, Josie, with assistance from Hanover, helped them both move on.

"I wonder if this will hurt their ghost tour business," said Dave, pointing at the brochure.

"I don't know, and I don't care," said Josie. "I can't leave them here just so someone can make money off them."

"You're right," said Simon. "It would be like a human-ghost zoo."

"Eww, I think you just ruined zoos for me," said Jenna.

"For me, too," agreed Dave.

"But it was really cool that she was able to move that rock," said Jenna longingly, thinking of the missed opportunity to get evidence.

When they left the fort, they drove around Lake George and stopped for a picnic lunch by the lake.

"I just got a text from Daniel. He was able to switch his afternoon off to tomorrow," said Josie.

"Okay," said Jenna. "That should work."

"What will work?" asked Rachel.

Jenna looked nervously at Josie. "Um, well, Daniel wanted to take us hiking at a place called Black Mountain. He wanted to take us today, but we didn't know you guys had stuff planned. So, he switched his day off to tomorrow. Can we go?"

Rachel exchanged a look with Angela that was nearly identical to the look Josie and Jenna had just exchanged. "We'll see," she said.

"Such a typical parental answer," Jenna grumbled, turning away from her mom.

"We'll make it happen," said Josie quietly.

After lunch they walked the trails through the Stone Bridge and Caves Park, then stopped at the winery where the adults stocked up on wine, and then Rachel and Greg treated them all to ice cream. After dinner at the steakhouse where Josie helped cross over a former cook during a trip to the rest room, they played one round of mini golf, and then piled back in the van to go back to the resort.

By the time they made it back to the cabins, the sun had set, and the stars were out in full force.

"Who wants to play 'Cards Against Humanity'?" Greg called out.

"We'll bring the wine," said Charles.

"Our parents have problems," Josie said to Jenna and Simon.

"Your parents are awesome," said Dave.

"Aw, they're practically your parents, too," said Jenna, wrapping her arms around him and snuggling into his chest.

"Yeah, I'm the son they always wanted," said Dave.

"Hey!" said Simon, throwing a punch at Dave's arm.

"Whatever, man, you know it's true," said Dave.

"Sure, well, you're the sister I've always wanted."

"Hey, why are you dragging me into this?" asked Jenna, throwing a kick towards her brother that he dodged with a step back, sending him colliding into Josie and stepping hard on her foot.

"Ow!" Josie shouted and jumped back, hopping on her one good foot the way her dad had earlier when hit by the rock.

"Oh, no! I'm so sorry!" Simon said, grabbing at her arms to help steady her. "Josie, I am so sorry."

"It's fine," she said, holding her foot, her flip-flop discarded.

"Here, sit down," said Simon, helping her hop to the porch.

"Josie, I'm sorry," said Jenna. "That was my fault."

"It's okay, both of you. I'm not made of glass," said Josie, dropping into a chair.

"So, since you're okay, you don't mind if my girl and I go for a walk, right?" asked Dave.

"I don't need three nurses," Josie said.

"I'll take that as a yes," said Jenna. "Simon?"

"What, like you need my permission to go off with your boyfriend?"

Jenna and Dave headed down the hill towards the lake, hand in hand. Giggles from Jenna could be heard floating on the air back to them as Simon took the seat next to Josie.

"Can you believe they've been together for over a year?" Josie asked.

"Longest year of my life," Simon grumbled.

She rubbed at her sore toes. "You don't have a problem with them still, do you?" Josie asked.

"No, but it's just changed everything. He's not my friend anymore, he's Jenna's boyfriend. That's his new title. Like he got a promotion."

"He's still your friend," said Josie.

"It isn't the same. He's more boyfriend than he is friend."

"I'm sorry," said Josie. "I don't really know what it's like. I mean, Jenna and I have known each other as long as they've been together, so I don't know anything different, but I do know that there are lots of times that I have to be the third wheel in order to spend time with her. It's always nice when you're around, so I don't feel so awkward."

"I didn't realize," he said.

"That's okay. Why would you?"

After a minute of silence, Simon said, "I guess I was being selfish, not thinking how it affected anyone else."

"Why should you?"

"Well, it's not a bad thing to think about other people. It would have been nice of me to maybe consider your feelings in those situations."

"You've had a lot going on, Simon. Senior year and all."

"I guess."

"There's no reason for you to consider my feelings, anyway."

"What do you mean?"

Josie avoided his eyes. "Just that – I mean, I know we're friends, but really, I'm Jenna's friend – and like I said, you've been busy with Senior year stuff. It's not a big deal. I don't usually mind being a third wheel. And I really like Dave. He's a good guy, a good friend."

Simon sighed. Several minutes of silence passed between them. He pulled something out of his pocket and passed it from one hand to another. Then he said, "So… I want you to know that I don't always think only of myself."

"Simon, I know you don't—"

"Do you? I want to show you…." He held out the thing in his hand. In the dim light she saw a pouch that looked like it was made of a dark colored velvet. "I saw this in the gift shop at the Stone Bridge, and I thought of you."

"What? This is for me?"

"Yes."

"But… why?"

"Do I need a reason?"

Josie didn't reply, unsure what to say.

"Take it. Open it."

She took the pouch and pulled at the draw string at the top. She reached in and pulled out a long strand of beads in a shade of rich, earthy red with swirls of dark gray. At one place in the strand, the beads were joined together with an amber-colored bead and a tassel in red, silky cord.

"Simon, this is beautiful!"

"The girl at the store said it's called a wrist mala, whatever that means. I thought it was a necklace at first, but she said you're supposed to wrap it around your wrist a few times."

She put it around her wrist and wrapped it around three times. "It's perfect," she said.

"It's a great color on you," he said. "Oh, and there should be a piece of paper in the bag that says what kind of stone it is."

Josie reached into the bag and pulled out the paper. "Red Jasper. It brings balance to the wearer, stimulates the chi – or life force – and can relieve stress. Associated with the root chakra and aids in grounding," she read. "That's very cool. Thank you, Simon. That was very sweet, very unexpected."

"You're welcome."

"It… it must have been expensive," she said.

He shrugged. "I've been working a lot. And it just… felt like something you needed to have."

"Thank you," she said again. She looked at his wrist, happy to see that he still wore the cuff she had given him as a gift when he announced what college he chose.

"I need something to drink," said Simon. "Want anything?"

"Water would be great."

He returned from the kitchen with two bottles of water. "Our parents are having way too much fun in there. I heard things just now that I can never un-hear."

Josie laughed.

"How are your toes?"

"No permanent damage," she replied.

"Good. So, what do you think is going on with that Mystery Mountain place?"

"That's a great question, and one I don't have an answer for," she replied. "I've never experienced such an instant physical reaction like that."

"And you're sure it was from that place? I mean, right before that you had gone through the fight with your dad. You were really upset, and you didn't eat much."

"Always the skeptic," she said.

"I don't mean to be—"

"It's fine, Simon. We need someone around who thinks that way. It keeps us from making irrational judgements."

"Exactly!"

Josie smiled. "But I'm certain that what I felt was a result of where we were, of something or someone there. It probably didn't help that I was upset and hadn't eaten much, but I don't think I would have felt sick if we'd just come back here. Did *you* notice anything weird?"

Simon shrugged and sipped his water. "Not at the time. At the time, I was more concerned for you. But afterward I remember just feeling really uncomfortable. Like something was just not right with that place."

"And you're okay with going back to check it out?"

"No, not really. I wouldn't go back there if it wasn't for you and Jenna. But I'm not letting either of you go there without me."

"Dave and Daniel will be there, so you don't have to go if you really don't want to," Josie said.

"Are you trying to keep me from going?" he asked.

"No, I'm just saying, that if you're worried about our safety, we'll have two other guys there with us. Not that we need guys to protect us."

"That's not what I mean. There's safety in numbers. I wouldn't care if Daniel was a black belt or if Dave was the Ultimate Ninja Warrior. Or if either you or Jenna were the female MMA champs. I'd still want to be there."

"It's not like any of that stuff helps against ghosts, anyway," Josie said.

"*If* that's even what we're up against," said Simon.

"You're right. We have no idea what's out there."

"But if you don't want me to go – if I'm getting in the way of anything, being a fifth wheel or whatever – just say the word and I'll stay here."

Josie hesitated, fingering the smooth, cool beads of the bracelet on her wrist. Her silence made him nervous when it was only that she was choosing her words carefully. Finally, she said, "I want you there. Of course I want you there. I just… I don't want you to feel obligated."

"Why would I feel obligated?"

She shrugged. "I don't know. Because of Jenna, because we're friends, because being there to help is what you do, even if it's something you don't want to do. But I don't want to be anyone's obligation. Like my parents. My *adoptive* parents. I feel like an obligation to them right now. Or at least to my dad. Like he feels he must suffer his way through all this just because they adopted me. It's not a good feeling."

"Well, I want to be there. Yes, because we're friends, and yes, because I want to help. But it's also because I care, Josie. Not because I feel any misguided sense of obligation."

She didn't respond. Simon didn't like the silence.

"You believe me, right, Josie?"

"I don't know," she said, still fidgeting with the beads of her bracelet.

"Well, if you don't believe that, maybe you'll believe this." He leaned over, took her face in his hands, and kissed her.

Part III

1

She was shocked at first, but then something deep within her responded. Every particle in her body suddenly came alive with the memory of kissing him on the beach. It was the same.

No. It was better.

They pulled slowly away from each other in a synchronized movement. Simon sat back and tried to steady his breathing and calm his heart. The act of kissing her again validated what he told himself for weeks hadn't happened in Florida, that when they kissed, there had been some kind of conscious electricity bonding them. He felt it again now, he just didn't know what exactly it meant.

All he knew was that he'd had to do it. In that moment, to not kiss her would have been like not breathing.

They sat together in silence, but Josie decided that silence was okay. It was nice, just sitting there. She could still feel his lips on her. There was a tingle that went from her lips down into the core of her. She didn't want to speak, she just wanted to enjoy it. Simon had kissed her. *He* kissed her. She wasn't sure what it meant, and she didn't want to think about it. She just wanted to enjoy it.

Behind them every now and then they could hear a burst of laughter from their parents. Ahead of them lay a dark landscape under a starry sky. Crickets chirped in their musical pattern. Every now and then a bird would let out a screeching call, and a moment later there would be an answer, and Josie wondered if it was Achachak out with some friends.

Thinking of Achachak made her think of Daniel and thinking of Daniel in that moment made her heart plummet into her stomach. Meeting Daniel and getting to know him had become one of the best things to ever happen to her. He understood her in a way that no one else in her life ever had. She had felt so alone lately, and he made her feel less alone. His presence had started to fill that deep, heavy, hollow pit within her. But he didn't erase the connection she felt to Simon.

Jenna and Dave came walking back up the hill, their shadows emerging out of the darkness long after the sound of their voices could be heard. Josie noticed that their hair was wet, but their clothes were remarkably dry. Josie didn't need to ask what they had been doing. The smiles on their faces and the looks they exchanged spoke volumes. Josie chuckled to herself and shook her head.

"Well, I need to go get my equipment in order for tomorrow. Good night, guys," said Jenna.

"I'm going to bed, too," said Josie. "Good night."

"Good night," Simon said to Josie, touching her lightly on the arm as she walked away.

Josie lay in bed while Jenna sat on her own bed, cameras and recorders and other equipment spread out before her.

"I'm so excited for tomorrow," said Jenna. "I don't know what it is about that place. I don't even know if it's haunted, but I know we need to be there."

"Yeah, Simon and I were talking about it earlier. I've never had a reaction to any place like I had there. There's something extra weird there, and I want to know what it is." She tugged at the mala bracelet, fingering the round, smooth stones. "Don't get me wrong, I'm terrified too, but my curiosity is overriding the fear."

"Hey, where'd you get that bracelet? I don't remember seeing that before," said Jenna.

"Oh… yeah, Simon gave it to me."

"He did?"

"Yeah."

"Oh."

"What?" Josie asked.

"Well, what about Daniel?"

"What about Daniel?"

Jenna shrugged. "Never mind. I need some water. You?"

"No thanks," she said. Josie frowned at Jenna's back as she left the room.

* * * * *

Josie woke the next morning confused. It was too dark. She looked at the time on her phone and again thought that it was too dark. Then she heard it. Rain was pounding down on the roof over her head.

Josie rolled over, not surprised that Jenna was already up and gone. She forced herself out of bed, went to the kitchen, and poured herself a cup of coffee.

"Where's Jenna?" Josie asked her mom.

"I think she went next door," said Angela, taking a bite of a bagel.

"That smells good. Are there more?"

"Yup," said Angela. "On the counter."

"It's raining."

"Yes, it is."

"When will it clear up?"

"I'm not a weatherman, but it's supposed to last all day."

"All day?" Josie hadn't meant to say it in a whine, but she couldn't help it.

"Really, Josie, it's just weather. We've been lucky so far."

Josie sighed and watched her bagel toast in the toaster oven. "So, what are we going to do today?"

"Probably just hang around here. Play games, read, relax."

Josie sighed again.

After a long, hot shower, she took her time getting dressed in leggings and a long-sleeved purple t-shirt. With her new red jasper mala bracelet on her wrist, Josie made her way over to the LaPage's cabin. She was nearly soaked to the skin in the short run from one cabin to the other, where everyone else was already gathered. Jenna, Dave, Simon, and Greg were deep into a game of Monopoly. Josie sat on the small couch with another sigh.

She took out her phone and sent a text to Daniel. IT'S NOT LOOKING GOOD FOR TODAY, IS IT?

She didn't wait long for the reply, NO. MAYBE TOMORROW?

MAYBE IT'S JUST NOT MEANT TO BE, she replied.

When Jenna had won Monopoly, everyone joined in for a round of Uno, and after that they played two games of Jenga. When the clock reached noon, Greg brought out lunch meat, bread, and condiments for everyone to make their own sandwich. The rain continued to pour down heavily.

Josie went to the window and looked out. She could hardly see the lake through the rain.

"Who wants to see a card trick?" Charles asked.

"I do!" said Dave.

"You know card tricks, Mr. York?" asked Jenna.

"I sure do. I'm a little rusty, but I'll give it a shot." He shuffled the deck of cards in his hands a few times, then held them out, face down, in a fan shape. "Dave, pick a card. Show it to Jenna and I want you both to remember the card. Okay. Are you good?"

Dave and Jenna nodded.

"Okay now put the card back somewhere in the deck," said Charles, holding out the stack. Dave returned the card, and Charles laid the whole deck in the palm of his hand. "Alright, now, which position do you want your card to end up – the first card, the second, or the third?"

Dave looked at Jenna, then said, "Third."

"Okay. I'll give the deck three good taps," he tapped the top card with his finger. "And now I have to give it three good blows to move the card." He cupped them in his hands and gave three short puffs of air between his thumbs, and then held the deck out. "One… two… three," he said as he flipped cards, holding the third one out. "Is this your card?"

"Yeah, that's totally my card. That's crazy!"

Charles gave a little bow. "I am 'The Great Salami'!"

"Dad, we're not ten," said Josie.

"What's 'The Great Salami'?" asked Dave.

"It's my magician's name, from when I'd do magic tricks for Josie and her friends."

"I like it," said Dave. "And not just because salami is delicious."

"Do you know any more tricks?" asked Jenna.

"Sure do. You want to see another?"

Josie watched from a chair by the window. Charles did one trick where the card they picked magically ends up in Jenna's back pocket, and he did another one where he ripped the card in eight pieces, put it in his pocket, and made it appear in the middle of the deck. She watched her friends' faces as he did the tricks, how they were mesmerized and in awe. Josie could remember feeling the same way when she was little, and he would entertain her friends at sleepovers and birthday parties. Her friends thought he was amazing, and she had, too. She was so proud to be his daughter.

That had all changed with one sentence.

She sighed. Watching her father with her friends made her heart ache with a love that had been beaten up. A tear slipped from her eye. She rose and went out onto the porch and breathed in the clean, cool summer air. She sat in one of the chairs and put her feet up on the railing, feeling the warm rain on her toes.

The steady drumming of the rain as it hit the roof, the grass, the leaves, was mesmerizing. Josie felt herself slipping down into a meditative state of relaxation.

And then the screen door squealed open. She looked over, surprised to see Dave.

"Hey," she said. "Is The Great Salami done his show?"

"Yeah," he replied. "Mind if I sit?"

"Of course not."

"Jenna challenged him to a game of Scrabble, and I think Rachel and Angela joined in."

"That should be interesting. My dad's pretty competitive when it comes to Scrabble."

"And Jenna's competitive when it comes to everything."

Josie laughed. "True enough. Hey…. So… can I ask you a question?"

"Sure," he said.

"Well, okay, if you don't want to answer, if it's too personal, just say so."

"Alright," he said with curiosity.

"I'm just wondering, like, I imagine you're pretty mad at your dad about what happened. Jenna said that you've stopped speaking to him. And, well, I'm just wondering how you deal with that… that kind of betrayal when you have the blood connection."

Dave frowned a little, then said, "I haven't thought about the 'blood connection', as you put it. For me, when I found out what he did, it destroyed any respect I had for him. I realized how different he is from me. I can't imagine ever doing what he did. He is a coward who couldn't tell his wife he was unhappy, so instead he had an affair. And now he's hurt a lot of people and turned lives upside-down. If he'd just had the balls to talk with my mom, even if it had ended in divorce, at least maybe they could have done it in a better way, without so much hurt and anger. So, I guess to answer your question, the blood relation means nothing. He isn't a good person, he isn't someone I want in my life, and even though we're genetically linked, I know I can choose not to be like him."

Josie frowned in thought.

"Can I ask you a question now?" asked Dave.

"Sure."

"Does the reason you asked that have anything to do with your own parents?"

"Yeah," she said. "Things with my dad… they're bad. I don't know if Jenna told you—"

"She's mentioned things have been rough, but I don't know the details."

"Long story short: he thinks I'm not really talking to ghosts, that I'm schizophrenic. And then when we were in family counselling, when we were talking about behaviors of parents versus children, he said that I'm not really his kid."

"Ouch," said Dave.

"Yeah."

"Man, that's rough."

"Yeah."

"Well, I don't know if I can help you with that, Josie. Except to say that, from what I've seen of your dad, he seems like a genuine guy. He seems to treat you well, despite all that other stuff. He may have said that, but his actions – that I've seen – contradict that statement," Dave shook his head. "And I don't know if the blood thing matters. Blood doesn't always mean better. Look at the LaPage's. Aside from my mom and brother, those people are the closest people in my life, and I'd take a bullet for any one of them. Seriously. They are just as much my family as my blood relations. Maybe more so. Maybe that's better. They're my family by choice. Your parents are your family by choice."

"I've never thought of it that way," said Josie.

"Blood doesn't always matter. You can have some of the strongest connections with people who you aren't blood-related to, and sometimes the people you share DNA with are terrible people."

She thought of the kiss with Simon the night before. "You're right."

"You know I consider you one of my family too, right?"

Josie smiled. "Aw, thanks. You, too."

"Good. So, that being said, my advice for you is: don't give up on your dad."

She nodded. "You know, when I first met you, I didn't think much of you."

"Gee, thanks," Dave chuckled.

"I'm sorry, but —"

"No, Josie, don't be. I appreciate the honesty."

"What I mean is, I made a judgement that was wrong. And I'm glad I was given the chance to find out how wrong I was."

"Thanks," he replied, sincerely.

"Jenna sees it. She's so smart with that. She knows what she wants in life, and she just goes for it. I envy that."

"You can have that, too, you know."

Josie shook her head. "I don't know. I don't think I know myself the way Jenna knows herself. And it's all gotten so complicated."

Dave shrugged. "It's something to strive for."

"I guess."

They lapsed into comfortable silence, letting the sound of the rain take over again. Josie's mind wandered back to her dad. Being connected by blood had never been an issue before. She had never felt odd, or out of place, or less-than because she was adopted. She almost never thought about it because it just didn't seem to matter. Then… everything changed last summer on that camping trip. Her life changed. Things that didn't matter before were suddenly thrust in her face.

She wished she could talk with her birth parents. It was something she'd wished for often. She'd begged her guides for information on them, or to bring them through to her. What good was being able to see ghosts if you couldn't see the ones you wanted to see?

The porch door opened, and everyone piled outside.

"What's going on?" Dave asked.

"We're tired of being cooped up inside, so we thought we'd go to the arcade for a bit and then back to the pizza place for dinner," said Greg.

"Who won Scrabble?" Josie asked.

Jenna turned away to Simon as though she hadn't heard Josie. "I won one game and Jenna won the other," said Charles.

"No tie-breaker?" Josie asked.

"Maybe later, right Jenna?" Charles asked with a smile.

"You got it, Mr. York!"

Charles ran for the van and backed it up to the porch so they could jump in without getting too wet.

The drive into town was slow and quiet, aside from the thrumming of the rain on the van roof. Charles dropped them off at the sidewalk in front of the arcade. It was virtually empty inside, so they started a skee-ball tournament. Rachel was the winner at the end of nearly forty-five minutes, and Josie was surprised to come in second place.

After crowning Rachel with an oversized plaid felt top hat purchased with the tickets won from their games, they made a mad dash through the rain to Village Pizza. They were seated quickly and ordered three large pizzas – one extra cheese, one Hawaiian, and one meat lovers – two plates of garlic bread and several salads. They were just starting on their salads when Daniel came in. He walked straight to the counter without seeing them.

"Daniel!" Josie called, finally getting his attention with a wave.

"Oh, hey!" He waved back and approached the table.

"What are you up to?" asked Greg.

"We're in our rainy-day mode. We've got movies playing on the tv in the game room, and we're providing pizza and sodas for the guests," said Daniel.

"Oh, I wish we'd known!" said Josie.

"Hey, are we going on that hike tomorrow?" Jenna asked Daniel.

"My dad is giving me the time off, so I'm good to go if you all are," he replied.

Josie looked at her parents. "We can go, right?"

"I don't know, Josie," said Angela.

"Why?" asked Josie.

"Well…."

"I'll tell you why," said Charles. "We are all concerned that you kids are ignoring William's warning and you're going to sneak off to that Monster Mountain place instead of wherever you say you're going. But I think we should let you go."

"What?" said both Josie and Angela.

"Josie, you think I don't trust you, but I do. I trust you to make the *right* decisions for yourself and the people you're with," said Charles. "Whatever and whoever that may be."

"Wow, okay," Josie replied, unsure. "Thanks, Dad."

"Okay," said Angela, eyeing her husband cautiously. "If your dad is okay with you going, then I am too."

She looked at Rachel and Greg. "Okay with us. We trust you guys."

"Awesome," said Daniel. "We should probably leave around twelve. Does that work?"

"We'll be ready," Josie said.

"Okay, well, I need to get these pizzas back. Good to see you. Stop by for a movie when you get back if you want."

"Okay. Bye," said Josie. She watched Daniel go with a little flutter in her stomach. She continued to be awed by him: the sight of him, his spirituality, his cultural knowledge, his openness to her… it all captivated her. But in that same moment, she felt Simon's arm brush hers, and her skin tingled with the electricity that always seemed to be there between them, linking them.

Why does life have to be so complicated? she lamented to herself. Part of her hoped someone would answer, but she knew enough to know that spirit guides weren't there to help her pick a boyfriend. She looked at Jenna who was listening to something Dave was saying, and felt a pang of sadness, knowing that she couldn't talk openly about it with her, either, despite their agreement to complete transparency. They may have meant it at the time, but there was still something off between them, some murkiness clouding the air between them. Just like with her parents. Her mom was under the impression that things were better with her and Charles. The way Angela was gazing at Charles across the table told her that, but the truth was, nothing had changed. Or had it?

"Josie?" said Simon.

"Huh?"

"I just said that it was weird, right?"

"What was weird?"

"The way your dad gave us permission to go."

"Oh, yeah," she nodded. "Definitely weird."

Josie lapsed back into silence, absorbed in her thoughts. Jenna was looking at her phone screen and making notes in a small notebook. Simon looked at Dave, asking with a look if he thought something weird was going on. Dave just shrugged.

The rain was finally starting to let up as they arrived back at the resort. While their parents went back to playing games, Jenna, Josie, Simon, and Dave gathered in Simon & Dave's room.

"So… I guess we should talk about tomorrow," said Jenna. "Whatever possessed Josie's dad to give us his blessing to go with Daniel… well, I'm grateful."

"He knows," said Josie.

"I agree," said Simon.

"You think?" said Jenna.

"Definitely. It was weird. Like, he meant what he said, that he trusts me. That alone is weird after everything that's happened between me and him. But I think he knows we're lying about hiking, he knows we're going to Mystery Mountain, and he's okay with it. Like he knows there's something there that we need – maybe I need – to do at that place."

"That doesn't really sound like your dad," said Jenna.

"I know. That's why I know."

Jenna frowned. "Okay, well, whatever the reasoning behind it, I'm relieved it's working out. The weather should be nice tomorrow. I just hope the place isn't a giant mud puddle after all this rain."

"Hey, nothing wrong with throwing a little mud wrestling into the adventure, is there?" asked Dave with a smirk.

Jenna rolled her eyes at him.

"Yeah, I'm gonna take a pass on that," said Josie. "Jenna, are you planning on hanging out here for a bit?"

"Yeah, I guess so. Why?"

"I want to meditate and maybe get a heads up about what we're in store for tomorrow, talk with Hanover."

"Ok, I'll give you your space," said Jenna.

* * * * *

Josie dashed through the rain and stopped on the porch. Everyone was occupied in the other cabin, so she settled into a chair and put her feet up on the railing like she had done earlier. She leaned back and breathed slowly, deliberately, feeling her body relax with each breath. Her eyes slowly closed as she listened to the patter of the rain on the roof overhead mixing with the dull thumps as it hit the earth around the cabin. She sunk into it until she found that place where everything in the world around her turned hazy and she was able to open herself to the spirit world.

A scene formed before her inner eyes: the rain was gone, the night was gone, and the sun was shining down from a blue sky onto a grassy hilltop. She stood and stepped off the porch. She could feel the soft, warm grass beneath her bare feet. Not far ahead, Josie noticed a circle of grass that was darker than the rest. She walked to it and as soon as she stood in the middle, Mother Elk Spirit appeared in front of her. She smiled gently at Josie and held one hand up, palm facing Josie in the universal signal to stay where she was.

We have some gifts for you, said Mother Elk Spirit.

We?

The spirit made no answer but suddenly Josie could hear movement of something large coming from the stand of trees just behind Mother Elk Spirit. Josie watched the shadows, seeing movement in the spaces between the branches, her heart pounding with excited anticipation. Then, a moose stepped from among the trees into the sunlight. In his teeth he tenderly carried an enormous sunflower with a clump of earth still attached to the roots. He approached the circle of grass where Josie stood. She could feel the thumping of his hooves through the ground. At the edge of the circle, he lowered his head and softly set the sunflower down. Josie watched as the sunflower roots instantly sunk into the ground at her feet and took root. She looked at the moose whose head was lowered to be level with hers, their eyes meeting, and he said *Earth: the seed of life*, in a thick, deep voice. Josie looked at the sunflower which began to wither and dry. Its seeds dropped from its head into the grass, and in a blink, dozens of new sunflowers started to grow. The growth, death, and rebirth process repeated until she was completely surrounded.

Then a great gust of wind blew, and the sunflowers swayed in unison like a chorus of ballerinas. Josie looked up to see an owl that she recognized as Achachak flapping his great wings to stir the air around them. He landed on the right antler of the moose, looked at Josie with his dark, piercing eyes, and said in a silky voice, *Air: the breath of life.* He took a large breath in, his feathered chest puffing out, and then let it loose from his beak with a force that stirred up a small cyclone around her, lifting her hair and tossing it around her face before dissipating.

Just as the air settled, the ground beneath her began to rumble. Next to where the moose stood, a hole appeared and grew like a yawning mouth, and out flew a dragon with silver skin. It did a loop in the air and landed next to the moose. It looked at her with sparkling red eyes, and in a strong, feminine voice, the dragon said, *Fire: the passion of life,* and roared a great gust of fire from her mouth at Josie. The fire formed a ring around her and then closed in, dancing in great orange, red, and blue lapping-tongue flames, growing closer and closer to where she stood. Then one of the large flames swooped under her feet, causing her to fall back only to be caught by the flame as if it were a giant hand. The other flames joined in and lifted her high in the air. Within her, she felt a great burning desire growing as the flames grew and lifted her higher in the air. She stretched her arms out wide and closed her eyes, soaking in the ecstatic feeling of joy and euphoria as it raced through her veins.

Then she heard a rushing sound. She opened her eyes and looked down to where the moose, owl, dragon, and Mother Elk Spirit stood. Behind them Josie saw a tiger running with a roaring river of water racing along behind him. The tiger stopped but the water continued until it reached the flames, which the water easily conquered. Josie fell from the sky as the flames disappeared below her but managed to land softly upright on her feet. The tiger looked at her with his intense yellow-green eyes and said, *Water: the purifier of life.* His voice wrapped around her like silk.

Mother Elk Spirit stepped forward and said, *We are all earth, air, fire, and water. Each one of us contains each element, and each one of us has a role to play.*

Just then, Josie was startled from her meditation by a loud thump. When she came to, she couldn't tell whether it had been something in her meditative-state or if it had been real. She looked around and saw nothing that could have made the noise, but she noticed that it had stopped raining. It still dripped from the roofs and tree branches, but the clouds were beginning to part and Josie could see a few stars peeking through. She looked around again, searching for the source of the noise, feeling like there were eyes watching her somewhere in the darkness.

She got up, went inside, and climbed right into bed. As she lay there staring at the ceiling, she replayed what happened in the meditation over and over until her eyelids closed and she fell into a deep sleep.

* * * * *

In the next cottage, in the room identical to the one Josie and Jenna shared, Jenna sat with Dave and Simon.

"I saw the bracelet you gave Josie," Jenna said to Simon. Simon said nothing, just continued to look at something on his cell phone.

Dave looked from his girlfriend to his friend, suddenly uncomfortable and regretting that he was sitting between them. "I'm gonna get a soda. Anyone want one? No? Okay, I'll be right back," said Dave, hurrying from the room.

"What's up with the bracelet?" Jenna asked when Simon remained silent.

"What do you mean?" Simon asked in reply, his eyes still glued to his phone screen.

"I mean why did you buy Josie that bracelet?" Jenna asked, her tone thick with anger.

"Why do you care? Can't I give a gift to someone?"

"Not Josie!"

Simon finally put his phone down and looked at his sister. "Why?"

"Because! You're going to lead her on and make her think there's something more there than there is!"

"How do you know there isn't something more between us?"

"Because I know you," Jenna scowled. "You can't tell me you actually have feelings for Josie."

"What if I do?"

"You can't be serious!"

"Why is it so impossible for you to think I might really like her? Is it that you think I can't have feelings for her, or that you don't want me to?"

Dave froze in the doorway, a soda can in one hand, the other hand gripping the door frame.

"That's it, isn't it?" said Simon, frowning at his sister. "You don't want me to have feelings for her, do you?"

Jenna continued to scowl, then said, "Forget it. I'm tired. I'm going to bed." She pushed past Dave and left.

After the cabin door slammed shut behind Jenna, Simon looked at Dave and said, “Your girlfriend is a whole boatload of crazy.”

2

Josie woke when Jenna came in, huffing and slamming things. She wondered if she should say something, but the image of the fire-breathing dragon came into her mind, only this time Josie was certain the fire would scorch her, so she pretended to be asleep.

Josie turned her mind again to the images from the meditation, running through them over and over, how the four elements each related to one of her four friends. Yes, Daniel was at the very least a friend now and probably would be for life. Just like Jenna, Dave, and Simon.

Earth, the seed of life. Air, the breath of life. Fire, the passion of life. And water, the purifier of life, Josie said in her mind. Her heart swelled with gratitude as she repeated those words. *Earth, air, fire, water. But where do I fit into it all?*

A knowing struck her that she would find out soon.

She heard Jenna tossing and turning in bed, the springs squawking in protest. It was unusual for Jenna to be restless and unable to sleep. That was Josie's thing. She wondered if something had happened with Dave but decided probably not. Perhaps she was just nervous about going out to Mystery Mountain, though Josie found that equally unlikely. Jenna wasn't one to be apprehensive about such things. Again, that was Josie's thing.

She wanted to help her friend with whatever was going on with her, but she felt that it would be best to let Jenna be for now. Josie frowned into her pillow. Though she and Jenna were friends again, their estrangement over, she couldn't ignore the fact that things were different. One of her biggest fears of telling Jenna about her feelings for Simon was that it would change their relationship, and it had. Something was missing that had been there before. Josie knew that was the nature of relationships. Things changed and evolved, and fights – arguments or disagreements or whatever you want to call them – were often the catalyst for the change. Sometimes they were a breaking point, but even if it didn't completely destroy the relationship, it still changed the landscape of it. Battles left wounds that would eventually turn into scars. Was Jenna still wounded? Or was she just trying to figure out how to navigate the new, altered landscape of their friendship?

That hollow place that had been within Josie since telling her parents about Ethan told her that she had foolishly gone back into her friendship with Jenna acting like nothing had changed when that was far from the truth. Jenna had layers of knowledge that she didn't have before. Not just knowledge of Josie's feelings for Simon but the evolution of those feelings, from the crush that started at her locker on her first day of freshman year to the connection she felt to him that was cemented in her when she thought he was dying in that house in the woods of Maine. Add the layer that Josie had kept it from Jenna for almost a year. Then add two more layers for the fact that both Dave and Simon knew before Jenna, and another one for the kiss – *Two kisses!* Josie reminded herself – that they exchanged at the end of their vacation in Florida. Then there were the layers of whatever Jenna felt in regard to all of it. Josie's heart sank at the realization that she would never again have the same friendship with Jenna that they'd had before.

Josie didn't realize she had drifted into sleep again, but as she did, she saw herself growing like a sunflower from a perfectly circular spot of earth. The sun's fire warmed her and nourished her and helped her grow. Birds came and ate her seeds, and rain fell from the sky, cleansing her leaves and filling her with purity. A gust of wind came and scattered her remaining seeds, and as she wilted into nothingness, she saw her seeds growing into more sunflowers that looked just like her, being nourished by the sun and rain. And she didn't feel sad at her own demise, but hopeful at the sight of her offspring that would grow and spread the way she did.

* * * * *

Next door, Dave lay awake, concerned about his girlfriend while Simon drifted off quickly into sleep. Sleep soon merged into a dream, and Simon found himself standing in a run-down old house in the middle of the woods. A storm raged outside. He could hear the wind and the thunder. He could hear rain lashing aggressively at the fragile walls and roof of the crumbling structure. He hoped it would hold.

A fire roared in a large fireplace, and he went to stand near it. He looked at Josie who sat on the floor near the fire, shivering and still wet from the river. He knelt in front of her and handed her his sweatshirt.

"Here. Put this on. You need to warm up," he said.

"Thanks," she replied, and quickly pulled the hoodie on. It would smell like her later when she gave it back. Like honey and lavender.

"How does your head feel?" he asked.

"Okay. A little better," she replied. Her eyes shimmered golden and amber in the light of the fire. They were hypnotic. He had to look away. Jenna and Dave huddled together nearby, and other people were around, standing in the shadows, but he couldn't remember who they were.

A gust of wind whipped around the house and the entire structure groaned. Then came the very distinctive heel-toe-heel-toe thumps over their heads. Everyone looked up, as though they could see through the ceiling to the floor above.

Josie stood. "There's a ghost up there," she said. "I can help him. I *must* help him."

Simon frowned. A ghost? But that wasn't possible. Ghosts aren't real. Fear gripped his stomach. Josie headed for the stairs.

"I can't let you go up there alone," he said. She turned to him and smiled and took his hand in hers.

He didn't remember climbing the stairs, but he knew they did. They stood in a room with a bed and a dresser on one side and a wall of bookcases on the other. In one corner was a table with an old CB radio system that Dave and Jenna were trying to fix.

"Oh, hey guys, what are you doing here?" Jenna asked.

"We're here to help the ghost," said Josie.

"Oh cool. Can I watch?"

Simon turned to tell her no, but his sister was no longer there. Instead, a tall man in an old, decaying, dust-covered suit pointed a rifle at him. Under the brim of his hat his face was gray and gaunt and even more decayed than his clothing.

"Simon, do you see him?" Josie asked from behind him, her voice barely audible. He nodded. She pressed herself up against him. He could feel her breath on his neck. "I can help him. Step aside."

"No, Josie. I can handle this," Simon replied. The man before him, though clearly sick and dying, was no ghost as far as Simon could tell.

"You can't protect her," the man sneered. There was a click and a BANG! A blinding flash and then darkness. Josie screamed. Simon's chest burned, and he found his legs would no longer hold him up. He collapsed.

Simon knew was dying. *But isn't this where I usually wake up?* he thought. *Isn't this just a dream?* It was a dream he'd had many times before, but he always woke before his last dying breath, an ache still resonating in his chest. Now, however, he wasn't waking up, so maybe it wasn't a dream. Maybe he was really dying.

Josie sobbed over him. With what little strength he had, he wove a hand into her hair. It was like silk. "I'm sorry," he said, his voice barely a whisper. "I couldn't protect you. I failed."

"No, Simon," she sobbed. "No. You can't die!"

He felt his heart slow, and his vision became fuzzy. In the next moment, he was outside his body, looking down on himself and Josie. She was bent over him, still sobbing. He could see into the hole blasted into his chest, a chaotic mess of flesh, blood, and unidentifiable goo. Something inside the hole twitched, perhaps his heart trying for one last pump.

Then he noticed his body being illuminated by a bluish-silver light. He moved closer and realized it was coming from Josie's face. It was a tear dripping down her cheek, and it emitted a tiny, beautiful glow.

He watched as it slid down her cheek to her chin and then fell into his wound. He heard it hit the bloody mess with a ping as though striking crystal, and a beautiful sound resonated from his heart. The glow from her tear spread and multiplied until it radiated from within him in chorus with the angelic sound as it intensified. Higher and more intense, the sound rose, the light grew, and then a blast engulfed the whole scene in the most beautiful light and sound.

When it faded, he was standing in darkness with only a tiny candle flame nearby. He faced Josie, who looked at him with liquid golden-amber eyes and a small smile on her perfect lips. He reached out and stroked her cheek with one finger. Three words repeated in his mind, begging to escape his mouth, to be said to her.

Simon didn't know what woke him from the dream in that moment, but the words were still on his lips, ready to be given to her. Realization dawned on him as sunlight entered his room. She was not there, he was very much alive, and Dave was snoring in the next bed. He covered his face with his pillow and sighed.

* * * * *

As always, Jenna rose early the next morning, put on her running gear, and headed out on the trail that ran along the lake.

She hadn't slept well, but she couldn't figure out why. Why was she so irritated that Josie and Simon were getting closer? She didn't think she was jealous. Was she?

She shook her head. Running would help. It always helped. It was a beautiful morning with the sun streaming through the trees. Despite the rain of the day before, the trail was dry except for a few puddles she had to leap over or navigate around. She finished her run at the beach and stretched on the sand, enjoying a moment of quiet and solitude. The lake before her was as still as glass. Occasionally it rippled with a small movement from under the surface. The light blues and pinks of an early morning sky were reflected perfectly. A bird cut through the image in a swift flight from one tree to another.

Jenna sighed.

Movement from behind her caught her attention. She turned to see William Lightfeather sweeping around the firepit.

"Good morning," he said to her with a nod.

"Good morning."

"Nice view you have there," he said, and used the small broom in his hand to motion out to the lake.

"One of the best," she agreed. "It must be nice to live here and see this all the time."

He came and stood near her, his gaze on the lake. "Better than any television show I've ever seen."

Jenna nodded.

"It's okay, you know," said William. When Jenna looked up at him, he added, "To feel what you're feeling. Don't beat yourself up for feeling something. Allowing it is key."

Jenna frowned. "How did you…?"

He shrugged. "I could sense a storm in you. It isn't uncommon in teenagers. You're figuring out the world. Resisting makes it harder."

"Thanks," Jenna replied, a frown still furrowing her brows.

"Well, back to work for me. Enjoy your day. Should be a beautiful one."

As William walked away, Jenna pondered his words and marveled at his ability to read her. It shouldn't surprise her though. Daniel was obviously gifted in similar ways, so it wasn't a surprise that his dad was too.

And he was right. Normally she could process these things easily, but there was just too much right now. And she was beating herself up over it all. She shouldn't be mad at Josie because Simon liked her, she shouldn't be mad at Simon for liking Josie, she shouldn't be jealous of Josie because of her ability to see ghosts, and she shouldn't be upset that Josie and Dave seemed to be close friends now. She shouldn't feel confused about her friendship with Josie, she shouldn't be mad at Josie's dad for not believing her, and she shouldn't feel terrified to go to Mystery Mountain.

Jenna told herself she *shouldn't* feel those things, yet she did. And William was right. Telling herself she was wrong only made her hang on tighter to those feelings. What had he said? "Allowing it is key"? *So, I needed to allow myself to feel how I feel. Okay, easy enough,* she thought.

She leaned back on her elbows in the sand and allowed herself to feel. She felt the frustration, the anger, the hurt, and told herself it was okay. She was okay, even if she felt that way. She let out a long, slow breath of release and looked up at the sky. A cloud drifted by that looked like it was formed in the shape of a dragon. She tilted her head at it and said, "Is that a sign?"

She watched the cloud as it drifted from view and morphed into some unidentifiable shape. The sun was starting to get warm and felt good on her bare arms and legs. She would have a lot more freckles by the time this trip was done, but she didn't care. She liked her freckles.

"Hey, Babe," said Dave. She turned to see him standing at the edge of the sand.

"Hi," she replied with a smile.

He walked to her and sat in the sand next to her. He leaned over and cupped her face with one big hand and kissed her long and deep. She never stopped marveling at how his kisses always made her tingle all over.

"Good morning," she said, a little breathless.

"How're you doing today?"

She shrugged. "I'm okay," she said. "I'm nervous about later. I mean, *really* nervous in a weird way, but I'm okay with that."

"I'm nervous too. There's something totally off about that place," he replied.

"But we can't not go," said Jenna.

"But we can't not go," Dave nodded.

"Is everyone awake?" she asked.

"I think so. Your dad's making French Toast and bacon."

"And you're sitting here with me? Wow, you must *really* love me," she said, offering him a playful smile.

"More than anything," he said, and drew her into another deep, toe-curling kiss.

* * * * *

When Jenna and Dave reached the cabin, the smells of frying bacon, melted butter, and warm maple-syrup greeted them.

Simon stepped out onto the porch. "Want to let Josie know breakfast is almost ready?" he asked Jenna.

She gave him a one-shouldered shrug. "Naw. You can tell her," Jenna said, and followed Dave inside.

Simon stared after Jenna in surprise, then headed to the next cabin. He stepped inside. "Josie?" he called tentatively. The screen door banged shut behind him and his heart banged in his chest as it did so often around Josie, though it was different now that he finally admitted to himself that she was the cause.

"In here," she called back.

He stepped to the doorway of the bedroom she shared with Jenna.

"Hi," she said. She stood at the dresser brushing her long, raven-black hair.

"Hey," he replied. He leaned casually against the doorway and drank her in. He wanted nothing more than to run his hands over the soft skin of her shoulders and down her arms, to kiss her in the scoop of her neck, and bury his face in her silky hair. *Oh yeah, I'm hooked*, he thought to himself with an inner chuckle. *How did it take me so long to see it?*

"What's up?" she asked. She put down her brush and turned to face him.

"Dad's cooking breakfast," he said.

"Oh, French toast?" she asked.

He nodded.

"I thought I smelled heavenly aromas," she said. She smiled and her eyes glittered.

Simon smiled. "You're very vibrant this morning. Sleep well?"

"Actually, yeah. And last night when I meditated, my new guide came to me!"

"That's great," he said, a little forced. "I'm really happy for you."

"Are you?" She frowned and tilted her head at him.

"I am. I really am," he said, moving from the doorway and stepping into the room. "I had a strange dream last night and it kinda made me realize something. Can we talk for a minute?" He sat on the bed.

"Yeah, sure," she replied. He could see she was nervous as she sat next to him, turned to the side, one leg bent in front of her so she could face him. He wondered if she knew how much he was tortured by his close proximity to her, how much he just wanted to kiss her and let the world stop and fall away like it had in Florida.

"The dream took place in that house in Maine," he started, fidgeting with a loose thread on the bedspread. "It wasn't exactly like it was. You know how dreams are. You know where you are even if it doesn't look exactly like it's supposed to."

She nodded.

He went on to describe the details of the dream he could remember leaving out only the last part with the candle and the words that he longed to say. Now wasn't the time for that. Instead, he told her, "What I realized was that a big part of why I've struggled with this ghost stuff is because it makes me feel so helpless. Yes, I saw them that night, but you were the one to save me, you were the one to help them. And you've helped all those other ghosts too. I can't do that."

She shook her head. "Simon… it's—"

"Let me finish," he said, with a smile. "It took me a while to realize that it isn't my job to protect you from ghosts. You don't need protection from them. It's your job – your ability or your gift, whatever you want to call it – to help them. Why would I protect you from that? It would be like someone trying to protect me from helping an injured person. So… I just wanted to tell you that and apologize again for being so weird about it all for so long."

She smiled, relief clear on her face. "Simon, really… you have nothing to apologize for." They sat in silence for a minute and then she stood. "Should we go get some breakfast before Dave eats it all?"

"Probably," Simon chuckled and stood too. "But first there's one more thing."

"What?"

"I'd really like to kiss you again."

Her smile fell. "Oh… um, Simon, I don't—"

"Oh, you don't want… oh, okay, I'm sorry."

"No, Simon, it's not… it's just that… everything is so… complicated right now. My head is… not on straight. And Mystery Mountain is…."

"And Daniel," Simon said flatly.

"And Daniel…."

Simon looked at her, hopeful for a second, and then frowned. "I'm not going to lie. I like Daniel a lot, but…."

"But?"

Josie shook her head. "I don't know. I'm sorry, but it's all just too much for me right now. I need to focus on Mystery Mountain. I'm really sorry."

When he saw tears glistening in her eyes, he pulled her into an embrace. "You have nothing to be sorry for, Josie," he said into her hair, his hands wrapped around her back. Her skin was so warm, so soft. "I'm sorry. I should have known. Let's just focus on getting this Mystery Mountain thing figured out. Okay? I'm not going anywhere."

"But you are," she said, muffled, her face pressed to his chest.

"What?" he asked, frowning as he stepped back.

"You're leaving soon. For college. Remember?"

"I know, but...."

She shook her head. "It doesn't matter right now. I'm sorry. We can talk about all this later."

"Promise?"

"Promise."

"Alright. We should probably go see if Dave's eaten all the French Toast," he said.

* * * * *

Josie thought her head might explode into an infinite number of particles just from the knowledge that Simon LaPage wanted to kiss her again. But it was bittersweet for her, too. There was just too much going on and she had too many unanswered questions.

Josie had spent so long telling herself it would never happen. Then she switched to being afraid that if it did happen, that she had built it up in her mind so much that the real thing could never live up to her fantasies. And then they kissed in Florida, and it was more amazing than she could have dreamed. But he'd run away from her. He didn't run away the other night, and then this, so what did it all mean? She would need answers eventually. She deserved to know. But she wouldn't ask yet. For now, she would put it out of her mind and focus on the task she would be facing that day.

The LaPage's cabin really did smell heavenly when they walked in. Greg – knowing how Dave eats – had two plates set aside for Josie and Simon, which he heaped with French toast and bacon when they arrived.

She thanked him with a smile and ignored the curious look from her mother. Simon was a part of her life and hopefully would be for a long time to come, so Angela would just have to get used to seeing them together.

Josie sat on the floor in front of the coffee table and Simon joined her. He sat next to Josie, close enough that his knee brushed up against her leg and continually sent shocks and tingles through her.

Josie's phone buzzed in her back pocket to signal that she had a new text. She read it and smiled. "Daniel says he should be done working around 11:30. He wants to know if we want to leave early and get lunch in town."

Jenna shrugged and looked at Dave. "Sounds okay to me."

Josie wondered if Jenna was avoiding meeting her eyes.

"I'm good with that," Simon added.

"Okay, I'll let him know." Josie frowned over her phone as she responded. Something about Jenna was off. She wasn't her usual perky and optimistic self.

Now is not the time to worry over such things, came a voice she knew for sure now was Mother Elk Spirit. *There will be a time and place.* Josie couldn't see her but sensed her nearby.

"We're heading down to the beach," Rachel said. "You kids are on clean-up duty when you're done eating. And do not go anywhere without letting one of us parents know. Got it?"

"Got it, Mom," replied Jenna, with a bit more perk.

Josie eyed Jenna carefully. "Okay, Daniel will meet us in the parking lot of the office at 11:30."

"Cool," Jenna replied, avoiding Josie's eyes again.

"Josie, I think you got some syrup in your hair," said Simon. He reached over and gently wiped at the beads of syrup on the strands of hair, his finger brushing the curve of her chin.

"Yuck," Jenna grumbled. She turned away and looked at her phone screen.

Simon looked at his sister. Without thinking, Josie grabbed his hand below the table. He looked at Josie. She gave him a barely perceptible shake of the head to tell him to let it go. For now. She released his hand. He sighed and looked at Dave who just shrugged. Josie felt bad for Dave, constantly in the middle of it all.

"Now that the adults are gone, I have something I'd like to share with you guys," said Josie.

"What's up?" Dave asked. As usual, he stepped up when Jenna needed to step back.

"I met my new spirit guide last night," she said.

"Cool," said Dave. Jenna continued to look at her phone.

"Jenna, if now isn't a good time, that's okay. I can tell you all this later," said Josie calmly.

Jenna looked up from her phone and finally looked Josie in the eye. "What? Oh, sorry, guys. I don't know what's wrong with me today. I'm just… grumpy."

"Everyone's allowed to be grumpy. It's okay," said Josie. She felt like their roles were reversed. Suddenly Jenna was the sullen one and Josie was the wise-sage cheerleader. "Do you want to hear about what happened with my guide or wait till later?"

"No, I definitely want to hear what happened. Go ahead," she said.

"Okay, so…." Josie told them of her meditation with Mother Elk Spirit and the visit from their four animal guides.

When she was done, Dave said, "You saw my moose? That's so cool!"

"Yeah, it was. Seeing them all was really cool. Like they're telling me that the four of us and Daniel are a good team. Earth, air, fire, and water. All essential."

"But that's only four elements, and there are five of us," said Jenna.

"I know," Josie replied, stifling a sigh. "Your animal guides are just a part of you, just like the element each gave to me is just a part of you. Each of us has all those elements to us. Literally and figuratively."

"Not literally," said Jenna. "We aren't literally made of fire."

"Actually, yeah, we are," said Simon. "Stars – like our sun and all those other ones up there in the sky – are giant fireballs. I read an article, I don't know, maybe a month ago, about an astrophysicist and a physician who teamed up and discovered that we are all made up of star dust, remnants of stars that exploded. So yeah, we are *literally* made of fire."

Jenna scowled at her brother. "You're such a know-it-all sometimes."

He shrugged. "I can't help it if I know it all."

"Shut up," she said, throwing a napkin at him. Not playful. She was angry. It was so unlike Jenna. "I need to get out of here. I'm going down to the beach. You guys clean up for a change."

Jenna stood and strode from the cabin.

Dave looked at his friends with uncertainty.

"Dave, you can go with her. Simon and I can handle cleaning up," Josie said. She gathered up the remaining plates from the coffee table.

"You sure?" He looked from Josie to Simon.

Simon nodded. "I think she'd rather be with you than either of us right now."

Dave nodded. "Okay," he said, and followed in Jenna's wake.

After the screen door slammed shut behind Dave, Josie said, "She's upset. It bothers her that things are different… changing… between me and her, between you and me, even her relationship with Dave will change soon when he goes off to UNH…. It's a lot."

She ran the water in the sink and scrubbed at a plate more aggressively than necessary.

"Did she tell you that or did 'they'?" he asked. He pointed a finger to the air with the word 'they'.

Josie shrugged and handed him the plate to dry. "Neither. It's just… obvious. I mean, all the changes are freaking me out too. And Jenna's usually very upfront with everything, so she's not exactly subtle when she's holding back."

"I never thought of it that way, but you're right," he replied and took another plate from her to dry. "But I can't help feeling that there's more to it than that. Something is just a bit *off* with her." He didn't add that he had been sensing something similar in her, too.

She focused on the dishes. It was like the world had turned upside-down. Jenna was being like Josie, and Simon was acting different…. Thankfully Dave seemed unchanged, or she'd really be freaked out. But Josie couldn't help but wonder if there was something going on, something outside of their control altering their behavior. Or at least influencing their behavior. Though Simon's behavior had changed more slowly than Jenna's had, his was more drastic. He'd gone from telling her she was like another sister to wanting to make out with her, something she never thought would happen. But it had happened. Was it for real or was something making him think he wanted to do these things with her, feel these things for her? Was it the fact that Daniel was around, paying attention to her? For the brief time she was with Alex, he had been rude to Simon because he could see their connection and was jealous. Could that be it, just jealousy? She shook her head. Her heart would break if that were the case. Maybe Jenna was thinking the same thing, that Simon's feelings for her weren't genuine and she didn't want her to get hurt.

It was all too much to consider.

"You okay, Josie?" Simon asked quietly at her shoulder. He leaned in close, and she could smell him. Like mint, fresh soap, and sweetgrass.

"Yeah, just thinking about Jenna. I think I took it for granted that things were okay between us, thinking that they'd go back to the way they were, but they can't, can they?" She focused on the dishes, so she wasn't tempted to dive into the blue pools of his eyes. She handed him a coffee mug without looking at him.

He dried it with the dish towel. "No, I guess not. I think a lot of people think that, though. That's why people break up and get back together a hundred times. Like Mary Alice. I couldn't understand how she could get back together with Rob. He'd treated her like dirt at the end of their relationship, but she thought things would go back to the way they were with him when things were good. Maybe they did. I don't know. But I can't think that way. When we were fighting, me and Mary Alice, about camp and Rob and whatever, I just can't forget that stuff. It's part of it all. Part of the picture that is that relationship. Does that make sense?"

Josie nodded. "Yeah. It does. I just wish I'd been paying attention to the new picture of my friendship with Jenna." She handed him the last plate from the sink.

"It will be fine, Josie, don't worry. You and Jenna are solid. You'll get through this, and you'll probably have a stronger friendship for it," he assured her. He dried the plate and put it in the cabinet.

She dried her hands but didn't respond.

"Hey," he said. He put his hand on her shoulder and turned her to face him. "It *will* be okay."

She looked up into his blue eyes, so vibrant behind his thick, dark lashes. He pulled her to him again and wrapped his arms around her in an embrace. She leaned into him wholly, her head on his shoulder, her face in the crook of his neck.

"It will be okay. This isn't going to break you guys. It's like you said, we're a good team, all of us." His voice vibrated in his chest. She absorbed it like her life depended on it and she inhaled his scent deeply. In that moment he could have told her that the earth was made of candy, and she would have believed it. Or at least wouldn't care if it were true.

She stepped back and leaned back against the counter.

"You know," he said. "That dream I had last night also made me remember how much we've been through, the four of us. I don't think there are four friends anywhere who have been through as much as we have."

"But you're okay with Daniel being there, too, right?" she asked him.

"Oh. Yeah. I mean, he was part of your… vision thing… right? So, yeah. Of course."

She raised her eyebrows at him.

He shrugged. "Let's go find Jenna and Dave."

"Is it true what you said earlier?" Josie asked as they walked down the hill toward the beach. "About people being made of star dust?"

"Yeah," he replied. "I mean, I've only read a bit about it, but it looks like the science backs up the claims. We know that star dust is made up of things like iron, sulfur, carbon, oxygen, and nitrogen, which is all stuff we're made of. Stars are exploding all the time and the dust and particles come to earth. We breathe them, they become part of a plant that we consume, they're in the water we drink. And, our planet was formed of those particles, too. Everything around us, including us, is made of those particles."

"That's pretty amazing," she said.

"I know, right?"

Josie smiled. She liked to hear the passion in his voice. "I spend so much time thinking about the spirit world that I forget sometimes just how incredible the physical world can be."

"I'm reminded how incredible the physical world is every time I look at you," he said.

Josie stopped and looked at him. Her mouth hung open.

He stopped and turned around then laughed at himself. "I didn't mean it… well, I mean, yeah… look at you, but that's not how I meant it. I just meant that you are here in this physical world and you're incredible. But now it just sounds kinda ridiculous."

He laughed at himself again, his cheeks flushed with embarrassment. She had to admit she enjoyed seeing it.

"It's okay, Simon. I get it. The attempt was... sweet," she said, chuckling. "And I'm glad to not be the one embarrassed for a change." Then she frowned. This was weird and not like him. She had never seen him fumble like that with anyone. Was this a normal change for him? Part of being jealous? Or was it something else? Could it be paranormal?

Josie sighed. If Jenna was being herself, they could talk about it all, about hers and Simon's changed behavior. But she wasn't sure Jenna was receptive to talking about that or anything else with her. She didn't want to think about the possibilities of what might be happening to them, but she couldn't help it. It had happened before. Could something like that be happening again? She knew well enough that ghosts could mess with them in various ways. When she was supposed to help the ghosts at Fishkill Pond, they tried to stop her by frightening her, and one of them even took over Simon. His behavior certainly changed that night as he and Dave fought and ended up in the pond. Then, it happened again when she was supposed to help Ophelia, and Mark messed with Josie's life to try to keep her from going to Florida.

Now, they were preparing to go somewhere strange. Was there something there that knew they were coming and was trying to stop them? Could something mess with the behavior of her friends like that? *No. Jenna's just in a bad mood. And Simon actually likes me. It's nothing more than that*, she said. She hoped for a spirit to respond, either Hanover or Mother Elk Spirit, but she heard nothing. Her stomach twitched in nervous anticipation.

Jenna and Dave stopped playing frisbee when Josie and Simon got to the beach but. "Hey guys. Sorry about before," Jenna said. "I don't know what's wrong with me. I think maybe I'm just anxious about today. I can't find much online about it, and I don't like going there with just some word-of-mouth stories."

"Do you want to forget about it? We don't have to go," said Josie, not believing her own words.

"No, we *need* to go there. I just wish I knew more. I don't feel prepared."

"We weren't prepared when we went out to Fishkill Pond," said Josie. "We'd only had the stories from Mary Alice."

Jenna shook her head. "But that was different. I didn't really understand what we were doing back then. God, that feels so long ago."

"It'll be okay, Babe," Dave said. He put an arm around her and pulled her close.

Jenna smiled and visibly relaxed. Josie watched them. There was a time when seeing them like that would make her jealous and wish things could be like that with her and Simon. But now Simon was acting so differently towards her. She could hardly believe it was real. Was it real? No, she wouldn't go there. Not now. They had Mystery Mountain to face soon, and she needed to focus on that. She couldn't worry about Simon. She would save that for when all of this was over, after she knew what was going on at that strange place.

She had gone into her meditation the night before hoping to get some idea of what they might be facing at Mystery Mountain, and though she did get something, it wasn't what she was hoping for. Like Jenna, she felt unprepared. Though she never prepared to the extent that Jenna might, she at least knew in the past that she was going up against ghosts. But she wasn't sure what she would be facing in that place. She remembered the sick feeling she had when they were there in the parking lot. With so many unknowns before them, Josie was definitely uneasy.

"We only have half an hour till we have to meet Daniel," said Jenna. "I'm gonna go get my stuff ready."

"Need any help?" Josie asked.

"No, but thanks. I think some time alone might be good for me." She looked at Dave. "I love you, but I mean *real* alone time. I need to get my head straight about this. Okay?"

"Okay," said Dave. His expression showed he was only slightly wounded.

When she was out of earshot, Dave turned to them. "So, what's going on with you two?"

Josie's cheeks flamed, so she looked away and turned her attention to the lake.

"Not sure that's something we need to talk about right now, buddy," said Simon.

"Got it. No problem," Dave replied, eyeing them curiously.

"Want to talk about what's going on with Jenna?"

"Touché, man. You've made your point."

"But seriously," said Josie, turning back to them. "It's not just us, right? She's not her usual self, is she?"

Dave looked at the sand, then at his friends. "No. Something's not right with her. But she's not talking to me about it."

Josie frowned. "Well, we all know how Jenna is. If we try to make her talk to us, she'll just get mad." *Fire-breathing dragon*, Josie thought.

"You're right," said Dave with a nod. He remembered all too well how she was when he and Simon tried to talk to her about her fight with Josie.

"So," Josie continued, "until she's ready to talk to us about whatever it is, or until it passes, we all need to agree to just keep an eye on her. Okay?"

"Yeah," said Simon with a nod.

"Agreed," said Dave.

"But she won't like it if she finds out," said Simon.

"I'll take that risk to protect my girlfriend."

Josie checked the time on her phone and saw a text message from Romy. Josie realized that she may not be able to share with Jenna right now, but she could share with Romy.

* * * * *

Simon saw her texting. "Daniel?"

Josie shook her head. "Romy."

"Who?" Simon asked with a frown.

"I met her at that group for young psychics. She's really cool. She has prophetic dreams of these big disasters, but through the dream she is able to help cross over the people that die in the disaster. And she can hold an object and get a reading off it. It's called 'psychometry'."

"Oh, cool," said Simon. He felt relief. She had another friend that was like her, that could see spirits, which meant Daniel wasn't the only one she knew that could do that. He wasn't so special after all. He knew he was jealous of Daniel. How could he not be? The guy was a link to her heritage that no one else could give her. And it was obvious that he and Josie had a connection. He didn't want to be jealous, but he was. It had taken him too long to realize he wanted to be with Josie, and this guy had a good chance of keeping it from happening.

But – he had to remind himself – like his dream showed him, he and Josie were connected too, on another level. He felt it whenever he touched her, whether with his hands or his lips. He felt confident that it was stronger than whatever she might share with Daniel.

That didn't mean he wouldn't keep a close eye on the two of them for the day.

* * * * *

Josie watched as her dad expertly steered a canoe back to the dock then helped Angela climb from the boat.

"I'm gonna go talk to my mom, let her know we're leaving soon," she said.

"I'll go get Jenna," said Dave.

"I'll meet you guys up there," she said.

Her mom saw her approaching as she crossed the beach. "Hi Josie," Angela called with a smile while Charles hauled the canoe back to the boathouse. Josie was happy that her mom seemed so much happier and more relaxed since they'd been on the trip – not including the fight with her dad a few days ago. She and Charles seemed to be getting along better, which made Josie happy. Maybe they wouldn't ever be a family like they were before, but she hoped their marriage would be okay.

"Hi Mom. You guys have fun out there?"

"Yeah. It's relaxing," she replied. "At least for me. Your dad does all the paddling. I just enjoy the sights."

Josie smiled. "We're heading out with Daniel soon. We're gonna grab some lunch on our way."

Angela frowned. "I'm still not sure about this little adventure of yours," she sighed.

"Mom, come on. You can't just take back permission now. We're about to leave!" Josie tried to keep the panic from her voice.

"I'm not, Josie. You can calm down. But I'm your mom so I am going to worry. Just promise me you'll be safe."

Josie crossed her arms and tilted her head at Angela. "I promise, Mom. I'll be safe. I'll have my phone with me the whole time. I'll be with my friends. And Daniel knows his way around this whole area probably better than most people."

Angela sighed again. "You guys have fun. Check in once in a while and let us know when you're on your way back."

"We will." She hugged her mom.

"Love you," said Angela.

"Love you, Mom."

3

Jenna was waiting on the porch with Dave and Simon when Josie reached the cabin. "We should go meet Daniel," said Jenna.

"Okay, I just want to grab a sweatshirt first," replied Josie. Inside she found her faded teal zip-front hoodie and put it on. It was a warm day, but Josie was chilled with apprehension. Back outside, she said, "Let's go."

They found Daniel in the small parking lot by the office leaning against a large car the color of pea soup that had to be at least twice as old as him. He smiled as they approached. "Ready?"

The back seat was large, easily accommodating Dave, Jenna, and Simon – who didn't like conceding to Josie sitting in the front next to Daniel. But he comforted himself with the fact that there was enough room for a small boat to fit between them.

They stopped at a small roadside gas station with a deli at the back. Daniel promised them that they had the best sandwiches in town, so they loaded up on foot-long subs, chips, drinks, protein bars and beef jerky. Jenna deemed it necessary for them to be prepared for anything.

"Are you planning on us spending the night out there?" Dave joked as she piled up snacks on the counter.

"You never know. But the way you eat, this won't get us through dinner," she shot back.

Dave shrugged. "You're not wrong."

A little further down the road, Daniel pulled over. The lake was before them and there was a clearing along the edge with several picnic tables.

"I thought we could eat here," Daniel turned the engine off.

"We're not far from Mystery Mountain, right? Can't we just get there?" Jenna whined.

"I figured you guys would be eager to explore once we get there. This way we can just eat and hang out first."

Josie sat with Simon on one side of her and Daniel on the other. She passed around the sandwiches while Dave set out drinks and chips. Jenna pulled a notebook from her backpack and put it on the table next to her.

"You really can't tell us any more about this place? There's *nothing* else about it that you can tell me? Nothing you've heard?" asked Jenna.

Daniel swallowed a bite of his sandwich and shrugged. "Not really. I'm guessing you searched online and found nothing, right?"

"Aside from a couple of old, grainy photos and a very general history, there is nothing," replied Jenna. "So, if there's nothing online, nothing reported in any newspapers or anywhere, how do *you* know about it? How do we know you're not just making it up to scare us?"

"Jenna!" said Josie with a scowl.

But Daniel smiled at Josie. "It's a fair question," he said then looked at Jenna. "My dad has been on the volunteer fire department forever, so when something happens – like hikers going missing – they tend to call him in. As a kid I'd sometimes go along with him, and now I'm old enough to volunteer myself."

"And you've been out there and actually witnessed some of this stuff?" Jenna asked.

"I've been there but I can't say I've witnessed anything. I've only been there for two missing persons cases. In one case, it was an old man with Alzheimer's who had wandered away from his home about a mile away. He was found on the property of Mystery Mountain. In the other case, the people turned up somewhere else. They claimed they got off the trails that run nearby and ended up finding their way back along the road."

"Have there been other cases that you weren't there for?"

Daniel shrugged. "A couple, I think, but I don't remember the details."

"What about the lights and sounds you said are reported?"

"I've never seen anything like that," he answered. He took two more bites of sandwich.

"Babe," Dave said with a nudge of his elbow at Jenna. "Maybe you should eat instead of interrogating Daniel."

"It's okay," said Daniel. "She can ask anything she wants."

"Good," Jenna said, and gave Dave a triumphant smile. "So, if you've never seen those things, how do you know about them?"

"People talk," he replied with a shrug.

"Do you believe them? What do you think they are?"

"I don't know. I do know that most people don't know what natural animal sounds are and most of the sounds might seem strange to someone who's in a spooky place, but I would bet it's something normal, like a fox in heat or a coyote. As for the lights? No clue."

"But you've been there, and you've never experienced anything odd or unusual? Unexplainable?" asked Jenna.

Josie had to admire Jenna's interrogation techniques, but it made her uncomfortable to watch her use them on Daniel. "You don't have to answer her, you know," said Josie.

"I really don't mind," he said. "I know you're all curious. I'm not surprised. Most people are when they see that place. But to answer your question, Jenna, the only thing odd I've experienced there is just an uncomfortable sensation of being watched."

Josie nodded. "I felt that too, just standing in the parking lot." She remembered it well, that feeling that there were eyes on them, eyes that watched and waited for them to step through that archway onto the grounds of Mystery Mountain.

"Josie, you really should eat more," Simon whispered.

She looked down at her sandwich that she'd only taken a few bites from. She also remembered the nausea she felt there. She shook her head at Simon.

"You've *really* never experienced anything else?" Jenna pressed.

"Not that I know of," Daniel replied. "But I don't like that place. I never go there unless I have to. I wouldn't be going now if it weren't for you guys."

"Why? What is the big deal?" Jenna asked.

Daniel sighed. He put down the last bit of his sandwich. "When I was a kid – probably five or six years old – my dad got a call to respond. My mom wasn't home. It was early winter, and we didn't have any guests, so he took me with him. He parked in the parking lot and told me to wait in the car. He told me that under no circumstances was I to get out of the car. It wasn't hard to do what he asked. The place creeped me out and I had no desire to tempt fate. I sat there, watching the volunteers walk through the place, searching for… I don't remember who. It got dark while we were there, so that at one point all I could see were their flashlights. Next thing I know, everyone's running. My dad came sprinting to the car, too. He got in, white as a sheet, started the car, and drove away. I asked him what happened, and he told me to never ask him about that moment ever again. I never have. And I've only ever gone there for an emergency because I had to. I didn't need to know what happened that night. Seeing the fear in the people that night, people like my dad who are strong, tough, fearless… I don't ever want to experience that ever again."

They were all silent. Jenna's face showed a mixture of shock and curiosity.

"Well now I'm totally freaked out," said Dave to break the silence. "But we're going anyway, aren't we." It wasn't a question. No one said anything in response. Dave shrugged. "I guess it can't be crazier than Florida, right?"

"What happened in Florida?" asked Daniel.

"Well, let's see… there were the sand dunes that came to life as zombie skeletons and attacked us, and the quicksand. Oh, yeah. Jenna got trapped in a jail cell, and there was an earthquake that *should* have killed us all. All done by one little ghostie guy," said Dave.

Daniel raised his eyebrows at the group of them. "Is he serious?"

"I wish I could say he wasn't," said Simon. He added, "We've been through a lot together."

"Wow," Daniel replied. "I had no idea."

"You really should eat," Simon said to Josie again, quietly.

Josie turned to him and looked in his eyes. They matched the sky above him, a bright cobalt blue. "Tell me… in your medical opinion, is it better for me to have a little food or a lot in my stomach when we get there, and I vomit?"

"You won't. I'll be right there with you. You'll be okay. You need to eat. Food is nourishment, strength."

She frowned, forced a bite, and glanced at Jenna who glared at her and Simon. Josie found herself hoping that Jenna's behavior *was* caused by something paranormal. It would be a lot better than to think she really didn't like the idea of them being together.

Josie forced another bite. At least Daniel had been right, the sandwich was delicious.

"So, do we think the guy that created the place might be haunting it?" asked Dave. "Or something else?"

"It's definitely not the guy that created Mystery Mountain," said Jenna.

They all looked at her.

She went on. "Daniel's dad said the other day that he thought the guy was in a nursing home somewhere, and he's right. While I couldn't find anything online about weird things happening in that place, I found one short article on the place that named the guy who started it. Then I searched for information on the property in public records." Jenna looked around the table proudly. Josie was glad to see a remnant of her old friend back.

"When did you find this?" Josie asked.

"I finally found it just before we left, after I left you guys at the beach. Once I knew who I was looking for, it was pretty easy. The guy's name is Rod Youth-Eden, and he's about 90 years old. He purchased the property in 1976 from a Ms. Mary Otwell who passed away six months later. There were about 16 acres at the time, and he purchased another ten acres over the next four years. Mystery Mountain opened in the summer of 1980 and closed down exactly ten years later, after the summer season of 1990. I was able to find records of five separate attempts to sell the property that never actually happened for some reason. And yes, the guy is in a nursing home in the town of Glens Falls, New York, which I guess is less than an hour from here."

"But we do know that you don't have to be fully dead to haunt, right, Josie?" Dave asked.

She nodded. "True, but... my gut says it's not him."

"Okay, so if he's not our culprit, who – or what – is?" asked Dave.

Jenna shrugged. "*That* is the mystery we're going to have to solve, isn't it?"

* * * * *

Jenna became increasingly antsy as they all finished eating. Josie was the last, feeling the tension of Jenna's expectations. Finally, she balled up her sandwich wrapper and said, "That was delicious."

"Can we go now?" Jenna asked.

Daniel looked at Jenna. "Hey, guys. Can I have a minute to talk to Josie privately?"

Simon frowned, instantly suspicious.

"Yes, you can," Josie answered for them. She didn't need anyone's permission to talk to Daniel.

Dave, Jenna, and Simon moved nearer the car while Daniel and Josie walked toward the edge of the lake.

"Is everything okay?" she asked.

"I just want to make sure you are truly okay with going to this place. I know you have gifts that the others do not. That I do not. When I am there I feel things I cannot explain, as do many, but I worry about what you might be able to *see*," he replied.

"I know. I get it. Really. I'm nervous but I think it's one of those things that the more I hear I shouldn't go there, the more I know I need to go there."

"Okay. I figured as much," he shrugged. "And I get it. I just thought I'd give you one final chance to get out of this... in case you were being pressured by your friends."

Josie should have been offended, but she said, "There was a time when that might have been the case, but not anymore. I've accepted that this is a part of my life. And a big part of it is helping the souls trapped in places like this. The guy that caused the earthquake and stuff in Florida, I helped him. I've helped a lot like him. It's pretty amazing."

"That's cool. I can get behind that. But if it gets to be too much, for you or any of them," he pointed to her friends who all stared at them, "just say the word and we will leave. Deal?" He held out his hand to her.

"Deal," she said. She took his hand, and while she held it, she said, "And I'm sorry if we're making you do something you don't want to do."

"My life needed a little adventure," he smiled his bright, warm smile.

* * * * *

The guy has about three seconds to let go of Josie before I go over there, Simon thought as he watched Josie and Daniel. He thought they were just shaking hands, like on a promise, but they didn't let go right away.

Then Josie released his hand and they both headed towards the car, and Simon let out a sigh of relief. He then held open the front passenger door for her, which allowed him the opportunity to touch her arm. He felt the electricity pass between them and when she looked up at him to thank him, he knew she felt it too.

"How far are we?" Josie asked Daniel as he pulled away from the picnic spot.

"It's only about 15 minutes from here," he replied.

"Okay.... We should be there by 12:30," she said, taking several deep inhales.

"You good, Josie?" asked Dave from the back seat.

"Yeah," she said with another breath. "Just needed to know how much time I have to get mentally prepared."

"Same," said Jenna.

Josie glanced back at her friend and gave her a small smile. When she turned back around, she thought, *We will get through this, and Jenna will be herself again.* She didn't know that Dave was thinking the same thing at that moment.

Hanover, are you with me? Josie then called out in her mind.

She felt the familiar tingle around her neck. *I'm here, Josie.*

Is Mother Elk Spirit with me, too? Can I talk to her the way I talk to you?

I am here, Josie, said the calm, smooth feminine voice. Then she manifested into view sitting between Josie and Daniel.

I'm guessing neither of you can tell me what to expect at this place?

It is not our place to tell, said Mother Elk Spirit.

Josie sighed inwardly and rolled her eyes. *As I figured.*

We will be with you, Josie, said Hanover, *should you need us.*

* * * * *

Daniel sensed a shift in the air between him and Josie. *Is that you, Mom?*

Yes, my wonderful son. I am here, he heard, a smile in her voice.

Good. I have a feeling we're going to need you.

No need to worry, Daniel. I'm here. For you both.

* * * * *

Josie could see it, just up ahead and around the bend where the trees gave way to a clearing with a pine-covered hill that rose beyond. Her heart quickened and her stomach churned with nerves. The anticipation was agony, unlike anything she'd experienced before.

However, she expected nothing less than chaos. In the woods of Maine, with the mad Phillip Stillwater, she had no clue she could see ghosts, but it was chaos. With the ghosts of Fishkill Pond, she had known more of what she was in for, but it was still chaos. In Florida, she hadn't expected ghosts in the fort on the island, but still there was a *lot* of chaos.

Daniel parked and turned off the engine. An unnatural silence seemed to settle over them. Up ahead lay the wooden archway topped with the sign for Mystery Mountain. Josie opened the door and stepped out, expecting to be hit immediately with chaos but felt....

Nothing.

4

"Is it just me… or is it…?" Josie turned slowly towards her friends.

"Different?" finished Simon. He stepped to her side.

She looked at him. "Yeah." They both turned back to gaze with matching frowns at the field before them. The sun was scorching and did nothing to enhance the decaying structures scattered throughout the overgrown weeds and grass. Like a bunch of shriveled creatures that fear the sun, the leaning walls, collapsing roofs, and broken beams seemed to be failing under the weight of the light.

"What do you mean, 'different'?" asked Jenna behind them.

Josie turned. "I'm not feeling what I did before. It was instant unease. Instant nauseating pain in my stomach. Now… nothing."

"So, it's weird when you feel stuff and weird when you don't. We just can't win," Jenna scowled. "But that does *not* mean we're leaving."

"I don't think anyone was implying that," Josie replied defensively.

"Good. Then I want each of you to strap on a recorder," said Jenna. She held out a voice recorder and a Velcro armband for each of them. "Left arm," she added.

"What's this for?" asked Daniel.

"EVP's – electronic voice phenomena, when a voice or sound is heard on a recording that wasn't heard at the time – are one of the most common paranormal phenomena," Jenna explained. "If we each wear a recorder, then we have more of a chance of picking something up, and I'll know if it was one of us speaking or not because I can hear it on other recorders when I align them."

"Wow, you are no joke with this stuff," said Daniel.

"I could have told you that," chuckled Simon, as he wrapped his armband around his left bicep and secured it in place.

"And I have two cameras, both with night-vision. I'll take one and… Simon, I want you to take the other."

"Me? Why me?" he asked his sister.

She shrugged. "I figure I'll be with Dave most of the time and you'll probably be sticking by Josie most of the time. That way we get two perspectives." She didn't say it with bite, but her words made Josie uncomfortable.

"We're splitting up?" asked Josie.

"Not right away, but I assume at some point we might want to. Cover more ground, you know?" Jenna replied.

"I didn't realize this was so organized and official," said Daniel. Jenna looked at him, still frowning. He added, "I like it. I feel like I'm in one of those TV shows."

Josie didn't think Jenna bought it, but she appreciated his attempt at appeasing her. Josie wondered if he sensed the change in Jenna as well.

"When you all have your armbands on, I'll come around and make sure everyone's recorder is on," Jenna said.

Josie struggled with her armband, unable to get the strap through the loop. Simon saw and went to her. "Let me get that," he said. He handed her the camera and took the armband from Josie. He wrapped it around her upper bicep, looped it, and pulled it tight. "Too tight?"

She shook her head. "Thank you." She looked into his eyes. Even through her sweatshirt he sent electricity through her with a touch.

"You're okay so far?"

"Yeah. So far. Nothing like last time."

"Well, let me know if you don't feel good," he said and leaned in closer. "I just might try to use Reiki."

She looked at him with her eyebrows raised. "You don't *want* me to feel sick, do you?"

"No, just looking for an excuse to put my hands on you."

Simon enjoyed it when Josie's cheeks flushed at his words and her eyes brightened as she looked at him.

"Are you flirting with me?" she asked quietly, matching his soft tone.

"Yes. Yes, I am," he smiled.

When Jenna called their attention back to her, he realized with a sinking heart how much he would give to be anywhere else with Josie. He would give up college and his entire savings account if they could just be back at the resort, on the beach or swimming to the platform, or out in one of the canoes. To lay in the sun with her until the stars came out and then watch the stars until the sun came up. To be anywhere but this place where the absolute emptiness of life – no bugs, no birds, no squirrels – creeped into his insides.

"Okay, I'm going to check your recorders," said Jenna, "and then… we go in."

"Let's get this over with," he grumbled, taking the camera back from Josie.

"You know how to work that?" Jenna asked him as she checked his recorder.

"Yes, Jenna. I know how to work a video camera," he said.

"And do you think you can keep your hands to yourself long enough to check this place out?"

He frowned again. "That's not why I'm here."

"Could've fooled me about sixty seconds ago," she said, and moved on to check Josie's recorder.

When Jenna was checking Dave's recorder, Daniel came over and said, "Are you just going to let her get away with talking to you guys like that?"

Josie shook her head. "Jenna's not herself right now," she said softly.

"That's not an excuse for her to treat her friends like crap," he replied.

"Actually, it might be," said Josie sadly. Both Simon and Daniel looked at her with concern. "Let's just do this and we'll figure that out later."

* * * * *

Jenna stood next to Josie just outside the gate. Behind them were Dave, Simon, and Daniel. They all looked up at the "Mystery Mountain" sign atop the thick wood poles. Once upon a time, that sign lit up in an attempt to draw attention and bring in guests. Now, it was dirty, broken, and dull.

"Nothing yet?" Jenna asked.

Josie shook her head. She then turned and looked at Jenna who had her camera running and pointed at Josie. "But there is still something very much not right about this place, guys," Josie looked at each of them. "I don't know what it is. I don't know if *anyone* – even the guy who built this place – knows what it is. So, we all need to be extra careful. Okay?"

They all nodded, looking grave. Jenna nodded too but Josie thought she looked… hungry.

Josie sighed. "Okay, let's go in."

* * * * *

Jenna's heart raced in her chest. Though everyone else seemed to think something bad might happen, Jenna only had high hopes. Now that she knew she had seen a ghost when she was a kid – not just once but all the time! – she was sure she would see something in this strange place. She agreed that it had an odd feel to it, but it was an odd place. A defunct, deteriorating roadside amusement park… how could it not have an odd feel? Normally she would try to get them to understand her point of view, but instead she was just irritated that they didn't just get it.

Jenna blamed it on Josie. Josie couldn't see anything but Simon and apparently hadn't for about two years – not that she'd known anything about it for the year they'd been best friends. And now Simon was being blinded by Josie. She couldn't believe how fast it happened. One minute he had no interest in her and the next... well, it was enough to make her sick. It wasn't that she didn't want Simon and Josie together. It was just that it felt... wrong somehow.

Then there was Daniel. Perfectly drop-dead gorgeous with his tall, muscular body, long hair, dark, almond eyes, and deeply tanned skin. Jenna could tell he liked Josie as more than just a friend, and if she could take her focus from Simon for more than a second, she might see that he could be really good for her. They had a lot in common. Not just their heritage. He had an openness to the spiritual world that Simon would never have. That had to be an asset to Josie, whose own father didn't believe her. Sure, he lived hours away, but in a few weeks, Simon would also be hours away at college, so either way, it would be long-distance for Josie.

Well, I can't bother with all that now, Jenna thought. She gave herself a mental shake and looked ahead of her at the scene. She stood taller, her spine steeled and strong. She felt confident and ready for whatever may come.

"Ready?" she asked, though she didn't pay attention to their responses. Part of her wished they would all go back to the resort and leave her there to investigate. But she was their leader, she had the most knowledge of the paranormal, and they were already there. She would just have to make the best of it. "Let's go."

Jenna went first through the archway. The sand and gravel crunched under her sneakers. She didn't notice how quiet it was there. No bugs hummed in the tall grass that was mostly dried and burnt in the sun. No birds chirped in the trees on the hill that was a backdrop to the field. Nothing stirred. Not even a summer breeze. She just walked on, following the wide path that was still plainly visible.

She didn't know exactly what she had expected when she passed under the sign, but it didn't feel any different than it had in the parking lot. A moment of disappointment passed through her, but she shoved it away fast. She wasn't going to get down about this place. Not yet. No negativity. *No negativity!* she silently ordered herself.

She stepped into a broad dirt circle. In the center were the remnants of what looked like it was once a ticket booth, now just a square frame of wood on the ground with a few yellow and red paint chips left on it. Around this, four other pathways joined together.

"Which way, Boss?" Dave asked her. Dave, the only one she could truly count on right now. The only guy not distracted by Josie, and the one person she knew would always have her back.

She smiled up at Dave and then looked around. She considered, and then pointed to the path that went from the right side of the circle to the carousel. "That way," she said. Jenna led the way, walking with clear purpose with Dave at her side. Josie followed with Simon, and Daniel trailed behind.

The fencing around the carousel was jagged and broken in many places, and very rusted, with a gate chained with a large padlock. It resembled a broken, toothy grin of someone sinister sending a warning.

"Should we climb over?" Dave asked.

"I wouldn't," said Simon. "If this rusty metal scrapes any of us we'll need a tetanus shot."

"Maybe we can break it," suggested Josie.

Dave shrugged and looked around him. He picked up a large fallen branch and took one swipe at the rusty chain, instantly breaking it in two. He pushed at the gate which swung open with a high-pitched, metallic groan.

"That was easy," said Simon.

"Too easy," said Josie.

Jenna raised her camera and stepped over the threshold.

5

Charles slowed the van as he approached a crosswalk. A family of four crossed. The two kids – a girl about ten and a boy about eight – pulled and tugged at the hands of the mom and dad, their faces lit with eagerness and joy. Charles envied the simplicity of their life.

As they drove on out of the downtown area, Greg said, "*Now* will you tell me where we're going?"

"Glens Falls," said Charles. He tapped his fingers nervously on the steering wheel.

Greg raised his eyebrows at Charles. "Glens Falls?"

Charles focused on the road before him and nodded.

"Why? What is in Glens Falls that we have to do without the ladies?"

Charles pretended to ignore him, using the hand-written directions in the center console as an excuse.

"Does this have anything to do with where the kids are?" Greg asked. "You don't believe they're hiking, right?"

Charles studied the directions, peered at the road signs, and tugged at the collar of his golf shirt. "No. I'd bet my life on it they're at that Mystery Mountain place."

"I've no doubt," said Greg. "I mean, really… I'd have done the same. You should see the place."

"Yeah, from what Ang told me, it's old, crumbling, and spooky. Which all adds up to potentially dangerous. An irresistible combination for teenagers," replied Charles darkly.

"Come on. You remember what it was like to be that age, don't you?" asked Greg. "To do things that you think your parents don't know about, things that are kind of risky, and to do them with the girl you like… that's teenage gold."

"Wait… what do you mean 'do them with the girl you like'?" Charles frowned.

"I guess Simon and Josie are… kind of… into each other," said Greg. "Rachel told me. I was clueless."

"Oh… geez…. Well, I can't even get into that right now."

"What does Glens Falls have to do with this?" Greg asked to distract Charles.

"I don't know. I'm probably being stupid," Charles shook his head. "You know that things have been rough with Josie lately. She doesn't believe I want to make it right, but I do. Saying it isn't going to help. I have to show her. So… I thought maybe you and I would do a little investigation of our own."

"Again… why Glens Falls?"

"William said that the guy who created that place is in a nursing home there. He was right. I made a couple calls and found the guy."

"We're going to visit him?"

"Yup."

"What are you hoping to find out?"

Charles shook his head again. "No idea. But I have to try something."

"Fair enough."

"You don't mind that I've dragged you into it?"

"Of course not," replied Greg. "Look, Josie has become part of our family over the past – what has it been? – year or so, and I care about her. She's a great girl."

"Thanks. I appreciate that more than you know."

"And I want you to know… I trust her experiences."

Charles looked at Greg with a frown.

"I don't know how much Angela told you about Florida, but Josie… she talked to my mom. My mom who's been dead for six years."

"I didn't hear that part."

"Yeah, well, Josie said things that she couldn't have known. Really, truly no way. I know the skeptical side of this stuff. There are ways to learn things about people to fool them. But there is no internet search or accidental find in my desk drawer that could give her the information she said to me that day. I don't understand how, but she is doing what she says she's doing. She's talking to dead people."

"I… I hear you, and I appreciate it. I really do. And I'm…," Charles took a breath and let it out slowly. "I guess I'm willing to admit that she can do… that. But if we can't see or hear the person she's supposedly talking to, how do we know if she's talking to something or someone good? Someone telling her the truth? What if she comes across something… evil?"

Greg thought for a minute, then said, "What if she does?"

"How can I help her? How can I protect her?"

"Charles, you know we can't protect our kids from everything. We can't protect them from most things in life. That's parenting. That's *life*. Life is about our kids learning to do things for themselves, having experiences, making mistakes, learning how to tell the difference between good and bad, right and wrong. From what I've seen, you and Angela have given Josie the tools she needs to go into the world and figure things out. Sure, she might get hurt a little or stumble along the way – like most of us have at some point. And yes, she might encounter someone – living or dead – who isn't the best person, but I'd bet money she will handle it well. And that's what's important, isn't it?"

"You're right."

"And she's got a great support system in you and Angela. And I'd like to think my kids are a pretty good part of that system, too. Even Dave."

"You mean, your future son-in-law?" asked Charles, smiling for the first time since they got in the car.

"Hey, don't go there just yet!" Greg laughed.

"Sorry. But you're right. Josie's got a good team. And it's time I get back in my place on her team again."

"I'm happy to help. And, you know, if Simon and Josie get together… who knows? We could be in-laws for each other's kids someday," Greg smiled.

"Hey! Okay, definitely not ready to go there! Your retaliation is complete! Can we talk about something else now?"

* * * * *

"Simon, are you recording?" Jenna asked, an edge in her tone slicing through the air.

"Yes, Jenna," he replied, trying not to respond with irritation.

"Okay, let's explore," she said with a sigh.

"But be careful," said Daniel.

Simon turned his camera on Josie, watching her alternately through the tiny screen and with his own eyes, watching for any signs that she was distressed. So far, she looked okay.

Simon followed her as she moved slowly towards the carousel, and he stopped when she stopped. He followed her gaze to the ground, where there was an elaborately painted sign that had obviously been on the ground for a long time, victim to the elements of all seasons, the writing on it was just barely visible. "Carousel of Beasts," Josie read aloud the curling script. She looked at him, and just then he heard what sounded like a hoof hitting the packed down dirt path behind him.

He spun around. "Did you guys hear that?" he asked too loudly.

"Hear what?" asked Jenna.

"I didn't hear anything," said Josie.

Simon shook his head. "Never mind."

They continued to move slowly closer to the carousel. Jenna approached the steps leading onto the platform and went up.

"Anyone coming with me?" Jenna asked. She looked at Dave. "You have to come with me cuz you have the camera."

"Just be careful where you step," said Dave, following her. The wooden platform was soft underfoot and broken in places, giving way to weeds and creeping vines that climbed up the poles, up into the canopy overhead.

"I'm gonna look over this way," said Josie, keeping her feet firmly planted on the hard dirt path.

"I'll stay with Josie," said Simon.

"Me too," said Daniel.

Jenna rolled her eyes at him. Simon rolled his back at her.

"Fine," Jenna huffed. The floor under her feet moaned with every step as she and Dave walked away from them.

Simon returned his attention to Josie. "So, no ghosts yet?" he asked her lightly.

"Nothing I can see," she said with a shrug. She turned around and looked at Simon. "Do you feel anything?"

He looked at her over the camera at her. "Me? No. Should I?" He wouldn't admit to her that – as much as he wanted to be supportive – he was more nervous than he'd expected. He didn't want to experience what he did in that house in Maine where he was shot by an insane ghost, nor did he want to experience a ghost trying to take over his body like when they were in the woods at Fishkill Pond. He wanted to leave that stuff to Josie and Jenna.

Josie shrugged again. "I don't know. Just thought I'd ask," she said.

They were at the back of the carousel. Beyond the fence that surrounded the ride was the park fence. Beyond that were some small trees and shrubs hiding the road that curved and disappeared into the distance. In front of them, the monstrous creatures of the carousel were frozen in time with snarls and eerie grins. Like everything else, they were weathered and chipped. The form of a werewolf with a saddle on his back leaped at them, its jaws dripping with mold, one red eye flashing accusingly at them. Looking at it through his camera, Simon thought he saw the eye blink. He looked up quickly and stared at it, but nothing moved.

He frowned.

"Simon?" said Daniel. "You okay?"

"Yeah, fine," he replied, still frowning. "Josie, what do you think?"

Josie matched Simon's frown as she gazed at a sea serpent petrified in its undulation through the air. "I just don't know," she shook her head. Then, her eyes widened.

"What is it?" asked Daniel. She grabbed at her stomach and doubled over. "Josie, are you okay?"

"I saw… I thought I saw…." She pointed behind Simon and Daniel. "Something moved over there, heading back the way we came." She took a deep breath and straightened.

"Maybe it was Jenna and Dave," said Simon.

"We're right here," Dave said, emerging from behind the center pole of the carousel.

"Did you see something?" Jenna asked as she came into view.

"Are you okay?" Simon asked Josie.

"I'm fine," she said, rubbing at a stitch in her side. "I'm fine. It's passed."

From over their heads came a loud BANG! Their heads snapped up.

"What the hell was that?" Simon yelled.

* * * * *

"So how are we going to see this guy?" Greg asked Charles as they walked across the parking lot of St. Joseph's Home.

"I told them on the phone that he was friends with my dad. He has no living family, so they said we could visit since we're in the area on vacation."

"Ah, sprinkling a little truth in with the lie," nodded Greg. "Smart."

"He's an old man with no family. I have a feeling they don't care if we don't really know him," said Charles, as much to convince himself as to convince Greg.

Greg didn't need convincing. Jenna inherited from him an open-minded sense of adventure along with the innate confidence that it would all work out. He thought this was a good idea, a good way for Charles to show Josie he cared. "Have any idea what you're going to say to the guy?"

Charles shook his head. "Not really. I'm just flying by the seat of my pants here."

Greg held open the front door. "Cool," he said with a smile.

Inside, Charles gave their names. "We're here to see Mr. Rod Youth-Eden."

The man behind the check-in counter gave them a thorough look-over and said, "Friends of the family, right?"

Charles nodded. "Yes, Sir."

"Do you know if the guy has any living family? Anywhere? Second cousin? Great niece? Step-granddaughter's boyfriend?" the man asked, brushing the strands of gray hair at the side of his balding head with his fingers.

Charles frowned. "I... don't know. Why?"

The man looked around and then lowered his voice. "If you don't mind my saying so, Mr. Youth-Eden is a, well, challenging resident."

"How so?" asked Greg.

"Can I be honest?"

"We would prefer it," replied Charles, throwing Greg a quick glance of curiosity.

"Well, it's just that...," he tugged at the corners of his mustache. "He talks of things... that aren't natural. Things that aren't normal. He frightens the other residents."

"Can you be more specific?" asked Greg.

Again, the man looked around, and then he leaned forward on his elbows. "He talks of things called skin-walkers. He talks of shadow people and Bigfoot and aliens. He says they still visit him in his room. He has his own room now. Not because he's got money, 'cause he doesn't anymore, but because he scares his roommates."

"He's always been an eccentric man," said Charles in a tone he hoped was casual and fearless.

The man looked at him and tugged at his mustache again. "Eccentric… right," he said, clearly disappointed that Charles and Greg didn't appear as distressed as he was. "Down the hall, take a left. He's all the way at the end on the right."

"Thanks," said Charles with a nod.

"Sounds like they've got him as far away as possible," Greg said to Charles under his breath as they walked the corridor.

"Sounds like they have good reason to," replied Charles. He instantly regretted his words. "I'm sorry. That's why Josie hates me right now, because of things like that." He shook his head.

"Don't be so hard on yourself, buddy," said Greg. "It's not an easy thing to wrap your mind around. I kind of grew up with it, so it wasn't such a foreign concept to me."

"But things like that, like that guy, the way he talked about this old man… that's what Josie's dealing with, right? She's going to have to deal with that her whole life," said Charles, his frown deepening.

"Yeah, probably," said Greg, very matter-of-factly.

They reached the door at the far end of the hall. It stood open. Charles looked in and lightly rapped his knuckles on the door. "Uh… Mr. Youth-Eden? Rod?"

"Ay, who is it?" grumbled the old man. He was propped up in the only bed in the room. A radio on a table in the corner played instrumental music softly.

"My name is Charles York," he replied and took a tentative step into the room.

"Ah, the 'family friend' the nurse said was coming," Rod said with a skeptical tone. He then cackled. "Don't worry. I didn't tell 'em you're a liar." The man then looked at Greg with his watery gray eyes.

"My name is Greg LaPage, Charles's co-conspirator."

"I'm sorry, Mr. Youth-Eden. We won't waste your time," said Charles as he took a step back.

"Nonsense! I didn't rat you out, so you owe me a visit," he said, pointing at Charles with a finger gnarled by arthritis.

"Oh. Well, alright," said Charles.

"Sit down. Both of you. Close, if you don't mind. My eyesight isn't good. There's plenty of chairs here."

There were exactly two chairs. Charles and Greg pulled the chairs near the bed and sat.

"Besides," the old man went on, "you can't go until you get what you came for."

Charles frowned. "Oh yeah? And what is that?" he asked with a light chuckle.

"Information, of course. For your daughter. Actually, for both your daughters."

Charles's face fell and he looked at Greg.

"I'm sorry… but what are you talking about?"

"You don't have to be afraid," said Rod.

"Sir," began Greg. "What makes you believe we need information for our daughters?"

"They told me," Rod replied.

"Who? The staff? A nurse?" asked Greg.

"No."

"Then who?" asked Charles.

A smile crinkled the corners of Rod's eyes. "The spirit of the mountain…."

* * * * *

"Is everyone okay?" Josie asked.

"Yeah," Jenna replied. "But what made that sound?"

"Nothing fell from the ceiling?" Simon asked.

"Nothing near us, not that we could see," said Dave.

"I saw something," said Josie. "Right before the bang."

As expected, Jenna's focus shifted. "What did you see?"

"Just movement, but it was big, like, person-sized."

"Did it move right to left?" asked Jenna.

Josie shook her head. "No. Left to right."

"Could you see form to it?"

"Not really. It was just kind of a blur of movement."

"Color?"

Josie shook her head. "Dark. Shadowy."

Jenna looked at Simon. "Did you get it on camera?"

"No," said Simon. "Josie was facing me so what she saw was at my back."

"Ugh. It figures," Jenna grumbled. She looked at Daniel. "Did you see it?"

He shook his head.

Jenna turned back to Josie. "What do you think it was? Do you think it was what made the bang?"

Josie shrugged. "Probably not. It was moving away from here."

Jenna sighed. "Okay. I guess we should just keep looking around. Maybe it will happen again. Just try to get something on camera next time."

Simon turned with a roll of his eyes as Jenna and Dave turned away.

Josie went up the steps onto the platform.

"You're being awfully quiet," Simon said to Daniel as they followed.

"Just trying to keep an eye out."

"For what?"

Daniel shrugged. "Everything."

"Look, there's a door here," Josie said.

"It probably leads to the motor and the music box," said Simon.

Josie pulled at the door and Simon took a step forward. A gust of wind blew through suddenly and the entire structure seemed to shiver. Another gust blew, and something creaked. Then there was a loud crack, and Simon fell backward as the werewolf pounced on him. He landed on the ground with the werewolf pinning him to the decaying floor.

"Simon!" Josie cried out. Her mind immediately went back to that night when he was shot by a ghost.

"I'm okay, I think," said Simon. "But I need a hand, please."

"What happened?" Jenna asked as she and Dave hurried back over.

"The werewolf fell on him," Josie said, her heart still racing. She took the camera from Simon while Dave and Daniel lifted the creature off him, then each took one of Simon's hands and pulled him to his feet.

"You alright?" asked Dave.

"I'm fine," said Simon.

"You're bleeding!" Josie said, pointing to his shin where blood was smeared.

Simon wiped a thumb down his leg. Underneath the blood, the skin was whole. "Um… the blood isn't mine."

* * * * *

"You'll have to excuse us," said Greg. Charles had gone as pale as the sheets on the old man's bed sheet, and Greg didn't trust him to respond well. "We're… well, new to this stuff. Can you explain what you mean by that?"

"New to this stuff?" repeated Rod. "That's rubbish. More lies! Why do people lie so much? I will never understand it. People lie so much they cannot hear when the truth is spoken. I always speak the truth, yet I am often accused of lies. Oh, maybe not outright, but I read between the lines. I hear it in the mocking tones in their voices, the looks of disbelief in their eyes. They humor me and think they appease me. No mind, though," he waved a hand in the air. "Got me my own room, didn't it?"

"Sir, please," said Greg. "Can you answer my question?"

"Yes, yes. I'll get to that. But first, you tell me you're new to 'this stuff' but that isn't the truth. *You*," he pointed at Greg, "know much about it. You've seen them. You've likely talked to them. Although...." He broke into a fit of laughter. Greg and Charles exchanged a glance. Finally, his laughter slowed. "You likely didn't know you were speaking to anything other than human. Why should you? You had no reason to believe it was anything abnormal. You had no context. It was normal in your home to have these beings present.

"But you," he went on, this time pointing at Charles. "Yes, I suppose you haven't experienced it as much. Remarkable considering your daughter. But I'd wager you wouldn't admit to any of it even if it smacked you right in the face!" Again, Rod broke into a fit of laughter.

Charles shook his head, clearly frustrated by the man. Eccentric was the word he'd used to describe the man before he even met him and now found that it was a gross understatement. He was about to stand to take their leave of the man when Greg put a hand on Charles's arm. When Charles looked at him, he shook his head.

He wondered if his friend could read his mind, then scolded himself for thinking something so ridiculous. But he acknowledged that he needed to be patient. *For Josie*, he thought.

Rod finished his laughter again and continued. "I just wanted people to know it, to experience it, to be open to it." He shook his head, then went on. "Yes, truth I suppose is a difficult concept. Sometimes there are truths we must deny for our own best interests, or for those we love. You love your daughter, do you not?"

"Of course I d-do," said Charles, surprised when his voice caught in his throat.

Rod nodded. "Then it is time for you to open your mind to *my* truths. Can you do that, young man?" He squinted his eyes at Charles.

"I'll do my best," said Charles with a sigh.

Rod nodded again. "Alright, then. I'm going to tell you boys a story. A *true* story…."

* * * * *

"How is it not your blood?" asked Jenna.

"I don't know but look. The skin isn't broken. I'm not bleeding."

"Is it even blood?" asked Dave.

Simon shrugged. "Looks like it but there's not really enough to tell for sure. I guess it could be rust."

"Is anyone else bleeding?" Dave asked, and looked at Josie, Daniel, and Jenna.

They all checked themselves. "Not me," said Josie.

"Me either," said Daniel.

"Okay, none of us are bleeding," said Jenna. She moved close to the werewolf now lying unthreateningly on the floor, crouched down, and pointed both her camera and a flashlight at it. "I don't see anything here. No blood, no rust… nothing that could look like blood." She stood. "Why did it fall?" she asked.

"How should I know? A breeze blew and the thing fell on me. This whole place is crumbling, so it's not improbable."

"I think," said Dave, "you need to be more careful where you step."

"I think we all need to be more careful," said Daniel as he and Josie went back down the stairs. "This whole place, not just this carousel, is old and that can equal dangerous."

"Daniel, I want you to know that we *are* careful," Josie said. "We… I… understand all the levels of potential danger."

"No offense, Josie, but I don't really think you do," said Daniel.

Simon heard this and turned his attention and the camera on them. Jenna and Dave lingered too, listening to the exchange.

Josie shook her head. "Maybe I don't know what is affecting this place... yet... but I know that people – living people – have been affected. I think of the families who lost someone who went missing on this property who'll probably never know what happened to their loved ones. I think of the souls who may be trapped here. I feel the weight of those souls. Whatever else is here... we'll figure it out. But those souls of the lost and missing and trapped, the living souls of those people are why I'm careful. I'm not here for fun or so I have a cool story to tell at school. I'm not here because this place is a cool, spooky anomaly. I'm here to help. And I'm confident that my guides wouldn't have wanted me to come here if I couldn't handle it."

Josie felt a tingle at her neck at her words, and then she saw Mother Elk Spirit manifest into view near Daniel. *You tell him, Josie*, she said proudly, with a wink.

"I thought you were on my side," Daniel said to the air over his shoulder.

Josie frowned. "Who are you talking to?"

"My mom. I told you I can hear her sometimes."

"What did she say?"

"She said, 'You tell him, Josie'."

Josie's frown deepened. "No, it was my guide, Mother Elk Spirit, who said that."

Daniel closed his eyes and let his chin fall to his chest. "Mom?"

Yes, Daniel, replied Mother Elk Spirit.

"Is it time?"

If you wish.

6

"Daniel, what's going on?" asked Josie.

Simon was suddenly at her side. "Josie, what are you two talking about?"

She shook her head, not taking her eyes from Daniel and Mother Elk Spirit. "That's what *I* want to know."

"Okay, but can we move away from this thing?" Daniel asked.

Josie immediately turned and walked back out to the main path.

"What is going on?" Simon asked. "You guys… the rest of us can't hear what your guide is saying so you need to fill me in." He looked at his camera screen.

Josie put her hand up, palm out, to Simon while she kept her eyes on Daniel. Simon wasn't going to get an explanation yet. "Daniel… tell me."

"First, I'll show you," he said. In a swift movement, he pulled his t-shirt up and off. He turned his back to Josie to reveal a tattoo that covered the upper half of his back between his shoulder blades. It was an intricately shaded sketch of a bison and an elk with an owl flying with outstretched wings over them. "This was a gift from my dad for my birthday. I am owl, he is bison, and my mom…."

"She's elk," Josie finished. "But is she… I mean, she couldn't be, could she?"

Daniel put his shirt back on and turned back to Josie. "She's not your mother, but she *wanted* to be."

"What?" asked Simon. Josie couldn't speak. Her mouth hung open, speechless with disbelief.

"My mom told me after you told me you could see her and my dad confirmed it," Daniel said. "I guess when your parents died

– your *birth* parents – there was something in the newspaper about you, trying to find some relative to take you in. Mom wanted to adopt you if no family claimed you, and I guess they tried. But… for some reason… it didn't happen."

It wasn't meant to be, said Mother Elk Spirit. Josie looked at her and she transformed into the image of the woman she'd seen that day as Daniel watered the flowers. *I can see that now. But I vowed to look out for you if I could, however I could.*

"Dad said that when your adoptive parents showed up here with you, he almost lost it. He couldn't understand it. He felt like it was a real blow to the Indian community. Because here they were, my mom and dad, already with a son, trying to adopt a Native baby, but she ends up with a Wasicun – a non-Native – family. It was hard for them to understand."

But then you visited us again, when you were older, she said. *And William and I saw how happy you were. Healthy, smart, and very loved. You'd already been taking dance lessons for a couple years at that time, and I remember watching you dance all over the beach.*

"Oh, yeah. I remember that now," said Daniel.

"Remember what? Josie, what's happening? Did your guide say something?" Simon asked. He was growing frustrated at only hearing part of the conversation. "Jenna's not gonna like it if we don't get it all on camera for the investigation."

Josie frowned at him. "This has nothing to do with the investigation. This is personal!"

Simon took a step back and lowered the camera. "Oh…." He backed up and turned away. Never before had he wished he could hear ghosts. Usually, it was only Josie who could hear or see them, but watching her and Daniel, he found he was feeling left out and clueless.

Dave and Jenna moved up behind him. "What's going on?" asked Jenna.

"They need a minute," he said, with a head nod at Josie and Daniel.

"Uh oh. Trouble in paradise?" Jenna asked him, unable to contain a smirk.

Simon rolled his eyes at her. "Shut up, Jenna."

* * * * *

Josie shook her head and looked up at Daniel. "You were almost my brother…." She said and laughed.

"I know. Crazy, right?" he smiled.

"Yeah. Wow. My life is so not normal." She shook her head.

"Normal is boring."

"Maybe, but sometimes I'd still like to know what it's like."

"Fair enough," he nodded. "I'm not sure you'll ever have that, but it's good to have dreams. Right, Mom?"

You can have whatever kind of life you want, Josie.

Josie turned to her. "So, you *are* Mother Elk Spirit, right?"

Yes.

"So why do you show yourself to me one way and to Daniel another way?"

I was not trying to trick you, Josie. I can take whatever form I wish to take. When I came to you to guide you, I took a form that represents my soul. This form represents who I was in human life as Daniel's mother.

"Your mom's name was Anna, right?" Josie asked Daniel.

"Yes."

"Can I call you Anna no matter what form you take?" Josie asked her.

Yes. If that is what you wish to call me, you may call me Anna.

Josie frowned then and looked at the ground.

"What is it, Josie?" asked Daniel.

She looked at Daniel, then at Anna. "If you're with me as a guide, then that means I'm taking you away from Daniel and William. I don't want to do that. He's so happy whenever you're near, and when William heard that I saw you...." She shook her head. "I just can't do that to them."

You aren't taking me away from them, Josie. I can be with all of you, whenever and wherever.

"How?"

Time and space are not the same for me as they are for you. Those things are necessary for human life only.

"I'm not sure I understand," Josie said.

It isn't something I can go into now. Your friends are waiting patiently for you. She pointed to where Jenna, Dave, and Simon waited. Jenna looked anything but patient. *But there is one more thing you need to know. Time and space don't work right here. Look at your clocks.*

Josie pulled her phone from her pocket and pressed the button to display time. It showed 12:45. "How is that possible?"

* * * * *

"I was just six years old," Rod began, "when my family drove from back home in Indiana to visit my mother's very best friend. My mother and Mrs. Mary Otwell had been best friends from the time they were little girls, but she had moved to upstate New York after getting married and they hadn't seen each other in ten years. Mrs. Otwell – Mary, as I would call her later – was happy to have us. She lived in a nice farmhouse across from a big field at the foot of a hill between Lake George and Red Drum Lake. My dad spent his days fishing while my mom and Mary visited. I would play in field and in the woods on the hill, hunting for sticks to use as spears, playing cowboys and Indians. In those days, it wasn't offensive to play cowboys and Indians.

"We had been there for four nights. That fourth night, I woke up suddenly and found myself outside, standing in the field. All around me were...." He closed his eyes and laid his head back.

Charles and Greg waited a minute for him to open his eyes. When he didn't, they exchanged a nervous glance. Greg shrugged.

Finally, Charles cleared his throat. "Uh, Rod? Mister… Rod?"

Rod's eyes popped open. He looked at Charles and Greg with a frown. "Who are you?"

"Um… we're—"

Before Charles could finish his reply, Rod Youth-Eden broke into laughter again. "Relax, boys. I'm not that far gone," he laughed. "Just wanted to give you a dramatic pause."

Greg laughed but Charles shook his head. "Mr. Youth-Eden, Sir, we don't really have time for this," said Charles.

"You want to help your daughter, then you will make the time," he said.

* * * * *

"I think we should leave," Simon said, after Josie and Daniel filled the others in.

"Simon, no! We can't leave yet," said Jenna.

He crossed his arms and took a wide stance facing his sister. "I knew you'd say that, and you'll probably win this fight like you always do, but I'm still gonna fight."

"Why bother then?" Jenna asked.

"I don't like this," he said. "Something is messing with time, Jenna. Do you get that? Josie saw something near that carousel, and I'm not so sure that the werewolf fell on me because of wind or age. This place is seriously messed up and bigger than just a ghost or two."

"I agree with Simon," said Dave.

"Thank you," said Simon.

"Hey!" said Jenna.

"Babe, I can't always agree with you. Especially when I don't agree with you," said Dave.

"Alright. So… why do you agree with him?" she asked. She tilted her head and crossed her arms like Simon.

"Because this has happened before," said Dave. They all looked at Dave questioningly. "Seriously… none of you remember?"

"Remember what?" asked Daniel.

"I expected you of all people to remember, Jenna. It's in your book thing. Your 'Paranormal Journal'…." Dave waited for someone to remember. "You guys! It's what started all of this. How do you not remember? Last summer in Maine… we were only in that house for one night, but the rescue team said they'd been looking for us for *three days*."

"Of course I remember that," said Jenna, "but we have no way of knowing why. We don't know if that was paranormal."

They all looked at Jenna in surprise.

"Hey," she said, defensively. "I don't always assume everything is paranormal."

"Of course it was paranormal," argued Simon. "Missing time like that is anything but normal."

"And something Josie said is bugging me," said Dave. "She said that Anna told her that time and space are necessary for human life. *Human* life… so if time is messed up here it's probably because of something *not human*. And if space is out of whack too, well, I can't even begin to comprehend what that could mean for us."

"But that doesn't mean it's necessarily a bad thing," said Josie.

"Thank you!" said Jenna.

"I'm sorry, guys," Josie looked at Simon and Dave. "I think you're right that there's something non-human here. I can't see or sense anything definite, but I *know* it. I know something – not someone – is here, but I also know that I need to find out what it is. I need to know if it needs my help."

Simon looked at Dave. "We never win against them, do we?"

Dave shook his head and shrugged. "But if they're not leaving, I'm not leaving."

"Same," replied Simon with a resigned sigh. "So… where to next?"

* * * * *

"…The next thing I remembered was my mom shaking me awake. I wasn't in my bed. I was still in the field. My mom was worried about me, but I felt… happy. I told her what happened, but she thought it was a dream. Thought I was sleep-walking, but I knew. I knew it was real."

Charles and Greg stared at Rod. Charles was frowning deeper than before, and Greg's mouth hung open awkwardly.

"My mother was so disturbed by what I said that we left that day, but I never forgot what happened. My mother would chastise me if I talked about it in front of her, so I didn't, but I thought about it every day of my life. Occasionally, as I grew up, I would tell someone about it, but no one ever truly believed me. I even had one guy, my friend Eddie who I'd known and worked with for years… I trusted him with my life, one of the best guys I'd known so I thought maybe… but he too laughed at me and called me crazy. It broke my heart.

"That was when I decided I needed to prove it to them."

* * * * *

Rachel pulled the cork from the bottle of Chardonnay and poured two glasses. She returned to the front porch of the cabin and handed a glass to Angela. She sat in the Adirondack chair next to her friend.

"Thank you," Angela said, and took a sip.

"You know none of them are where they say they are," said Rachel.

"I know," Angela sighed.

"How is it, do you suppose, that we know that?"

"Mother's intuition," Angela said. Her texts to Charles were going unanswered and she was tired of waiting for a response, so she put her phone down on the small table between them and focused on her wine.

"Yeah… mother's intuition. Funny how it works for our husbands, too," laughed Rachel.

"Well, when they act like children themselves, it's not that surprising," said Angela with a shake of her head.

"True enough," replied Rachel. "So, are we going to do anything about it?"

"Not yet. Let's just enjoy the peace."

Rachel let silence fall between them for a few minutes. Then she said, "You know, I'm not so sure my mother's intuition was something that I acquired after I became a mother."

"What do you mean?"

"I mean, 'mother's intuition' is a term for when a woman has a knowing about what their kids need, and sure, I have that," said Rachel. "But before I became a mom, I think I had pretty good intuition. I always trusted my gut – which is intuition. Intuition is having a knowing without knowing *how* you know it."

Angela sat up and looked at Rachel. "What is this all about?"

Rachel sighed. "Ever since we were in Florida, I've been thinking a lot about all this. Josie told us things… like Greg and Simon are something called 'an Empath'. Well, I didn't know what it meant, so I started doing some research of my own. And I found a website for a medium, Jessica something or other. She's not around here. I think she lives in California, but she talks of how everyone has intuition, and we've had it as long as people have existed. But in modern society, we've been conditioned to trust only science and our five senses. As a result, we've forgotten how to use our sixth sense – our intuition."

"You believe that?" Angela asked.

"You don't?"

Angela shrugged. "I didn't say that. I guess… I've just never really thought about it."

"Maybe that's the problem. If we had grown up around people who used their intuition, who knew how to use it and trust it, then we would've learned it too. We *would* think about it. Greg grew up like that. His mom read cards and things for many years, but after Greg's dad left…." She shook her head. "Well, she kind of shut down after that, so he's not a great example. But I guess the point I'm trying to make is that maybe we all have a little bit of what Josie has, we just have had ours turned off, or turned way down, and we only use it when it's acceptable. Like when it's called 'mother's intuition'."

Angela frowned into her wine glass. "It makes sense. And it means…," Angela swallowed away the tears that jumped into her eyes. "It means that Josie isn't so different from me and Charles."

* * * * *

Josie followed slowly behind Jenna and Dave as they made their way up the path that led to the Ferris Wheel. Simon wanted to ask if she was okay but didn't want to annoy Josie.

As if reading his mind, she stopped and turned to him. "Simon, you need to stop worrying."

"I can't help it."

"I appreciate that you care," she said, "but if you want to know if I'm okay, why don't *you* tell *me*."

"Um… what? How?"

"Use your Empath sense. Tell me what you feel from me, from my energy."

"Um…." Simon looked around and saw that Daniel had come up behind him and Jenna and Dave had also stopped and were listening.

"I'm not trying to put you on the spot. I think this is something you need to try. Go ahead," Josie urged. "I'll be honest and tell you if you're right or wrong. Tell me how I am feeling."

"Well, uh... okay. I'll try." Simon fidgeted, frowned, and took a breath. Then he focused on her: the way she stood, the way she shifted her weight from one foot to the other, how she tilted her head and crossed her arms at him. He inhaled, closed his eyes, and tried to do what he did to her leg when they were in Florida when she got stung by a jellyfish, to imagine what was happening underneath the surface. Swiftly, it came to him. "Physically you're fine. Nothing is affecting you that way, making you feel sick like before. But you're... you're not afraid. You're anxious. A little nervous, but confident."

He opened his eyes and looked at her. After a long moment, she said, "You're a hundred percent correct."

"Really? Wow."

"Awesome, my brother's a psychic too," said Jenna, her tone biting. "I can't tell you how thrilled I am. Oh, wait, Simon... why don't you *feel* how thrilled I am?"

"Geez, Jenna," said Simon. "I didn't ask for this."

"Whatever. Can we just get moving?" Jenna turned and walked away without waiting for a response from anyone.

Dave shrugged at his friends and walked after Jenna. Josie, Simon, and Daniel exchanged a wary look with each other and slowly followed.

The Ferris wheel was too choked by vines and weeds for them to get near it, but Jenna got as close as she could, waving various pieces of equipment at it with a determined frown while the rest of them watched in uncomfortable silence. Simon, doing his best to not trigger any more of his sister's wrath, kept Josie in his viewfinder while also trying to get some images of the Ferris wheel. Another breeze disturbed the leaves of the tree growing alongside the structure; Simon watched as Josie turned towards him, a frown forming slowly on her forehead.

"Do you feel that?" she asked, her words getting lost under the chattering leaves at her back. Then, Simon saw a thick strand of Josie's hair lift, but not from the wind. It was like two invisible fingers were lifting it away from her.

"Josie!" Simon said, pointing.

"What?" asked Josie, but then the wind kicked and swirled, then shot at them. As quick as it came, it was gone, and everything fell silent again.

Jenna looked at them. "Was that…?"

"Freezing?" Dave finished for her.

"Like a giant freezer door was opened," said Daniel.

"Simon, why were you pointing at me right before that happened?" Josie asked.

Jenna turned to Simon. "Did something else happen? What did you see?"

"I…." Simon looked at Jenna who stared at him expectantly. "I don't know. No, nothing happened."

* * * * *

"Would one of you boys get me a Coca-Cola?" asked Rod Youth-Eden.

Charles and Greg looked at each other. Greg stood. "Yeah. Sure. I'll go…."

"What did you do to prove it to others?" Charles asked, unwilling to wait until Greg returned from the man's errand.

He thought Rod would be difficult and wait for his soda, but he went on. "I took a leave from work. I'd been at the factory for more than ten years by then, I was a shift manager, so I had time to take, and I'd been able to save some money, too. Didn't have a family to support, you know. Never was the marrying kind, as much as my mother wanted a daughter-in-law and grandkids. She never let on, but I knew I was a disappointment to her in that way. But I tried not to let it bother me, and I tried to be the best son I could be. Anyway, I packed up a suitcase, put a map on the passenger seat, and headed east for New York."

Greg came back with a tray holding three cans of Coke and three cups of ice. He popped one and poured some in a cup then handed it to Rod before popping one for himself. Charles waved off Greg's offer and watched as the old man took a few sips and smiled. "Ahhh, that's good stuff. Anyway, I got to New York and had a moment of feeling ridiculous. Wondered if I was a fool for coming all this way because of what really might have been a dream. But I decided I had to at least see the place. I thought if I saw the field and the hill, I'd know if it was real like my heart told me, or if I was crazy, like others thought.

"I'd gotten the address for Mrs. Mary Otwell from my mother and drove right to her house. It was after dinner time, but it was summer, so it was light out still when I got there. And it was exactly as I'd remembered. The moment I saw it all, I knew I wasn't crazy, and I knew I hadn't dreamed anything that night all those years before. But I still needed proof. I *wanted* proof! And I suppose I also just really wanted to know more about what happened that night.

"I was nervous when I knocked on Mary Otwell's door, like a schoolboy on his first date. But she knew who I was when she opened the door. She invited me in and warmed up leftovers from her dinner for me. She'd been a widow about five or six years by then, and she welcomed the company. Over coffee after dinner, mixed with a little brandy for nerves, I told her what I'd experienced that night. She remembered it." He paused and sipped his Coke. Greg poured more from the can into the cup. "She remembered my mother telling her of what she called my 'dream' and claimed I'd been sleepwalking – something I'd never done before and haven't done since… that I know of. Mrs. Otwell also said that my mother was very nervous and told her they needed to leave a couple of days early because of a forgotten appointment back home, but there wasn't any appointment.

"I asked her the question then. I asked her if she believed it was a dream. She said she knew it was not. She said she'd known of it all as long as she'd lived there. And she said that I must be special, because it didn't show everyone the same friendliness that it showed to me."

"What does that mean?" asked Greg, as he drank the last of his own soda.

Rod did the same, then eyed the unopened can sitting next to Charles. Charles picked it up and handed it to Greg, who popped the tab and poured some into Rod's cup. "Precisely what I asked her. She said, 'I don't really understand it, I just try to honor it, and leave it alone.'"

"That's it? She didn't tell you anything else?" Charles asked.

Rod went on as though he didn't hear him. "She invited me to stay in her guest room, but I insisted on camping outside in the field. I'd purchased a small tent and equipment before I left home. I wanted to be where it happened, to experience it again. But this time, I had so many questions.

"I didn't expect anything to happen the first night, yet I had trouble sleeping," said Rod, sipping happily at his Coke which Greg had topped off again. "Every sound I heard had me on edge, waiting for something to happen. But nothing happened. A week passed, and I hadn't experienced a thing. I spent my days helping Mary with chores, and each night I waited. Then, one Sunday, Mary had gone to visit a friend, so I spent the day just wandering through the field. I climbed the hill and back down, I walked every inch of the field, I sat by a tree for hours and meditated. Still, there was nothing. But deep in my gut I felt that I was exactly where I needed to be."

* * * * *

"Guys, what just happened?" Jenna snapped.

Josie sighed. "Just before the breeze started, I got that feeling… that feeling of being watched."

Simon matched her sigh. "And I saw a strand of Josie's hair lift up."

"What!" Josie cried.

"That could have just been from the breeze," said Daniel.

"No," Simon shook his head. "It didn't lift like that. It was like someone, or something, was lifting it."

"Please tell me you got it on camera," Jenna said.

"Actually, I did. I saw it happen through the viewfinder."

Jenna's face lit like a lightbulb. "Yes! Finally! Recorded evidence! I measured the temperature drop 25 degrees in only a few seconds. This is amazing!"

"No, it's not," Josie said.

They all looked at her.

"Talk to us, Josie," Daniel said with a frown.

She started to pace. "I felt it, whatever that was, I felt it. Watching us. But if Simon is right, and something was close enough to me to touch my hair, why couldn't I see it? I should be able to see it, right?" She stopped pacing and turned to face them all, looking at them with wide, panicked eyes.

"Not necessarily," said Jenna. "Remember last spring, you had that ghost guy haunting your house. You caught his voice as an EVP on the recorder, but you didn't see him, right? And at the fort, we had all kinds of things happening, but you didn't see him until you found Ophelia."

"Yeah… you're right," said Josie, calming a little, but then frowning. Jenna *was* right. She couldn't see everything. But that still didn't seem like a good thing.

"Energy is weird, Josie," said Daniel. "There's so much we don't know about the spirit world. Many people even call it the 'Invisible World' and for good reason."

Josie frowned in thought. "I still don't like it."

"Do you want to leave?" asked Simon.

"You're welcome to go, Simon," Jenna snapped.

"You know I'm not going to leave you guys," he said and followed her.

"I know you're not going to leave Josie," Jenna replied.

"Jealousy does not look good on you, Sister," Simon said.

Jenna opened her mouth to respond then closed it so fast that the click of her teeth echoed in the air.

Josie rolled her eyes and shook her head. For a split second, the old Jenna had returned, but she was gone in the next instant. "I don't want to go."

"Okay, so that's settled… for the next five minutes, anyway," said Dave with a sigh. "Where to next?"

Jenna just huffed, turned, and walked away. She had only gone a few steps when she stopped so suddenly that Dave had to jump sideways to keep from crashing into her.

"The snack bar… I wonder if the cold air came from there. They must have had freezers and coolers," Jenna said.

"There's no way," said Daniel. "This place hasn't had electricity in decades."

"Let's check it out anyway," she said.

Dave shot a nervous look over his shoulder as he hurried after Jenna and then jogged to get in front of her. "It's all closed up, Babe," he told her, seeing the thick wood panels covering the windows. He hurried to the side. "Big padlock on the door, too."

"Hmm, so they don't want anyone getting in there," Jenna said.

"It's kind of strange that this place isn't more vandalized," Josie said.

"Yes, it is strange," Jenna replied.

"I have a feeling that anyone who stepped foot on this property with the intent to do harm would find some reason to leave it real quick," Daniel said.

"What do you mean by that?" asked Simon.

Daniel shrugged. "Just that my gut… my *intuition*… tells me that whatever is here would find a way to deter vandalism. I can't explain it any more or any better than that."

"I think you're right." Josie glanced at the dome on the other side of the clearing. It beckoned to her, and she didn't like it.

* * * * *

"I became obsessed with the place," said Rod. "Nothing happened that was out of the ordinary, but I felt if I just waited, it would. I felt that it would happen to me again someday if I was patient.

"Mary said it was nice to her because it liked that she took good care of the land, letting most of it go to the wild. So, I thought I would help with that. She wanted me to move into the house, but I didn't feel right doing that. Instead, I converted a shed at the far side of the property to a little one-room thing with a bed and a wood stove. I did eat my meals with Mary, though, but the rest of the time I was in the field. Eventually, I quit my job back home and had all my stuff put in storage. Never went back for it, not to this day. I didn't care. My focus was like a laser. But I had to earn my keep and earn a living still. I did mostly odd jobs for folks in the area and worked at a bar on some weekends. Just waiting for the time when something would happen again."

He paused to drain the last of his second soda, then went on. "I guess a couple years went by. The only thing that happened was that every now and then I would feel like someone was watching me, but as soon as I tried to locate it, or as soon as I spoke out to it, the feeling was gone. Then, Mary became unwell. Her family came to talk about moving her into a nursing home. She agreed on one condition: that I purchase the house and the property from her and continue to care for it. The family didn't like that. They thought I was some weirdo out to take an old lady for everything, but she insisted. I had quite a bit in savings by then, and in the end, we were able to come to an agreement that made them happy enough.

"And that was when things started to change," said Rod. His eyes grew wide and lit up with the memory.

Then a nurse came in. She eyed the empty cans of soda on the tray near the old man. "You know this man's a diabetic, right?" she said to Greg and Charles.

Charles opened his mouth to apologize, but Rod said, "Oh, Patty, don't give them a hard time. It's not like I'm ever gonna walk outta here alive. Let me indulge a little with my guests."

"Fine. This one time," she replied with a frown. But she gave him a smile and a wink before leaving the room.

"They have to pretend they don't approve, but they know. I'm not gonna live much longer so why deny me?" Rod told them. "Now where was I. Oh, yes… I became owner of the property and the house. Of course, the family took a lot of furniture and stuff they felt was valuable and whatnot, which I didn't mind. It wasn't about the house for me.

"It was about two weeks after I became official owner that I finally… I finally had an experience. I was walking through the field late one afternoon. The sun was setting. It was kind of cloudy so the colors in the sky were blazing oranges and pinks. And it was almost winter, so most of the leaves were off the trees. I had spotted something that looked like trash – something tossed from a car window maybe or blown from a neighbor's yard – and was walking towards it when I tripped and fell forward. In the few seconds of falling and righting myself, something happened. The sun was suddenly high overhead in a cloudless sky and all the leaves on the trees were fresh and green. The grass was wet like it had rained recently. I heard a noise and looked up to see a man, an Indian man, running straight toward me with a look of pure terror on his face, like he was running for his life. But then he spotted me and stopped in his tracks. It only took him about half a second, though, before he looked at me like I was his ticket, and he started running at me, charging at me, a long spear held over his head. Terrified for my own life, I stepped back, stumbled again, and when I righted myself this time, I was back in the sunset and the autumn, and my attacker was gone."

* * * * *

Jenna tugged at the lock and pounded on the plywood window coverings, but nothing budged. She walked around to the back of the building. "Another door. Locked." She frowned deeply. "There must be something in there. They wouldn't lock it up otherwise."

"Why is it that locked doors only make you want to know what's behind it?" asked Simon.

"What are we going to do, break in?" Dave asked Jenna. "Did you not hear what Daniel just said?"

"I don't want to break in," Jenna replied. "I just want to know what's in there. *My* gut, *my* intuition is telling me that there's *something* in there."

"Why? What good will it do?" Daniel asked. "The cold air didn't come from here. There's no way the way it's locked up."

"Daniel's right, Jenna. It's not like we'll find a set of keys lying around," said Josie.

Jenna turned to Josie and said, "Geez, Josie, will you just stuff a sock in it!"

7

"I stepped forward, and nothing. I checked the ground for whatever I tripped on. Nothing. It was the strangest thing. There and gone so fast. But it *was* there. Like I'd stepped through a doorway and then back out.

"That night, as I ate my dinner, I thought about what had happened. It didn't make sense. It was like I'd stepped through a doorway into another time. I sat on the front porch and just watched the field, as if a door would just suddenly appear. But I couldn't just sit there. I grabbed a flashlight and walked the field. I was terrified but pumped with adrenaline. I think I walked every inch of the field three times, zig-zagged in and out of the tree line, climbed the hill and came back down. All was as it had been before.

"But I wasn't satisfied. It drove me nuts, trying to figure out what happened. I tried to recreate it, but never could. I waited for something else to happen. Nothing. Weeks passed. Then, one night, I turned the television on. I didn't watch a lot of television, but that night, I just needed something to distract me from my thoughts. But… you know that saying, 'Everything happens for a reason'?"

"Of course," said Greg.

"Well, I turned the channel to 'Star Trek', and in the episode, Captain Kirk, Spock, and McCoy are checking out some planet with a guy that has a machine with a time portal. They all travel through it, but Kirk goes to one time and Spock and McCoy to another. I watched the show, riveted. There's another saying…."

"Truth is stranger than fiction," Charles said.

"Yes," said Rod heavily. "Yes, and I kept thinking, we create these fictions from true things, so there must be some science, some *real* science to this portal stuff.

"The next morning, I went straight to the town library, but the librarian there, nice lady, told me that they wouldn't have what I was looking for. Too small. She recommended I try a college or university. So, I drove out to Skidmore College, about an hour away, and went to their library. And that was when I met Drew."

* * * * *

The tension was palpable among the five of them as the echo of Jenna's words still hung in the air. No one dared speak.

Finally, Jenna turned and continued on, and they hesitantly followed. They stopped in front of the ski lift; a large wooden sign overhead was so faded from weather and sunlight that it was hard to make out the two words on it.

"Sky Watch," Jenna read.

"What does that mean?" Dave asked.

"I bet there's a good view from up there," Josie replied.

"There is," said Daniel. "There's a viewing platform up there."

They all turned to look at Daniel. "How do you know that?" asked Jenna.

"I've been up there," Daniel replied.

"Why didn't you tell us this before?" asked Jenna.

"You lied to us," Josie frowned.

"Ha! Not as perfect as you seem," said Simon.

Jenna turned to him. "Jealousy does not look good on you, Brother."

"Shut up, Jenna," said Simon.

"How about you all shut up," said Dave, "and let Daniel explain."

They all looked expectantly at Daniel. Daniel sighed. "I didn't lie, exactly. I told you about all the times I'd been on this property except...."

"Except what?" said Jenna and Josie at the same time.

"Give the man a chance to speak!" said Dave.

Daniel looked at Josie. Josie could see Mother Elk Spirit – Anna – standing just behind him with a hand on his arm. He patted the spot where her hand was. He sighed again and then said, "It was last fall, I came out here with my two buddies, Jack and Henry. We drove by but didn't stop. Instead, we went and parked around the other side of the hill. There are some trails."

"Up to there?" asked Jenna.

"No. Jack was the one who wanted to climb to the top of the hill. I didn't want to give in but, you know, I didn't want to—"

"Be a chicken," Simon finished for him.

"Well, yeah. You know how it can be with your friends. So, we went off trail and climbed up the back of the hill. We made it to the platform; all that's left is some planks of wood with a railing, but it gives a great view of the sky, and you can see the whole park down here. Jack wanted to stay until it got dark, but I didn't, and neither did Henry. Henry was getting weird about it, too. He was visibly uncomfortable up there, all nervous and twitchy. Jack was stalling and kind of being a jerk. Henry and I wanted to leave. It was getting dark, but Jack wouldn't go, and we wouldn't leave him behind. And then... Henry had to take a leak.

"He went to find a tree but first gave me a look begging me not to let Jack pull any pranks on him – which is something Jack would do. I kept my eyes on Jack. He didn't do anything out of the ordinary but too much time went by, and Henry didn't come back. I was just about to tell Jack that we had to go look for him when we heard a yell. I looked toward the sound, and saw him, Henry, down here, running this way," Daniel indicated the path they were on, gesturing in the direction of the dome structure. "Jack and I went back down the hill as fast as we could, got in the car, and came after him, but by the time we got over here, he was gone.

"Gone?" asked Josie. "Like, vanished?"

"Not quite," said Daniel. "We were sitting in the parking lot, trying to decide what to do, when we saw the flashing lights up the road. Jack and I were scared out of our minds of what we were about to encounter. But it was not what we expected."

"What happened to him?" asked Jenna.

"Let the man talk," Dave said gently to Jenna.

Daniel shook his head. "He was okay. Sort of. Someone driving by had seen him sitting on the ground on the side of the road, crying. He wouldn't stop crying even long enough to tell them his name, so they called an ambulance. We stopped and told them he'd been hiking with us but must have gotten lost when he went to pee. They asked if we'd been at Mystery Mountain. Jack denied it first, but I knew it was best to also say no. It was mostly true. We'd only been up on top of the hill, not in the park. Henry didn't contradict us, either, once he talked. But he never said what happened. To them, to us. All he said was he got lost and was scared and he'd overreacted."

"And that was it?"

"No. First, because my dad is on the volunteer fire department, he heard about what happened and I got grounded for two months. And Henry stopped hanging out with me and Jack. I asked if he was mad at us, and he said no. But he avoids us to this day and has new friends now."

"You have no idea what happened to him?" Jenna asked.

"No clue," said Daniel.

"Why didn't you tell us about this before?" Josie asked.

"Because I have no idea what happened. I have no idea if this place had anything to do with what happened and I can't even say for sure it was him I saw down here in the park. I just… I don't know. I don't like talking about it. I don't like thinking about it. I lost a good friend because I gave in to peer pressure. I'm not proud of any of it. I'm sorry I didn't tell you sooner."

Do not be mad at him, Josie, said Anna.

"It's okay, Mom," said Daniel. "She has every right to be mad at me."

Josie shook her head. "I'm not mad." Simon huffed, and Josie shot him a look. She went on. "I understand why you didn't want to tell us, and I think if everyone here used a little *empathy* they would understand, too. But I do wish you had told us."

"He should have told us, Josie," said Jenna.

"He has now," replied Josie calmly.

Jenna scoffed and shook her head. "Whatever. Okay, so, question: did he have enough time to get from where you were to down here?"

"That was one of the weird things. He was wearing an orange sweatshirt that day, and that's why we thought we saw him down here, but it had only been maybe ten minutes from when he went to pee until we heard the scream and saw him. I don't think he could have done that even if he ran full sprint down the hill."

"That might be true anywhere else but here," Simon said. They all looked at him. "Have you forgotten already that time doesn't work right here?" He held up his phone. The time showed 1:08 pm. "This," he said, pointing at the time, "is impossible. Yet it's happening."

* * * * *

Charles looked at his phone and ignored another text from his wife. It was getting late, and Angela and Rachel were getting concerned that they weren't back yet or responding to their texts. But the old man talked on to his captive audience.

"I was sitting at a table in the back of the library with a pile of physics books and my head in my hands. I didn't understand any of it and had no idea where to begin. Drew saw this and came to my table. He was in the PhD program at the school in their physics department and could tell I didn't belong there. At first, I told him I was just doing some research. He asked what I was researching. 'I had something odd happen at my house,' I told him.

"'Tell me about it,' Drew said. I wasn't sure. He seemed nice, but how do you tell someone, a stranger at that, you think you stepped through a portal into another time?

"'You'll think I'm crazy," I told him.

"But he said, 'Look, I'm done classes for the day and was about to go get a cup of coffee. Why don't you come with me and tell me your crazy story? I promise to listen with a completely open mind and if it's something that can be found in these books, I'll tell you exactly where to look. How does that sound?'"

"Well, I had nothing to lose, and I was overwhelmed to say the least. So, we went to a little coffee shop near the school, and I told him my story. My whole story. It just kind of poured out of me. Probably because I hadn't had anyone to talk to about it in such a long time. And to my amazement, he didn't laugh. In fact, he was fascinated. Genuinely. He asked if he could come out to my house to check the place out, and I couldn't refuse. It was such a relief to have someone to talk to about it all. I hadn't realized until that moment just how lonely I was.

"Drew came that Saturday. He brought all kinds of weird equipment and books and notebooks. I showed him around while his things beeped, and he took lots of notes. I asked him to stay for dinner, and we talked until the stars came out and kept talking until the sun came up."

Rod paused, a sad, faraway look in his eyes. He shook his head and went on. "He came back a lot after that and we became close. He wanted to solve the mystery as much as I did. Eventually, I asked him to move in, and he did, despite having almost an hour's drive to school. Beyond trying to figure out what happened to me on that land, we liked being with each other.

"Time passed and life started to settle into something almost normal. I continued to spend my time working odd jobs, walking the property, talking to things that I couldn't see but suspected were listening. Drew and I worked with his instruments; I never quite understood what any of it did, but I did my best to help.

Nothing happened, though. I didn't get discouraged. I believed that when the time was right, something would finally happen, and I would get answers.

"It was late winter. The snow was melting, and the air was starting to warm when I had the dream. I don't think it was just a plain dream, but something *more*. I was to make an amazing place out of that field. I would show people things. But not in a way that was obvious. They would learn of possibilities without knowing they were learning. Open their minds without them knowing we were opening them. As soon as Drew woke that day, I told him about the dream, and to my surprise, he got as excited as I did. For the next two days we planned and sketched out the whole thing. We barely ate or slept but when we were done, the idea was clear. We called it 'Mystery Mountain'.

"Everything fell into place: the money, the materials, the labor… I almost didn't have to do anything, it happened so easily and quickly. As we worked, I started to have experiences again. Strange and wonderful and confusing experiences. I didn't understand most of them, but they drove me forward with the place. We opened it that summer, right on Independence Day. Business was good the first few years. And I continued to experience what was unexplainable to Drew's scientific mind. He had started as a skeptical scientist, but the more that happened that he couldn't find explanations for, the more frustrated he became. And he took that frustration out on me. The longer this went on, the more it affected Mystery Mountain. Soon, we just knew that something just wasn't right.

"What do you mean by that?" asked Greg.

"We had been open for almost a decade at that point. Mystery Mountain, I knew, would never be as big as Disney, you know, but people came. Most enjoyed it while some poked fun at it. I didn't care, so long as some of the people liked it. I thought we were doing the right thing. But then bad things started to happen."

* * * * *

"Alright, so, what now?" Dave asked.

"We're not leaving," Jenna snapped.

"Did I say anything about leaving?" Dave asked her.

Jenna turned to Daniel. "Is there anything else that you haven't told us that we should know?"

Daniel shook his head. Jenna looked at Josie who looked at Anna. Anna nodded at Josie and Josie said to Jenna, "He's telling the truth."

Jenna huffed and turned. "Fine. Let's keep going," she said over her shoulder. She marched up the next path to the crumbling structure of the haunted house. She stopped in front of the door with the "Enter at Your Own Risk" sign and let out a roar. "Arg! It's locked!"

Another big gust of wind whipped by them as they caught up to Jenna. The door rattled in the wind, knocking against the decaying wood of the jam, and the knob jiggled like someone on the other side was trying to open it. Then there was a click and the door swung open with a squeal.

Jenna's eyes were as wide as dinner plates as she turned to the rest of them. "Please tell me someone got that on camera."

"I think I might have caught it," Simon said, "but Jenna, it's an old rusty lock. It was probably already open, and the wind just moved it."

Jenna rolled her eyes at him. "Of course you would say that."

"Yes, because not everything is paranormal," Simon replied.

"But it could be! Simon, if you would just open your mind a crack, you would see the truth in all of this. But I get it, you're afraid. Too afraid that precious science isn't the end-all be-all. Too afraid that you don't know everything!"

"Jenna, I don't think you're being fair," Dave said.

"Oh, you're taking his side?" She shot daggers from her eyes at him.

"I'm not on anyone's side. I'm on all our sides. I want us *all* to get out of this place without losing our minds or our lives!" Dave said. "Or maybe I should say, without losing our souls!"

Jenna frowned at him but pressed her lips together, a good sign in Josie's mind. *How much longer are we going to allow her to get away with this behavior?* Josie asked, casting a glance at Anna who stood behind her son.

That is up to you, Anna replied. *How much longer do you want to let her get away with it?*

Josie's frown deepened. Her irritation with Jenna was mounting, and Anna's words hit hard. Josie said, "We're never going to find out if it's paranormal or not if we just stand out here arguing, so maybe we can finish this later?"

The pressure that had been building evaporated, though Josie was sure it wouldn't last. Without another word, Jenna pushed the door open the rest of the way and stepped inside with Dave at her heels. Josie hesitated. A shiver ran up her spine and dread tightened her throat as she stepped forward and crossed the threshold. Before her eyes could adjust to the darkness, she heard Jenna say, "I don't believe this."

Josie looked around as Simon and Daniel stepped inside behind her. The door swung closed with an echoing thud. "This can't be possible."

"Josie, what is it?" Daniel asked.

Josie just shook her head at him and looked at the others. Dave frowned and Simon looked pale in the light of their flashlights they had each clicked on.

"Guys, what is going on here?" Josie asked.

Simon swallowed hard. "It's got to be a—"

"If you say this is a coincidence, I will disown you as my brother," said Jenna.

Simon closed his mouth and shook his head.

"What's the big deal, guys?" Daniel asked. "What's going on? It's just a house, right?"

Josie looked at him. "It's an exact replica of the house in Maine," she said.

"What house in Maine?" Daniel asked.

"The house in Maine where we took shelter. Where I first saw a ghost," she said.

"Where I got shot by a ghost," added Simon.

"But it's just a house," said Daniel, shining his flashlight around. It landed briefly on the fireplace that Josie sat beside that night, trying to warm up, her head pounding; the light flicked over the furniture covered in dusty sheets, and the cabinet full of knick-knacks left behind.

"It's exactly like it," Jenna said, her tone full of awe. She had her backpack off and was pulling out a familiar notebook. "I drew a floorplan of the house. Look," she said.

Daniel went to examine it, but Josie didn't. She didn't need to see the drawing to remember the exact location of the dining room at the back, the hallway on the other side that led into the library where she'd found the scrapbook, and the stairs that led up into the darkness where he was waiting for them….

"What is happening to us?" Josie asked in a low, strangled voice to Simon.

It was what Simon needed to snap out of it. "Josie, listen to me," he said, looking deep into her eyes and putting one hand on her arm, warming her with his touch. "This might look just like that place, but it isn't the same. Philip is gone, right? Don't doubt that, Josie. Philip is gone. He's not here, he's not going to hurt us. Whatever is going on here, we will figure it out, and we will beat it, just like you did with Philip. Okay?"

As the warmth from Simon's hand spread through her body, her fear melted and the anxiety that gripped her chest released. "Okay, yeah. You're right," she said. "Thanks," she added.

"Alright, guys," said Simon. "This place is… weird, to say the least. I don't understand how it could look exactly like that house, hundreds of miles away, but even I can't deny it."

"Thank you!" exclaimed Jenna.

"But it seems like it's just a house. Maybe they had trick lights and hidden speakers or something to make it spooky. Now, it's just a house. A weird house, but a house. So, I think we should keep moving and get out of here."

"We can't just leave," said Jenna. "We need to look around first."

"Seriously, Jenna? There's nothing here!"

"Fine, Simon, leave if you want to leave. I know you're terrified of this place. I know you still have nightmares about being shot. So, you can go ahead and be a big chicken and leave. Just give your camera to someone else."

Simon's face revealed shock, betrayal, and then anger in a flash before he thrust the camera into Daniel's hands, turned, and walked to the door. The light of his flashlight bounced as he struggled with the door. He turned and pulled, but it didn't budge. They could hear him jiggling and pulling at the doorknob with no luck.

"Um, Simon?" Dave called.

He stopped pulling at the door and returned to the room. "It won't open," he said.

"There has to be another way out of here," said Dave. "Let's just look around, and if we can't find another way out, well, I'll break the door down because I am not spending the night in this freaky place."

Josie chuckled uncomfortably.

"Alright, well, I'm going to check upstairs," said Jenna defiantly, moving toward the staircase.

"I doubt you'll find a way out up there," Daniel said.

"In case you haven't noticed, Genius, I am not the one freaking out about getting out of this place. I'm the one trying to investigate, which is what I'm going to do."

"Jenna!" Josie admonished.

Jenna ignored her and started up the stairs. Dave followed close behind. Daniel and Simon both looked at Josie, waiting to see what she would do.

Josie shook her head again. "I can't believe this is happening. This… this is where it all started. For me, for her… it's like a really bizarre reminder of how it started. Why would this be here of all places?"

"Don't look at me," Simon replied. "I have no clue."

"Does it really look exactly like that other house? Not just similar?" Daniel asked.

Josie nodded. "It's smaller scale, but yes, every detail is the same."

"Agreed," said Simon.

Daniel frowned.

"What?" asked Josie.

"I'm not sure. I think there's purpose to this, but I'm not sure what that purpose is."

Over their head, floorboards squealed with that familiar heel-toe movement. Even though she knew it was Jenna and Dave, Josie shivered.

"Well, let's at least look around for another way out of here," Josie said.

"Let's get this over with," Simon replied.

* * * * *

"One of our newer additions that summer had been a barn and a small petting zoo," Rod went on. "The smaller kids especially loved it. But one night I got up to take a pee, looked out the window, and saw the barn on fire. Killed all the animals. It was awful." Rod paused. He swallowed hard and fidgeted with the blanket over his lap with his crippled fingers. His eyes glistened with moisture. "But it was nothing compared to what happened next. There had been a small pond at the back of the field that we expanded into a pool and made it into one of those water bumper-car games. It was shut down for about a week because the timing mechanism was broken, and the parts were on order. A little two-year-old boy wandered away from his family and fell into the pool. By the time he was found, it was too late. He was dead. We were devastated. We were sued by the parents, of course. What had seemed like a dream come true was becoming a nightmare. We never reopened the ride, and we filled in the pool, but that didn't help anything.

"And then the final straw came late in the summer. A young couple was on the sky lift. They were engaged and would be getting married the following weekend. Well, he was stung by a bee and went into anaphylactic shock. He was struggling to breathe, and in his struggle, fell out of the lift. Landed… well, let's just say it wasn't a fall he could survive. We shut down for good that day."

"That's terrible," said Greg.

"It was, and it destroyed me and Drew. We had insurance and lawsuits hanging over our heads and the stress was too much. Our relationship didn't survive. He moved out and returned to the college. I never allowed him to take the blame for any of it. It wasn't his idea; he was just there to help me build my dream. Didn't see why his life should be ruined too. I tried to sell the place to pay all the lawyers and things, but every time, something got in the way. It was like someone had cursed us. It was the land. It was mad at me."

"What? You can't be serious," Charles scoffed.

"Charles, I don't think—"

Rod held up a hand. "It's fine. I don't know if I'd believe me either if I hadn't lived through it."

"Do you really believe this stuff you're saying?" asked Charles.

"Young man, if you would just open your mind a crack, you would see the truth in all of this. But I get it, you're afraid. Too afraid that precious science isn't the end-all be-all. Too afraid that you don't know everything," Rod said, nearly echoing Jenna's words spoken miles away.

Greg leaned forward. "With all due respect, sir, I don't think you're being fair," Greg replied, nearly echoing Dave's response to Jenna.

Rod shook his head. "Forgive me. I've spent a long time being called crazy, not being believed about any of it because it's all so ridiculous and fantastical. But I will go to my grave holding fast to my conviction that there is something going on beyond the norm on that land. And sometimes I get defensive. Because the really crazy thing is, I still love it there. I'll never stop loving that land. I don't think it's bad. I just think it's misunderstood."

"Why?" asked Greg.

"Good and bad is so ambiguous, really. It's kind of like… it's like a toddler who is trying to get attention but is going about it in the wrong ways. You know?"

"I understand the analogy, Sir, but… well, how is any of this supposed to help me with Josie?"

"Let me ask you a question. Do you believe any part of the story I just told?" asked Rod.

Charles sighed and looked at his hands, then up at the man. "I think… that what you experienced was very real to you."

"Precisely!" Rod replied and punctuated the air with a gnarled finger.

"Pardon?" asked Charles.

"You don't believe me. Not entirely. But you respect that I believe me, yes?"

Charles frowned in thought then said, "Yes, actually."

"That's all you have to do. Respect that it's real to her, even if it isn't real to you."

"Makes a lot of sense to me," said Greg.

"Me too," said Charles, almost sounding disappointed.

"But there's more," said Rod.

Oh, great, thought Charles. He braced himself for more weird talk.

But Rod pointed at a cardboard box that sat on a stool across from the foot of his bed. "That's for you to take. For your daughter. And yours, too," Rod added, pointing at Greg. "I think she'll also like what's in the box."

Charles went to it, lifted the lid, and looked at Rod.

"It's my notes and journals. Everything I ever did for Mystery Mountain, everything I experienced, is written down and is in that box," the old man said, his voice tinged with sadness. "I've no one to give it to. No family. But both of your girls will find use in what's in there. If you boys don't mind taking it to them."

"You don't even know our daughters," said Charles.

"See, that's the thing," Rod replied. "Time and space don't work the same on Mystery Mountain as it does other places."

"I don't understand," Charles said.

"You don't need to," said Rod.

* * * * *

"Jenna, what are we doing?" Dave asked.

"Investigating," she replied casually, but he heard the suppressed bite.

"But…."

"I just want to have a look around," she said. There was something more she wanted to say, but she was holding back. Dave didn't like it. She was not his usual Jenna, and that worried him. Something was happening to her; something was affecting her in a bad way, and he didn't know what it was or how to get rid of it.

"This place freaks me out," he said, hoping his admission would spark something in her.

"I think that's the point," she said. She continued down the hall, the floorboards groaning under her feet. A shiver ran up Dave's spine and he glanced over his shoulder, expecting to see a looming shadow behind him, but there was nothing he could see. Nothing he could see, but he sensed something, something different from the things they'd encountered before.

"Jenna, there's nothing up here," he said, unable to hide the tremble in his voice. "Let's go back downstairs with the others."

Just then, the lights on the K-2 meter in her hand jumped. "Not yet," she said. "I think there's something here." Jenna followed the lights of the meter as they flickered and jumped from green to yellow to orange to red as she turned slowly. She looked up at Dave, then past him, and her eyes widened. "Don't move. I think there's someone at the end of the hall."

"Josie? Or Simon?" Dave asked, though he knew the answer. He wanted to turn around, but his feet wouldn't move.

Jenna stepped past him, the lights of the meter bouncing. He wanted to stop her, but he couldn't. Fear gripped his insides and tightened his throat. Then, he felt a warm tingle in his spine and everything else eased. Released from his terror, he turned toward Jenna as a deep, comforting voice in his head said, *You must let it happen.*

"What?" Dave said.

"Shhhhh," said Jenna.

He shook his head and watched her take another step forward. Then, the shadow charged at her, and Jenna let out a blood-curdling scream as her feet went out from under her. She fell flat on her back before Dave could catch her. The air around them was charged with electricity, and a moan vibrated through the entire hallway. And then, it was gone, and all was silent.

Josie, Simon, and Daniel were at the bottom of the stairs when Dave carried Jenna down. Her face was buried in his neck, and she was crying hysterically. "We need to get out of here," he said.

"We haven't found another way out," said Simon.

Josie went to the door and tugged at it, but it still wouldn't budge. "Arg! Let us out!" She yelled. The door popped open.

She frowned at it as she pulled it open the rest of the way and they all hurried back out into the hot summer sun.

"That was weird," said Josie. "Jenna, are you okay? What happened?"

"I was attacked!" said Jenna, as Dave set her on her feet. "I don't know what it was, but it knocked me over."

"Are you hurt?" asked Simon.

Jenna shook her head. "I don't think so. It just scared me," she said, calming. She then turned to Josie, her eyes flashing. "Why didn't you warn me there was something… demonic up there? What's wrong with you?"

Josie felt as though she'd been slapped. "What? What's wrong with me? What's wrong with you, Jenna? You have been nothing but mean to me, to all of us except Dave, for days! I can't take it anymore!"

"Oh, I've been mean?" Jenna repeated and looked at Simon and Dave.

Simon kept his mouth shut but Dave stepped forward. "She's right, Babe."

"What?"

He put one hand on each arm. "Jenna, you are the sweetest, perkiest, most optimistic person I have ever met, but you've been a nightmare lately. You aren't you. I think this place is doing something to you, and I don't like it. I want to get you away from this place as fast as possible."

She looked at him with wide eyes, but then her face crumpled. "I know!" she said. She scowled and folded her arms across her chest. "I feel it. But I can't help it!" She leaned her head against Dave's chest, and he hugged her to him. "I'm sorry. I just can't help it. I'm trying, though. I really am."

"I know you are," Dave said.

Jenna straightened and stepped back. She looked at the others. "I'm sorry. I know I'm being a huge jerk. I'm sorry."

"It's okay, Jenna," said Josie. "We know it's not you."

"But we can't leave. I don't think this will go away until we've done… whatever it is we're here to do."

"Unfortunately, I agree," Josie said.

"Josie, can I ask you a question?" Jenna asked. "Do you know who or what was in there?"

Josie looked back at the house, the front door still open, and frowned again. Something about it looked different, but she shook the thought away. "I'm sorry, Jenna. This place is… well, I can't get a grasp on anything here. Whatever was in there, well… I don't know if it was a thing or a person or something else. I'm really sorry."

Jenna frowned. "You don't have anything to be sorry for."

"Babe, you're sure you want to stay?" Dave asked her.

Jenna nodded. "I am."

"Me too," said Josie.

Dave, Simon, and Daniel all exchanged a look of resigned exasperation. Jenna went to a nearby bench and sat and pulled a bottle of water out of her backpack. "Why is this happening to me?" she asked as she gulped down water.

Just then, the sound of tires crunching over dirt and gravel filled the air. They all turned toward the parking lot to see a gray sedan pulling to a stop near the entrance.

"Uh oh," Dave said under his breath.

A man stepped from the car. He was tall and slender with a full head of thick white hair. He walked to the archway, looking at them with furrowed brows over his sunglasses. They were all frozen in anticipation of what this man was about to do.

They stared at him, he stared at them, and then he turned, got back in his car, and drove away.

8

It took a little while to extract themselves from Rod. He asked if they'd come visit him again, and Greg told him that they would do their best.

"I feel bad for the guy," said Greg. "No family. Wasting away in the back corner of a nursing home." He shook his head.

The man at the front desk heard them approaching and smiled. "Had a nice visit?"

Charles put the box down on the desk and made a note of the time next to their names on the visitors' log. "Actually, yes. We had a very nice time with him."

"Did he tell you any crazy stories? Bigfoot visit lately?" The man cackled at himself.

"I found his stories rather… enlightening. How about you, Greg?" asked Charles.

"That guy's one of the coolest guys *I've* ever known," answered Greg.

"One of you gonna take him home with you?" the man winked.

"We'll go talk it over with our wives and flip a coin. See who wins the pleasure of his company," said Charles.

"Excellent," he replied, not picking up on the sarcasm in Charles's tone. "Get him outta our hair."

Charles picked up the box and turned away. "Not like you have much hair left," he muttered.

"What was that?" the man asked.

"Have a nice afternoon," Charles said over his shoulder. Once back in the car, Charles turned to Greg. "I don't know how I'm going to do it. How am I going to help Josie fight this fight for the rest of her life? Fight the disbelievers like me, fight the skeptics and the outright jerks like that guy?"

"I think she already knows how to fight them. She fought you, didn't she?"

He flinched at the realization. "Good point," he nodded.

"How did she fight you?"

"Do you mean, aside from the actual yelling and screaming?"

Greg laughed. "Yeah."

"Well… I guess she… she didn't care that I didn't believe her. And the thing she said to me that had the most effect on me… she looked me right in the eyes and asked me why I was afraid. Until that moment, I didn't realize not only that I was afraid, but how afraid I was."

"That's the thing, Charles. You don't have to help her fight anything. It's only a fight if *she* allows it to be a fight. I saw it with my mom. People would call her a witch. She let them. She didn't care. She even played it up sometimes when it suited her. But looking back, I remember her doing things like Josie does. She would do a Tarot card reading, and the person would leave in tears of joy, hugging my mom and thanking her like she'd just given them the best gift in the world. *That* was what mattered to my mom. Not the people who didn't believe her. She just didn't make time for them in her life. That's all you have to help Josie with. Not fighting anything but learning what to let go of."

Charles shook his head. "Is it that simple?"

"I think so. That and respecting her in her experiences, like Rod said in there… I think it will go a long way," said Greg.

Charles started the engine and sent a text to his wife that they were on their way back to the resort. "I hope you're right."

"Do you think our wives are going to kill us?" asked Greg.

"No. They'll be mad when we tell them what we did, but if we show up with that box and the amazing story to go with it – and maybe some flowers and steaks for the grill – I think they'll forgive us," Charles replied.

Greg laughed. "That sounds like a smart plan."

* * * * *

"What was that all about?" Josie asked. "Do you think he's going to the police?" She looked at Daniel.

He shrugged.

"That can't be good," said Simon.

"I'm not leaving. The police will have to drag me out of here," Jenna scowled.

"Then we'd better get a move on it so we can cover as much ground as possible before they get here," said Dave. "Where do you want to go, Babe?"

"Maybe we'd all better have a water break first," said Simon, passing a bottle to Josie.

"Okay, but not too long," Jenna said, then she turned to Josie. "Why do you think this is happening to me?"

Josie sat on the remnants of a post near Jenna while Simon and Dave paced. Daniel sat nearby on the ground.

"I think the energy of this place has gotten to you," said Josie.

"But it started before we got here. I've felt… well, not quite right since yesterday… maybe the day before." She shook her head. "I'm not quite sure. So, if I've been *off* for that long, then it couldn't be this place, right?"

"Not necessarily. I don't think time or distance matter. Remember the ghost of Mark in Florida was messing with me all the way up in New Hampshire weeks before we ever went to Fort Roday. I think if something here wants to mess with you, it can do it however and whenever it wants to."

Jenna sighed. "Well, that makes me feel a little better. Sort of. I mean… that it's not just me suddenly being horrible to you all. But I want it to stop, Josie."

"I know," said Josie. "Me too."

"Will you help me figure this out?"

"That's what I've been trying to do, but this place isn't making it easy," Josie replied. She looked at her phone for the time. It showed 1:14. "I wish I knew how long we'd really been here. Feels like closer to two hours than 45 minutes."

"That actually might work to our advantage," said Jenna.

"How so?"

"If time's moving slower here than out there and we're here for what feels like six hours but turns out to only be three, then hopefully we can figure out what's going on before our parents find out where we are and flip their lids."

Josie chuckled. "You have a point."

Jenna stood. "Okay. Let's get back to investigating."

"Where to? Back in there?" Dave asked, hitching a thumb at the haunted house.

Jenna shook her head. "I want to go back in there and find out what knocked me down, but I want to check out the rest of this place first. Let's go to the dome, and if that guy isn't back with the police by the time we're done there, then I'll go back in."

Josie could sense fear in Jenna. Simon could, too. Even Daniel knew it wasn't normal. Dave was doing everything in his power to hold things together for Jenna. "Sounds like a plan," Dave said, mustering as much casual cheer as he could.

They headed down the path, but Josie found herself rooted to the spot. She looked at the domed structure and a shiver ran up her spine and shook her whole body.

"Josie?" Simon said, turning back to her.

"Yeah, I'm fine. I'm coming," she replied.

As she forced her feet to start to move, Daniel leaned in close and said in her ear, "I feel it, too."

She smiled at him, grateful for offering comfort, but there was nothing anyone could do or say that would quell the anxiety that had turned all her insides to jelly. There was something about that looming structure, the pimple on the landscape, that bothered her more than the grotesque merry-go-round, more than the rusted skeletal Ferris wheel being choked by vines, and more than the house that was a near-replica of that horrible house in Maine.

Anna? Hanover? You're with me, right? Josie immediately felt the familiar tingle on her shoulders and neck, and then she heard Anna's voice softly say, *You can do this.* Josie took a bracing breath and charged forward until she caught up with Jenna.

Jenna and Dave had paused before the entrance to the dome. A small alcove of pitch blackness stood before them, inviting and foreboding at the same time.

"I don't like that the doors are wide open like that," said Simon. Unlike all the other structures, this one wasn't boarded up, locked, or chained. "There could be homeless people living in there," he added.

"I doubt anyone would want to live in there," said Daniel from behind Josie.

"We have to go in. See what's in there," said Jenna, her usual confident tone sounded less convinced. "Or who." With a fluid motion, Jenna had a headlamp pulled from a pocket of her backpack and positioned it on her forehead. She clicked it on, then clicked on her hand-held flashlight. Everyone else did the same, clicking on their own flashlights, and she started forward with Dave at her side and Josie behind them with Simon and Daniel at her heels.

The darkness engulfed them. Had anyone been standing outside the dome entrance, they wouldn't have been able to see anyone in that moment. Then, as quickly as the darkness had overtaken, they stepped through into a cavernous space that seemed to glitter with thousands of diamonds reflecting their flashlight beams. When their eyes adjusted from the dark to the bright light, they could see that it wasn't diamonds reflecting the light but dozens of panels of glass and mirrors.

"What is this place?" asked Jenna.

"Looks like a hall of mirrors," said Dave. "Like the one at Canobie."

Simon shook his head. "This is not at all like the one at Canobie, dude."

Dave shrugged.

"It says it's the 'Labyrinth of Lost Souls'," Josie read, shining her light on a sign just inside the entrance that was in near-perfect condition, aside from a thick layer of dust. Josie brushed it away with the sleeve of her sweatshirt. "It says, 'Beware! Reflections of the truth can often be hard to face. Follow the path, make the right choices and you may find the way to reward! Make the wrong choices and you may end in despair!'"

"Well, that's not ominous," Simon said, his tone dripping with sarcasm.

Josie frowned. She shined her light toward the wall of glass. Rows of stanchions linked by a thick rope created their own maze that at one time would guide park guests to the entrance. Josie wound her way along, zigzagging back and forth until she reached the gap in the panels of glass that marked the starting point. She could hear the others talking, their voices echoing off the high domed ceiling, but she didn't hear what they were saying. Until, that is, she stepped forward into the maze and heard Simon shout, "Josie! No!"

* * * * *

"Josie! No!" Simon shouted. "Don't go in there alone!" But it was too late. She was in the maze of mirrors and glass now. He rushed toward her, ducking under the ropes, camera still in one hand, flashlight bouncing light off the glass panels in the other. He paused at the entrance to the maze. He could see Josie through the glass and reflected in the mirrors. His heart jumped to double-time though he didn't know why. He stepped into the maze. It was instantly overwhelming. Some panels were glass, some were regular mirrors, some were two-way mirrors. With the darkness of the room and the refraction of the light from the flashlights, it was hard to know what he was seeing.

"Josie!" he yelled, but his voice seemed to disappear. He followed the path but didn't see her. Then he did. She was on the other side of a glass panel, looking at him. But the maze took him in the opposite direction from where she was.

"Josie!" he yelled again.

"Simon!" he heard her call back. He hurried forward, but then there was a loud bang and the sound of gears grinding. "What is going on?" he heard her say.

"Josie, don't go anywhere!" he called back, but she didn't hear him.

* * * * *

"My K-2 meter is going crazy!" Jenna said, holding the equipment out in front of her. The multi-colored lights lit in succession then fell and repeated this over and over.

"Do you think there's electricity here?" asked Dave.

"Possibly, but I doubt it. The only other place this meter lit up was that stupid haunted house," Jenna replied.

"Uh, Jenna? Dave?" said Daniel.

"What?" Jenna snapped.

Daniel frowned. "Josie and Simon are in the maze."

"What!" Jenna and Dave exclaimed together.

Suddenly there was a loud bang and the sound of gears and movement. "What is going on?" Jenna said.

The sounds of banging and gears grinding grew louder and louder, echoing off the high metal ceiling and walls of the dome around them. Jenna's meter lights jumped all over the spectrum, then all their flashlights went out, and their cameras died.

* * * * *

Josie froze as terror overcame her. "Simon!" she tried to yell, but her voice caught in her throat. "Can anyone hear me?" She had never experienced a darkness so complete. There wasn't a speck of light coming from any direction. She could hear sounds, but she couldn't tell what they were or where they came from. *It must be my friends*, she thought, but they sounded very far away.

"Why did I go into this stupid maze?" she lamented, her voice bouncing off the glass walls and metal dome above her. *Hanover? Anna? Can you help me?* she pleaded in her mind, but there was no response, not even a tingle on her neck from Hanover. "This isn't good," Josie said.

* * * * *

"I'm right here, Babe," Dave said to Jenna with a firm grip on her arm.

"It's so damned dark!" Jenna said.

"Is everyone accounted for?" came Daniel's voice. "Simon? Josie?"

"I'm here," Simon said, having felt his way back to the mouth of the maze in the pitch blackness. "But I think Josie is somewhere inside the maze."

"What do you want to do, Jenna?" Dave asked, his voice level and calm.

"I- I don't know.... I guess... let's try to find our way outside," Jenna said, sounding uncertain.

"I'm not leaving Josie in here in the pitch darkness," said Simon.

"Me either," said Daniel. "She's probably terrified."

"I'm scared too, but if we can't see anything in here, we aren't doing her any good," Jenna replied, sounding more confident. "I have extra batteries in my backpack, but I have to be able to see in order to find them and change them."

A sigh was heard in the darkness. "Fine," Simon said. "But we stay near the door."

"Fine," said Jenna. "Dave and I will go first."

The sound of feet shuffling along the floor could be heard, then another sigh from either Simon or Daniel. Simon leaned back into the maze, listening for any sign of Josie. He couldn't believe she wouldn't be shouting for them. Then, suddenly there was light as Jenna and Dave opened the outer door and daylight came streaming in.

"Simon, come on!" Jenna said.

He frowned, looked back into the maze, and shouted, "Josie, if you can hear me, we'll be right back! We'll find you, just hang on and don't move!"

* * * * *

Josie thought she heard a voice but couldn't make out words or even whose voice it was, then everything went silent, the kind of silence where she could hear nothing but the static in her own head. Then, her flashlight flickered in her hand and suddenly lit. Josie breathed a sigh of relief. The only problem was, she now had no idea which way she had come. She looked behind her, and it didn't look right. But neither did the path in front of her.

"Guys? Simon? Daniel? Jenna? Can anyone hear me?" Her voice echoed. She listened but heard nothing. Josie frowned. "I couldn't have gone too far in.... Well, I guess I should just try to find my way out before my flashlight goes out again."

* * * * *

Simon stayed by the door as Jenna crouched on the dirt path and pulled stuff from her backpack.

"No sign of that guy or cops," Dave said, shading his eyes from the sun with his hand as he looked toward the parking lot.

Simon nodded and watched as Daniel started walking around the side of the dome, running his hand over the metal. "Where are you going?" Simon asked him.

Daniel peeked back around the dome. "I'm going to see if there's a back door into this place."

Simon frowned. "Holler if you find anything."

Daniel waved as he disappeared behind the structure. Simon took another step back towards the inside, his ears perked for any sounds from Josie, but it was oddly quiet inside. "Jenna, can you hurry up, please?"

"I'm sorry, Simon! I know they're in here somewhere. Ah!" She handed Simon a square battery. "For the camera," she said. He popped out the dead battery and snapped the new one in place. The camera instantly came back to life. She handed a second one to Dave.

"Flashlight batteries?" he asked.

She passed him a handful of double A's. "Put the extras in your pocket in case it happens again."

Daniel reappeared around the other side of the dome. Jenna passed him a handful of batteries. "There's no other door into this thing," he said. "Seems weird to me. There should at least be a fire exit."

Dave shrugged. "Less regulations when this place was built."

"I still think it's weird," Daniel said.

"I agree," Simon said. "Are we ready to go back in? We can't just leave Josie in there."

"Everyone's batteries working?" Jenna asked. They all nodded. "Good. And at least it seems the audio recorders are still working. Okay. Simon, lead the way."

With his camera and flashlight on, he started back inside the deep, thick darkness of the dome. *Don't go out. Don't go out. Don't go out,* Simon ordered his equipment with his mind and pleaded with whatever energy or helpful spirits might be lingering, on the off chance they were listening. *Please help me,* he added.

* * * * *

Josie pleaded in her mind for her flashlight to stay on. She stepped slowly forward along the pathway created by the panels of glass. Twice she jumped and shrieked when her own reflection startled her. "Simon?" she called. "Daniel?" She called out every few steps or so, but no one answered back. "Why can't they hear me? Where is everyone?" she grumbled.

She wondered what the maze had been like when the park had been open, deciding that there had to be more to it than just a maze of mirrors and windows. It certainly was challenging and confusing, because the windows reflected images that were more transparent, like ghosts, while the mirrors reflected clearer images, but combining the two and having them play off each other had a weird, dizzying effect. Even in the light of her flashlight she thought she saw extra people in some of the reflections, only to look again and see only various angles of herself. Maybe that was the point, to not know at any time which reflection was real.

She reached a fork in the path where she could go two different directions and she stopped. One went straight while the other went to her left. She knew enough about mazes to know that just because you thought one option would be more direct, that didn't mean it would stay that way. *Hanover? Anna?* She called again to her guides with her mind and again was disappointed with no response.

Then, there came a bang and another bang, and then the grinding of gears.

"Oh, no," Josie said. Her flashlight flickered again and blinked out.

* * * * *

Simon didn't hesitate as he stepped into the maze. Every few steps he glanced behind him to see Daniel on his heels with Jenna and Dave not far behind. He didn't want to lose sight of any of them like he had with Josie.

He made one turn in the maze, checked that everyone was still behind him, and went on. Another turn. Checked again. Still there. He stopped and motioned for them to be quiet, listening just in case Josie was calling out, but there was nothing but the sounds of their breathing. Simon moved along slowly and then as he turned another corner saw the clear reflection of Josie from the side. "Josie!" he yelled, but her reflection didn't show any signs of hearing him and she disappeared. He rushed to the glass where he had seen her. It was a mirror. He turned to see where the reflection could have been coming from, but none of it made sense and he turned in a circle. Then, it happened. The bangs and the gears grinding. The flashlights flickered. The camera screen flickered. Everything went dark.

"Not again!" Jenna and Simon yelled in unison over the noise.

But this time as the noise subsided, their lights and camera screens flickered back to life. Simon turned to Daniel but instead, he found a wall of mirror. "What the…?"

* * * * *

Jenna was already searching her pockets for the extra batteries when her flashlight came back on. She breathed a sigh of relief that then caught in her throat. She hadn't moved a muscle when the noises started up and the lights went out, but everything was different now. Around her were mirrors and glass walls. Gone were Dave, Daniel, and Simon.

"Guys?" Jenna called out.

She could hear sounds, but they were distant, muffled, and indistinct.

"But that's not possible!" she lamented to no one. They had been right there only seconds ago. Dave had been practically attached to her. And now she was in the maze alone, the glass and mirrors reflecting only various angles of herself.

However, reason told her that the building was only so big, and that if she just worked her way through, she would eventually either find her way out or find someone else, or both. "Alright, let's get moving," she said aloud to herself.

* * * * *

Dave would swear to the end of his days that at the moment the lights went out again, he felt two hands on his chest shove him backwards away from Jenna. It caught him off guard and was strong enough to knock him onto his rear end.

When his flashlight and camera flickered back to life, he picked himself up off the floor. "Jenna! Can you hear me?" Dave shouted. "Simon! Daniel!"

He strained his ears, but he couldn't hear any of them. It made no sense. He could tell a wall had moved and cut him off from Jenna. She should have been on the other side of the mirror right in front of him. He pounded on the wooden frame and shouted, "Jenna! Jenna, can you hear me?" He pounded harder, the mirror rattling in the frame. If Jenna was on the other side, she would have to hear that, but no sound returned to him. "Jenna! I'm coming for you!" he shouted as loud as he could. He turned to the pathway that had opened up and hurried forward.

* * * * *

As soon as the noises started again, Daniel froze. Every cell in his body was telling him that this was a situation they had to navigate carefully.

When the light in his flashlight came back on, he looked around and said, "Oh no."

* * * * *

"Well, this ought to be good," Angela said as she and Rachel watched the van pulling up the drive. Gravel crunched under the tires as they came to a stop between the cabins. They just watched, full wine glasses in hand, as their husbands approached them looking sheepish, Charles more so than Greg. Charles carried a cardboard box with him, and Greg had a grocery bag and two large bouquets of flowers.

"I don't think I've ever seen two men who think they need forgiveness more than the two of you," Rachel said with a chuckle.

"Let's just rip the bandage off. Tell us what you boys did wrong," said Angela.

Greg looked at Charles. This was his gig, and he knew Rachel knew it. Charles sighed. "We went to see the man who owns that place. Mystery Mountain."

"You did what?" That was not what Angela expected.

"His name is Rod, and he's probably the weirdest person I've ever met," said Charles.

"Why did you go see him?"

"I think we all know the kids aren't hiking," said Charles. Rachel and Angela both nodded. "I'm just trying… I don't know. I'm trying to help Josie. I don't understand what she is doing, why she's doing it, or what she sees when she says she sees ghosts. I respect that she believes it, even if I'm still not quite sure. But what I am sure of is that there are real live people associated with that place, so I thought maybe Greg and I could talk to the guy and get some information that may help Josie. And in turn, maybe she won't resent me so much."

Angela's eyes overflowed with tears. She quickly put her glass down and stood to embrace her husband. "Oh, Charles. Thank you."

"You're not mad?"

"I wish you had just told us where you were going, but no, I'm not mad. I'm incredibly pleased and I'm proud of you." Angela planted a kiss on Charles.

"The question is: are we going to go get the kids?" asked Greg.

Angela looked at Rachel. "Not yet. Let's give them a bit more time to do their thing. And while we wait, you can tell us all about your visit with this man while you cook up whatever is in the bag."

* * * * *

Josie took several turns – left, left, right, left. She saw no sight other than her own reflection and heard no sound from anyone other than herself. Occasionally there would be a groan or a bang from the structure. She would pause, expecting the noises again, but then nothing would happen. Every now and then she would stop and shout as loud as she could for her friends, but she never heard a response.

Her heart pounded hard in her chest. She didn't like anything about this situation. She felt like she had fallen into deep water and didn't know which way was up. And the fact that her spirit guides were not responding unsettled her even more. But she pressed on, because that was the only thing she could do, figuring that eventually she would have to either find her way out or find one of her friends.

She took a corner that bent to the left and was surprised to find that one wall of the path ahead was not a wall of mirrors or windows but the wall of the dome. "Yes! I must be almost out!" She quickened her pace; she could see a door at the end of the passage now and she rushed on. The door had one of those black rectangle stickers with gold lettering that said, "Employees Only", and instead of a doorknob had a silver metal bar that you had to press to open the door.

Her brow furrowed and her heart pounding in her chest, Josie cautiously pressed the bar down and pushed. With a loud groan, it gave way and opened into a dark hallway. She nearly jumped for joy when her flashlight lit up an emergency exit sign over the door at the end of the short ramp. Relief flooded her as she ran for the door. She pushed it open and was blinded by the sun. She closed her eyes, breathing hard. She heard the door snap shut behind her. She let her eyes adjust and then slowly blinked open.

What she saw was not Mystery Mountain.

9

When her eyes adjusted to the light, Josie wasn't standing in the burnt and aged field of Mystery Mountain. Instead, she was looking up the walkway to the front door of her own home back in New Hampshire. The front door stood open and directly inside she could see moving boxes stacked and labeled "kitchen" or "living room" or "storage".

She slowly made her way up the walkway and leaned in the door. "Hello?" she called. She stepped further into the house. "Hello? Anyone here?" As she stood there, waiting for her dad to come walking into the room or for her mom to call back to her, she realized that while it was most certainly her house, it was a bit different. The wall colors were different in the living room, and the cabinets in the kitchen were white instead of a light wood. It had a different feel to it. It was odd.

She stepped further in, and then she heard the voices. They were coming from upstairs. "Hello? Is there someone here? I could use some help!" Josie called. The voices continued in their chatter – too far away for her to hear exactly what they were saying but they should have been able to hear her. Slowly she climbed the stairs.

At the top of the stairs, she turned towards the voices, more audible now. They were male and female, and they were coming from the room that would have been hers. "Hello? I need some help, here!" she called, as she moved towards them.

The people talking didn't respond. She was almost to the doorway when she heard, "I just can't do this anymore, Charles. I've told you a thousand times. I'm not going to change my mind."

"Angela, please," Charles responded. "Please let's just talk about this."

Josie stopped in the doorway. It was her room, but it wasn't. It wasn't painted ballet pink like her room was, but a plain white, and it had a queen-size bed that had no sheets or comforter on it. It was a cheap-looking dark wood headboard, with a matching bedside table and a small dresser with a mirror. She'd never seen this furniture before. Her parents sat on the bare mattress, facing each other.

"No, Charles. We've talked it to death. I'm done," Angela replied. Josie looked at her parents. They looked different, too. Younger? She wasn't quite sure.

"I don't believe it," Charles replied. "We took vows, and I cannot believe you're willing to let this end."

Angela stood. "You make it sound like I decided this on a whim! It's been seven years, Charles. Seven years since we buried our little boy. We broke the day he died. You know this. And we have been trying for seven years to make this right, but we're still broken. It's not fair to either of us to drag this on any longer. We need to move on. I want to move on."

Charles hung his head. "I can't imagine my life without you, Ang." His voice was quiet.

"And I never thought I'd have to imagine my life without Ethan. I never imagined I'd live a life without watching him grow up, to find out if he likes soccer, or baseball, or maybe music. To see him have his first crush, his first heartbreak. To go to prom, graduate high school… get married. You are a constant reminder of all those moments and every second in between that I will never experience with my son."

"And do you think I don't get that? Do you think it's not the same for me?"

"It doesn't matter. How many times are you going to make me say this? I cannot be married to you anymore." Angela looked up and out the window. "The movers are here. Sign the divorce papers, Charles. Let's be done with this. I'll mail you the check for your half of the house after the closing next week."

She walked to the door. Josie stepped back and bumped into the wall.

"Angela, please."

"Goodbye, Charles. I wish you well. I hope someday you can do the same for me."

Josie watched her mother disappear down the stairs and looked back at her father. He remained seated on the bed, his head hanging again.

Seven years. Angela had said it had been seven years since Ethan died. But according to everything she'd learned just a couple months ago, they adopted *her* five years after he'd died. So, what was this?

Josie had wished often enough – especially recently – to know what life would be like if her birth parents hadn't died. Is this what she was seeing? But it had seemed logical that such a wish would give her a glimpse into what her life would have been like with them. Instead, she was getting a glimpse of her adoptive parents' lives if her birth parents had lived. Had they lived, they wouldn't have adopted Josie. Is this really what would have happened to them?

"This isn't fair," Josie said, a deep frown creasing her brow as she looked at her father. He stood and went to the window. Josie went and stood next to him, and they watched Angela directing the movers on where to put what in the moving truck.

"This isn't fair," Charles said.

Josie flinched. "Dad?" She wondered if he could hear her.

"I thought I had this," he went on. "I thought we were on track to fixing things. If only we'd been able to have another child." He stepped back and looked up at the ceiling. "God, I know I don't talk to you much, or pray, or whatever. And I'm not going to stand here and ask for you to bring my wife back to me. But I would appreciate some answers. Yes, I want to know why. Why did you take our sweet little boy? Why weren't we blessed with another child? Why couldn't I convince Angela to consider adoption? What am I supposed to do now? How am I supposed to move on from this?" He shook his head. "What do I need to do to get some answers?"

Josie wiped her cheeks. She hadn't realized she'd started crying, but she could hear the pain in her father's voice. Was he even still her father? Could she still call him that? She didn't even know where she was, if she was dead, or if this was the cruel trick of the mirrored maze of Mystery Mountain. "Be careful what you wish for," she said to herself, and then realized it was appropriate for Charles, too. He might think he wants the answers to those questions, but chances were good that he wouldn't like the answers.

She turned and left her father, who had resumed his vigil looking out the window. She went downstairs where Angela was directing the movers. "My boxes have a big 'A' on them, and my furniture has a pink tag with an 'A' on it," she said. She lifted one of her boxes and carried it outside. Josie followed.

Angela handed the box to one of the movers and then she stepped back out of the way. "Mom, why are you doing this?" Josie asked. Her mom wiped her cheek and brushed a tear away. Josie had thought Angela was unaffected, resolved in her decision, but she was hurting too. "You're upset! You don't want to leave Dad. I know you don't!"

Angela pulled a tissue from her pocket – her mother's only disgusting habit had been that she seemed to always have a crumpled and possibly used tissue stashed somewhere on her – and she blew her nose. She then went back inside and got another box. She put it in the truck and then turned to a large man with the bushy goatee and bald head. "I'll see you at the other house in a few hours?"

"Sure thing, Ma'am," he replied.

Josie watched her mom walk to her car, a car she remembered seeing photos of when she was little, and she hurried over. She was able to jump inside the car when her mom paused and turned to look at the house before getting in and driving away.

"Mom, I wish you could hear me," Josie said as they drove. "I'd tell you that you're making a big mistake."

They hadn't gone very far when Angela abruptly pulled over. She shoved the gearshift into park and then broke into sobs, laying her head on the steering wheel. Josie squirmed in her seat. She'd never seen her mother like this, and she didn't know what to do. She was helpless. Angela couldn't hear her. Josie reached out and put her hand on her mother's back in the way her mother had done so many times when she was sick, upset, mad, whatever. She could feel Angela. She felt real to Josie, so why couldn't Angela see or feel her?

Angela sat up, pulled several crumpled tissues from a pocket, and blew her nose. "I'm doing the right thing, right? Of course. I didn't make this decision lightly. I *am* doing the right thing. I am!" Angela shifted the car into drive and pulled back onto the road.

* * * * *

Dave moved through the maze as quickly as he could without making too much noise, constantly listening for any signs of his friends and Jenna. He didn't like being alone in this place. He didn't like that they were separated from each other. By now, though, he knew better. *Something* wanted them alone, and it was going to make sure they stayed that way. At least for now.

"If you can't beat 'em, join 'em," he said quietly and continued on. The path turned a few times, and he lost his sense of direction. Then he reached a point where the maze split in two different directions. He stopped and examined each path. Frowning, he turned back to look at the path he'd already taken and as he moved, he saw movement reflected behind him in the glass and mirrors. He spun, but it was gone. "Jenna, is that you?" he called, but the image he'd seen looked taller than him. He turned around again, and again he saw movement. This time, when he looked, he saw his father standing behind him. Dave jumped and spun but no one was there. He looked again in the mirror and his dad's image was gone.

"What the hell is going on in this place?" he grumbled. He looked again at the two paths before him. "Right. Because right is right. I hope," he said and continued down the right-hand path.

A couple more turns, and the path went straight for a bit. As he walked on, he noticed just beyond the beam of his flashlight there was a door standing open. What lay beyond was darkness. He moved slowly towards it. His flashlight beam getting swallowed by the darkness. Then, like before, he felt a pair of firm hands on his back, and he was shoved over the threshold into the pitch blackness.

Dave was surprised again at the strength of the unknown hands as he stumbled in the dark. He heard a door close somewhere behind him with a snap. When he regained his footing, he saw that he wasn't in total darkness. He was standing in a dimly lit hospital room. Before him, Jenna lay in a bed, unconscious. Tubes and wires were attached to her, and machines beeped and hissed. Her family was gathered around her, and they were all crying.

A terrible memory came back to him from only a few months ago when an intoxicated driver hit his car as he was driving Jenna home. Jenna had been unconscious for hours because of it. The scene before him looked eerily similar to that.

"She's going to be okay," Dave said to her family. No one said anything. It was like they didn't hear him.

"Son, it's time you face the truth." The voice came from behind him. He jumped and whirled around to find his dad standing there.

Dave frowned at him. "What are you talking about?"

"I know it's hard for you to hear, but I'm only going to tell you *one* more time," his dad said, sternly. "The doctors said that Jenna is brain-dead, and they don't expect her to make it through the night."

"What? No! That's not right! She'll come out of it. I know she will! She's not brain-dead. She'll wake up! And she'll be fine."

An alarm sounded from the monitors at her bedside. A nurse bustled into the room and turned the machines off. A man in a white coat came in and bent over her, then said, "I'm sorry. She's gone." Jenna's mother wailed. Her father hung his head.

Dave looked in awe and disbelief at the scene. "No. No, she cannot be gone. Jenna's indestructible! She can't die!"

He then realized Simon was looking at him. No, not looking at him. *Glaring* at him in a malicious, bloodthirsty way.

"You! You killed my sister!" Simon roared. He charged at Dave with his hands out. Dave half-expected Simon to disappear before he reached him, so he was surprised when Simon's hands closed around his throat. He squeezed hard, and Dave felt his windpipe collapsing beneath Simon's thumbs. He couldn't speak to protest, to apologize, to plead. He grabbed at Simon's hands, but he couldn't break the grip. He was weakening, his head was starting to get fuzzy from lack of oxygen. He would lose consciousness soon. He almost welcomed it. If Jenna truly was dead, he didn't want to live without her.

Dave gave in, willingly accepting his death.

Then suddenly Simon let go, and air rushed back into Dave's lungs. He gasped, sputtered, and choked as he collapsed to the floor and rubbed his sore neck.

"You're dead to me," said Simon. "Deader to me than Jenna ever will be."

Dave tried to reach out, to plead for forgiveness, for understanding. It wasn't his fault; it was the idiot driving drunk! But his voice wasn't working.

When he was finally able to stand, Simon, Jenna, and their parents were gone. The door opened and a young woman with bleached hair, wearing too much make-up, and holding a baby, came in and put her arm around his dad. "Come, dear. Let's go home."

"Okay," he smiled at her and then looked at Dave. "Well, it's time for me to go back to my *real* family. Goodbye."

"What? No! Dad! *We're* your family!" Dave yelled, though his voice was raspy, and it hurt to talk. His father either didn't hear or didn't care to hear. He disappeared out the door with the woman and baby.

"It's fine, Son." Suddenly Dave's mom was there. "Let's all move on. You're old enough now. You don't need parents anymore."

"What? What do you mean?"

"I'm leaving, too," she said. "I'm going to travel the world and find myself. Have a nice night, honey." She kissed him on the cheek and disappeared out the door like his father.

He turned to the empty room. He was all alone. All the people he'd cared about in the world were gone. How was he supposed to go on? Could he go on? He didn't know how. He didn't know how to live without Jenna. He couldn't remember a time when she wasn't in his life. Even when he and Simon had been kids in elementary school, she was always there. He and Simon would play G.I. Joe's and she would join in with her Barbie dolls or My Little Pony's. He loved her even back then. He would never love anyone the way he loved Jenna. He didn't even want to try. He knew it wouldn't be possible.

"What am I going to do?" He dropped into the chair Simon had been in and put his head in his hands. His throat still hurt but that didn't compare to his heart. His heart ached in his chest. It felt like someone was strangling his heart, squeezing the will to live right out of him.

He stood and paced. Then he noticed a bathrobe that lay on the hospital bed. It was a mint-green fleece robe that he'd seen Jenna wear hundreds of times. How many times had he slept over their house and seen her come downstairs in the morning, her strawberry curls all over the place, her blue eyes bright and shining with eagerness to start the day, wrapped in that mint-green robe?

He picked it up and held it to his face. It smelled like her, like honey and sweet apples. He breathed it in deep and let the memories flood his mind. He walked to the window and looked out. He was up high, the parking lot at least six stories below.

Dave looked at the gray sea of pavement below and wondered if he was high enough for it to end him. He had nothing. His girlfriend, gone. His best friend, gone. His dad, gone. His mom, gone. No one was left to help him deal with his grief over her loss and he didn't want to live with only memories. Memories of all the small moments and the big ones. Birthdays, graduation, countless Christmases, the time his mom had to have her tonsils removed and Dave, his brother and dad all camped in the living room and then had cake for breakfast the next day. His first day of school. The day he and Simon became friends. And then there were the memories of Jenna. The first time they kissed, the first time he told her he loved her, and she'd said it right back. The first time they'd…. Small moments of stolen looks across the LaPage dinner table when Simon wasn't looking, the laughter they shared during so many drives home from school, holding hands in the movie theater because they both actually wanted to *watch* the movie, something they also both found funny. Suicide seemed the only alternative to a lifetime of being haunted by those moments. Moments like just the other night when they'd gone swimming in the lake. He remembered the looks Simon and Josie gave them as they walked back to the cabins, their hair wet and their clothes dry. He and Jenna had laughed about it later.

He shook his head and opened the window. He didn't want to live with only memories of the people he cared about. He wanted to move forward and make new memories with them, but they were all gone from his life now.

Dave climbed up on the windowsill and looked down. "I'm ready for it to end. For the pain to end," he said. A sharp gust of wind whipped by and slapped him in his face. He frowned. "Wait a minute…." It was just the other day that he and Jenna had gone skinny-dipping in Red Drum Lake. The car accident was months ago. They were in New York on vacation. They were exploring a weird domed building in a field. Jenna *wasn't* dead. Simon was still his friend. They were both in the maze somewhere not far away.

He turned back into the room and jumped down. "No, this isn't right." Sure, his dad had left them, but his mom hadn't. Not yet, anyway. "But I don't have to let it be that way," he said to the empty hospital room. Yes, he was hurt by his father, but another memory came back to him then. It was from the *real* time he and Jenna had been in the hospital a few months ago. Dave was wracked with guilt over Jenna's injuries. His dad had sat with him and put an arm around him. *You can't take responsibility for someone else's mistakes, Dave. The man who hit you guys,* he *made a big mistake today, and he'll be paying for it. Don't you worry about that. But the best thing you can do is to find forgiveness. Maybe not right away, but eventually. Everyone makes mistakes. We're all human. Some mistakes are bigger than others, but it isn't up to us to be judge, jury, and executioner. Your anger at him isn't going to change a thing. All it will do is eat you alive.*

Dave wondered now if his dad had been preparing to leave his mom then, if he knew he'd been making mistakes and was trying to ask Dave for forgiveness. Well, whether he was or not, eventually he would find a way to forgive his dad for making such a big mistake. He was only human.

He rushed to the door of the room, determined to find his way out now that he knew the truth. He pulled the door open to find a large, bear-like man standing there, smiling at him in a serene way.

"You did well," he said, his voice deep and thick like velvet.

"What?"

"I have a gift for you." He held out a gigantic hand, a single large seed the size of a half-dollar resting in it. "Please take it."

With complete trust, Dave lifted it from the man's hand. The man stepped aside, then pointed down the hall.

"Go straight ahead. You'll find your way out."

"Thank you," he said, pocketing the seed and rushing forward down a very long, very dark hallway. In the light of his flashlight, he could see an unlit exit sign above a door. He pushed on the metal bar and stepped out into a dimly lit room. As his eyes adjusted and he shined his flashlight around he realized he was in a basement. He saw stairs going up and hurried to them, climbing up and through another door that took him into a dusty and very outdated kitchen. He looked around again, and a quick glimpse out the window told him exactly where he was.

Dave shook his head as he stepped out the front door onto the porch of the house across the street from Mystery Mountain. He settled himself into a chair that felt surprisingly sturdy that gave him a view of the dome and rest of the park. He couldn't see any movement and wondered where everyone else was but a velvety voice inside him told him to stay put, so he did.

* * * * *

Rod Youth-Eden was lying in his bed, near drowsing, and feeling more content than he had in years as his favorite song, "Salut d'amour" by Elgar, played on the radio, when a light knock on his door roused him.

He blinked and looked to the doorway, but his age and his health made his vision blurry. "Who's there?" Rod asked.

"You don't recognize me, old friend?" said the visitor in a gentle tone.

"I'd know that voice anywhere, but I would swear…," Rod's voice caught in his throat. "I'd swear that the person it belongs to said I was dead to him, so it can't be. Unless one of us is a ghost."

The man stepped further into the room. "I'm no ghost, and neither are you," he replied. "And I'm sure you know as well as I do that time gives you a chance to regret things you've said, and sometimes it gives you a chance to try to make things right."

"Come closer. My eyesight is terrible."

Drew stepped to the foot of Rod's bed. "How are you?"

"I'm dying."

Drew nodded. "There are people at Mystery Mountain."

"You saw them?"

"I was in the middle of writing when I had a… a feeling. It just overcame me. I had to drive out there."

"And?"

"And I think… I think… it's them. Finally."

Rod smiled. "I think so, too."

10

The maze had changed, Daniel knew instantly. And he didn't like it.

The mechanics of it must not be connected to electricity. "Smart," he said under his breath. He looked at the pathway beneath his sneakers and wondered if there were triggers in the floor. "Must be," he concluded, though he didn't think he was the one who triggered it.

"I know what you're doing," he said. "It won't work with me, so just let me out of this place." He sensed a change in the air at his back and his flashlight flickered and failed again.

You've done well, Daniel, came a strange voice. It was silky and carried the tones of several voices woven together. He shivered.

"I didn't do it for you," he replied. "I did it for Josie."

You care about her.

"Of course I care about her," Daniel grumbled at the darkness. He didn't need the light. He wouldn't be able to see it either way. "And I doubt you expected anything different."

You're a smart boy, the voice chuckled.

"I want to talk to my mom," he demanded.

I'm here, Daniel. His mother's voice came from somewhere in front of him.

"Prove it's you."

Daniel, I was with you earlier. You should know it's me, she replied.

"I don't trust you," he said. "I don't trust anything happening in this place."

I understand, she said. *You have a mole on the inside of your right knee that is shaped like a dinosaur, and you named it 'Tommy the T-rex' when you were five.*

Daniel sighed. He was wearing shorts. He needed more. In his mind, he saw a young version of himself sick in bed with his worried mother looming over him. She tucked him in bed, mopped his brow,

When you were eight, and you were really sick, remember I sat with you the whole time, and I made sure your bunny rabbit was with you. He was yellow and had only one eye. Do you remember that?

"Sure. I remember that because I just made it up."

What? No. Daniel....

"Yeah. I've never been *that* sick and I never had a stuffed rabbit. I made it up. And you pulled it from my head like I knew you would."

You are *a smart boy, Daniel,* said that other voice, chuckling again.

"Yes, I am, and I'm in no mood to play games."

But that's exactly why you're all here. To play the game.

"Oh yeah? And who determines the winner? Is it even possible for us to win?"

It isn't about winning or losing.

"Then what is it about?"

That's not for you to know.

"I want to talk to my mom."

She's busy.

"You're lying. I know it doesn't work that way. Now... I want to talk to my mom."

It's not up to me.

"Stop lying!" he yelled. Just then, his flashlight came back on in a sudden burst of light and Daniel heard a familiar screech from over his head. He lifted his right arm and felt talons of his friend

Achachak close on their perch. Wings flapped and rustled his hair. "Hello, old friend. I need your help," Daniel said to the owl.

* * * * *

Jenna wasn't one for regret, but as she made her way through the maze with her flashlight bouncing off the glass and mirrors, she regretted ever laying eyes on this place. *Why can't I just be happy with a normal vacation?* she scolded herself. *Well, no more. I'm done with this stuff after today. I just want to hang out with my friends, kiss my boyfriend, go swimming in the lake....*

"Mystery Mountain makes no sense. No wonder it failed," she said with bite. Frustration grew rapidly in her. She clenched her fists and yelled, "None of this makes any sense!" and without thinking, she kicked at the glass panel closest to her. It shattered and created a cacophony as the glass broke into countless slivers and rained down. Jenna shrank away but couldn't escape the shower of shards.

"Ouch," she said, picking a few of the pieces sticking out of her skin and dropping them to the floor. She shook her head and more shards fell from the tight curls of her hair. She wondered if any of the others had heard noise she'd made, but there was nothing but silence again.

She didn't like being alone. She was already feeling off and the only thing that had kept her from losing it so far was Dave. Even though logic told her that he had to be close, he suddenly felt a thousand miles away.

"Why are you doing this to us?" she yelled. Her voice echoed against the walls and reverberated. Jenna covered her ears, and the glass rattled in another panel and shattered.

"STOP THAT!" she roared.

Another panel popped and shattered, and then another and another.

"I'M ANGRY!" Jenna yelled. More glass panels shattered and dropped their pieces.

"I'M ANGRY! I'M SO ANGRY AT JOSIE AND SIMON! EVEN DAVE! THEY ALL LIED TO ME! THEY KEPT SOMETHING IMPORTANT FROM ME AND I'M STILL SO ANGRY!"

More glass panels popped and shattered around her. Jenna was panting as she looked around at the destruction she was causing with her anger. She was so angry, and she had tried for so long to hide it, but it felt really good to let it out.

"JOSIE BETRAYED ME! SHE LIED TO ME! AND ALL I'VE EVER DONE IS TRY TO HELP HER, BE THERE FOR HER! HELP HER THROUGH ALL THIS STUFF THAT SHE WHINES ABOUT! THESE GIFTS THAT SHE DOESN'T EVEN APPRECIATE! SHE TAKES IT ALL FOR GRANTED! AND NOW WE'RE TRAPPED IN HERE BECAUSE OF HER! WHY?"

She could hear more panels shattering and the glass pieces clinking as they fell to the floor. "SIMON BETRAYED ME! HE TOLD ME JOSIE WAS LIKE A SISTER! HE LOVED SOMEONE ELSE! WHAT IF HE BREAKS JOSIE'S HEART? HE WILL DESTROY OUR FRIENDSHIP! AND I WILL NEVER FORGIVE HIM! I WILL NEVER FORGIVE ANY OF THEM FOR THE LIES AND THE HURT!

Jenna bent over, hands on her knees, panting. She could feel the energy of the anger churning inside her. She straightened, ready for one last blast.

"I'M... SO... ANGRYYYYYYY! AHHHHHHHHHHH!" The remaining glass panels exploded as Jenna released her rage.

Jenna looked around and smiled. She felt good. Lighter. Better than she had in a long time. She hadn't realized how much pent-up anger she'd been holding on to. Releasing it was a rush.

She shined her flashlight around at the destruction. Every glass and mirror panel had shattered, leaving only the frames standing their sentinel, now endless doorways instead of walls. Then she realized that she could see everywhere, and there wasn't a single other person in there with her. "Dave! Simon! Where is everyone?"

She shook off more shards of glass and started forward, peering into the dark beyond her flashlight beam, but there was no one else there. Then she saw the door with the "Employees" sign. Assuming the others had already found their way out, she headed quickly towards the door, broken glass crunching beneath her feet, but before she could reach it, the door popped open and Josie and Simon strolled in from the darkness beyond, hand in hand.

"What are you two doing here?" Jenna frowned.

"Can you believe all the ghosts that are here?" Josie said to Simon. "This place is a paranormal gold-mine!"

"What? It is?" said Jenna. "Why didn't you tell me!"

"I know," he agreed. "I've never seen so many in one place before."

"Are you going to tell your sister you can see ghosts too?" Josie asked. Jenna moved closer to them.

"No way. What she doesn't know won't hurt her," he replied. "Or rather… won't hurt me. She'd kill me if she found out."

"Hey! I'm right here! I can hear you!" Jenna said.

"I don't want that. We just finally got together," said Josie, as she wrapped her arms around Simon and looked up at him with inviting eyes. "I don't want you taken away from me so soon."

Simon smiled down at her. "And I don't want to be taken away. I want to be right here with you."

"And you'll help me fight all the ghosts?" she asked.

"Of course. It's you and me against the spirit world," he said, then bent his head to hers.

Jenna turned away, her face scrunched. "Yuck."

"What do you think Jenna will do when she sees us making out?" Josie asked Simon with an uncharacteristic giggle.

Jenna turned back to them with a frown.

"I don't know," said Simon. "But I've had to watch her suck-face with my best friend for a year now, so I don't really care."

"There's been so many times when they've been… you know, doing *whatever*," Josie said to him, "and I was so jealous. She really had it all. An amazing family, a great boyfriend who is practically part of her family, so she gets to see him all the time… on top of having great grades in school and being a star athlete…. It all just seems so easy for her. I don't think she knows how much I have envied her."

"What? You envy me?" Jenna said, but they still didn't seem to hear her.

"But now…," Josie stood on tiptoes and kissed Simon again, then went on. "I think I might finally be catching up."

"Josie's jealous of me?" Jenna asked and turned away again. "I can't believe she's jealous of *me* when I've been so jealous of *her*."

"It hasn't been easy to watch her and Dave together," Simon said. "To see her become the best friend to my best friend.... I've been replaced by my sister. I hated her for it at times."

"Can this be true?" She asked "Am I a horrible person? I've been so jealous of Josie, and then of Simon… and this whole time *they've* envied *me*!

"You know she'll be mad when she finds out all the ghost stuff that's been going on that we didn't tell her about," said Simon.

"Guys! Seriously… this isn't funny! I can hear you!" Jenna yelled. Somewhere in the darkness she heard glass pieces falling from a frame.

"She shouldn't be. I mean, really, we can't be her personal ghost detectors twenty-four-seven!" Josie replied.

"I think she expects that of you," Simon said.

"If only she could see it from our perspective," Josie said. "But she just doesn't get it."

"Guys! Stop it!" Jenna yelled. More glass pieces rattled and popped somewhere behind her. "I'm trying to see it from your perspective! Don't you get that?"

"Jenna won't ever be able to understand it, Josie. She'll never be able to do what we do," Simon said.

"We could teach her," said Josie.

"You can teach me?" Jenna exclaimed.

Simon chuckled. "Do you want to?"

Josie looked up at him and laughed. "No. Then she'd have even more of a superiority complex."

"What! I don't have a superiority complex!" Jenna shouted. More glass popped and fell somewhere in the darkness.

Simon put his arms around Josie again. "*You* are the superior one," he purred. "She doesn't know it, but you have so much more than her. More than she'll ever understand."

"Stop it, Simon! I know you're just trying to make me mad!" And it was working. *Pop! Pop!*

"Thank you, Simon. That means the world to me coming from you. And… I should tell you… you *are* the only reason I became friends with Jenna. I really have been using her this whole time."

Simon laughed. "Can you imagine how angry she'd be if she found out?"

Josie and Simon laughed together while Jenna's anger grew.

"WHY ARE YOU BOTH DOING THIS TO ME?" she yelled. *Pop! Pop! Pop! Pop!*

They continued to laugh at her.

"STOP! PLEASE! STOP!" She roared.

Simon pulled a lighter from his pocket. "I think it's time this place was destroyed. What do you think, Josie?"

Josie nodded. Simon flicked the lighter and a flame leaped in the darkness. He held it close to the wooden frame nearest him; it caught immediately and went up in a gust of fire. Jenna gasped. The fire moved from one wooden frame to another and another. Then, she heard Josie scream. Jenna looked between the empty panels and saw Josie, alone and surrounded in flames. The tips of Josie's hair burned. Jenna could smell it.

"Jenna, why are you doing this to me?" Josie asked, shouting over the roar of the fire.

"You did this to yourself!" Jenna yelled back.

"You want my ability? Is that what you want?" Josie opened her mouth wider than normally possible and put a fist inside. Josie coughed once, then pulled from within something that glowed whitish-purple through the red-orange flames. She pulled and pulled until she held in two hands a large, sparkling mass resembling thick spaghetti. "Here! Take it! If that's what you want, then take it!"

The flames parted as Jenna stepped close and looked at the pulsing, sparkling strands in Josie's hands. She frowned.

"Take it!" Josie commanded. Jenna looked at her. Josie's cheeks were wet with tears, her hair was singed, her clothes smoking. "Just take it!"

"No," Jenna replied. The flames fell to nothing more than candle flames and then vanished. "No. I don't want it."

"Yes, you do," Josie frowned. "Take it already!"

Jenna shook her head. "No. I thought that's what I wanted, but no. I don't."

"But I want you to have it," Josie said, holding the glowing mass toward her. "It will make everything better."

"No, it won't," Jenna said again. She shoved Josie's hands holding the blue-silver spaghetti away from her. It was starting to freak her out. "Because it wasn't meant for me."

"Are you sure?" Josie frowned.

"Yes, I'm positive," replied Jenna.

Josie put her face into her hands and sucked the glowing mass back into her. But the glow from the substance seemed to be spreading over Josie's face, hair, and down her body, growing brighter and brighter until Jenna had to shield her eyes. The glow formed a column of purplish-white light that Jenna recognized.

You've done well, said a gentle female voice that came from within the light.

Jenna frowned. She felt like her heart had been torn from her chest and stomped on. How was that doing well?

As though reading Jenna's mind, the voice said, *You cannot walk another's path, and you've seen that. Your path may follow beside Josie's sometimes, they may cross, and someday they may part ways, but they are never the same path. Hers isn't better than yours. Never forget that. Do not envy the path of another, just focus on your own path and taking the best steps for you.*

Jenna nodded.

I have a gift for you, the soft, soothing voice said. In a swift movement, something like an ethereal arm extended from the column of light and handed Jenna a crystal of transparent red. *You can go now.*

Jenna moved towards the door again, broken glass crunching under the soles of her sneakers and said, "Get me out of this crazy place," as she pushed on the metal bar of the exit door.

* * * * *

Simon instantly took several long, slow, deep breaths in an effort to keep himself calm and steady. He wasn't going to let this place get to him.

"The only thing to do is to find a way through this maze," he said to himself, having seen that the way back to the beginning was now blocked. He put the strap of the camera around his neck and let it dangle, not wanting to be burdened with it. Then, with another deep, bracing breath, he took one step forward then another and another.

When he came to a break in the walls where there was more than one direction to go, he paused only briefly and followed his gut, knowing it was his best option. Josie would call it his intuition, and thanks to her he understood that they were the same thing.

He moved along at a swift but steady pace. In his peripheral vision he kept seeing movement and shadows in the reflections of the windows and mirrors and odd flickers of light, but he refused to pay attention to any of it. Unless he encountered someone actually in his path, he wasn't going to let this weird labyrinth confuse him.

But as hard as he tried, he couldn't help but see the strange things happening in the reflections. Something glittered in the light of his flashlight. He tried to keep walking, his head down, focused on the path before him. It worked until he came to another break in the path where he had to choose which way to go. He looked up at the paths before him and saw that there were more glittering objects reflecting light in the reflections of the glass and mirrors. With a sigh, he looked closer, and then frowned. It looked like snow.

Simon shivered. He hadn't noticed until then how cold it was in the maze. Abnormally cold, considering the blazing heat outside. But it didn't matter. All that mattered was finding Josie.

At the thought of Josie, he closed his eyes and sighed again. *Hang in there, Josie. I'll find you*, he thought, wondering if she would receive his mental message.

With rescuing Josie as his driving force, Simon continued on, following his intuition as he had before. He could see the snow falling in each reflective surface and his breath came out in white clouds before his eyes. The impossibility of this lingered at the edges of his mind as he worked to remain focused on finding his way out or finding Josie and the others – whichever came first.

He turned a corner, hit a dead end, and turned back, then went in the other direction. He shivered. It was getting colder. Didn't Jenna say that a drop in temperature could be a sign of paranormal activity? He couldn't see any ghosts, not that he was looking for them.

He hit another dead end, turned around too quickly, slipped, and fell flat on his back. The wind was knocked out of him momentarily, and he gasped for breath. The ground beneath him was cold. When his breathing returned almost to normal, he put his hands down to prop himself up, and pulled them back quickly. He looked at his palms, and saw they were wet. He sat up and looked around. The ground below him was covered in snow, snow that was now visible to him not just in the reflections. He shivered again.

"What is happening?" he asked.

He jumped to his feet and continued in the direction he'd been going when he fell. At least he thought he went in the same direction. But after a dozen careful steps with the snow crunching under his sneakers, he started to think he was going the wrong direction. He turned around and looked down at his footprints, hoping to follow them back, but the snow was falling fast and all signs of him on the path behind him were already wiped away.

"How is this possible?" Simon asked. He stopped and turned around, looking in all directions. He shined his flashlight upwards but couldn't see the domed ceiling; all he could see was darkness and snow falling.

He shook himself. Snow fell from his hair and shoulders. He couldn't stay still. He had to find his way out or he would freeze to death. He looked at the directions he had to choose from, took a deep breath, and went left. He flexed his fingers as he walked. They were stiff with cold. Flakes were piling up on his shoulders and hair, and he was wet now, which made the cold even colder. But he could handle it. He was a New England guy. He could handle some snow and cold. He was less worried about himself than he was about Josie. She was somewhere in this maze, too. He wondered if she was experiencing what he was, or if the maze did different things to each person. He wondered if she was okay or if she was scared. He walked faster, as fast as he could without slipping again.

He shivered again, found himself in a dead-end which he told himself was not one he'd already been in, turned around, and walked on. He didn't notice that the snow started to fall faster. He slipped again, but this time he reached out and grabbed for the wooden frame of the mirrored panels. Just as his hand closed around the wood, his flashlight went dark and everything around him was silent. He straightened himself and moved his foot. There was no snow beneath his feet, and he felt warm and dry.

Simon frowned in thought and released his grip on the frame. His flashlight relit the scene: snow coming down on him again and had accumulated up to his ankles. He grabbed for the wall again to see what would happen and all was dark and dry once more. He took one large step in the direction he was heading and reached out for another panel. When he removed his hand, his light came back on and this time the snow was up to his shins.

He grabbed at another panel and shook his head. "Geez… it just keeps coming down!" He reasoned with himself that his best way forward was in the dark, so he clicked off his flashlight and put it in his pocket, and as he fumbled, something knocked against his chest. With renewed hope, he lifted the camera and opened the viewfinder and breathed a sigh of relief. He could see with the night vision mode.

"Okay, this is how I will find my way out of here without being crushed by a freak blizzard," he said. And just to be sure, he lifted his hand from the panel and found the snow now up over his knees. Quickly he touched the panel again and breathed a sigh of relief when the storm disappeared. "Alright. Let's get moving."

He had to move slower to keep one hand on the glass and wood panels and one hand on the camera. He only slipped up once when he came to another junction where his gut was telling him to take the path opposite the wall he was gripping. But he couldn't juggle the camera without breaking his grip, and when he did, he found the snow had accumulated up to his thighs. He struggled to push through it as his legs quickly chilled. He stretched to reach the wall and finally gripped it. The snow was gone once more, and he was dry, though still chilled. "I never thought I'd hate snow so much."

He continued on. The next time he came to a junction, he let the camera fall to his chest instead of trying to juggle, allowing him to reach from one side to the other without losing grip and being plunged back into the snow. He followed the path through several twists and turns before reaching a straightaway. At the end, through the camera's night vision, he saw an opening. He assumed it was either the entrance or exit to this mad-house, but when he reached it, he found an octagonal-shaped space of mirrors with only one way in or out.

"Be careful, Simon," he told himself. He stepped into the space keeping his hand on the wall. Through the viewfinder, he could see what he thought was a star on the floor in the center of the room, but as he looked more carefully, he could see lines crisscrossing from one end to the other forming a complex pattern. The name of it tickled the edge of his mind… sacred geometry? It was one of those things that he'd overheard Josie and Jenna talking about that had piqued his interest, though he still knew little of it. However, if it was here, it must mean something.

He knew in his gut what he needed to do next, but hesitated wondering what would happen when he took his hand off the panels. "Only one way to find out," he said.

Simon lifted his hand from the wood and stepped into the center of the space. He had expected the snow to be up to his chin. Instead, he took the flashlight from his pocket and shined it around, revealing snow tumbling in through the opening he had come through but otherwise the octagonal room was snow-free. In the hallway, the snow was at least waist high. So, he knew he needed to be in this room. He just didn't know why.

"What am I supposed to do?" he asked. His voice echoed. "What do you want from me?" He was cold, and he was irritated. He just wanted to find his friends, find Josie, and get out of there. But no, if he was going to be an ER doctor, he couldn't allow anything, even a crazy, mixed-up place like this, to rattle him. He shook himself and said, "Okay, I have to look at this the only way I know how." *And at least I'm not up to my ears in snow in here*, he thought.

Then he heard a strange sound, out of place for where he was. It was the beep of a heart monitor.

"Dr. LaPage, what should we do?" came an unfamiliar voice. He spun towards it. Suddenly, the windows in the octagonal room were like windows into an operating room. Before him were three hospital beds and a nurse in full head-to-toe scrubs and mask, only her eyes visible, staring at him expectantly. Then he realized that each bed held a familiar body: Dave, Jenna, and Josie.

"What is going on?" he asked.

"Dr. LaPage, as I said, we don't have enough resources to save all three of these patients. Who should we save?"

"What do you mean? I can't choose one life over another. Especially them!" Simon frowned.

"You must, Doctor. Either one of them gets to live or they all die," the nurse said. Her voice echoed strangely in the mirrored octagonal space from the other side of the glass.

Simon's frown deepened. "No. This isn't right."

"You must choose. Who lives and who dies?" the nurse asked.

"This isn't right. This isn't right!" He said again, and then, he believed it. "This isn't right. You're trying to trick me. Ha! You can't trick me!"

An idea came to him then. Simon frowned, took a bracing breath as he stuck his flashlight back in his pocket, and placed both palms flat against one of the mirrored walls. He closed his eyes and focused. Taking slow, deep breaths, he focused on the feeling of the cold glass and hard wood frame. He imagined that the room was his patient, a sick patient, and he had to find out what was going on under the surface. What was happening to make the room behave this way?

Simon slid his hands along the wall. He could feel something underneath the surface of the painted wood and glass. It was faint, almost like the thrumming rhythm of the flow of blood in a vein. "Show me the truth," he said. "What are you trying to tell me? How can I help?"

He could feel it. It moved through the wall, into his hand, and up his arm. He felt it spread through his chest and wrap around his heart. Then, he felt the change in the air. He opened his eyes to darkness. He felt triumphant that the sad, dying forms of Jenna, Josie, and Dave were no longer before him, but that was quickly replaced by something else. He was feeling… feeling the truth, as he had asked, and it was overwhelming. Simon sank to the floor, his hands sliding down the wall, and he wept like he had never wept before in his life.

11

When Angela pulled into a gas station, Josie jumped out of the car in the few seconds she had before the door slammed shut. The whole way there, Angela gave herself a pep talk about how moving on was the best thing for them both and that she was doing the right thing.

"The lady doth protest too much, methinks," Josie had said, proud of herself for successfully quoting Hamlet. She wondered if she could get extra credit for that from her English teacher, but then she wondered if she would ever go to school again. "Maybe this is Limbo," she said. "Some sort of weird in-between thing. Just wait till I tell Jenna about this."

Josie walked away from the gas station. She couldn't stand to watch her parents like this anymore. It couldn't be Limbo. More likely it was Hell, because it felt like torture. "It *is* torture," Josie said to the sky, "because it isn't the truth. Charles and Angela wouldn't divorce. Not like that. After Ethan died, they came out stronger on the other side. You can't convince me otherwise. *I'm* not what held them together. Their love for each other did. They would be *fine* without me! Now get me out of here! Whoever is doing this to me, do you hear me? Get me out of this place!"

Nothing happened. Josie continued to walk. She was on a street lined with trees on both sides. She was sure there was a neighborhood around there somewhere, but if she were in a time when she would only have been two years old, maybe the neighborhood hadn't been built yet.

The sun shone through the trees, and she could see that it was sinking low in the sky. It would be dark soon. She wondered what time it was. She felt in the back pocket of her shorts but there was no cell phone there where it usually was. Figures. She doubted there was service in Hell or Limbo, anyway. But if the sun was going down, she'd need to find somewhere to go for the night. Then, coming from somewhere in the nearby woods, she heard voices that sounded young. They sounded like her friends.

She saw an opening in the undergrowth, a well-worn but narrow path. She veered onto it and headed for the sound of those voices. They were music to her ears. As she got closer, she was sure she could hear Jenna's voice. Then she heard Dave and Simon.

Yes! She'd found her friends! Maybe whoever had put her in that nightmare had taken her out!

But she heard other voices too. Some were familiar, but she couldn't quite place them. She hurried on, and when she came out into a large clearing and a sandy beach at the edge of a river, she stopped in her tracks.

This part of the river was calm and smooth. She saw her friends on the sand, talking and laughing in the late day sun. But it wasn't just Simon, Dave, and Jenna. She saw Adam, Christine, Jeremy, Brandon, and even Reagan. There was only one person she didn't recognize. A girl was talking to Simon and smiling up at him from beautiful hazel eyes. He brushed a strand of her light-brown hair out of her face and tucked it behind her ear.

Josie's heart clenched and her stomach heaved. "What is happening?" she whispered. She stepped closer to the scene. To her left, she could see the check-point tents, and she could smell the food the staff was cooking for them.

"Hey, Adam. Can we go swimming?" Jenna said.

"Sure, but be careful," Adam replied.

Josie remembered this day last summer on their hiking trip, so she wasn't surprised when Dave said, "Let's play *Chicken*!" as they all got in the water. "Jenna on my shoulders, and Sam on Simon's."

No, this was all wrong! Josie clutched the sides of her head as she sat in the sand. "Why are you doing this to me!" she yelled.

"Hey, Adam," Reagan said, sauntering up to him with a swing in her hips that telegraphed trouble. She looked at him and batted her eyelashes in an obvious way. "Is there anything I can help with?"

"Sure," he replied, smiling back at her in a way Josie had never witnessed before. "Want to help me check the raft equipment?"

"Okay," she said.

"What alternate universe did I stumble into?" Josie asked. She frowned at the scene before her as tears slid down her cheeks. Simon and Sam won one round against Jenna and Dave already. "We make a great team," Simon said to the girl. They high fived and Simon ducked back under the water to hoist her on his shoulders.

"Is it that easy? I'm that replaceable?" Josie yelled at them. They didn't reply. "I suppose she can talk to ghosts, too, and she'll be the one to save you all from Philip Stillwater."

"No, she can't see ghosts," said Brandon.

Josie jumped, and her heart pounded in her chest. She hadn't noticed that he came to sit in the sand nearby. "You can hear me? How? Are we dead?"

Brandon smiled at her. Brandon, with his round, ruddy face, was a welcome relief from being ignored. "I'm invisible to people most of the time, so it's easy for me to slip into the world of the invisible."

"Huh?" Josie frowned.

"Don't worry about it."

"Will they see you talking to me?" she asked.

"Who? Jenna and Dave, who only have eyes for each other? Or Simon and Sam, a blossoming romance neither one will admit to? Or Christine and Jeremy, who are both off in their own world? Maybe Adam or Reagan will notice me? Ha… now that's funny. Reagan never notices me. Girls like Reagan are programed to see right through guys like me. And with her in his line of sight, Adam won't be able to see me either."

"Is that really how it is for you?" Josie asked.

Brandon nodded. "You noticed me, or you would have, if you'd existed in this world. But I guess you did something to change it all. And now, this is what we're stuck with."

"What's going to happen when the raft flips and you all get stuck in that house?"

"It won't happen," Brandon said.

"What do you mean?"

"The raft flipping, the storm, the house, the ghosts. None of it will happen to us. That was *your* fate. Because you were on that trip with us, our fates got tangled up with yours. But without you, things will happen differently for this group."

Josie dug into the sand with her foot. "So that's it, huh? I screwed up everyone's life by being here, and without me… their lives are easier, better? Wow… how hurtful can the universe be?"

"I don't believe that anyone's life is better without you. It's just… different," Brandon replied.

Josie shook her head. "You know, you deserve way better than someone like Reagan. I always wanted to tell you that."

He smiled again. "Thanks."

"Last I heard, she was dating some big, popular football player from my school. Or what was my school, I guess."

"Yeah, I figured. That's okay. In what was your world, I have a girlfriend."

"You do?"

"You don't need to sound so surprised," Brandon chuckled.

"No! I'm just… happy for you! How did you meet her?"

"At a church dance. Her family was new to the area. Her name is Molly, and she has red hair – not like Jenna's though. It's a darker red. She's beautiful, and she's smart, and she's really nice to me."

"Good. That… that makes me feel better. I mean, there is *some* good in this crazy, effed-up world that put me here."

"Thanks for that," he chuckled.

When Jenna, Dave, Simon, and Sam all ran from the water and wrapped towels around themselves, Josie stood. "It's getting late. I guess I should go and… I don't know… figure out if I can get out of here."

"Mind if I walk with you?" Brandon asks.

"No, but won't they notice you're gone?" Josie asked, and motioned to where Adam was sitting by the fire with Reagan, Jeremy, and Christine.

"Naw. Like I said, I'm already invisible to them."

They started to walk back up the path Josie had come down. "So, how is it again that you know all this?"

He shrugged. "I'm pretty interested in quantum physics. The way I see it, quantum physics is all about the study of particles that cannot be seen with the naked eye. They can't be seen, yet people know they're there. I'm kinda like that. Most people can't see me, but they know I'm there. I started thinking about that, and I started to try to be a quantum particle… being in two or more places at once. I guess it worked. It's pretty neat, actually. I'm able to know what's going on in the other places when I need to."

"So… I'm in another place? Am I dead?"

"Well, see, that's the tricky part. I'm not sure that death *isn't* another reality. I'm pretty sure it is. But, I'm not sure exactly where this place is or what state you're in. It just… *is*. You just… are."

"Well, that clears things up," Josie scoffed. They were back at the road she'd been walking on earlier. Twilight was in full bloom, giving the woods around them that deep, blackness while the sky overhead was still pale blue that faded to indigo.

"Unfortunately, that's quantum physics for you. More questions than answers."

"That's most of my life lately," said Josie.

"Speaking of questions, I have one for you. Do you know how you got here? To this place?"

"Well…." Josie went through the whole story of vacation, finding Mystery Mountain, the dome. She went through what she saw of her parents, and then how she ended up finding him.

"Hmm," was all he said, when she finished.

"What?"

He shrugged again, though it was dark, and she could barely see him. "It sounds like a weird version of that movie *It's a Wonderful Life*, for one thing."

"That really depressing black-and-white movie my parents always watch at Christmas?" she asked.

"It has a happy ending, but yeah," he replied.

"Great. What does that mean?"

"I don't know. It's strange that you experienced a reality with your parents from a time when you would be – what did you say? – two years old, and then you ended up in a reality from a year ago. It sounds like you are jumping realities without knowing it. I'm wondering if someone you can't see is taking you through these specific places. Like the angel does in the movie."

Josie frowned. It made more sense than anything else so far. One minute she's with her parents in Centerwood fourteen years in the past, and the next she's in the woods of Maine one year in the past. And now… she looked up and could see streetlights in the distance. She wasn't sure exactly where they were now.

"Could you be the one bringing me? I mean, you're the only one so far that I've talked to."

"Maybe, I suppose. Though, if I am, I don't know it."

"Or you do but you're not allowed to tell me."

"Perhaps."

"How do I know you're even really Brandon?"

"What do you mean?" He frowned, clearly caught off guard by her question.

They were closer to the lights now, and she could see his cheeks redden. She stopped walking and stood in front of him. "I mean, maybe you're not really Brandon, but some other person or spirit or… God-knows-what here to help torture me."

"Torture you? I thought we were having a nice chat," he said. She could see beads of sweat on his upper lip now.

"Yes, torture. Showing me my parents' marriage imploding, showing me my best friends having a great time without me and replacing me so easily."

"What were you thinking about when you were in that mirror maze?" Brandon asked.

"I was thinking about how badly I want to know my parents. My *birth* parents. I've wanted that since I started seeing ghosts. I don't understand why this is all happening. *This* is torture!" Tears were flowing freely from her eyes, soaking her cheeks.

"Josie, you can't blame me for what the mirrors reflect for you," he said.

Josie frowned at him. "Who are you really?"

Brandon leaned in close to her and replied, "Wouldn't you like to know!"

* * * * *

Brandon was gone. Josie didn't see him leave. She just blinked, and he wasn't there. She sighed.

"Hanover! Anna! Is anyone there? Can anyone hear me?"

She continued walking towards the streetlights. It was better than staying in the shadowy woods where any number of nocturnal creatures with the ability to see in the dark could see her as prey. She found that the streetlights hung over a gas station and country store, the kind that sold everything from sandwiches – like the ones they'd eaten earlier with Daniel – to gallons of milk to aspirin to batteries, and everything in between. The gas pumps looked old. They didn't even have a slot for credit cards. She didn't think those existed anymore. Then again, she wasn't sure she existed anymore, so maybe she was in good company with the old gas pumps.

There was a weather-worn bench along the front wall of the store. She looked at the road ahead and saw nothing but darkness and the same behind her. She went to the bench and sat, suddenly exhausted. "Hanover? Anna?" Josie said again. "Where are you? If I'm dead, shouldn't you be with me? Guiding me?"

Then the door to the store opened with a tinkle of a bell, and a woman walked out. She was old, her face wrinkled like a crumpled paper bag, and her long white hair hung around her face and over her shoulders. She turned and saw Josie and smiled at her, her small eyes crinkling.

"Young lady, you shouldn't be out by yourself at night," she said. Her voice was crackly and thin. She reminded her a little of Aunt Pauline, and suddenly Josie missed her aunt with a fierce ache.

Josie smiled back politely but said nothing. She didn't trust anyone or anything in this place, wherever she was.

"Mind if I sit?" the old woman asked. Josie shrugged at her. The woman shuffled her feet along the dirty pavement to the bench and slowly heaved herself down. "Not feeling very talkative, are ya?"

"I'm not supposed to talk to strangers," Josie replied flatly.

"Ah, well, then. My name is Malayou." She held out her hand. Josie didn't respond and she didn't shake her hand. "You see, this is where you introduce yourself."

Josie shook her head. "I know that game. I introduce myself, you say all sweetly that now we're not strangers, and next thing I know I'm tied up in your basement, being held hostage. No thanks."

"Oh, come on, Josie! You've watched too many movies!" she said.

Josie looked at her with her eyes narrowed. "How do you know my name? I didn't introduce myself."

"I know it because we're not strangers," Malayou replied. "Not really. I'm the one who brought you here."

Josie's insides went cold. "Why?" Josie asked without looking at her.

"I beg your pardon?"

"Why? Why would you do this to me? This is torture!" Josie replied. "Seeing my parents divorcing and my friends happily enjoying life without me! It's terrible! Who are you that you would want to put me through this?"

The old woman clicked her tongue and shook her head. "Typical. You humans are so ungrateful!"

"What do you mean 'you humans'? Ungrateful for what?" Josie asked.

Malayou went on as though Josie hadn't spoken. "You all cry and complain that life is unfair, and you think you know what will make it better, then when we give you what you want, you complain about that, too! And this isn't a simple thing, young lady. It isn't as easy as just flipping a switch to change things. Steps must be taken! There are big gears to shift here! Bringing people back from the dead, wiping memories. It's all very complicated! So, a little gratitude would be nice!"

Josie turned and stared at the woman, her eyes wide. "Did you say, 'bringing people back from the dead'? Am I actually going to get to meet my parents? My *birth* parents?" Josie started to shake from a mix of excitement and fear. What would they be like? Would they like her? Would she like them? Where would they live?

"If that is what you *truly* want, then… yes."

"Of course it's what I want! Let's go! What do I need to do? How can I help?"

"Fine! Fine, but slow down. There are things you must know first," Malayou said.

"Like what?" Josie asked, impatiently.

"What you have seen so far is… will be the new reality for the people you know and love. They will not exist in your life, and you will not exist in theirs." Josie frowned and picked at a fingernail. "You won't remember them, and they won't remember you."

"At all? Nothing?" Josie asked, her voice a whisper.

"Nothing. Also, this change will be permanent. If you don't like what happens, it's too bad. You cannot go back."

"So, it's not just getting to meet my birth parents. I'm not going to just get a glimpse of what my life would have been like with them?"

Malayou shook her head. "It's one or the other. The life you know or the life you don't know but think about all the time. You don't get both."

Josie put her hands to her stomach and took a deep breath. Her stomach churned like a raging hurricane. "I don't like this," she said. "It's not fair!"

"Life isn't about fairness, honey," Malayou chuckled.

Josie frowned at her. "What would you know about life? What are you, anyway?"

"What I am is difficult to explain to simple human minds. I am a conscious being, and that is all you need to know."

"None of this feels right. At all. I don't like this," Josie said again, shaking her head. She continued to breathe deeply, hoping not to lose her lunch, if that was even possible at this point.

"You must decide," Malayou said. Suddenly, they were standing, face to face, in the middle of the road. She looked back towards the way she came. At the tree line, she saw her parents – her adoptive parents – standing with Jenna, Simon, and Dave. They all smiled at her and waved. Josie then looked in the other direction, down into the long darkness of the road ahead, and all she could see were two shadows of people she hadn't yet met. She looked at those shadows for a long time until Malayou moved to stand in front of her. "Go forward or go back. But you must choose."

* * * * *

Josie looked at the shadowed figures before her. All she had to do was go to them, and all her questions would be answered. Actually, all her questions would disappear along with the life she'd lived for the past sixteen years. No more Angela and Charles, no more Jenna and Dave. No more Simon.

No more wondering.

There would be no regrets because she'd never know anything different. No memories of those she loves in the present.

Her stomach hurt and her chest felt like it had been torn open and her heart ripped out.

A memory rose to her mind from health class. Along with the always-horrifying sex-ed, they learned about babies. She remembered reading that babies can hear in the womb sometime around eighteen weeks, a little more than halfway through the pregnancy. Josie wondered if she'd remember her mother's voice from being in her womb. Or maybe her father's. Maybe he talked to her while she was in her mother's belly. Would she recognize them? Would they already love her? Would she love them the way she loves…?

Josie turned back and looked at her adoptive parents. Her dad had said some hurtful things to her in the last few weeks, but what about all the years before that? He taught her how to play guitar and appreciate music. He had the best hugs that always made her forget whatever upset her. He sat through endless dance classes and recitals and plays. He paid for singing lessons and dance lessons and guitar lessons. He never said no to something she was passionate about. He always wanted her to try whatever it was. If he ever complained, she never saw or heard any of it. She wondered if he ever thought about what it would have been like if Ethan hadn't died. Would he have been a typical son, sharing in sports and cars and all that? Did he miss that? If Josie chose her birth parents, she would be denying him a chance to be a father at all. It wouldn't give them Ethan back. Was she being selfish?

She looked at her mom. She remembered the look in Angela's eyes when she talked about losing Ethan. And she remembered how she sobbed just an hour or so ago against the steering wheel of the car over her marriage ending. Would Josie be responsible for that if she chose her birth parents? Would her birth mom nurse her through the flu and strep throat and ankle sprains like Angela did, with endless cocoa and soup and unconditional love? Would her birth mom teach her to love books about King Arthur while also encouraging her to be a strong, independent young woman the way Angela did?

But how could she turn down an opportunity to know the people who created her? She didn't even know what they looked like. The only thing she'd ever had, which she didn't allow herself to utter or even think very often, were their names: Jason and Leah Whitehall. For so long it had felt like a betrayal to her adoptive parents to give names to the idea of her birth parents. Now, she was only a few steps away from erasing it all.

Malayou touched Josie on the shoulder. "Well, honey? What will it be?"

* * * * *

"If I get to live life with my birth parents, then I want my adoptive parents to have Ethan back," Josie said to the old woman.

Malayou narrowed her eyes at Josie. "There's no bargaining in this place. You take what you get."

"I don't accept that," Josie replied. She crossed her arms over her chest and thrust one hip out. "And by the way, where exactly is 'this place'?"

"I think you know I can't tell you that," Malayou answered.

"Come on!" Josie tilted her head at the woman. "I'm not your average person. I talk to dead people. I saw my great aunt die. Like, watched her soul move on. You can tell me where we are. Another dimension? Limbo? Hell? It's not like I'll remember it, right?"

"What are you trying to do? Stall? You must choose. We cannot stay here forever," Malayou said. She put her hands on her hips and tapped her foot at Josie, a too-human gesture.

"What are you? A genie? An alien? Bigfoot in human disguise? Is this a punishment for something? Because it seems like a punishment."

Malayou lifted her chin. "You think you're pretty smart, don't you?"

Josie shrugged. "I think I've had one hell of a year, and I'm not the person I used to be."

"You've made your choice?"

"Will you answer one question for me?"

"You can ask. I can't guarantee I'll answer."

Josie shrugged again. "Which one do *you* think I should choose?"

The old woman raised her eyebrows at Josie. "You want my opinion?"

"Yeah. Why not? I'm assuming that, whatever you are and wherever we are, you've been witness to a few of these dilemmas. I'd like your input."

Malayou rubbed her hands together and her tongue flicked out, licking her lips. It disturbed Josie but she did her best not to let on. "No one ever asks for my opinion," Malayou said.

Josie frowned. "That's not very kind, is it? I imagine you have a lot of wisdom to share."

"I do!"

"Good. Will you share it with me?"

Malayou looked around, then looked up at the sky. "Well… alright. In *my* opinion… you should go with your birth parents."

Josie gave a small nod. "Why?"

"It's what you have wished for! For so long! The longing for them is deep in your heart, is it not it?"

"Yes," Josie replied.

"You've dreamed of this your whole life, haven't you?"

"Yes."

"Well… it seems obvious. You have an opportunity most people will never get, to live a different life, the life you were *supposed* to have."

Josie frowned in thought. She looked to where Charles and Angela were standing with Jenna, Dave, and Simon. Then she looked again at the shadowed figures of her birth parents.

"And I can't talk you into giving them Ethan back?" Josie asked.

"I'm sorry," she shook her head. "That's just not part of this."

Josie sighed. "Okay, I've made my decision."

"You have? Wonderful," Malayou smiled. "I hope I helped."

"You did. More than you know," Josie replied.

"Alright, so which shall it be? Old life, or new life?"

Josie looked once more in each direction. She then looked at Malayou, standing with a streetlight behind her head like a halo, casting her almost entirely in shadow. Then, Josie braced herself and ran straight at the woman. With all her might, she planted both hands on the woman's chest and knocked her flat on her back. Josie jumped over her body as she flailed and screamed. "I choose neither!" Josie yelled over her shoulder as she ran around the side of the country store and took off as fast as she could.

12

Josie's heart pounded in her ears. She slowed to a walk, heaving great gasps of air into her lungs. Maybe she should start running with Jenna.

Josie stopped at the thought. Would she ever see Jenna again? How would she get out of this place?

A glance back over her shoulder showed her that the convenience store was no longer in sight. All she could see was a vast, sun-burnt field. She turned in the direction she'd been running. The field stretched on in front of her, the setting sun hovering low in the sky. Going forward was always better than going back, right?

She walked on for what felt like an hour, though the sun did not move any lower in the sky. She tried to ignore the terror creeping into her, the fear that she would walk like this forever and never get anywhere. And if she did get somewhere, would there be another strange being like Malayou there? Would she ever find someone to truly help her? All she wanted was some trees for shade and maybe a friendly face or two.

Josie looked up from her thoughts then to see that the landscape was finally changing. Far in the distance she could see a small copse of trees breaking the monotony of the burnt field. She hurried her pace out of curiosity. When she got closer, she noticed a rustic gazebo on the edge of the trees. In the light of the still-setting sun, she could see the silhouette of two figures sitting on a bench inside the gazebo, one male, one female. Her heart quickened in anticipation. It had to be her parents. Her birth parents. She was going to meet her birth parents despite having not chosen them.

* * * * *

"Uncle Frank! Aunt Pauline!" Josie exclaimed at the pair smiling at her from the gazebo bench. She was disappointed that it wasn't her parents, but not surprised. She had chosen neither path.

"I know we're not who you wanted to see," said Aunt Pauline, rising easily from the bench. She was in a form similar to when Josie saw her crossing – long, dark flowing hair and smooth, young skin. Uncle Frank, too, looked younger than she was used to seeing him.

Josie embraced Aunt Pauline, surprised she was able to feel her. Again, she wondered if it was because she was also dead.

"You're not dead, Josie," Uncle Frank said, also rising from the bench.

"I don't understand. Where are we?" she asked.

"Unfortunately, we cannot answer that," said Aunt Pauline.

"Figures," Josie scoffed.

"What we can tell you, is that this place is an anomaly. It shouldn't exist, but it does, and there are… things, energies, if you will… that have learned to use it to their advantage," said Uncle Frank.

"Like tricking people into thinking their dead parents can be brought back to life?" asked Josie, angrily thrusting out her hip as she crossed her arms.

"Josie," said Aunt Pauline, "I know you want to meet your birth parents, but I'm afraid that isn't going to happen."

"Why?" she asked, defiantly.

"You see how I look different than I did when you knew me in life?"

"Yes, you're younger."

Aunt Pauline smiled. "Yes, I present myself to you as a younger version of the me you knew, but I am not that person."

"What do you mean?"

"I mean… the person you knew me as was a living person, like yourself. You have a physical body and a spiritual body. But you also have another body, a layer of human existence that is formed and shaped solely from your experiences in your human body. It's like a filter. What you see of me now, standing before you, is only the spiritual body. When my physical body died, I shed the experiential body as well, to become this. I am not the Pauline you knew."

"But you're still with Uncle Frank!"

"Because our spiritual bodies are connected."

"Why are you telling me all this?

Aunt Pauline looked at Uncle Frank, and he took a step closer. "You never knew your birth parents. Who they are now is not who they were when they were alive in your time. Because of that, you will not be able to get from the experience what you want."

Josie frowned. "I don't understand. Wouldn't they remember me? Remember their lives?"

"Yes, but…."

"But what? This makes no sense."

"I know it's confusing, and I wish we could explain it better," said Aunt Pauline.

"But you won't," pouted Josie.

"Can't," said Uncle Frank. "We've already told you too much."

"Of course. Why would this ever be easy?" asked Josie, throwing up her hands in exasperation.

"We do have someone who would like to meet you," said Aunt Pauline.

Josie's head snapped up. "What? Who?" She was both excited and wary. "Wait, how do I know I can trust that you're actually you, and not someone like Malayou?"

Aunt Pauline and Uncle Frank exchanged another look, then they both held out a hand. "Take our hands, Josie."

She did, but with a suspicious frown. A familiar, wonderful, warm tingle flowed through her fingers, up her arms, and into her heart. "Okay," said Josie softly. "Who is it that you want me to meet?"

Aunt Pauline looked at Uncle Frank, and Uncle Frank turned to look over his shoulder. That was when a shadow that Josie had thought was just a tree moved in closer to reveal a man. He reminded her a little of Daniel's father William, only broader, but with similar long, dark hair and light golden-brown eyes. Then she realized that the eyes were very similar to the eyes she saw whenever she looked in the mirror.

The man stepped cautiously into the gazebo.

"Who are you?" Josie asked, anticipation clenching her lungs and making it hard to breathe.

"In your life, my name was Joseph Whitehall," he replied, his voice soft, gentle.

"Whitehall…? That was…."

He gave a small nod. "I was the father of Jason."

"So, you're my… my grandfather?" Josie's heart did a leap in her chest at the words.

"Yes."

"We're going to go now and let the two of you talk for a bit," said Aunt Pauline.

Josie looked at her in panic. "But—"

"We won't be far, Josie. Frank and I are always watching over you. And you will see us again."

Before Josie could say anything else, Aunt Pauline and Uncle Frank had faded into the golden sunset.

"Will you sit with me?" Joseph asked, gesturing to the bench.

Josie sat. Questions swirled in her mind, but she couldn't force any of them out of her mouth.

"I am sure you have a lot of questions," said Joseph. "Though I am not sure I could answer many of them. But I will tell you what I can.

"My life as Joseph Whitehall was not a good one. At the time when your parents were in the car accident, it had been five years since Jason and I had spoken. I was not a good father. I did not even know they had died until you were already adopted, and until then, I did not even know Leah was pregnant. But that was a good thing. I could not have parented you. And my life ended when you were about four years old. Those last few years of my life, I was wasting away, trapped inside a bottle, trapped inside a body that was eaten away by poison."

"You were an alcoholic?"

"Yes. I made a lot of mistakes in that life, and instead of facing my mistakes and facing life's challenges, I numbed myself to it all. So, I could not have been there for you in any meaningful way. I was not there for Jason, and I was not able to be there for you."

"Can… can you tell me about my father… about Jason? What was he like?"

Joseph shook his head. "I cannot tell you much. His mother and I divorced when he was five, and my downward spiral accelerated at that point. I saw him rarely. He did not want to see me, and I cannot blame him. It was hard to stay in that numb place. The more I drank, the harder it was to stay there. So, when he and I did see each other, I was usually drunk. But I do remember that he was very clever. He liked to invent things, build things. He was in school to be an engineer when he married your mother. She was a chef. She was a beautiful person, inside and out. I ruined their wedding reception because… well… you know, and she was still kind to me. She always treated me with kindness and compassion. I do not think she did it for me, though. I think she did it for Jason. Because he could not. She was a very special person."

Josie wiped tears from her cheeks. "How do I know this is true? How do I know any of this is real?" she asked. She wanted it all to be true. She finally had more pieces to the puzzle of who she was and where she came from, and her heart ached for it to be true.

Joseph sighed. “I do not know that I can offer you anything to prove what I say. But you can take my words with you, sit with them, feel them, and feel if they are the truth.”

“Do I have any other family related to either my dad or mom?” Josie asked.

“I do not know,” he replied sadly.

“Do you know how I can get out of here?”

He shook his head again.

This time, Josie sighed.

“But I think the way will show itself to you when the time is right, and I do not believe you will be here much longer. Until then, I would like to share with you the keys to living your best human life,” said Joseph.

“Yeah, sure, but how? My spirit guides are always less than generous with actual, real information. They’re always telling me that I need to figure it out for myself.”

“And they are right, but first of all, wherever we are right now, the rules are not the same. And second, just because you know the keys, that does not mean you will do anything with them. That is up to you.”

Josie was torn. Her mind warned her to be suspicious, but her heart was open and trusting of this man. There was something familiar in him, and something that she liked. “Okay then. Go on.”

“Alright. Well, the first key is that everything you do in your life should be done from the heart. Do you know what I mean by that?”

“I think so. Well… no, I’m not sure.”

Joseph smiled. “That is okay,” he said, and paused, thinking. “What is one thing in your life that you love to do, that you cannot live without?”

“Easy. Dancing,” Josie replied.

“Okay, dancing. When you dance, you feel joy?”

“Yes,” Josie nodded.

"Do you feel lifted, raised, more alive?"

"Yes," she nodded again, more emphatically.

"And do you feel something like a tug in your heart – not your physical heart, but that center of you?" he asked, pointing at the center of his own chest.

Josie paused and then said, "Yes. Yes, all the time. Dancing is like breathing for me, but better."

"Okay, so imagine that every time you do something, every time you say something, every time you interact, every aspect of what you do comes from that place where you feel that tug, and it gives you some level of that same feeling. Does that make sense?"

"Yes, I think so," Josie replied, frowning in thought.

"It is not realistic to think that you can live that way one hundred percent of the time, but if you try to incorporate it into your life, then you will live from your heart the majority of the time, and when you live from your heart, you need not fear anything, you need not regret anything. You will live from the energetic heart, which is the seat of your higher self, the core of who you are, and you will radiate joy, kindness, empathy, love…."

"Higher self?" asked Josie.

Joseph nodded. "The higher self is the place where your soul comes from. It is the essence of your pure self. You have access to that place, here," he said, tapping the center of his chest again. "Does this make sense?"

Josie, still frowning, shrugged. "It's all very overwhelming," she said. "I don't understand why you're telling me all this."

Joseph sighed. "I confess, my motives are somewhat selfish," he said, which caused Josie's heart – her physical heart – to jump into double-time and her stomach to churn with nerves. "In life I was not able to guide my son in how to be a good man, and I could not guide him in death as a spirit guide because he died before I did, but I can help guide you, and maybe become just a little bit of the person I should have been in life had I made different choices."

"So… are you one of my spirit guides now?"

When he shook his head, Josie was surprised to find she was disappointed. "Maybe someday. For now, I have been given the opportunity to give you some information."

"Okay. You have more to tell me?"

"Yes. The second key to life is to know that everything, and I mean *everything*, has a purpose. But nothing is out of your control. Do you understand?"

She frowned in thought. "You're saying there's purpose in things like war, cancer, drug addiction, mass shootings?"

"It is not an easy concept to believe, and I understand why you would have trouble with it. But there is a yin and yang to everything in human life. A push and pull. Because you cannot recognize the light without the dark, the good without the bad, the highs without the lows."

"You sound like cliché song lyrics," Josie scoffed.

Joseph chuckled. "Maybe I do, but it is true. However, it is all to varying degrees. And you always have a choice in how you respond to both the highs and lows. Let me demonstrate, okay?" He stood and went to the gazebo entrance and scooped up a handful of gravel, and then he walked to the opposite side of the gazebo. "Please come stand with me," he said.

She rose and went to the railing where he stood.

"Find me a leaf, if you would," he said.

Josie bent and picked up a fallen leaf from the floor and held it out for him. He lined up the pebbles and stones along the railing. He took the leaf and twirled it by the stem between his fingers.

"Everything has a purpose because everything has an effect. Sometimes it is a big effect, sometimes it is small. Sometimes you are aware of the effect, and sometimes you are not," he said, studying the leaf. He gestured for her to step to the railing. He held the leaf out and let it go. Josie watched it flutter down into a small pond she hadn't noticed before.

"The leaf represents a person," said Joseph. He held up one of the smaller pebbles between his fingers. "This represents an event in that person's life. A small event. When dropped into the water near the leaf, watch what happens."

He released the pebble and it fell with a small plop into the water. A small ring of ripples undulated outward, causing the leaf to rock a little but stayed mostly in place.

"Now with a bigger event," said Joseph, holding out one of the larger stones. It fell into the pond with a bigger plop and splash, and the rings of the ripples sent the leaf on a ride further out into the water. "But people have an advantage that leaves do not have. When something causes ripples in your life, you can choose how you respond. Will you go with the ripples, or fight against it? When you are faced with cruelty, will you respond with cruelty or kindness? When faced with a challenge, will you meet the challenge or run away from it?"

"But wait. You said everything has a purpose. What is the purpose of the kids you see on those tv commercials with cancer? What was the purpose of your alcoholism? What is the purpose of my father – adoptive father – thinking I'm a nut because I talk to dead people? How can those things have a purpose?"

Joseph sighed. "Those questions are harder to answer," he said.

"I knew it. You can't answer them."

"I did not say that. They are harder to answer because the possibilities are endless. You have something close to eight billion human lives existing on the planet right now, and that means there are infinite possibilities for any given event. Again, some are big, some are small. Look...." Joseph waved his arm again, and a breeze stirred the tree. A dozen small leaves fluttered to the surface of the pond and settled. He cupped his hands together, and they were instantly filled with pebbles of different sizes. "Imagine that the leaves represent a portion of the population, and these stones are events." He tossed the pebbles and they spread out through the air, and each plopped into the pond causing countless ringlets of ripples. The leaves rocked and spun along the surface of the water, some bumping into each other, others moving further away.

"You are living in a crowded, noisy world, so if you have events causing ripples going off all around you, it takes a lot of focus to know what is yours and what is for someone else, and to decide how much effect it has on you. But the possibilities are endless. Perhaps someone who loses a sister to cancer will grow up to find a cure for that form of cancer. Perhaps the mother who loses a child to gang violence will work with inner city youth and change lives for the better. There are so many possibilities. My alcoholism… well, that was a result of my running from life's challenges, but even that had a purpose. I do not know what it was. Perhaps it was to keep me from Jason's life. Perhaps you would not exist to help trapped souls if I had been a good, active presence in his life. Perhaps he would have made different choices if I were a better father, that would have kept him from meeting Leah. One of the amazing things about human life is that there are all these possibilities for what could happen at any given moment. It can be scary, but it is mostly just a miracle. And it is always purposeful.

"As for your adoptive father, I cannot give you answers, but if you trust that you are responding to the challenge of his behavior in the best way you can, I believe you will have an outcome that is good for you both. Perhaps you are meant to stretch his limits of belief, to teach him to be more open to things in your world that so many humans do not understand. Again, the possibilities are endless, and you are the best person to answer the why's and how's."

Josie, frowning again, turned and went back to the bench. "I'm not sure any of that was very helpful."

Joseph returned to his seat on the bench next to her. "I am sure that if someone had told me any of those things in my human life, I would have called them a crackpot. All I ask is that you hang on to all I have told you, try it out, see if any of it fits at any time in your life, and do with it what you can. Just do your best, okay?"

"Okay," Josie nodded.

Joseph smiled at her.

"So, what now?"

* * * * *

"Do you trust me?" Joseph asked.

"I don't know why exactly, after everything that's happened, but yes. I trust you."

"Okay, then," he smiled warmly. "Will you come with me?"

"Where?"

"If you trust me, does it matter?"

Josie frowned in thought but took his outstretched hand.

They stepped from the gazebo and walked in the direction of the setting sun which still didn't seem to be getting any lower in the sky. "What made you run away from that woman, Malayou?" Joseph asked her.

"I knew something wasn't right about her when I asked her opinion of what I should do. She was excited and flattered. None of my guides would react that way, and so it just seemed odd to me. Something told me not to trust her or the situation. So, I chose option number three," she replied.

"You are a smart girl," he said, shaking his head in admiration.

"And you don't know anything about her, who – or what – she is, and where we are?" Josie pressed.

"Unfortunately, no. I was brought here by Frank and Pauline to help you, but that is all I know. But…."

"But what?" Josie said, her curiosity piqued.

He scrunched his face in thought, as though fighting an inner battle over whether to speak or not. Then he let out a puff of air and said, "I am not saying this is what it is, but back in the day, before alcohol took over my life, I would listen to the stories from the others in our tribe of men who walked through doorways into other worlds, worlds that were like ours and not like ours. Depended on which door they went through."

"Do you mean in meditation? Like astral projection?" Josie asked.

"Yes, and no. Both. I heard stories of men who were out hunting with the others who vanished before everyone's eyes, only to turn up miles away days later. Or sometime not at all. But the ones who came back described all different kinds of experiences, meetings with beings that were often very different from us. Some were kind, some were not. But the one thing that was the same was this," he made a gesture like his hands were forming around an invisible column that ran within him. "Our core self. You call it intuition. It is that thing that told you Malayou may not have good intentions. And those who listen to their core self when they pass through those doors are usually the ones lucky enough to come back."

Josie's face turned to a sudden, deep frown.

"What's wrong? Did I say something to upset you?"

Josie shook her head. "No, not at all. It's just that… I spent so much energy focused on wanting to meet my birth parents that I never even thought about other family, like a grandpa. And I am so grateful to know you now, that I feel bad I didn't think about you before…."

"Oh, Josie, do not feel bad about that." He stopped walking and they faced each other. "Your focus on your birth parents is what brought us together. I am also grateful for that. We must focus on the gratitude. Okay?"

Josie nodded even as she wiped away tears.

"And to answer your next question, yes, you have more family like me, in the spirit realm at this point. But you are blessed with the blood of a people whose ancestors remain very connected to them even after death. So, while I am not a guide for you at this point in your life, I may be at some other time, or other ancestors may step forward to help guide you. We are always nearby, ready to help if it is needed."

Josie felt a familiar tingling warmth spreading throughout her entire body, as though many spirits were holding her close in love all at the same time. "Wow," Josie breathed.

"Yes," said Joseph with a warm grin as if he could feel it, too.

A comfortable silence fell between them as they continued to walk on through the golden field towards the sun that didn't seem to want to set, until Joseph stopped again and broke their silence.

"It feels as if we are almost there, but first—"

"Where?"

"To the door you need to take to get back. But first, we need to talk about your father. Your adoptive father."

Josie frowned again, but the feeling from her ancestors was stronger than the hurt she still felt from him. "What do I do about him?" Josie lamented.

"What do you think you should do about him?" Joseph asked.

Josie tilted her head at him. "Spoken like a true spirit guide," she said with a chuckle and a sigh. "I hate referring to him as my 'adoptive father'. He's my father, like it or not. He's the man who raised me. No disrespect to the man who gave me half his DNA, but the bottom line is, he isn't here. Charles is. And I don't want to go through the rest of my life angry or resentful at him. I need to find a way to fix it with him. If he is willing."

Joseph smiled proudly at her. "He is willing," he said. "Alright, we must say goodbye for now," he said. He motioned to the air behind her, and she turned to see a vertical patch of air shimmering like a pool of water.

"That will take me back?" she asked.

"Yes, back to your friends, who are anxiously awaiting your return."

"Does it sound weird to say that I'll miss you?"

"No, it does not sound weird. I am blessed that you feel that way. But remember, I am never far. And sometimes you may see me in other forms. Turkey is one of my favorites."

"Are you saying that I may see you in the form of a turkey?" she chuckled.

"Exactly. When I need to get a message to you, I may show up as a turkey. For now, anyway," he chuckled, too.

"Can I hug you?" she asked, getting serious again.

"You can and you must," he said. It was strange because he felt so solid in their embrace, so warm, and so full of energy. Good energy. "I love you, my beautiful, wonderful, amazing granddaughter."

"I love you, too, Grandpa Joseph," she said. "Thank you. For everything."

With that, she turned toward the shimmering pool of air and walked as quickly as she could through it.

13

"Being a college professor seems to have served you well," Rod said. "Tenured and published all kinds of books. I'm glad for you."

"You've followed me?" Drew asked, his eyes softening on Rod.

Rod nodded. "Always hoped for good things for you."

"I'd hoped the same for you," Drew replied.

"I appreciate that. Unfortunately, I just couldn't… I couldn't let that damned place go," Rod said with so much sadness.

"More like it wouldn't let you go, my friend," said Drew.

"Huh," Rod grunted. "Perhaps. Mutual."

"Well, perhaps today things will change for the better for you."

"You think?"

Drew nodded. "Would you like to go for a ride?"

Rod's eyes lit up.

* * * * *

Simon could hear voices as he stepped into the basement. It was easy enough to recognize Dave and Jenna's voices, so he followed the sounds and climbed the stairs. When the squealing of the screen door notified them of his arrival, Jenna said, "It's about time!"

"Where's Josie?" Simon asked.

"She's the only one who hasn't turned up," Daniel said with a deep frown.

"And we didn't want to go looking for her until we were all together," said Jenna.

"Does that mean that you…?"

"Are no longer being a grumpy bee—"

Somewhere inside a door slammed shut, cutting Jenna off, and making them all jump.

"Maybe it's her," said Jenna.

"I don't think so," said Daniel.

"Me either," said Simon.

"Well, we should go see what that was," said Dave.

"I agree," said Simon.

"Okay, Dave and I will check upstairs," said Jenna, "while you and Daniel check the first floor and basement."

The screen door squealed in protest again as they went back inside. "I assume you guys checked the place out already?" Simon asked Daniel as they moved through the first floor rooms and headed toward the basement steps.

"Yup. Doors to all the rooms were open, closets and things were closed," Daniel replied.

"Did you talk about your experiences in the maze?"

"Not yet."

Daniel had reached the bottom of the stairs. The door to the tunnel that led back to the maze was standing wide open.

"Exactly how I left it," said Simon. They shined their lights around, looking for anything that could have made the sound.

"I don't see anything out of place," said Daniel. "No other doors."

"Same. Let's go back upstairs. I don't even like being near that tunnel."

"Me either," Daniel grumbled and hurried back to the stairs.

Jenna and Dave were coming down from the second level when they reached the hall. "Nothing amiss that we could see," she said.

"Okay, well, I say we forget it for now. We need to find Josie," said Simon.

“I’m really worried about her,” said Daniel.

“We’re all worried about her,” said Jenna gently.

“Can we go back outside? This house gives me the creeps,” said Dave.

They all shuffled back out the door to the front porch. “Anyone have any ideas?” Simon asked.

“The way I see it, we have to decide if we go back the way we came,” said Jenna, “back into the maze, to look for her, or if we should just go across the street and search.”

They all stood in silence, looking at each other, waiting for someone else to make the decision that no one wanted to make.

Finally, Jenna said, “Simon, what do you think we should do?”

He frowned and looked over their heads at the field across the street, still baking under the hot summer sun. And then something caught his eye.

“What is that?”

* * * * *

Simon hurried across the street. Daniel was fast at his heels, but Dave and Jenna moved a bit slower. Jenna would admit later how foolish she felt for rushing into it all without a care and with a lot of arrogance. Now, however, she was frightened enough to be more cautious when something odd was happening before them, and Dave could sense the shift in her, so he moved at her pace.

She paused when she reached the threshold of the park. The broken sign overhead now looked ominous instead of invitingly mysterious. She shook her head at herself.

“You good?” Dave asked, standing at her side.

She smiled at him. “As long as you’re next to me, I’m perfect.”

* * * * *

"Have you ever seen anything like that?" Simon asked Daniel as they hurried across the field.

"Nope," was Daniel's reply.

Simon's heart pounded and his head spun. He had never seen anything like this before. It was like a big oil-slicked puddle was hanging vertically in mid-air. It shimmered in the sun in a way that was beautiful, but he knew enough now not to trust anything, especially if it looked inviting. The fact that Jenna wasn't rushing to be first there with all her equipment was almost equally concerning. He wouldn't have gone near it except that something told him it might have something to do with Josie's disappearance.

Six feet from it, he stopped. Daniel stopped next to him. They waited for Jenna and Dave to join them.

"Is that a…," Jenna started, "a p—"

"Please don't say it," Simon cut her off.

"It's a portal. It has to be a portal," she said, frowning in awe and disbelief.

"Portals don't exist," Simon said.

"Then what are we looking at, if you're so smart?" asked Jenna.

"I…," Simon said, "I don't know."

"Okay. Well, whatever it is, I have to get data on it," Jenna said. "Dave, can you get it on camera? I want to take EMF readings," she said.

"Camera's dead, babe," Dave said, frowning at the camera in his hand.

"What?"

"Died as soon as I turned it on."

Jenna turned to Simon who held the other camera. He lifted it up, pushed a button. "Dead."

"Seriously?" Jenna lamented. Then she looked at the EMF detector in her hand. "Geez, this is dead, too!" In seconds, Jenna had her backpack off and was handing out fresh batteries.

"Babe, it's still not working," Dave said.

"Same," said Simon.

Jenna hit the EMF detector against her palm. "What is going on?"

"Just a guess, but I think this thing is draining the batteries," Daniel offered.

"Ah-ha!" Jenna exclaimed, her arm in her backpack up to her shoulder. She pulled her arm out and showed them a small rectangular object.

"A disposable camera?" asked Simon.

"Yes! I put one in here in case of emergencies! It doesn't use batteries!"

Dave smiled, happy to see the Jenna he had known and loved for so long finally coming back to them.

Jenna started snapping pictures of the thing shimmering in the air in this field. Jenna clicked away, moving around the shimmering mass in a wide circle when it started to ripple.

"What is happening?" Simon asked, taking a step back.

"Jenna," said Dave, "maybe you should move away." But in typical Jenna fashion, she kept taking pictures.

"Wait, I see something… someone…," said Daniel.

In a blink, Josie was standing in front of them, her eyes wide as she looked around. "Whoa, that was weird," Josie said. The shimmering puddle of air was gone.

"Josie!" Simon grabbed at her and pulled her into a hug, then Daniel, then Jenna and Dave bear-hugged her together. "We were so worried about you."

"It is you, right?" said Jenna, chuckling, yet they all looked a bit nervous.

"It's me… I think…." Josie said with a weak smile.

"What happened to you?" asked Daniel.

Josie shook her head. "So much. And I want to tell you all, and I want to hear about what you guys have been through. But first, we need to fix this place."

"How?" asked Jenna.

Josie took a bracing breath. "Alright, let me explain…."

* * * * *

Rod and Drew sat in the idling car and watched as Josie stepped through the doorway back into the field.

"Wow," said Drew.

"Yup," said Rod. He swiped a tear of joy away from his eyes. "I knew it. I knew those kids were special."

* * * * *

"Follow me," Josie said, and started back through the field. "And I should add, I don't really mean 'fix'."

"So, what *do* you mean?" asked Daniel as he and the others followed her.

"I… I'm not really sure how to explain it," she said. The burnt and dried grass crunched underneath their feet as they made their way past the dome and back into the park. Near the entrance, in the dirt circle that housed the remnants of the ticket booth, she stopped and turned to look at her friends.

She held out her hand, palm up, displaying a rather large, oddly shaped and lumpy rock of green and brownish-orange. "I assume you all also received a… gift of some sort?"

One by one, they each held out their hands. Jenna showed them her opaque, blood-red crystal, and Dave showed them a seed the size of his palm. Daniel held out a long, thin, carved feather.

"Ivory?" Josie asked with a frown.

Daniel shook his head. "It's bone. I think it's an owl bone."

Then they looked at what Simon had. It was round and almost as big as his palm, rough on one side and smooth on the other, with a design resembling a spiral staircase. "It's called an ammonite. It's a fossilized sea creature that died over sixty million years ago," he said.

"And this…," Josie said of her object.

"It's raw copper," said Simon.

"Yes," said Josie. "Metal." Then she pointed to Dave and said, "Earth." At Daniel, she said, "Air." At Jenna, she said, "Fire." And at Simon, she said, "Water. Earth, air, fire, water, metal. All the elements are represented."

"What does it mean?" Jenna asked.

"I think we need to give these gifts to this place," Josie replied.

"How?" Dave frowned.

"I think we need to make an offering to the land," she said.

From behind them, came a voice. "We'd like to help."

They all turned. Two men, both old and gray, one looking very unhealthy, stood under the Mystery Mountain entryway.

"If you'll let us," the healthier of the men added, a shovel in his hand.

* * * * *

"What if someone drives by?" asked Dave.

"This is *our* property," said Drew. "You won't get into trouble. You have our permission."

"You're the owners of this place?" Jenna said, her eyes lighting up. "I have so many questions for you!"

"And we'd be happy to answer them but—"

"Can we do that later?" Josie asked. She looked at the circle of dirt. "We need to move this wood."

Simon, Dave, Daniel, Drew, and Josie went to work rearranging the remnants of the ticket booth out of the way.

"Watch out for nails," said Simon. "And splinters."

"Who is he, the mom of this group?" Rod asked, chuckling that then turned into a cough.

Jenna sidled over to where Rod stood, leaning on a four-footed cane for support, but looking more and more lively as the moments passed. "So… you're the mastermind behind this place." It was a statement, not a question.

"Yup," said Rod with a nod. "It wasn't ever great. It wasn't what I wanted it to be."

Josie turned, a board in her hands. "It wasn't your fault. You did everything right," she told Rod. "This place…." Josie tossed the board aside and put her hands on her hips, looking around, searching for the right words. The sun was finally sinking lower in the sky, though she felt like it should be midnight, hovering just behind the treetops. "The energy that caused… well, weird stuff to happen has been here for a long, long time. The land itself has a powerful consciousness. That's the only way I can describe it."

"What do you mean?" Drew asked, a frown furrowing his brows.

Josie frowned in thought. "It's like there is a portion of this land – most of this park and the field, and partway up the mountain – that is alive, aware, and conscious of everything that's going on. It's like this because something bad happened here, and the land got mad."

"What do you mean, something bad?" asked Jenna.

"Bloodshed of some kind," Josie shrugged. She bent and picked up the shovel and looked again at the circle of dirt. "A battle is my guess. Massive bloodshed and death. And all that death and blood and anger and sadness seeped into the land which became deeply angry and deeply sad and deeply aware."

They all stood in silence, each lost in their own thoughts.

"That's why I said that we can't fix it. We cannot change what happened, but we can honor the land with an offering, by giving it our gifts," Josie added. She planted the tip of the shovel in the center of the dirt circle, nodded, and started digging.

Dave stepped forward and said to Josie, "May I?" Josie nodded and handed the shovel over.

"So, the land made all these weird things happen?" Jenna asked.

"Yes and no," said Josie. "Let's do a ceremony first. Do you have any sage and a lighter in that bag, Jenna?"

"You know it!" Jenna replied, swinging her backpack off her shoulder. "Prepared for any situation."

"Impressive," said Drew.

Jenna smiled at him. "Thank you!" She passed Josie a bundle of dried sage and a lighter.

Josie looked at the neat hole Dave had dug quickly, piling the dirt nearby. "A little deeper, please," she said. Dave nodded and went back to work. Josie turned back to Rod and the others and went on. "Some of it was the consciousness of the land, but some of it was a side effect of the energy of this place. I think because of the battle, because of the land gaining a consciousness, it made a sort of magnet for weird energy. The phrase 'a thinning of the veil' comes to me, though I'm not sure why."

"The veil," said Rod, "is the barrier between our world and other worlds. Most think it's just the barrier between life and death, but I've experienced enough here to know there's more than just here and not here."

"I agree," Josie said.

Simon shook his head. "I wouldn't have agreed before today, not even with everything we've been through, but we all just witnessed you come through that 'veil'."

"I doubt any one of us would disagree," said Drew. "But… and I don't mean any disrespect… how is this ceremony supposed to help anything?"

"That's a fair question. As I said, it won't fix anything, but the land, the consciousness that is the land, is unhappy, and it's been largely ignored and sometimes abused, especially since the park closed down. We need to first acknowledge it and then we need to honor it."

"And how will we do that?" asked Daniel.

Josie motioned for Dave to stop digging. She knelt down at the edge of the hole, close to three feet deep and nearly as wide.

She lit the bundle of sage until it released a good, thick smoke, and tossed it in the hole. Then, she took from her pocket the piece of copper. She almost hated giving it up. Her grandfather had given it to her. Her *blood* grandfather. But she knew he gave it to her for a purpose. She ran the pad of her thumb over a smooth part of the copper chunk, and said, "I give this gift to the land in gratitude for showing me the way, for helping me to learn that what I want isn't necessarily what I need, and that love can transcend time, space, death, and blood." With that, she let the copper fall from her hand. It landed in the bottom of the hole with a dull thud, but then came two loud bangs, like that of a drum. *Boom-boom!* It reverberated in the air around them and shook the earth below them. They all looked at each other with wide eyes and raised eyebrows.

Josie looked at her best friend. "Jenna, would you like to go next?"

Jenna knelt next to Josie. She held out the red crystal that caught the sunlight and glowed like fire. She said, "I give this gift to the land in gratitude for showing me the way, for helping me learn not to hold in my emotions, and that instead of envying the gifts of others I need to focus on the unique gifts I have been given." Like Josie, she dropped the crystal in the hole, and again a loud *Boom-boom!* sounded like a giant's heartbeat.

Simon knelt at Josie's other side. Holding out the ammonite, he said, "I give this gift to the land in gratitude for showing me the way and for helping me learn that the truth is in what I feel, not just what I see." He tipped his hand and let the fossil fall. When it hit the bottom of the hole, there was another *Boom-boom!*

Next, Dave took his place by Jenna's side. He held out his palm with the extraordinarily large seed resting in it. "I give this gift to the land in gratitude for showing me the way to forgiveness." The seed fell into the hole followed by another *Boom-boom!*

Josie looked over her shoulder at Daniel. He went and knelt on Simon's other side, and he held up the feather carved from bone. He said, "I give this gift to the land in gratitude for showing me the way and for helping me learn to trust: to trust myself, my intuition, and to trust…," he looked at Josie, "others." He released the feather and it fell softly, but there came the same *Boom-boom!* heartbeat.

"We have gifts we'd like to offer," said Rod, moving around to the other side of the hole with Drew's help.

Josie nodded. "Yes, absolutely, please do."

"You don't have to kneel," Drew said to Rod as he started lower himself slowly.

"I do, actually. We're doing this the right way because I'm not dead yet," he replied. "But you all may have to help me back up."

They all chuckled softly. Drew and Rod knelt next to each other and gave each other a glance that anyone watching knew spoke volumes. Drew held out his hand first, palm up, showing two matching gold rings. "I give this gift to the land in gratitude for showing me the way and for helping me learn to love with all my heart, to love unconditionally."

He didn't let the rings go yet. He was waiting for Rod.

Rod pulled something out from his back pocket and held it out over the hole. It was a small frame with a dollar bill inside. "The first dollar we ever made," he said to answer the unspoken question. "I give this gift to the land in gratitude for showing me the way and for helping me learn to not let money and greed cloud my intentions, because prosperity comes in many other forms."

They looked at each other again and with eyes locked, they released their gifts into the hole. *Boom-boom! Boom-boom!*

Then, the earth beneath their feet swelled, lifting them all gently in the air a couple feet, and then released, as if the land just heaved a great big sigh of relief. Clouds then rolled in, and the sky opened up in a heavy downpour that drenched them, but it stopped almost as quickly as it started. And then then something else happened. The field around them came alive with the sounds of birds, bugs, squirrels, and other critters.

"Wow!" said Jenna as they all got to their feet.

Drew, Dave, and Daniel helped Rod to his feet.

"Does anyone else feel like the land just cried tears of joy?" Josie asked.

"Yeah, but… is that… it? Did we do it?" asked Jenna.

"Well, this is just a start. Someone will have to find a way to continue when we go home or else things will start to happen again," Josie replied. She gave a nod to Dave who motioned to the shovel, and then he began filling the hole with dirt.

"But are you sure?" asked Simon. "Usually we're battling against some mean, nasty ghost. This seemed too easy."

"Easy?" Josie looked at him with wide eyes. "I don't know about you guys, but when I was in that dome, or wherever the dome took me, I faced my inner demons, and that was anything but easy." She looked around at them.

"I… I didn't think of it that way, but you're right. That was tough in there," said Simon.

"Brutal for me," Dave agreed.

Jenna and Daniel both nodded.

"We can't expect these things to all look the same, I guess," said Josie.

"Okay, so what's next? You said that someone will need to continue this?" Daniel asked.

"Unfortunately, yes. This land is a conscious entity in its own right, and needs a caretaker," Josie replied.

"I may have a solution," said Drew.

"You do?" Rod replied.

"It's the reason I was coming to see you today. I decided to swing by and take a look at the place on my way and saw them here and… well, I just had a feeling that everything was lining up right. Finally," said Drew.

"It's still a work in progress, but…," he went on. "Well, I've done alright for myself over the years, with teaching and my books, and I didn't really have anything to spend it on. So, I have quite a bit saved, and I'd like to use it to put the land in a conservation trust."

"Wow, that's amazing!" said Josie.

"From there, I don't know. Sell off the stuff for scrap or whatever, maybe let it be just walking trails and a picnic spot or something," Drew added.

"Maybe… maybe we can turn the house into a kind of museum," Rod said, standing a little straighter. "Maybe we can do some research and find out what happened on this land and find a way to honor that through a museum."

"That sounds like a really good idea," said Drew.

"My dad and I could probably help with that," said Daniel. "He's pretty good with the histories of the tribes in this area. And I'd like to help however I can. Since these guys won't be here."

Josie smiled up at Daniel as his mom placed a transparent hand on his shoulder.

"Let's go home and talk about it some more. We can start making plans," said Drew.

"Aw, I've had so much fun. I don't want to go back to the home," said Rod, who seemed to be standing straighter.

"No, Rod. Not *the* home. My home. Your home, too, now. I don't want you to go back there, either."

Rod's eyes lit up and sparkled with tears of joy. Josie thought she felt a shiver of energy beneath her feet, like the land was joining in with the moment of happiness.

"Well, we should probably head back, too," said Simon. "It's getting late, and our parents are probably anxious to kill us."

"But I have *so* many questions!" Jenna lamented.

Drew handed Jenna a business card. "My cell is on there. Call me, and we can answer your questions. But I think we've had all we can take for today."

Jenna shrieked with joy and threw her arms around Drew in a hug, then did the same to Rod.

"Thank you. Thank you all for whatever it is that you've done here today," said Rod, again brushing away happy tears from his eyes. "I don't know what kind of magic you all stirred up, but I can easily say this is one of the best days of my life," said Rod, looking at Drew with eyes shining bright.

They all said goodbye and promised to stay in touch with each other, then Josie, Simon, Dave, Jenna, and Daniel all piled back into Daniel's car. The sun was sinking behind the mountains, splashing the evening sky with dazzling shades of pink, red, orange, blue, and purple.

They rode in silence all the way back to the resort. When Daniel shifted his car into park in the lot by the office, five heads from the beach turned to look at them. A large fire was roaring in the pit and hot dogs were roasting on the ends of long sticks held by Charles, Angela, Rachel, Greg, and William.

In silence they walked over to their parents. Their parents just looked at them. No one looked angry.

Finally, Angela broke the silence. "Well, what do you all have to say for yourselves?"

Josie, Jenna, Simon, and Dave all took a breath in, but Josie's voice was first with, "I'm sorry, but—"

And then the rest joined in with apologies and exclamations until finally William stood and said, "Hold it! Hold it! Quiet down!"

They stopped. William gave Daniel a knowing look that Daniel returned with a shrug. William sat and then said, "We know you lied, and we know you went to Mystery Mountain. We're not mad… anymore."

"Truthfully, we expected it," said Greg. "Because it's what we would have done if we were you."

"And now," said Angela, "we want you all to sit down, have some food, and tell us everything."

"Full transparency, right, Mom?" Josie said, taking a seat between her parents.

"Right."

Epilogue

One by one they each told their version of the days' events, including – at Jenna's insistence – the behavior changes that Jenna had experienced. They oohed and aahed at each other's stories from the dome and got gasps of surprise when they told of Rod and Drew's appearance. By the time they were all done, the sunset had long since faded and the stars were out.

"Alright, it's late," said Charles. "We should get to bed."

"I don't want to leave tomorrow," said Josie.

"Me either!" said Jenna.

"Let's all have breakfast tomorrow before we check out," said Greg. "William and Daniel, your presence is required."

"Are you sure?" asked William.

"You're now an extension of this weird motley crew of a family we are," said Angela, "so yes, we are sure."

As the LaPage's and the York's, along with Dave, walked up the hill toward their cabins, Josie could feel the team of spirit guides following them along. The amount of unconditional love that was radiating from them was intoxicating.

"Jenna, you have Brandon's cell number, right?" Josie asked.

"Yeah, why?"

"I want to reach out. We should see how he is, maybe hang out or something. I don't want him to think he was or is invisible," she said.

"I think that would be cool," said Dave.

"Me too," said Simon. "Brandon's a cool guy."

They had reached the cabins. Jenna went and sat on the porch with Dave. "Just for a few minutes," she said to Rachel as she and Greg passed by.

Josie stopped and looked at Simon, then at her parents standing on the porch of their cabin. "I'll be there in a minute," she told them. Then she turned back to Simon and took his hands in hers. "Thank you."

"For what?"

"For participating."

"What?"

"Usually, you're just going along with us in this stuff, but today, you participated. I know that in the beginning you were there to keep an eye on me, but you actually participated."

"You give me too much credit. That place didn't exactly give me a choice," he said.

"And how do you feel about it now?" she asked.

He frowned in thought for a moment, then said, "Like my life has been changed. My trajectory has been changed. For the better."

She smiled and nodded. "Because you participated."

"I'm glad that makes you happy."

"You make me happy."

"Ditto," he said. He leaned in and kissed her.

It's a shame that the living cannot see that, Anna said to Joseph. Hanover perched on Joseph's shoulder.

The energy they create is... magnificent, Joseph replied.

* * * * *

Inside, Josie went into the living room where her parents sat at the small table, a cardboard box between them.

"Can we talk?" Charles asked.

"I hoped we could," said Josie. She took the empty seat at the table.

"Did I ever tell you what I wanted to be when I was a kid?" Charles asked her. Josie shook her head. "I wanted to be a music teacher."

"You're kidding!"

"Nope."

"What happened?"

"Well, my dad didn't think teaching was… well, a respectable job for me. He pushed me into finance and accounting. He bullied me and pushed me and manipulated me, and, as you know, I ended up not being a music teacher. I came to resent my father for it and swore I would never do that to my kids. Then, when you asked me recently what I was so afraid of, I got to thinking. It took a while. I'm a bit stubborn, in case you didn't know. But I eventually realized that I was doing to you what my father did to me. And Josie, I do not want you to ever resent me the way I resented my father for so long."

"Dad, I want you to know that I understand if you can't believe in what I can do. It's okay and I'll try not to talk about it all too much around you."

"I don't want that, Josie," said Charles.

"Really?"

"No. I want to support you in what you do. I don't want to push you in a certain direction because it's what *I* think it's what you should do. I want to know what is going on in your life to help me understand it."

Josie nodded. "That's amazing, Dad. I'm glad you feel that way. And I want you to know that just because I do this ghost stuff doesn't mean I won't still do the other things or do something else. I'm only 16."

Angela chuckled.

"Your mother has said the same thing a dozen times," he chuckled, too. But the smile faded quickly. "And about that horrible thing I said in therapy…."

"Dad, you really don't have to. Not anymore," she said.

"Yes, I do, Josie. I want you to understand that I have never once thought of you as anything other than our child. You're a smart girl, and I know you know that sometimes people can say things they don't mean when they're upset and afraid."

"Fear makes people crazy," Josie nodded.

"See, like I said, you're smart. I was upset. At myself. Because I didn't understand and I didn't know how to react, and then the fear of what it all means if what you're saying is true, fear of not being able to protect you, fear of not knowing how to be there for you, and fear of losing you, it all just overwhelmed me."

Josie frowned. "You were afraid of losing me?"

"Your mom pointed out to me that this type of gift is likely in your blood, because of your heritage. I knew she was right. And I was afraid that you would leave us and go in search of people who you could relate to better than you could to us. That fear consumed me and amplified the rest, and I behaved…."

"Like an idiot," said Angela.

"Like a child," said Josie.

"Like a childish idiot," said Angela.

Charles looked from his wife to his daughter and watched their grins growing until they burst out laughing. "Yeah, well, you're not wrong. I started doing and saying things that almost made my worst fear come true."

"But it didn't," Josie said. "It won't."

He smiled. Then he said, "But wait, there's more."

"More what?"

"Well, in an effort to try to understand and to try to make up for at least some of my mistakes, I made a few calls and sent a few emails, and got this." Charles handed Josie a thick manilla envelope that had been lying on top of the box.

She looked at her mom who watched her eagerly, like when Josie was opening that one special present at Christmas. Josie didn't want to prolong the moment, so she undid the clasp and pulled out a stack of documents. On the top was a photocopy of an old, black-and-white photo of a face she recognized instantly. Below the photo was the label "Lieutenant Commander Mark Darcy, U.S. Navy". She looked up at her dad, her eyes wide and jaw hanging open.

"Look at the next one," he said.

She lifted the page to another photocopied photo, this one showing Mark standing next to a little girl in a fancy dress with shiny ringlets of hair. "That's him with his sister, Nancy. Josie, I nearly fell out of my chair when I found out they were real people. I cried."

"He did, Josie," said Angela.

"How did you get all this?" Josie asked, flipping through the other pages of historical information and more photos.

"I contacted the Wakefield, Massachusetts historical society, they sent me some of this, and some distant relatives supplied the rest."

"I cannot believe you did this!" Josie said. "Jenna's going to *love* this. Is this box stuff on Mark, too?"

"No," said Charles. "That is from Rod."

"Wait, what? You know Rod?"

"Your dad and Greg snuck off to meet him at his nursing home," Angela said.

"I didn't know what else to do. It was weird, though. It's like he was expecting us and knew why we were there without us telling him," Charles said.

"That doesn't surprise me," Josie replied. "Can I look?"

Charles pushed the box toward her, and she lifted the lid. Inside were drawings, journals, photo albums, and a few old pieces of memorabilia from Mystery Mountain. "Oh my god. This is amazing."

"I had no idea he'd end up with you guys."

"I think he knew," Josie chuckled. "I'm impressed, Dad. This is just amazing. All of it."

She rose from her chair and went to him. He received her in his arms and gave her the first bear-hug he'd given her in weeks.

"Can I ask a question?" Angela asked.

Charles released Josie from the hug. "Sure," she replied.

"So… you met your grandfather," Angela said.

Josie waited a few beats then said, "That's not a question."

"He was… your birth-father's father, right?"

"Yes."

"Did meeting him… make you want to know more of that side of your family?"

Josie furrowed her brows in thought and said, "Yes and no. I think that I was so upset about learning about Ethan, about it having been a secret for so long, and I just…. Well, like dad, I think that I was upset and afraid and it made me say things I maybe didn't mean and I became obsessed with things that weren't right.

"But I need you both to understand that even though I am still curious about my birth parents and blood relatives, I believe that I am living the life I am meant to live with the people I am meant to live it with. And I trust that if I am meant to know more about those other people, I will find a way, or the way will find me."

Tears poured down Angela's cheeks though she was smiling. "How did we get so lucky, so blessed, to have you as our daughter?"

* * * * *

Greg made his famous French toast, eggs, and bacon for their breakfast feast, to go with a large bowl of fruit salad. During the meal, they all came to an agreement that William and Daniel would visit them in Centerwood during their very brief off-season.

"You are both part of our extended family now, like it or not," Angela told William.

"That's really nice, thank you," William said, his cheeks a bit red. "It would seem that we are a bit more connected to each other than we realized already. Josie, when you were telling your story last night, you mentioned your grandfather, Joseph Whitehall, and I thought that the name sounded familiar. I didn't want to say anything until I was certain, but here…." William pulled a photo from his shirt pocket and handed it to her. It was a photo of two young boys, probably ten or eleven years old, smiling unabashedly at the camera with their arms slung over each other's shoulders.

Loopy handwriting on the back said, "Bill Lightfeather and Joey Whitehall."

"That's my grandfather?"

"He and I went to school together when we were young, and we were good friends."

"What happened?" asked Charles.

William shrugged. "I think his family moved to a different town, so he went to a different school. Back then, kids didn't keep in touch with each other across town lines. No cell phones," he said. "I understand from what you said that his life was challenging, but when he was a kid, he was good kid. He was a good, kind friend."

Josie held the photo out to him, but he said, "Keep it, if you like."

"Really? Thank you so much."

Then Charles said, "I want to thank you all. It's no secret that our family has been through a rough time over the past couple months, and I don't think we would have gotten through it without you all."

"And thank you to the kids," said Greg, "for being honest with us about what you went through yesterday. We are here to support you all, and we can only do that through honesty."

"Aw, thanks, Dad!" Jenna said.

Then Rachel spoke up. "I have a question for Josie, if I can."

"Sure, Mrs. LaPage. What's your question?" Josie replied.

"Well, in listening to everything you all went through, each of you experienced something different in that dome, but your experience, Josie, was more than the others. Have you considered why?"

"Actually, yes, I think I know why," Josie replied. They all looked at her expectantly. "I think the land – the consciousness that is the land – and I had something in common, and I think it recognized that in me. From Aunt Pauline's passing, and my guides leaving me, the truth about Ethan, and… well, the other truths that came out...." She gave a remorseful look at Jenna. Under the table, Simon squeezed her hand. "Well, it all created this awful feeling inside me. The land and I both had it. It was this deep, aching sorrow that made us feel... *hollow.*

"And I can feel that some of you right now want to say you're sorry for your part in that, but don't. Please. No more apologies. What I went through in the dome or in that other... world or whatever... showed me how to fill the hollow the *right* way. And I think we did the same for the hollow that the land felt. At least a little bit, anyway. It's a good thing. It's all good."

"Well, I'll say 'cheers' to that!" Charles said, raising his coffee cup in the air.

They all did the same and said, "Cheers!" or "To the land!"

They finished eating and everyone pitched in to clean up and then pack up. Daniel helped load the van, but before Charles and Greg could usher everyone into it, Josie pulled Daniel aside.

"You know, when I first heard about this vacation, I kind of dreaded it. My friendships were on shaky ground, I'd lost my aunt, and I thought that I might lose the rest of my family at any moment. I had no idea that it would end up this way," Josie said to him. "Things are good with my friends and my dad, I gained another grandpa, and I met you and your dad. I don't know what life has in store for either of us, but I think at the very least we will be great friends for the rest of our lives."

"I would like nothing more. You are forever my khe'kén, which means little sister. And you are forever my Kachina Kai," he said and gave her a big hug.

Simon approached then and Daniel took a big step back. Simon held out his hand and said, "You're a really good guy, Daniel. I hope I can call you 'friend'."

Daniel hesitated but then smiled and shook Simon's hand. "You got it, friend. Take good care of Josie."

"We'll see you in a couple of months!" Josie said. She gave William a big hug before climbing in the van. "Goodbye, William. Thank you for everything."

"Goodbye, Josie. And thank *you.*" Josie smiled at father and son standing shoulder to shoulder with the shimmering form of Anna behind them.

* * * * *

They were mostly quiet during the first part of the drive home. About halfway, they made a stop for snacks and a bathroom break, and then hit the road again.

"Hey, Jenna, send me Brandon's number before you fall asleep," Josie said to Jenna who looked drowsy as she leaned against Dave's shoulder.

Josie's phone pinged with the information a moment later. Josie opened a new text. HEY, BRANDON, IT'S JOSIE. HOW ARE YOU?

Josie closed her phone, not expecting an immediate response, but her phone pinged again almost instantly.

HEY JOSIE! GOOD TO HEAR FROM YOU!

JENNA, DAVE, SIMON, AND I WERE TALKING ABOUT LAST SUMMER. WONDERED IF YOU'D LIKE TO GRAB A PIZZA SOMETIME.

DEFINITELY! CAN I BRING MY GIRLFRIEND MOLLY?

SURE!

Josie watched as the bubble with three dots indicating Brandon was typing showed on screen and then his message came up. SO YOU AREN'T TEXTING ME ABOUT WHAT HAPPENED WITH REAGAN?

WHAT DO YOU MEAN? WHAT HAPPENED WITH REAGAN?

She anxiously watched the bubble, and then, SHE HAD A BIG PARTY AT HER PARENTS LAKE HOUSE THURSDAY NIGHT. SOME KID FROM YOUR SCHOOL WAS THERE AND HE WAS FOUND DEAD THE NEXT DAY. THEY THINK HE WAS MURDERED.

"What!" Josie exclaimed.

About the Author

Valerie Lofaso is a writer, an Empathic Medium, a Reiki Master/Teacher, and a paranormal investigator and researcher. Fusing her personal experiences with dead people with the stories that have lived in her head all her life, she is working to create a believable world in which contact with the dead can - and should - happen. Valerie lives in southern New Hampshire with her daughter.

Valerie is available for readings, books discussions and various lectures on writing, Mediumship, ghost hunting, and more. She also welcomes reader's comments or questions. Please email her at ValerieLofaso@hotmail.com

She can also be found on social media:
Facebook.com/ValerieLofaso
Twitter: @TangledWeb_JJSD

Available Books in the Tangled Web of Friends Series

Book I – Summer Camp
Book II – The Witches of Fishkill Pond
Book III – The Last Hour

Coming soon!

Book V – The Phantom of Newhall Theater
Book VI (untitled)

Printed in the USA
CPSIA information can be obtained
at www.ICGtesting.com
JSHW051123130923
48072JS00003B/10